MURDER & MAYHEM
IN THE GOD BOX
ON A BILLION DOLLARS A DAY

RYCK NEUBE - ROBERT B. SCHOFIELD - JUDITH TRACY

PADWOLF
PUBLISHING

I WOULD LIKE TO THANK THE CINCINNATI WRITERS PROJECT FOR UNITING THE THREE OF US. HANGING WITH MY FELLOW WRITERS IS COOL, BUT THE FRIENDSHIPS ARE THE REAL GOLD.
   -RN

FOR MAYNARD GOOD STODDARD, WHO INSPIRED ME TO WRITE.
   -RBS

I WOULD LIKE TO DEDICATE THIS NOVELLA TO MY HUSBAND, PETE PALMER. AMEN
   -JT

PADWOLF PUBLISHING INC.
457 Main Street, #384
Farmingdale, NY 11735

WWW.PADWOLF.COM

Padwolf Publishing & logo are registered trademarks of Padwolf Publishing Inc.

MURDER & MAYHEM IN THE GOD BOX ON A BILLION DOLLARS A DAY

MURDER, MAYHEM, AND MUSIC © 2006 Judith Tracy
GOD BOX © 2006 Robert B. Schofield
MARS ON A BILLION DOLLARS A DAY © 2006 Ryck Neube

cover art © 2006 Daniel Horne

Book Edited by Marc S. Glasser

ISBN: 1-890096-27-X

Printed in the USA

First Printing

MURDER, MAYHEM, AND MUSIC
Judith Tracy

Murder, Mayhem, and Music Application for Murder

This application of intent constitutes the entire agreement between you and Murder, Mayhem, and Music, and supersedes any prior agreements. You may also be subject to additional terms and conditions that may apply when you use affiliate services, third-party weaponry, or third-party apparatus or supplies. This partnership between you and Murder, Mayhem, and Music shall be governed by the laws of the Coalition of Planets and Galaxies. Our failure to exercise or enforce any right or provision of this agreement shall not constitute a waiver of such right or provision in the future.

Legalized murder, maiming, and destruction are still considered felonies, and by filing this application you will be labeled a 'Legalized Criminal' in accordance with Volume Twenty, Section A, Item 2927.02 of the Intergalactic Code of Being. The Ministry of Law Enforcement as well as the Intergalactic Department of Investigation will record all information provided herein. Once the murder is committed, you will be identified as a felon even though you will be exempt from punishment or imprisonment.

By affixing your signature to this document, you agree that you are bound by all the rules and regulations stated herein. The decision to grant a permit is final. You may, however, at any time after submitting all the forms in their entirety, withdraw this application of intent. Retracting said intent does not nullify the contract specifications of a full inquest, and you are still bound by this agreement and subject by law to an investigation if Murder, Mayhem, and Music Inc. deem it necessary.

Be aware that by signing this document, you forfeit the right to sit on a jury, the right to join the armed forces, and the right to be hired as an employee of any/all governments including, but not limited to, the Intergalactic Department of Investigation, the Intergalactic Revenue Service, and the Department of Sanitation and Recycling.

**** *Please note*: applying for permission to commit murder in no way affects your obligation to the Big M Music Club. All dues, fees, and orders will continue to be processed under the terms of our club agreement.

I/we (Print name(s))_____, have read the agreement and the disclaimer and agree to all conditions.
(signature(s)) _____
Date (Standardized Universal Date System (SUDS)) _____

PERMIT 2927K INTENT TO MURDER, MAIM, OR COMMIT MAYHEM

Name(s):_____   (Include aliases, nicknames, titles)
Galaxy - Quadrant - Sector - Planetary System: _____
Mailing Location: _____
Area of Residence: Check one of the following:
___ Above ground ___ Underground ___ Underwater
___ Inter-dimensional (List dimension/s on back of form)
Telecommunication Portal ID number: Home _____ Work _____
Intergalactic Identification Security Number: ____-_____-_____
Species Classification: _____
Age: _____ (Please use the Standardized Universal Date System (SUDS))
Habitation Status: Single _____ Married _____ Widowed _____
Divorced _____ Asexual _____ Other _____
Have you ever been arrested? Yes ___ No ___ Not Sure ___
If yes, explain:

Name(s) (including species, planet, and sector) of Life-Form(s) to be murdered:
(Use back of form if more space is needed)

Reason(s) for each request: (Use back of form if more space is needed)

I/we hereby declare that the above information is true to the best of my/our knowledge:
Signature(s): _____ Date _____ (SUDS)
_____
DO NOT WRITE BELOW THIS LINE
Case Number _____
Licensing Bureau _____
Interviewer _____
Date of Review _____
ACCEPTED _____ REJECTED _____

Chapter One

A speckled Geek, an Arachnid from the planet Spydor, and a Doubel were the first to bound into the lobby. Though Morlax could have installed a timer mechanism on the door, it would have deprived him of the view of the early-morning melee. Hovering in the dimly lit hallway, the Orfian watched the scene unfold. It was the high point of his morning routine that also included a cup of Peruvian java, an Earth-grown stogie, and four pounds of jerky of unknown origin (jerky constituents, along with the ingredients of Wild Turkey whiskey and musk fragrances, are best kept mysteries).

Morlax was an Orfian of few convictions. He didn't read labels, didn't step on a scale, and didn't own a mirror. Neither did he admit to having emotional or sexual needs. But when it came to speaking intelligently on a subject to be taken seriously, Morlax was an authority on Earth culture, specializing in tobacco and reprocessed, hydrogenated beef matter.

"Mister-Morlax-your-first-applicant-has-arrived," Mai-Z droned.

Mai-Z (short for Mechanical Android Intelligence, model Z) was typing in her chair behind a synthetic-wood-and-metal desk. Morlax had requisitioned the board for a 3055 model, hoping to get a new robotic assistant. He would have settled for one made sometime in the last two or three thousand planetary revolutions, but it wasn't to be. Money was tight and the competition fierce, even for the third-largest interplanetary conglomerate. Ever since legalized murder became fashionable, everyone and their clone had an application processing office, so he settled for what he could get—an occasional memory chip or a tube of grease.

Mai-Z, better than nothing but not by much, was in need of major repair. He knew it, the machine knew it, and so did all the dregs of the universe waiting in the lobby.

With things under control, Morlax hoisted his three layers of fat and jetted to the coffee machine. The black liquid glopped into his mug and he shrugged. Any minute now, Franzy would be back. Its two-week absence placed an unfair burden on Morlax, but in truth, he really didn't miss the non-gendered Nuet. As far as he was concerned, the company had made a big mistake hiring Franzy in the first place. Other than making the best cup of java in the galaxy, the creature was useless. Nuets were much too sympathetic and too easily swayed to be in a position of authority.

In Morlax's opinion, granting someone a permit to kill, maim, or destroy, was serious business. But what did he know? He was only the manager. The big blobs upstairs were only concerned with profit margins. Franzy worked cheap.

Morlax disliked Franzy; the creature hated being called anything but its formal name, Franzine, so he had made it a point to call it Franzy from the beginning. It irritated him that someone's wardrobe, a bad hair day, or a casually made death threat could sway the creature. Too often, its irrational issuances brought serious repercussions. Since Morlax was in effect its boss, he took the heat for Franzine's diminished analytical capabilities. That, he reasoned, justified snooping through its office to read its caseload files, which he did whenever the Nuet was away from its desk.

* * *

Murder, Mayhem, and Music Inc., one of the universe's largest interstellar conglomerates, opened its doors sometime in the twenty-third century, SUDS (Standardized Universal Date System), and was originally a musical recording business called Music Inc. It boasted of having represented some of the galaxies' most popular rock groups, and at one time had the largest membership of any club of any type, including the interactive book guilds.

Two galactic years ago, when the Coalition of Planets and Galaxies legalized murder, the big boys upstairs voted to diversify. They couldn't afford to forego the added revenue. The company had been losing money ever since the creation of SWS players. (Sound-Wave Synthesizer earplugs made hand-helds obsolete and were less expensive than the bulky palm players Music Inc. manufactured.)

Unfortunately, the government, learning from an earlier mistake, the legalization of marijuana and hallucinogens, enacted further legislation just one short GY after Murder, Mayhem, and Music (or The Big M™) set up its offices. The new laws severely regulated the murder industry, and the paperwork increased to the point where Morlax needed, but could not afford, to hire a full staff.

The glory days lasted less than three hundred sixty days. Business dwindled due to the competition, and the Big M's profits slipped to the point where the business didn't warrant more than three workers. Morlax was forced to fire everyone but Franzy and make do with a remanufactured robot assembled from spare parts.

Murder, Mayhem, and Music Inc.'s stock plummeted. Too much red tape. Too many deadbeat customers. And much too much paperwork. There were times Morlax feared for his own job. The big boys at Big M were threatening more layoffs.

They weren't the only company to suffer setbacks. During this time, smaller businesses were disappearing as fast as raindrops on the Andanuvian desert. Soon only a few corporations remained in the criminal-licensing business.

At one time Morlax planned to start his own company, Discount Death and Destruction. He had lined up all the hit men and a cache of top-notch, refurbished weapons, all ill-gotten, and of course, cheap. Dealing with the scum of the universe had its advantages.

It was a brilliant idea. Morlax would sub-contract the killers for a percentage of their fee. It kept the overhead down and did away with the need to pay unemployment insurance or workbeings' compensation. The weapons he would rent to the do-it-yourselfers. That, he calculated, was where the fortune was to be made.

Since Morlax was already familiar with the procedures and had the connections, he gambled he would be ahead of the recently-formed Elimination, Eradication and Extinction Inc., run by his one-time trusted assistant, Tarnak. The two beings never got along, and since Morlax had seniority, Tarnak had been the first to be dismissed.

Tarnak's absence from the workplace delighted Morlax, but only until the day E.E.E. Inc. opened its doors. Still, Morlax figured there was a place in the industry for a discount enterprise, and he was about to sign his blood away when the Coalition of Planets and Galaxies instituted a freeze on new businesses.

As in all other endeavors, Morlax had all the right answers to all the wrong questions. He was on top of business trends but too lazy to follow what the government was doing. He gave up his dream of being self-employed and to this day, he regretted his lack of foresight.

Tarnak was doing very well, acquiring two lightning air-coupes, a four-dimensional mansion on the planet Tacky, and a beautiful Venutian for a fifth wife. Morlax's salary barely kept him in ten-course dinners. But such is the business of life...and death.

* * *

"Send the first one in, Mai-Z." Morlax leaned back in his egg-shaped leather chair and beckoned for a cigar. The metal band on his pudgy wrist glowed, and a long brown tube floated through the air, nudging itself between his sixth and seventh fingers.

"Light," Morlax commanded, and the cigar began to smoke. He drew it to his slobbery lips and puffed. He was now somewhat ready to conduct today's business.

The Doubel peered into the office. Morlax first noticed the tearful eyes of the female half of this two-bodied creature through the plumes of smoke.

"Come in. Come in. Grab a chair and take a seat. In your case, take two. I don't bite. Don't have many teeth." Morlax grinned, exposing his gums. (Due to the effort it took to chew one's food and to brush, Orfians tended to lose their teeth early in life.)

The female side entered first. She was remotely attractive, Morlax thought, as she pulled a straight-back chair from the corner and sat. Clearly mammalian, the feminine side of the creature could be considered desirable, a two-point-seven on a scale of four. She had blonde and blue-streaked feathers on her head, plump, kissable lips (all three of them) and bouncing, quivering chest-mounds that resembled milk factories (there were three of those as well).

The creature removed at least a dozen articles from her tote bag, and smiled when she found what she was looking for—a ratty, bright red folder. With a flick of her jeweled wrist, she tossed it on his desk.

The male half leaned over, opened his briefcase, and removed his own folder, placing it atop the red one. He glanced at his partner and ran a finger through his raven, lion-like mane. Long, wiry whiskers bristled as he turned his head to make a face at his wife, who was licking and preening her feathers.

"Two folders?" asked Morlax.

"Yes, and why not? There are two of us," said the female, rolling her eyes and sneering.

"I see, I see. Forgive me for assuming that you are one entity."

The male snarled at his female side and said, "There's nothing to forgive. She's the one that's out of line. I tell you, it's a wonder we even made it into the room together. Some day her mouth is going to get us into real trouble. What do I mean, some day? Just yesterday she winked at a construction worker and the next thing I knew, I was defending her honor. I awoke this morning with a puffy eye." A finger pointed to an orange bruise. "You got to feel sorry for me. She gets us in trouble, and I do the right thing and defend her. I never learn." The male end sighed. "I'm cursed with her presence for a lifetime unless you help me. I want to kill her and put me out of my misery."

"What do you know of misery?" she asked. "Nothing. Living with you is like having an itch you can't scratch. If anyone is going to kill anyone, I should kill you." The female crossed her legs, kicking the thigh of the male half. "And that, Mr. Morlax, is why there are two folders. I want to kill him as much, no, more than he wants to kill me."

The half-Doubel wriggled in her chair and fluttered her three sets of eyelashes. "Can you blame me for wanting to get rid of him? Just look at him. That's all the better it gets: rumpled shirt and tie, scraggly mane, and a belly as large as his ego.

"I'm tired of fighting with him to get involved and do things. I hate wallowing in filth. I hate being fat because *he* won't watch what he eats. He refuses to move his lazy ass and exercise."

The female finished her tirade, looked at Morlax and gasped. "Sorry, sir, didn't mean to offend you."

"None taken. Orfians are fat. Everyone knows it, and it's to our liking. A society as advanced as ours, existing only to create creature comforts, naturally has some disadvantages. Now, if you will give me a couple thousand milliseconds to look over your files…"

"Insulting bitch. Always stuffing her feet in my mouth. Don't go making any decisions based on her assessment of me. I'm quite the rage, a beloved star in the Doubelan entertainment industry. I'm really quite famous. Known over three planetary sections for talent, compassion, and brains. Now the Mrs., she never thinks before speaking; shit, she doesn't think at all. My half retained all the intellectual cells."

The being fluffed his mane and raised his voice two octaves. "Just listen to her…get out and do things! Don't think for a minute I haven't tried. Many were the times I made reservations only to miss out because I couldn't pull her away from a mirror. If she spent less time primping and fussing, we might have had a bit of fun, but oh, no…"

"Quiet!" Morlax pounded the desk. "It's obvious I can skip over the section, 'Why do you want to murder this being?' If you continue to bicker, I'm going to kill you both and I won't need a form. Is that clear?"

The two faces glared at each other, stuck out their spotted tongues, and said nothing more.

"You must be Ola." Morlax glanced at the female side and rubbed his quadruple chin.

The female half nodded.

"And that leaves me to assume you are Bola."

The male half grunted.

"Let us see here," Morlax swiveled his chair, inhaled, exhaled, and blew smoke rings. "Both of you are filing separately. I must admit this is very unusual. I have dealt with a few Doubels before, and was under the impression the two halves were compatible."

"It's that way in most instances," Ola smiled, "but unfortunately, we are the exception. We have tried counseling, tranquilizers, and de-hormonizing, but nothing worked. As you can see, we also applied for a medical separation. Unfortunately, they turned us down."

"Hmmmmmmm...I didn't know they could do that."

"It has been successful, but only in rare cases, and then one half died and the other lived. Since our bodies' nervous systems are connected at the hips, it's an operation that has never been attempted on a healthy Doubel. Right now, the legislature and the medical society are looking for ways to make the surgery work. There are a lot more unhappy Doubels than our government realized. It's a real cause now—been on all the news shows. You might have heard of the slogan, 'One head is better than two'?"

Morlax shook his head. "Sorry, but I don't subscribe to any of the information channels. Too biased."

Bola nodded. "Well, it's cutting edge news, but it will be years before they make it a viable option. I can't live another minute with this thorn in my side. I would rather be an outcast than live with her nagging."

"Oh, yeah," Morlax mused. "I remember reading that half-lings are considered second-rate citizens."

Both heads nodded.

"Then why go through this?"

"Because it's better than living with a slob," Ola blurted. "I would rather be a pariah than exist another day like this."

"Oh, this is typical. Watch now. She's going to burst into tears. Got a mop?" asked Bola.

Ola hit Bola's arm. The male mumbled something under his breath, looked at Morlax, and shrugged. "Please read the files. If you have any questions, ask. We will do anything you want, but please, choose between us. Both of us are prepared to abide by your decision. This is the only solution short of a double suicide. Murder, Mayhem, and Music, at least for one of us, is our last chance at happiness."

The female hiked her skirt up above her knee and exposed her lacy garters. "I have never been more serious about anything in all of my twenty Doubelian revolutions. I deserve to be happy, and when I'm happy, I make others happy."

Bola's jaw hit the desk. "Why, you cheap roadside attendant! I haven't a chance with you promising that Orfian your goodies."

"Bola!" Morlax shouted. "I'm not allowed to accept bribes. Now sit down and let us finish this interview."

"Yeah, yeah, yeah. I'm no dummy. I know all about your kind. Orfians are a dying race. Your kind is either too fat or too lazy to do the horizontal bop. Both male and female find physical exertion disgusting. Even if you found something remotely erotic, the aesthetics make it improbable. If it weren't for sperm banks and artificial wombs, you guys would be extinct."

"What are you getting at, Bola?" Morlax blew a cloud of smoke in the male half-Doubel's eyes. "I enjoy the occasional bump and grind."

"Sure you do, as long as you can sit there and do nothing. Ola is a living, willing female and not a bad-looking one at that. She's probably offering you the first and only invitation you've received in ten Orfian revolutions. Considering the situation, she would do anything to lure you to her side, and I mean anything. No sir, don't tell me you're not salivating. I see the drool."

"Of course you do. Orfians constantly salivate and dribble. It's the no-teeth thing."

Bola didn't reply. Morlax could tell the creature was beyond reasoning by the low guttural groans and intermittent rumblings issuing from both halves. He was familiar with Doubels' ability to produce an echo effect by simultaneous vibrations of both larynxes. It was a duet of noises, parallel twangs like two plucked rubber bands.

Bola rose and stomped around the office, dragging the female along as he paced. Ola, unable to control her other side's temper, made the best of it and winked at Morlax every chance she got. None of it was lost on Bola. The antics of his female half infuriated him until finally, Morlax had to call in Mai-Z.

As soon as the Doubel saw the robot they calmed down. "We will behave. Please don't kick us out," said Bola.

"If this happens again, I will tear up your application. Do you both understand?"

They nodded.

"Good. I need to do some serious thinking on this matter. Give me until next first light to make up my mind. Now, if there are no objections, Mai-Z will show you out."

Morlax watched as Mai-Z shoved the Doubel out of the office. Ola, doubling back, managed to blow a kiss before being dragged out of sight.

She is a pretty one, thought Morlax, but the entity was trouble. Morlax could smell adversity a kilometer away. And—he puffed long and hard on the stogie— Bola was correct about his sexual prowess. It was, as with most of his species, almost non-existent. The one thing neither of them knew was that he really wasn't above taking bribes. *Definitely something to keep in mind.* Morlax rubbed his crotch and closed the file. It was time for a doughnut break.

* * *

The TP (Telecommunication Portal) lit up. Morlax reached over his desk, almost spilling his coffee, and clicked the button. A two-headed, three-dimensional figure about twelve centimeters high materialized on the platform. As soon as he was fully formed, Morlax recognized the being and sat upright in his chair.

"Identify yourself, Agent Eight-naught-eight."

"Is this really necessary, Mr. Nix? I can see you, and you can see me."

"Got to follow protocol, Morlax. Now identify yourself with the code."

With a voice that would bring up yesterday's lunch, Morlax began to sing. "Someday my prince will come. Someday…"

"Good, it's you, Morlax. Now listen. Cinderella dressed in yellow ran upstairs to kiss a fellow."

"A code yellow?"

"A code HBS39A443KKQIDNE-yellow. He has been spotted."

"Are you sure?" asked Morlax. "False sightings have become a regular occurrence. Oh, and why can't you just say code yellow? I will know what you mean."

"Can't. It's in the book. Must follow procedures, Morlax. That's why they put me in charge of this situation. Details are the crux of every successful operation."

Morlax shook his head, grateful the illusion on his desk was just that, an illusion. The urge to swat his boss overcame him, but he kept it in check. He didn't want to interfere with the transmission, though he sincerely doubted this sighting was the real thing.

"Where?" Morlax asked.

"On Chloriflorida. One of our sneakers was turned in a few hours ago. There's no doubt this time."

"Any deaths to report?"

"So far, nothing. He's acting like a tourist. Just as we expected."

"Hmmmmm," Morlax bent down and opened his file drawer, "hang on a minute."

"That's all you have to say? Hang on? What are you doing, Morlax? I can't see you. Morlax? Morlax? Do you realize how serious this is? He is back. Morlax? Are you eating again?"

Morlax resumed his position, holding a file, and opened it. Tiny particles of doughnut dust sprinkled the air as he wiped the crumbs off his hands and sneezed.

"Chloriflorida. Hmmm…eighty percent of the Elders bet on that planet. This really could be it."

"That's what I'm telling you, Morlax. Get with the program. It is He. I should have an illusio-tape for you to watch tomorrow. Go ahead and read the file again. It's crucial to be prepared. I'll be in touch. And Morlax, wipe the sugar from your chin. Very unprofessional."

The two-headed creature vanished. Morlax re-lit his cigar. Between the call from his boss and the shouting Doubel, he had a headbanger. Though more than half the work day remained, he decided to call it quits and tucked the file in his briefcase. If his boss was right, and He really had returned, the least Morlax could do was be prepared.

Morlax grabbed his hat and stopped by the front desk. "Cancel the rest of my appointments and all of tomorrow's, Mai-Z. Nix just called with a code yellow."

"Do-you-wish-me-to-alert-Franzine?" asked the robot.

"Not just yet. There's no reason to send that idiot into a tizzy. I just want you to be aware. Don't power off. Plug yourself in and stay on stand-by. I want you to be ready if any packages are dropped off. They're supposed to be sending me an illusio-tape, and I want to see it as soon as it arrives. Call me at home if it gets here."

"Is-there-anything-else-I-can-do-sir?"

"Nothing really. I know that you're just a bucket of bolts, but it wouldn't hurt to cross your digits. We need a miracle if the reports are true. No, my sweet Mai-Z," Morlax patted the robot's back, "just pray that if it's true, He has a sense of humor this time around, because we're going to need it."

Chapter Two

Too upset to eat his usual eight-course, mid-afternoon, pre-dinner snack, Morlax zipped his air-coupe through EarthlyPleasures' drive-through window for a tidbit to tie him over. "Four triple burgers with all the goodies, three large orders of fried potato strips, and a keg of cola to go, please."

The robotic voice crackled over the intercom. "That will be 8,000 credits. Please pull up."

Morlax rounded the corner and shifted into hover, stopping by the flashing neon lights. Highlighted in blinding rays were the universal numeric symbols displaying the amount the owed. Next to the sign was a mechanical bank teller, making it easy for Morlax to type in the required digits for an automatic withdrawal from his account. As soon as the transaction was completed, his meal, encased in a bottle, slid through the tube. Morlax lifted the lever, snatched the container, and examined the contents: four brown bricks, three yellow ones, and a cellophane bag of crystalline granules.

"They got it right for once," he muttered to himself. "They must have gotten their food synthesizer fixed. Happy days..."

Morlax leaned back in the cushy seat, realizing the paradox of his outburst. If He was back, really back, those happy days would come to an end. Even if the "sneakers" had been wrong all these thousands of galactic years, eventually, they would be right.

* * *

Thousands of GYs ago, planets, galaxies, wormholes and other assorted heavenly matter disappeared. Poof. No explanation, scientific or otherwise, accounted for this anomaly. (Weather balloons didn't work as a believable explanation in this instance.)

Teams of researchers, scientists and magicians, as well as the entire Department of Military Intelligence (all four generals and one assistant), visited the various "crime" scenes. The sapient races of the universe agreed to set aside their petty wars and disagreements to work together to solve the mystery.

They began a long, drawn-out investigation, correlating fact and fiction, supposition and conjecture, theory and coin tosses. After ruling out natural causes and mass-suicidal planetary syndrome, and after twelve and a half long years of recorded wavelength phenomena, the Committee for a Radioactive-Free Atmosphere made an educated guess. After many years elapsed and many millions of interplanetary taxpayers' credits spent, they concluded:

He did it. (The male pronoun was chosen as female pronouns were already in use naming violent galactic storms.)

It took the Committee another twenty years to prove it, and one more before they could agree on a name for Him: The Great Ordainer of Destruction of 2003.

And now He was back, approximately two thousand galactic years later.
* * *

"Why now?" Morlax asked out loud.

"Because we're tired of waiting for you to move your tin can. Sleep on your own time, buddy."

Morlax looked in his rear-view mirror. The vehicles were eight air-coupes thick and piling up fast. After making an obscene gesture at the Troglodyte yelling obscenities, Morlax shifted out of hover, and whooshed into mainstream traffic. The planet Orf's orbiting queue was backed up all the way to its two-ringed moon. Taking his turn, Morlax entered the atmosphere, found his marker, and swooped to within a few kilometers of home.

Home: Orf—one of the most beautiful planets in the galaxy, or any other for that matter, and similar to Earth in many ways.

* * *

It was thought at first that Orfians and Homo sapiens evolved simultaneously, but that theory was later disproved. Earth was first on the ladder of sentiency. Orfians evolved later, but faster.

The parallels between the two planets were uncanny. Even the life-forms, from beast to man, resembled those found on that primitive world. Orfians were shorter than most earthlings, not to mention green, but the species shared a common skeletal frame: two eyes, two ears, two arms, and two legs. The difference was in their thumbs. Orfians had two on each hand, and the joints could pivot, allowing for a full 360-degree rotation. Aside from that difference, they were human.

Some of the population denied the similarities between the two species, but they only made up a small part of Orfian society. Most didn't care that there were commonalities in their genetic make-up; after all, they owed most of their latest fantastic technology to the theft of Earth's ideas. Humans were imaginative and industrious, even if they were hostile, noisy, and petty.

Orfians were insipid and lazy. Their minds were far more developed, and could be considered organic computers. They could solve eight-dimensional differential equations in their heads because they found it tiring to pick up a pen. Soon after discovering Earth's technology, they had reduced almost every convenience imaginable to a gadget. Being a pedestrian was outmoded. Their chairs, air-coupes, and anti-gravity footwear replaced walking, and what their toys couldn't do, their wristbands did. Orfians ate and slept, and in between, they procrastinated.

* * *

Arriving home late, Morlax found that the hover-park at his apartominium was full. Even his designated space was taken. Morlax wrote down the ID number of the vehicle that had stolen his spot, and flew in circles until he got lucky enough to find someone leaving. Annoyed that he had to park in the visitors' lot, he made his way to the eletube on a cushion of air, making a mental note to report the idiot who took his space. It wasn't just the inconvenience; it was the principle. He paid for that spot. Morlax felt the burn in his topmost belly. It was one more aggravation to add to his list, making a completely dismal day.

There were three messages on the TP's answering machine. He could tell from the way the light flashed that two of them were solicitors. The third was a local call and flashed red for priority. Morlax decided to eat first, and called for his command chair along with the re-hydrating plate to place his dinner in. After inflating the cushions to fit the contours of his flab, and pressing the little button to recline and vibrate, he settled into his seat to answer his calls.

An old Orfian appeared wearing a white jacket. In one hand he held a laser pointer, and in the other a sandwich. Behind him was a board with two pictures of atrophied feet. "Do your arches ache from shrinkage? Do you suffer from pustules and boils? Then try…"

"Skip," Morlax mumbled between bites. The Orfian vanished. "Next."

This time a semi-attractive female emerged. She was wearing a tight, red dress that accented her lime-green complexion and highlighted the colors of her veins. "Hi there, big boy. Tired of sitting alone in your command chair module for one? Well, you're not alone. I too, spent many a night by myself until I called 'Dial-a-Date'."

"Skip. Next." Morlax almost choked when the image of his mother appeared. He hadn't called her since first light.

"You must be dead. It's been forever since I've heard from you. Is this the way to treat the woman who gave you life?" The obese figure of the aging Orfian sniffled. Opening the purse hanging on her shoulder, she pulled out a white hanky and honked. "Please call me, and in case you have forgotten, my TP number is 88-844-739572302347. If I don't hear from you by tomorrow, I will call the police."

"Replay." Morlax took a sip of his cola and watched the performance again. His mother was a born actress. Her histrionics were better than any of the programming on the Interactive Vision Module. Except for the Earth channel broadcast, Morlax rarely tuned in.

* * *

Earth. Once, ten GYs ago, he visited the planet, and met with some of their military people in an area named Antarctica. He was part of the Coalition of Planets and Galaxies' welcoming committee back then, and enjoyed the free trips and meals.

After thirty-two ER's (Earth Rotations, or days as they called them), they came to an agreement. Orf would supply the creatures with a few harmless technological upgrades. In exchange, the earthlings would provide Orf with tobacco, alcohol, and memorabilia (bumper stickers, pet rocks, animé, and toilet tissue).

Morlax was thrilled with the deal. He held great respect for a society that could be so idea-oriented, and that, even with such primitive technology, could still create some of the tastiest snacks in the universe.

* * *

Now, Morlax shuddered at the reality of the situation. If the sneakers really had spotted the Great Ordainer, there was a good chance this shipment of Cubans would be his last. Earth could be the first to go.

According to the top-ranked scientists of the forty-first century, all forms of life could be traced to Earth. Human DNA was the oldest of known nucleic acids. To the universal evolutionary theorists, hominids were classified with metazoans. In the hundreds of thousands of years of sentient existence, Earth was the only world where evolution failed to show progress. It was sure to attract His attention.

It was obvious the big "He" didn't like failures. Only sentimentality had spared Earth in the "Great Destruction of 2003." This time the odds weren't in its favor.

Morlax sighed and called his mother. It was getting late, and the last thing he needed was a visit from the authorities.

"You are alive, thank goodness!" the 3-D visualization shouted.

"Yes, mother. I have been busy. How are you?"

"As you would expect for an old lady of eighty-eight years. My vocal chords are rubbed raw, and my thumbs don't rotate like they used to. Verbo offered to take me to see the family practitioner, but your uncle has been drinking again and I'm afraid to ride in the air-coupe with him. Of course you're too busy to take me, but don't feel guilty. I will suffer in silence."

"Can't you ask Budgy?"

"Your sister? Hah. She's too engrossed with wedding plans to think about her dear old Mum. Which reminds me, Budgy told me you haven't responded to the invitation. Are you going? I know the two of you aren't speaking, but you must consider how this will look…"

"Mum, I'm going to have to call you back. My boss is on the other line."

Without waiting for a response, Morlax ended the conversation. The TP rang again, and he nearly jumped out of his chair. He'd only been using another call as an excuse to be rid of her.

"Morlax, is it true? Do you think He's really back?"

It was Franzy, a day late and hysterical as usual. "The evidence hasn't arrived, and until then, I will keep my opinion to myself. How did you find out?"

"Nix told me. That's why I didn't show up for work today."

Morlax tried to conceal his anger. Why the hell had Nix told Franzy? Morlax was in charge. This was his assignment. "So you had a meeting with him today?"

"Yep, yep, yep. One of his heads, anyway. The other one was on vacation."

"I see," said Morlax.

"You *are* angry. I can tell by the tone in your voice."

"I'm fine, Franzy. Can we discuss this at the office tomorrow? I have a lot of reading to do. There's a whole backlog of cases that need attention. A huge stack of files is piled on your desk."

"Well, that's another reason I called. I won't be in tomorrow. Nix and I have a morning appointment."

"Fine. Just fine. You go meet with him. I'll handle everything for another day."

"You're mad at me. I had nothing to do with this. It was an accident bumping into Nix while on holiday."

"I believe you. Everybody vacations on the planet Redun." (The planet Redun was in the most remote corner of the known universe. It was a perfect site for the Coalition to establish a headquarters. No water, no atmosphere, no intelligent life, no vegetation, nothing but sand and gravel. No one but government bureaucrats and journalists ever went to Redun¾except for Franzy.)

"It isn't important. Talk with Nix. I'm not angry. We can discuss this at length when you return. And that will be sometime this week?"

"Yep, yep, yep…well," the Nuet hummed, "the earliest I could be there is Friday and it seems senseless to come in for one day, so I thought I would take a long weekend. That is, unless you have a problem, and then I will work tomorrow."

"No problem at all. Take the weekend. Take all of next week—" Morlax disconnected in mid-sentence. He wasn't mad; he was furious. That double-dealing, conniving Nuet. It was after his job. *Well, if Nix wants to promote that incompetent creature, then I say, so be it. And if Franzy wants to stick a proton torpedo in my back, then let it deal with its own blunders. It can handle its own messes all by its lonesome. No way will I take the blame for its mistakes.*

By now the entire evening was ruined and Morlax couldn't concentrate. He had planned to read through the Doubel's file, but decided to watch the *Gilligan's Island* fest broadcast from the Earth Channel. He needed a diversion, a laugh, and a few minutes to call his own. Three episodes later, Morlax was ready to fall asleep.

"Bed." The chair clanked and chugged, turning into a cradle while its occupant was still inside. "Fluff." The pillows plumped. In minutes the Orfian was snoring.

* * *

The two suns blared brightly when Morlax awoke to the alarm. Tired from the past day's upset, he sputtered to the shower sans anti-gravity slippers. Hot water blasted from the vents placed at all angles around the stall. With so many layers of fat and body creases, Morlax had to lift and separate the folds and soap diligently. Even though Orfians were lazy, the bathing ritual was one form of exercise they took seriously. They were surprisingly sweet-smelling creatures.

Since only Mai-Z would be in the office today, Morlax decided to wear his crimson sack in lieu of a business caftan. The loose-fitting garment had a hole for the head and one on each side for the arms. Unlike his formal gown with its drawstring, it hung loose and was large enough to accommodate his bulk, no matter how much he weighed.

The office was lit when Morlax punched in the digi-code. Mai-Z greeted him by pointing to the chair at the opposite end of the room. "Ms.-Lyon-is-here-to-see-you."

Morlax turned to see a thin, green female basking in the glow of the artificial sun lamp. She seemed to be chatting with the philodendron hanging above her head, though Morlax couldn't see a mouth.

Except in pictures, Morlax had never seen a Chlorifloridian before. Only in the past few years had they allowed aliens to visit and mingle with the common vegetation. Little was known about these ambulatory greens. Morlax blinked and pretended he wasn't staring.

"Ms. Lyon, I'm sorry if you had an appointment today, but something important has come up. I'm afraid I must reschedule." Morlax extended his hand.

The stalk smiled and placed her four-edged leaf in the Orfian's palm. "Oh no, I'm not here to apply for a permit. Nix sent me over with the illusio-tape. And please, Ms. Lyon is so formal. You may call me Dandi."

"The tape." Morlax's eyes lit up. "Wonderful. In that case, please make yourself comfortable. I will only take a milli-moment to prepare. In the meantime, Mai-Z will set up the illusio-player. May I offer you anything? Coffee? Doughnuts?

Beef jerky?"

"No, but thank you anyway. Chlorifloridians don't eat solids, and except for a dusting of fertilizer every month, all we require is our soil, water, and UV rays. I have some chlorophyll pills given to me by the IDI (Intergalactic Department of Investigation) that are supposed to make up for the lack of natural sunlight. It was the only way I could travel. Your plant-lights help, but I prefer soaking in the rays of yellow stars whenever possible."

"Then allow me to set a lamp in the conference room and bring you a pitcher of water. It's the best I can do under these circumstances. Mai-Z, will you show Dandi the way?"

Morlax disappeared down the hall without waiting for an answer. Not wanting to seem piggish, he gobbled down a dozen doughnuts before jaunting to the conference room.

"Have you watched it yet?" he asked Dandi.

"Two or three times. I'm afraid the copy isn't as clear as the original, but I believe you will see enough evidence to convince you that He has returned."

"So, you think it was Him?"

"I would prefer to answer your questions after you've seen this tape. It's important that my conclusions don't influence yours."

"Fair enough." Morlax bowed and sat facing the screen. He smiled at Dandi, and as soon as she nodded, he ordered the illusio-player to proceed.

After a second of static, a sneaker appeared on the screen. Morlax circled his thumbs during the six and a half clock revolutions of its oration.

Watching a talking shoe was commonplace for Morlax. He had been aware of the spy technology ever since his training for the IDI. Sneakers (named after the popular athletic shoes manufactured on Earth) were actually an outer covering for the audio and video device that taped specific wavelengths, movement and sound. Installed in the front toe-bumper, it automatically clicked on when the atmospheric electrostatic wavelength signature registered in the upper microfarads.

Or something like that. Morlax was no scientist. All that mumbo jumbo meant little to him. What he did understand was that each creature had its own electric signature, and the device was set to recognize the Great Ordainer's code. That was all he needed to know.

* * *

At first, only agents from the IDI wore them. When the technology evolved to the point where those chips could be inserted in any foot-like covering, the Coalition passed legislation forcing all manufacturers to put the microprocessors in their products.

Of course, they weren't told of their real purpose. They were made to believe it was an accounting device. Since it was virtually impossible to monitor all the sneakers, teams of researchers devised a way to keep tabs.

Morlax and all Orfians had theirs installed in their "Cushies" (a name-brand footwear product that has paid this author quite a bit of Earth currency to be placed in this story). These foot coverings were made of a leather-like substance able to expand and contract under most atmospheric conditions and gravities. This material could also conform to every contour of any being's lower extremity.

They were so comfortable that they outsold all other shoes all over the universe (except on Earth, whose legislatures banned them because of something called capitalism, free enterprise, and Nike).

It was a scam, but a necessary one. If the chip recognized His frequency, it would begin to record. When it ran out of memory, the chip triggered the release of a dye that would cause the user's foot/feet to turn black. As the shoes' "Do Not Remove Under Penalty of the Law" tag carried a warning that this condition could be fatal, this would send the life-form rushing to the Ministry of Infection and Disease, sneakers in hand, to be examined. The doctor would then administer the antidote, collect the shoes "for research purposes", and transmit them to the IDI.

* * *

Morlax listened to the sneakers finish their speech, and ordered his magnifying glasses on. He needed them to see with precision.

There was no mention of the planet in the actual tape. In the past it had either been obvious, or easy enough to determine with a little bit of research. Nix had already told him it was Chloriflorida, but it didn't look anything like the pictures in the few available planetary travel books.

This world was a complete jungle, kilometers of endless vegetation. No roads, no buildings, no signs of anything that Morlax associated with intelligent civilizations.

He continued staring at the screen, hoping to catch a glimpse of an appendage that would give away the identity of the sneaker's wearer. Then it dawned on him.

Morlax looked at Dandi and she nodded.

"I saw Him," she said.

Chapter Three

Dandi might have seen the Great Ordainer, but there was nothing on the screen that confirmed her statement. Morlax saw some of the most outrageous and beautiful foliage in the galaxy, but nothing to prove He was there. Occasionally, some of the taller plants would bend to a breeze. Others were mobile to a degree, but that wasn't indicative of anything pertaining to the sighting.

"Where exactly are we on the planet?" asked Morlax.

"This is one of our nurseries. Our offspring are planted and tended until they're capable of mobility. I was visiting my sprouts when He came into view. I even spoke to Him." Dandi sighed. "He is wonderful. I will never be the same again."

Morlax fidgeted with his command bracelet. "Well, I don't see a damn thing."

"He's not on the screen yet. As in any endeavor, patience is a virtue."

"Orfians have never been patient. That's why we have filled the universe with time-saving devices."

"Well, actually, we were taught it was because your kind was lazy."

Morlax chuckled. "That too. Now, may we proceed? I'm interested in why you perceived this event as 'the event'."

"If you had been there, you would have felt His presence. I doubt you will understand because you can't capture on tape the emotion, the raw energy that was Him."

"Don't you worry your little petals. I'll recognize Him, if we ever get to that part."

"I guess it's taking a long time. I'm sorry the IDI didn't have time to edit the tape."

"May we fast-forward?"

"I suppose. It must be boring for you to watch baby pictures."

The tape fluttered as it zipped in fast mode. Although there was a peaceful beauty to the scenery, it was boring as hell. *If you've seen one forest, you've seen them all*, Morlax thought, but he held his tongue for the sake of etiquette.

All of a sudden Morlax caught a clump of grass moving. "Stop the tape. Is that Him?"

"Do you mean the pampas grass moving to the right of the frame?"

He pointed. "Yes, that plant, the one that's moving. I don't know the names of your sub-species."

Dandi clicked and the tape began to play slowly. "No, that's one of our toddlers taking her first steps. Isn't she cute?"

Morlax was glad the room was dark. He had little control over his eyeballs rolling. "Just adorable. How much longer?"

She didn't have to answer. In the middle of the screen, a sprout emerged from the bubbling soil. The stalk grew to be four meters tall in a matter of seconds. Arms and legs formed and rustled. Petals, as gold as Dandi's, burst into life, accenting the immense dark face.

"Rewind," shouted Morlax. "And this time don't have it on fast-forward."

Dandi smiled. "It wasn't. He just grew out of nowhere. If you don't mind, could we rewind it later? I want you to see the interaction. If need be, I will leave it here for you to review." She paused. "Look to your right. Those are my seedlings. To the far left, you can see Holly and her hocks. She's my best flower. Notice how Holly continues to go about her business?"

Morlax didn't know a flower from a weed, but he nodded anyway. "Yes, I can see them, considering there's so much static."

"Holly doesn't see anything. Neither do her sprouts. He walks right by Holly and they continue with their business. Nothing."

"And that means?"

"I suppose I have to explain it to you. You see Him, don't you?"

"Yeeeee-es," Morlax extended the vowel in a sarcastic tone.

"I see Him, and Holly doesn't. He is magical. Now just watch Him disappear. He will return in a few minutes. Please, say no more. We will discuss this further, later. The rate we're going, we will be here for hours."

Morlax agreed. He was determined to get through this tape and be on time for lunch. His double belly growled, and the bushes rustling reminded him of salad.

Since the tape had been made from the chip in Dandi's sneakers, she wasn't in the video. Morlax took her word for it that she was there; all he could see was a clump of ragged-edged leaves and an occasional hand patting the ground underneath them. He figured it was her appendage, but to him, all leaves looked alike.

A few hundred more feet of meaningless tape played until He was sighted again. The huge sunflower appeared in the distance and walked towards Dandi. A strange glow surrounded the huge plant, but since this was a copy it was difficult to tell if it was coming from the flower or just a quality-control error.

The voices grew silent. Dandi quit chatting with her offspring and the little ones stopped squeaking. In fact, there was dead silence, for all the surrounding plant sounds ceased…until He spoke.

"Lovely children. In fact, they're all beautiful. You have done well."

"Why thank you, Sir. It's a pleasure and honor to meet You."

Morlax recognized Dandi's voice and saw her hand in the frame as it shook the stalk's leaf. "You touched Him? Weren't you terrified?"

Dandi paused the tape. "Not at all. He was radiant, and the serenity surrounding His presence blanketed everyone and everything in the nursery. Even if they didn't see anything, everyone in the vicinity remembers feeling a rush of euphoria. It's all in the written report and the interviews. Now shush."

The stalk smiled and a clipboard appeared out of nowhere. Dandi waited and watched as the sunflower made notes.

"May I ask what you are doing, Sir?"

"This is My list of rules, and I'm checking it twice. I must be consistent. You see, Dandi, there are certain constants of the cosmos that must not be tampered with; I created it that way so things would work within a framework of logic. So," the sunflower's long stems extended side to side, growing far and out of sight, "if the universe is to continue to exist, even I must obey My laws. I can't expect others to be obedient if I, myself, refuse to comply."

"I don't understand."

"Forget it. All that matters is that you and your little ones are safe. Heck, I'm feeling generous. Make it the entire planet. Chloriflorida has pleased Me, and that is rule number one." The stalk laughed. "I never dreamed sentient vegetation would make the cut. "

"What cut?" she asked.

"I haven't made Myself clear. I am Man, Woman, Birth, Death, and Infinity. I have the power to destroy, but I'm reasonable. It would be unfair to demolish, say, a planet, on just a whim, so with Me now is a list of criteria I follow, as well as rules, and universal truths. If I didn't adhere to them, the whole platform that is the basis of life would crumble. Every couple of thousand years, I perform a quality control checkmake sure no one has stepped out of their boundaries, abused their gifts, and flouted My laws. You could say that My job is that of a shepherd; that I'm here to separate the goats from the sheep."

"What's the difference? They both eat us."

The sunflower laughed. "Your innocence is refreshing. I do have a sense of humor, you know. It's why I spared Pluto. Such strange creatures, and so amusing."

"I'm afraid, Sir, I still don't comprehend."

"Don't worry. If more planets were like Chloriflorida, My job would be easier. You can't imagine the pressure I'm under having to make such life-and-death decisions. And the guilt…" He rested His petals in the flat of the leaf. "It's too much at times. Sometimes it makes Me cry; other times I get so angry I blow up. Then, there's the remorse and depression that follow. It takes Me forever to build up the stamina to return and complete my mission. You just don't know."

Morlax looked at Dandi. She shrugged. He could tell from her facial expression that she was clueless.

"Just tell them I'm fair and reasonable. This isn't helter-skelter."

"Tell whom?" she asked.

"The Coalition. Those whose sneakers you're wearing."

Dandi said nothing.

"The Coalition will understand." The stalk patted Dandi's shoulder and collapsed in a burst of light. The Chlorifloridian soil by her feet shook. Black dirt bubbled around the stalk as it consumed the evidence. No one but Dandi felt the quake.

The rest of the tape was footage of the interviews that Dandi had spoken of earlier. There were four other forms of vegetation in the area, one only a sneeze away. None of them had seen the entity, nor had any of the plants heard a voice, but all felt exhilarated. It was eerie.

Morlax rewound the tape and listened to the scientific mumbo jumbo in the header. Though he didn't quite understand what they were talking about, he did comprehend the conclusions. All indicators were functioning properly. The levels were off the charts. There was no doubt it was Him.

"What do you make of His comment?" Morlax scratched his head.

"About being fair and having a sense of humor?"

"Yeah, and the shepherd-goat thing."

"I don't know. I wasn't aware my comment was funny, but His laughter was honest, not forced."

"Do you believe He was serious? You heard His voice, the tone, the inflections."

Dandi shrugged; the yellow leafy fringe framing her face drooped. "It's hard for me to conceive that someone so awe-inspiring, all-knowing, could be bent on destruction. In His presence, one only feels a sense of beauty and inner peace; but you also have to consider He was responsible for the Great Destruction of 2003. Still, He says His decision is based on criteria and not on personal opinion. Unfortunately, He didn't show me His checklist."

Morlax sighed. "Perhaps we can take advantage of His sense of humor and justice. I will have to think on it. I wasn't prepared for all of this. My bet was based on a guess of three thousand galactic years between comings. It's only GY 4004. I'm almost sorry I accepted my position with the Intergalactic Department of Investigation. In my worst nightmares, I never thought I would be dealing with this crisis."

"Why did you become an agent? Oh, and could you please turn on the lights? I'm beginning to wilt. Plants rest in the dark."

"Light." The room illuminated instantly and Dandi arched her head to look up at the ceiling. "Is that better?"

"Much, thanks."

Dandi removed her new sneaker and opened her purse. She took out a huge green pill, which she placed between two tips of her left appendage's root system (which resembled his six-digit foot). Morlax observed the instant change in the Chlorifloridian. A second ago she had seem shriveled and pale.

"Are those your chlorophyll pills?"

"Yes. They give us instant energy. I feel much more alive now." Dandi's petals brightened and the pale stems deepened to a hunter green. "So, why did you apply for a job with the IDI? I didn't mean to interrupt you."

"No problem, and I didn't. They sought me out. It was to their benefit to have an agent with tenure at Murder, Mayhem, and Music."

Dandi's eyes opened wide. "You must have been important. Someone with power."

"That's the funny thing. I was working in the mailroom then. It was a dead-end job with low pay. I have often wondered why they chose me. I presume it was because I could be bought."

"You think too little of yourself, Morlax. You are intelligent, well-mannered, and a born leader. I bet they saw those qualities too."

The Orfian laughed in a series of snorts and grunts. No one had ever complimented him before. The thought that he had any of those traits was hilarious.

"You're too kind. The truth is, the IDI bribed me with an additional salary and a yearly bonus to keep it a secret from the board of directors at the Big M. The only reason I accepted their offer was because I didn't think He would return in my lifetime. To be honest, I'm scared, and I want to run as far away as I can get on my savings. You could say I'm a loser."

"That can't be true."

"I'm afraid it is, pretty flower. All Orfians are losers to a degree, but I have taken it one step further. I have never aspired to be anything but lazy."

"I refuse to believe that. You didn't run. Here you are, doing what you were hired to do. No one could ask for more. The IDI is lucky to have you, and I feel lucky to have met you."

Morlax looked away as he felt his cheeks flush. "Why, thank you, Dandi. That's the nicest thing anyone has ever said to me. Would you like to have lunch? The cafeteria serves a decent meal and caters to hundreds of life-forms. It seems a good time to take a break, and I'm starving."

He turned to stare into the pupil-less eyes of the flower. Dandi was pretty in her own way, he thought. Two big brown orbs recessed in a face of yellow tufts; stop-sign-red lips that appeared when she spoke. The aroma surrounding her was delightful, and, since she had been visiting her offspring in the tape, there was a good chance she really was a female.

"I would be honored." Dandi batted her golden eyelashes.

Morlax flew her to the nearest lunch line. He chose a table in the far corner, preferring privacy to convenience. After unloading his full tray of multi-colored tubes and bricks, he sat. Dandi was watching him as he poured water in his cup and on the plates. She also waited until all his food materialized before setting her tumbler down in the only free space on the table.

"You're staring at me. You must think me a glutton to have so much food."

"Oh no. It's fascinating to watch you cram your orifice with so much matter. My constitution only allows me little. Eating is a new concept for me. I'm embarrassed to tell you this, but I have rarely ventured out of my solar system, nor have I dealt extensively with an alien."

"Really," he mumbled between bites. "I would never have guessed."

"It's true. I was nervous; terrified, really. My stem nodules were knocking. I'm surprised you didn't hear."

"Not a thing."

"You are too polite to be truthful. I like you, Morlax. You're a very handsome creature; everything about you is exciting and fresh."

He stopped shoveling bird giblets into his mouth. Dandi was flirting with him, or it seemed like she was. He wiped the gravy dribbling from the corners of his lips, using a fresh napkin. "For a plant, you aren't so bad yourself."

Dandi's petals fluttered. "Why, thank you."

She's shy, thought Morlax. *Sweet and polite, and she emits an odor quite like powdered doughnuts. An Orfian could do worse. Even better, she doesn't require food, and water is cheap. I don't care what others may think of Chlorifloridians,* Morlax thought, *I feel good when she's around.*

Morlax set his spork on the table, food still piled on the tines, and rose, knocking the pitcher of water to the floor. Everyone in the surrounding area, including the cafeteria help, quit chattering and clapped.

He bowed and most heads turned away. "Sorry about that. I'll clean it up."

"No need." Dandi stepped into the puddle and the water disappeared up her stems.

It was the most amazing thing Morlax had ever witnessed. Overcome with awe and emotion, he knelt beside Dandi's roots. The floor felt hard and cold as his flabby knee pressed against the tiles. It was the first time in ages that a part of his leg had come into contact with a solid object. A hush fell over the diners.

Morlax was making a spectacle of himself, but he didn't notice and didn't care. Imaginary music filled his ears as he took Dandi's leaf into his hand. His eyes sparkled as he gazed into Dandi's face. "Marry me, O beautiful flower of passion. I'm filled with a fire that never before has burned in my chest. It must be love. I would recognize heartburn."

Morlax saw the huge smile spread over Dandi's face and his chest inflated. She wasn't rejecting him, yet. "I want to spend the rest of my life with you. Say you will marry me. Please, say yes."

Chapter Four

All eyes were on the couple. Morlax's heart was beating so hard he felt nauseous. He hadn't meant to shout the proposal. Why, oh why, had his lips betrayed his thoughts? His mother had warned him about his impetuous behavior and how it would get him in trouble. He had met Dandi just this morning. She could say no and everyone would see his rebuff. He was mortified and wished for a cavern to crawl into. The odds weren't in his favor.

Dandi spilled the glass of water and knocked a plate to the floor. Morlax couldn't tell a thing from the expression on her face, but when she placed her hands in his, and turned her petals to whisper in his ear, he smiled.

"It's a bit sudden, and not at all expected. I'm not saying no. You are wonderful, Morlax; but Chlorifloridians don't have relationships. We experience a common alliance with the soil. Until now, I've never felt emotions like these. We have so many boundaries to break. None of my kind has ever pollinated out of our species. Sub-species perhaps, but never like this. Let's discuss this further. Perhaps we should try living together first."

Morlax sighed in relief and grabbed her stem in the middle, pulling her form against his. Dandi was lost in the blubber, but he still felt her elation. They kissed, and most of the beings in the cafeteria, the ones that were still watching, clapped.

After breaking the embrace, the couple returned to their seats. Morlax quickly shoveled the rest of the food into his mouth. After burping a few times, he reached for Dandi's foliage and the two left the room, hand-in-leaf.

Mai-Z handed Morlax his messages as soon as he entered the office. He glanced at them and tossed them on her desk. "Call Nix and set up an appointment for tomorrow. Make it as late as possible; the Doubel has an early appointment. Hold all calls. Dandi and I will be in my office. We don't want to be bothered unless it's an emergency."

Morlax held the office door open and Dandi entered. "I'm sorry it's such a mess. I've been so busy and the cleaning-bot isn't allowed in. Top secret information is kept in these files."

The room was a total disaster, although no more than usual. It had never bothered Morlax before, but he wanted to continue making a good impression. Piles of paper, folders, and filled ashtrays hid the simulated-oak desktop. At one time, the desk had rested upon an elegant, oriental carpet, but now the rug was faded, coffee-stained, and littered with wads of crumpled paper. A massive leather chair, large enough to provide comfort for the immense Orfian, tilted backwards behind the desk. It was worn and the arms were ragged and torn. Large cigar burns speckled the seat from carelessly flicked ashes.

This was Morlax's real home. He spent more time here than anywhere else. Once each winter, Mai-Z would help him organize the disarray. Clutter was not filth. He was disorganized, not dirty, and he never gave a thought to others' impressions. Criminals ventured into this habitat, and their opinions didn't matter. They were there for his approval to kill, maim, or destroy. They were there to impress *him*. They were there because they needed him, but today was different. For the first time, Morlax felt uneasy. He cared what Dandi thought.

In an attempt to fashion order out of chaos, Morlax shifted some of the files on his desk to the already brimming-with-paperwork bookshelves. Though he normally kept the heavy brocade curtains shut, he opened them, acknowledging her need for sunlight. The light that filtered in for the first time in years made the room seem musty. A mist of dust particles glistened in the sunshine that poured in from the two small windows.

If Dandi objected to being in the stale-smelling office, she didn't say. Morlax held out one of the straight-back chairs and waited for his girlfriend to be seated before leaning back in his own.

"All this paper you use. It's not...I mean you don't use real paper do you?"

"Of course not. No trees are killed. We aren't heartless people. All the materials used here are chemically manufactured."

Dandi sighed. "Thank goodness. I remember when our kind first made contact with your Ambassador. I was only a little weed then, but I do recall the huge controversy over the use of trees for materials. If the Coalition hadn't banned the senseless killing universally, Chloriflorida would never have joined."

"Times and situations make for great changes. At the time of our contact with your species, intelligent vegetation was unheard of. No one will harm your kind again. Even He is pleased with your planet. I'm afraid Earth and Orf won't be so lucky."

"It just doesn't make sense that He's a killer. He seemed so nice."

"He is and He isn't. Up until now, before we had the technology to imprint frequencies, no one knew He was responsible for all the mass destruction of planets and life. It all looked haphazard...coincidental."

Morlax began to float back and forth. "Meteor showers destroyed Gomorth. A wormhole swallowed Hilth. The burnout of Jorin's red sun froze all the inhabitants. I could go on, but you know the history. All these catastrophes were written off as natural calamities. It wasn't until 3013, a bit over a thousand galactic years later, we were able to prove they were His doing. In each case, His frequency imprint was observed. There's no doubt."

"I'm not arguing with you. You don't have to shout. It's just that, well, I met Him. It's difficult for me to believe someone who seemed so pleasant, so filled with serenity, is a mass murderer of planetary proportions."

"You're going to have put your experience aside if you're to be of any assistance, Dandi. He is capable of molecular reconstruction. He can look and sound like anything He wants to. He has the power to destroy by thought. Our laws, our governments, mean nothing to Him. Right now, the Coalition is trying to track Him. I'm sure that's why Nix is trying to get a hold of me. If all else fails, then it's up to us. We have to persuade Him to see things our way..."

"You're right. I'll help you in any way I can. It's not right for one being to sit in judgment of all life, no matter how powerful it is. Tell me what I can do."

Morlax's hover shoes were almost out of fuel, and he sat down in his chair. "Cigar. Light." He began to puff and leaned back.

Dandi gasped. "Is that what I think it is?"

"What? This cigar?"

The golden spikes surrounding her face turned red. "It's made of tobacco leaves, plant leaves. You could be smoking a distant relative. Why, that's cannibalism."

Morlax stubbed the stogie in the ashtray. "I didn't realize. I'm...I'm so sorry."

"The marriage is off. I could never marry a monster."

"Old habits are hard to break, but for you, because I love you, I will give them up and spend the rest of my life fighting the use of tobacco."

Between sobs, Dandi looked up. "Do...you...mean...that?"

"With all my heart. Please forgive me."

"I will do even better than to forgive you. I will forget it ever happened."

Morlax was humbled by Dandi's graciousness. "I only hope the Great Ordainer can be as generous."

"We can only pray," said Dandi.

"For now, that will have to do, because I haven't a clue how to stop Him."

* * *

On the way home to Morlax's apartment, the couple stopped by Dandi's hotel room to gather her few belongings. For the better part of the month, Dandi was to travel. The Coalition needed her to distribute the tapes and gather recruits. Her weekends were free, and staying with Morlax would indicate whether or not the two of them were compatible.

The Revelry Rooms for Rent hotels were comfortable and inexpensive, a home away from home. Noted for their interplanetary accommodations, they were the only lodgings that were owned by, and catered to, Chlorifloridians. One of the first things Morlax noticed was the oblong box by the sliding glass doors. It was filled with dirt and pebbles.

"It's my bed," said Dandi. "I really need to plant my roots every night. The soil is imported from my home town. It's a special blend. If I'm to sleep soundly, I'm going to need this. Do you think they'd sell this one?"

Morlax shook his head. "I doubt it, and I don't think we can sneak this one out. I have a large flowerpot at home, but I don't suppose it'll do."

Dandi sighed. "Not without my special soil."

"Why didn't you bring some with you? You knew you would be traveling."

"Because there are plenty of Revelry hotels, and they always have a few rooms with soil bedding."

"I guess we could stop by a gardening shop. Maybe they'll have something we can use, but what if there isn't any for sale?"

Dandi didn't answer, but crossed her leaves and roots. Morlax sat on the side of the bed and called a few shops, searching the universe for Chlorifloridian soil. After making a dozen calls, he found a small arboretum that sold the dirt by the bag. It wasn't until he saw the size of the bag that his delight turned to dread. The container held less than a tablespoon.

"It's a very specialized and enriched product. You won't need much of this. Mix it with your own dirt. One package per kilogram."

"It's for a Chlorifloridian. How many will I need?"

"Let me look this up. No one has asked this before, and we aren't talking about simple vegetation."

The elderly Orfian sputtered to his office and returned carrying a book. He laid it on the table and double-thumbed through the pages.

"Ahh. Here it is. Chlorifloridians require their native soil in pure form. Nope. Can't be mixed. Sorry."

Morlax wanted to scream. He began to hit his head against the counter. "How much is this going to cost me?"

The Orfian scratched his chin and asked, "How tall is your guest?"

"One and half meters, maybe."

"Let me see. I'll need my convertalator." The man punched in a few numbers. "The bed should be as long as the being is tall. I need to convert the height to cubic meters. We sell this by the tablespoon…you're going to need 33,333 packages at twenty-five hundred units a piece…That'll come to 83,332,500 units plus tax at fifteen percent. Total comes to 95,832,375.00."

"I don't have that kind of money!"

"You don't need to shout, sir. I don't have that much soil anyway."

Morlax rolled his purple eyes. "Then why go through this? Why didn't you say so earlier?"

"You needn't get huffy. You didn't ask me how much I had, just how much it would cost. Here at the Posey Patch Arboretum we pride ourselves on customer service. I've gone out of my way to be helpful. Chlorifloridian potting soil is extremely expensive to import and there's not much of a market for it."

"Sure there isn't. Who the hell can afford it?"

The doorbell tinkled. Both males looked up to see Dandi enter.

"Is there a problem?" Dandi walked over to Morlax and kissed him on the cheek.

"Oh, my," said the salesbeing. "Why didn't you tell me you needed it for a female Chlorifloridian to begin with?"

"Would that have made a difference?" asked Morlax.

"You bet it would. I wouldn't have wasted my time. Mixed couples? Disgusting. Get out of here now! This is my establishment and I don't have to do business with the likes of you."

Chapter Five

It took Morlax all night to calm Dandi. Even in the forty-first century, a time of wonder, ease, and peace, alien prejudice persisted as a universal problem. Technology could prolong life, solve hunger, and obliterate most diseases. It couldn't wipe out fear, violence, and hatred.

The salesbeing had infuriated Dandi. Ms. Lyon had reached over the counter, wound her leafy appendage around the Orf's neck, and choked the green out of his face. Morlax, caught by surprise, had stared until his senses returned. By then, she had released her hold. *Thank goodness*, Morlax thought. He rarely—no, never—fought. Fighting was too exhausting and dangerous.

With their ejection from the shop, any chance they had of purchasing the special soil vanished. The couple rode to Morlax's residence in silence. Dandi's almond-yellow petals covered her eyes. Morlax glanced her way, reached to touch her, but her leaves recoiled. He tried to make conversation, but Dandi ignored his words of reassurance. Defeated, he surrendered to the shallow pool of his thoughts.

"Chloriflorida," the console blared, "is a planet where gentle and intelligent life-forms (except for the weeds) exist in complete peace and camaraderie. (The weeds were eradicated in 2990.) Though it was accepted into the Coalition in the year 1001 by a small margin, most of its history has remained a mystery. Its ambassador invariably takes a pacifistic position when speaking or voting. No one on the council knows what to make of a planet of sentient vegetation that hasn't heard of war. The inhabitants are non-violent."

All but Dandi, Morlax thought as he turned off the computer displaying pictures of Chloriflorida's landscape. Moments earlier she had exhibited uncharacteristic aggression when her stems encircled the salesbeing's neck. Obviously the database was unaware of a Chlorifloridian's latent hostile tendencies. Morlax pondered his duty as a council member. Should he inform Nix? The council? His mother? Naw. Too close to dinner.

The air-coupe shook as he put it in park. Dandi jolted awake. "Take me back to the hotel."

"Why? Have I done something wrong?" asked Morlax.

"Not you. That salesbeing. I can't believe anyone in this day could be so prejudiced and offensive."

"Come on, sweet petal-face. Not all Orfians are rude."

"No, only the fat ones."

"We're all a bit overweight." Morlax huffed.

"Obese is more like it."

He wanted to smack her, but held his temper. "Let's not start name-calling. I've done nothing to hurt you."

Dandi sobbed. "No, not you, but your kind."

"Not all of us are intolerant."

"I suppose...still, I don't think it's going to work."

"Let's give it a chance first. Okay?"

Morlax succeeded in drying his beloved's tears with logic. Dandi was wilting from the loss of the water.

The Chlorifloridian fell as Morlax assisted her out of the vehicle. She was too weak to make it to the apartment on her own. Morlax had to carry her.

To revive her, he placed her in the shower. There she remained in an oblivious state for what seemed hours. Morlax left the flower reclining in the tub.

Dandi's crisis allowed him to check his messages. Luck was with him, as his female parental unit wasn't home. Nix wasn't in either, but his boss's Mai-ZXL9 relayed a communication: Morlax was to meet with Nix tomorrow, along with Dandi and Franzy. His own Mai-Z had left a recording to remind him of his appointment with the Doubel. There were three advertisements, one bill collector, and a musical download from his membership club with Murder, Mayhem, and Music.

Morlax glanced at his watch, and it related the time in unison with his grumbling stomach. He was hungry, too hungry to wait for Dandi to recover. Besides, he reasoned, one of the qualities he found so endearing about his fiancée was that she didn't require food. So what if he was cheap? There were worse personality traits.

Except for some minor wrist movements, Morlax had little to do to prepare his meals. Everything from beans to baked Alaska came in reconstituted packets. Hot and cold food items, differentiated by blue and red symbols, were heated or chilled as soon as the brick or powder hit Orfian air. A gourmet, twelve-course dinner could be made in a blink of an eye.

Lack of exercise was of little concern for the Orfian race. Obese and lazy creatures, they were constantly dealing with medical problems. Even muscular atrophy was a minor nuisance. They had a pill to cure it.

With his dishes in the washer and Dandi still out of commission, Morlax decided to review the Ola-Bola case. They would be expecting a verdict, and with all the commotion, he hadn't time to decide. Common sense told him to veto it. Perhaps he could argue that they were one entity, so that what they wanted to commit constituted suicide, not homicide; then it would be outside his jurisdiction.

There was also the possibility he could ask for an extension, using the excuse that he needed to research and conduct an investigation on body separation. It was all too much of a burden now that He had made an appearance.

Morlax shuddered at the thought. Why had the Great Ordainer of Destruction made an appearance now? "Because," he answered himself out loud, "I'm the unluckiest Orfian in the universe."

Dandi began to sob. "All you had to do was ask me to leave. And to think I believed you really wanted me to stay. You Orfians are all alike!"

He swiveled his chair and beckoned to the girl to join him in his chair. "I was talking to myself about His re-appearance. Why did you assume I was talking about you?"

Still racked with tears, Dandi snuggled in his arms. "That awful man in the shop. People aren't going to accept our species intermingling. I really care about you, and I'm afraid this relationship isn't going to work. I guess I transferred my fears to you. I thought you were experiencing those same doubts, too."

Morlax put his other arm around Dandi and kissed her on the forehead. "I do have doubts—no, let's call them concerns. We have a lot of issues to deal with that same-species couples don't, but we can find a way to work through them. We'll get you a box of dirt, no matter what the cost. I'll install repli-star lights all over the house so you will have the natural UV rays you need to thrive. We'll find a way. Okay?"

Dandi sighed. "You really mean it, don't you?"

"You bet I do. Now, are you feeling better?"

"Yes, I am. Thank you. You are a darling."

Morlax blushed. "So are you, and you smell nice too."

The petals surrounding Dandi's face turned pink.

"There, there. You're looking a lot better now. Think you could help me with a problem? I really need some advice."

Dandi nodded; her petals vibrated.

"Good, because I have a situation here that has me perplexed." Morlax handed her the Doubel's file. "Please look this over, please, and give me your opinion."

While she thumbed through the documents, Morlax switched on the Interactive Vision Module. It was time for one of his favorite Earth shows: *Lost in Space*.

Morlax was one of the few Terraphiles on his planet. Most Orfians held little interest in a planet considered so low on the evolutionary scale. It was probably a good thing, too, as Morlax stole quite a few ideas from Earth's technology. Of course, by the time they made it to consumers, these products no longer resembled the originals. It was one way Morlax made a few extra credits.

Though Earth wasn't officially part of the Coalition, contact had been made with the planet's military leaders. In exchange for Orfian non-violent technology, Orf was now able to tap into Earth satellite broadcasts, and had begun trading things like artificial hearts for cigars and remote controls for jerky.

After the Coalition had what they wanted, they'd forgotten about Earth, and contact ceased. It was what gave Morlax an edge—he was still interested in the third planet's culture. He marketed many an idea from their infomercials, and no one was the wiser.

"Strange creatures," Dandi said.

"Who?" Morlax had been thinking about humans, and wondered if his girl-friend read his mind. Or, maybe, she was thinking about Orfians.

"These Doubels. I'm not sure granting either half a permit will do any good."

"What?" Morlax was relieved she hadn't thought him weird, and only heard half a sentence, as he was entranced with the tin-can robot.

"If you're not going to listen to me, why did you ask for my opinion?"

He clicked off and sighed. "Sorry. I get so engrossed in these re-telecasts. Their spaceship resembles one of our garbage tankers. It's a real hoot, but you're right. I didn't mean to be discourteous. Go ahead. You have my full attention."

Dandi relaxed, crossed her legs and shook her roots side to side. "Do you think it could be a hoax?"

"I hadn't considered that. Why do you ask?"

"It's inconceivable they share the same body and can't get along. Nowhere in this stack of paper is there another case like theirs."

"There's a first time for everything. Besides, doctors evaluated them, and there's no medical or hormonal reason for their incompatibility. I need to make a ruling soon, so I can devote my time to the real problem. Based on what you've read, whom would you grant the license to?"

Dandi handed him the file. "I don't think either half should get dispensation. Bola and Ola are both disagreeable creatures. They most likely won't get along with anyone. This seems more like a lovers' spat than anything else."

"You don't think I should look into the medical-separation angle?"

"Why bother? It's not your concern. You take on too much. Your job is to look at the situation and make a simple decision. With more serious issues at stake, why get so involved?"

"I guess you're right. Besides, your assessment of this has given me an idea."

"Really? I'm glad I was of help. Are you going to reject both applications?" Dandi asked.

"Not sure. I need to think this through a bit more¾work out the variables. In the meantime, why don't we head to bed? I'm tired, and tomorrow we have lots to do."

Dandi nodded and slipped out of the chair. Morlax followed, putting his arm around her as they walked down the hall.

"Good night and sweet dreams." Dandi opened the door to the bathroom and stepped inside.

"Are you going to sleep in the shower?" Morlax asked.

"Did you have something else in mind?"

"Well, I was hoping we could cuddle for a while."

The petals surrounding Dandi's face straightened. "Cuddle? Oh, I get it now. Sex. You want to engage in this physical form of exercise that creatures of your kind perform for reproduction."

"It was a thought. It's not just to produce offspring, though; we show our affection this way."

"I'm afraid I don't know much about it. Chlorifloridians reproduce by spores. I don't think I even have the necessary body parts to comply."

Morlax had to bite his tongue. He wanted to ask her to lift her leaves, but felt it wasn't the most romantic of requests. Sexual incompatibility was something he hadn't considered. She had a face, arms, fingers, and legs. He'd assumed the covered portions of her body were Orfian-like as well.

The pause was uncomfortable. Morlax stood in the hallway speechless, trying to hide his disappointment.

"I'm willing to learn. Why don't you explain it in more detail? Show me your reproductive organs. Tell me what's involved in scattering your seed."

Morlax's face turned two shades of red. In combination with his green skin, the effect resembled some Christmas displays he remembered seeing on Earth. "Let's drop the subject for now."

"Have I embarrassed you?"

"No...er, yes. Let's drop it."

Dandi patted Morlax's back with her frond. "Perhaps if you have a book on the subject, it might help. You seem a bit uncomfortable about the process. I'm an asexual creature. Reproduction to my kind is a simple matter of scattering by the wind."

"The manual thing is a good idea." Morlax let out a long and deep sigh. "I can pick up one tomorrow."

Dandi smiled. "You have a full day ahead of you. The meeting with the Doubel will tie you up for a few hours. Why don't I run some errands and stop by the bookstore before we meet with Nix? I can be back in time for lunch."

"Great. Just drop me off at the office and you may use my coupe. You're insured, aren't you?"

Dandi nodded and stepped into the shower. Morlax ordered the showerhead to sprinkle lukewarm water. Tiny beads of water sprayed out as a mist and collected in a puddle deep enough to saturate Dandi's roots. "This will do. Thank you and good night, Morlax."

"You are most welcome." He turned off the light, shut the door, and paused in the hallway. It had been a long and depressing day. The optimism he had felt earlier was fading into depression. His heart ached.

Plopping back into his chair, he made himself comfortable before whispering to the closed door, "Good night, Dandi. Sweet dreams."

* * *

Morlax arrived at the office early only to find the Doubel waiting. He knew Ola and Bola were there, as their arguing could be heard as soon as he entered the eletube. The plastic walls of the shaft were a conduit for noise. The tunnel would have been quieter, but took too much energy. One had to use arm movements to float. Since the invention of the eletubes, elevating air-current channeled tubes, the tunnels were used in emergencies only.

The lobby was crowded. Morlax did a silent head count. There were fifteen creatures from all parts of the galaxy, pushing, shoving and grumbling. It was pathetic. So much hatred in one room. No wonder the Great Ordainer of Destruction had returned.

He was in no mood to placate anyone. What was one death, here or there, when the galaxy's fate was in question? Morlax grabbed the mail, poured a cup of coffee, snatched a few doughnuts, and entered his office. Only nine o'clock and already he was perspiring.

"Send the Doubel in, Mai-Z. Thanks."

"Yes-sir..."

Morlax ordered the intercom off. He wiped the crystal sugar crumbs off his mouth with the edge of his caftan and parted his slobbery chops in anticipation of his stogie. Dandi was nowhere around. She wouldn't know, and what she didn't know wouldn't piss her off. Giving up cigars was more than he'd bargained for in the deal.

The cigar floated in mid-air while one end was snipped and the other slithered between his waiting lips. A lighter flamed until the tobacco smoked. He puffed and pointed to the chair.

The Doubel sat. Bola spoke. "Have you reached a decision?"

Morlax handed the male half a folder and waited until he opened it. "Halitosis, Baby-Cakes," Bola jumped up. "Your days are numbered, Ola. Start saying your prayers."

Ola batted her eyelashes at Morlax and pouted. "How could you—and with all I promised you?"

He tossed Ola her file. "Open it."

The female sobbed and sniffled. "What's the use?"

"Just open it."

Ola did. She stared at the top page marked *Accepted.* "What's the meaning of this?"

"Yeah," echoed Bola, staring at Ola's application. "What the hell does this mean?"

The cigar bobbled as Morlax answered. "Both of you have cause and reason to want the other dead. I couldn't make up my mind. Neither of you realizes the seriousness of my position and the depth of my responsibility. Just because murder is legal, doesn't mean every Tom, Dick, and Doubel will get my okay. I have a great regard for life."

"Yeah, yeah, yeah," mumbled Bola, "But this isn't what we asked for¾"

"Please *don't* interrupt me again. I don't give a Doubel's ass what you want. You both wanted a permit to kill the other and that's exactly what you got. Now shut up and hear me out."

Bola sat back down. "I'm listening."

Morlax puffed and blew smoke rings. "As I said, each of you has good reasons to want to kill the other. I teetered back and forth until I realized I was going about this all wrong. Had you filled out one application instead of two, I would have been forced to choose. As it was, though, I had to determine separately the merits of each of your motives, and that's what I did. That's all I did. That's all I had to do."

"We're right back where we started," said Bola.

"Not my problem. Good day to you both. Please stop by the desk and pay Mai-Z. You may also want to consider purchasing my brochures, *Murder Management, Weaponry for Beginners*, and *Twenty Sure-fire Ways to Maim or Kill.* I've been told they're worth the credits."

The half-Doubels stared at each other.

Morlax stood. "Nice meeting you. Good luck. There's the door. Bye-bye."

It was the first time since he'd met the entity that there was silence from both halves. Morlax inhaled deeply and continued puffing. "Shut the door, please," he said, waving the cigar. "Merry murdering."

He chuckled as he swiveled the chair, reveling in the sheer brilliance of his decision. Though it wasn't his problem anymore, he wondered if the inseparable couple would learn to get along now that they both had permits to kill. Oh, he was a smart one all right.

The digital clock announced the time. It was still early, and he could see a few more applicants before his meeting with Nix.

How he dreaded those conferences. Nix was a stickler for protocol, wasting precious time with procedural amenities. Franzy could squander half a meeting asking useless questions and taking notes. Few things, if any, were accomplished, but until now it hadn't mattered. With the Great Ordainer's return, every moment counted. The planet Earth was in jeopardy¾even worse, his own planet, Orf. Orf was sure to be on the destruction list.

Morlax didn't want to die. He had so much to live for: food he hadn't tasted, worlds he hadn't visited, and women he hadn't... In light of the real problem, Dandi's sexual inadequacies didn't matter, but still the desire hovered in the back of Morlax's mind. He owned dozens of girlie magazines from all over the galaxy, and up until now, when the mood had struck him, he'd used his hand-held manipulator. The manuals and articles all spoke of an ecstasy that could only be reached by body coupling. Morlax didn't want to die before experiencing true intimacy.

He sighed. "I'm taking a break, Mai-Z. Hold all calls."

Morlax skimmed through the mail, finding the cover of the latest copy of *Alien Aberration*. It was one hot publication and he looked forward to each month's installment. This issue came with a 3-D video, a hottie, but it wasn't why Morlax went searching for it. The cover article about wooing and seducing aliens had caught his eye.

Morlax flipped through the pages and stopped when he reached the "Alien of the Month."

The commentary was entitled, "Candy is Dandi, but Lick-Her is Quicker." There in the centerfold, in bright colors and animation, was his girlfriend cavorting with a bird-like creature dangling a twenty-centimeter long, triple, flapping tongue.

Morlax freaked.

Chapter Six

The most annoying characteristic of Nix was the echo coming from his second head, named Nax. Morlax, still tipsy from the morning's wine-tasting, tried to stay awake as his boss read the minutes of the last meeting¾all forty-two pages, ten thousand or so words, spoken by two sets of lips under the control of one very tiny brain divided in half. If Nix had any sense, he would have been considered dangerous. How he had managed to climb from the bottom rung to become the head of the Intergalactic Department of Investigation and silent part-owner of Murder, Mayhem, and Music was enough to boggle even the keenest mind.

Without inflection, he read from the text appearing in the imbedded screen of his desk. The other head, the one staring into oblivion, looked lost, and indeed it was. It was still on vacation. Only its lips moved, as if a thread secured one head to another. Morlax saw nothing tangible. All he could see was the tufts of purple hair encircling Nix's bald spot. The shiny patch of skin reflected the overhead hover-light's beams in an array of rainbows.

Two arms, four hands, and twenty-two fingers gripped the edge of the desk and kept the top-heavy creature from falling. Morlax admired the custom-tailored suit and the large but muscular build pressing against the seams. Nix was big; Morlax was just plain fat.

"You are listening, Morlax, aren't you?" Nix cleared his throat and waited for a response.

"I can hear with my eyes closed, sir. The echo is making me dizzy."

Nix's one eye glanced at Franzine. "And you, you're getting all this down, aren't you, Franzine?"

"Oh my, yep, yep, yep, of course, wouldn't dream of missing a single word, your Eminent-ship."

Morlax's closed eyelids hid his burning eyes. "May we please discuss the problem? Considering the importance of the situation, I vote we dispense with normal procedures and discuss the issue."

"Your vote doesn't count." Nix snorted and continued reading.

Morlax lifted his lids a slit to read the wall clock. Nix's speech was running long. Franzy was busy brown-nosing, alternating smiles with nods. Dandi hadn't arrived.

The empty seat next to him made the situation intolerable. Dandi, his precious fiancée...a centerfold in an alien porno magazine. Morlax felt humiliated and curious, angry and proud, revolted and randy. Wanting to confront her with the evidence, he stared at the office door as if a bomb were ready to explode.

It had been an awful morning.

* * *

After seeing Dandi's photo, Morlax could barely concentrate on his job. His fifteen-minute break stretched into an hour. Had he more excuses, he might have relaxed and calmed down, but Mai-Z's constant reminders forced him to keep his next appointment.

Morlax activated his langulator, a tiny nodule embedded behind the ear that translated all known languages. (He was versed in nineteen languages, but that wasn't nearly enough to be effective in his line of work). He waited silently while the entity from the planet Vino ranted and raved about killing a worm.

"It's destroying my vineyards. It eats the roots, and my grapes turn to raisins. There isn't enough time in the day to keep abreast of this worm's path of destruction. As soon as I replant one section, it has destroyed another. It's ruining me."

How trivial, Morlax thought. *Wasting my time with a request to eradicate a common worm. Why doesn't the idiot just kill it? It's only a worm.* This murder-licensing legal rigmarole was being taken too seriously. Morlax nodded and agreed and nodded and agreed.

Backass, or something similar-sounding (Morlax couldn't make sense of the langulator's enunciation), was a silly-looking life-form. His scales were spotted, purple and red, most likely stained from years of pressing grapes. The parts of his torso not tinted in wine were yellow. He looked as if he had failed to duck when someone threw a paint can at him. Morlax would have laughed if he hadn't realized that Batchass, or something similar-sounding, owned one of the galaxies' largest vineyards and made an award-winning alcoholic beverage, similar to champagne and known all over the universe. It was a darn good thing he knew when to shut up; otherwise he might have made the creature angry.

Backash, or something similar-sounding, had brought evidence, and of course Morlax, in the interest of doing his job competently, had to sample it. The two beings finished off the first bottle of black wine, fermented from grapes grafted from the original vines in the Bubblingling region south of Effervescentia. They chased that bottle down with a rare white wine, and finally Bochass (the langulator's interpretation was getting annoying) pulled out a magnum of his cava.

Perhaps to a wine connoisseur, the special grapevines and age of the samples would have made a difference. To Morlax, wine was wine, good or bad, and he was impressed neither by the label nor the bouquet. Alcohol was expensive, and rarely was he able to indulge in the imported stuff. Being offered three bottles for sampling was a temptation he couldn't resist. Morlax couldn't find one good reason to deny himself such a pleasure.

To say Morlax got drunk would be an understatement. To say he remembered anything about the request to kill worms would be an exaggeration. Morlax could barely keep his eyes open as Bacchus (the langulator finally made sense of the accent) droned on and on about the mechanics and techniques of cultivation and fermentation, information that under any circumstances would still have been boring to Morlax.

When the purple creature begged him for a permit, Morlax, too inebriated to think clearly, could do little but stamp his application *Accepted.* Bacchus was delighted and donated two cases of his best wine. Morlax didn't see that as a bribe, but as a gift of appreciation for a job well done. It *was* a job well done, not like one of Franzy's irrational decisions, and that made it all right to keep the present.

Morlax called Mai-Z in to lug the cases to the closet and show Bacchus out. He then canceled the rest of the morning appointments and snoozed.

* * *

He'd been asleep when Nix arrived, and had been fighting the urge to return to slumber from the moment Nix began reading last week's minutes. Only the odor of powdered doughnuts forced Morlax to stir.

Dandi's entrance jolted Morlax to an upright position, though Franzy recorded in its notes that it was Morlax's own snoring that awakened the Orfian. If it hadn't been for the seriousness of the situation, Morlax would have been written up on the spot, but with the Great Ordainer on the loose, it was a grave state of affairs. Except for Nix, no one read Franzy's minutes anyway.

Dandi excused herself and took the empty chair next to Morlax. When Nix wasn't looking, Morlax drew the magazine from beneath his caftan and shoved the photo in Dandi's face as if it were a loaded gun.

"It's not me!" Dandi cried.

Franzy dropped its pen.

Nix quit reading. "Who isn't you?"

"Me," replied Dandi.

Morlax looked at the centerfold again. "Sure looks like you."

"All of us look alike." Dandi sneered at Morlax.

"I'll have none of that prejudicial posturing in this room. According to the galactic law books, volume 444, section 991, line 22—or is it line 23?...Franzine, get me the volume..."

Morlax pounded the page with his finger. "The name says Dandi. Right here under the blurb."

"Of course it does. We're all named Dandi."

Franzy rushed out of the office and returned with the book, handed it to Nix, and stayed by his side. Morlax and Dandi, arms folded, exchanged nasty looks.

"Do you mean to say everyone on your planet has the same name? I find that confusing as well as unbelievable." Morlax tucked the evidence under one of his folds.

"Give me that magazine."

Morlax took it out again and handed it to Dandi. "Gladly."

"I can't believe you are calling me a liar. What do you know about Chloriflorida? Nothing. All of us are called Dandi. Our last name is what differentiates us from the rest of the phylum. All of us are replicas, and our line can be traced back thousands of years. We don't share genetic material in the exchange of seed. We have everything we need to do the reproduction ourselves and with a little help from air currents, we sporulate. See?" Dandi pointed to the blurb. "Read it out loud."

Morlax read slowly. "A Dandi..."

"See? *A* Dandi, referring to a type, and not a name at all. I rest my case."

Morlax bit his bottom lip. "Well, I'm sorry. How was I supposed to know? I saw this photo of you and couldn't control my jealousy."

"Here it is. I was right. Line 22. 'The Intergalactic council hereby—'"

"Stifle it," shouted Morlax. "This has nothing to do with species bigotry."

"You're out of line, Morlax. I will mark you down for one demerit and it will show up as such on your next check. Franzine, take care of it." Nix rolled his one eye and pointed to the chairs. "Now sit, both of you. We're here to discuss what we're going to do about the return of the Great Ordainer."

Morlax shrugged. Dandi scrunched her nose. Both took their seats.

"It's about time," mumbled Morlax.

"That will be two demerits. Now, what do any of us know about the Great Ordainer?" Nix picked up a piece of chalk and stood by the board.

Franzy waved its hand furiously. "Yep, yep, yep. He is most powerful and nothing known to the universe can stop Him."

"Correct. And where was He last seen? Dandi?"

"On my planet, Chloriflorida."

"That's not fair," pouted Franzy. "She didn't have her hand up. No, she didn't. Yep, yep, yep."

Nix rolled his eye. "This isn't a game show. There are no winners."

"You can say that again. Knowing the disposition of the Great Ordainer, in time, all of us are going to be losers." Morlax folded his entwined green fingers on his lap.

"Very true. In my briefcase are four other tapes depicting the latest in planetary annihilations. That is, four in one day. Four out of five sightings ended up in disaster. That's an eighty percent kill factor. Unless we do something, we may be next." Nix removed the tapes. "You may view them later. Right now, we're open to suggestions."

"We?" asked Franzine.

"Yes, we. Due to the news, I was forced to call my other head back from vacation. He should be here any minute now."

As Nix spoke, the other head shook, blinked, and winked. "Darn. I was having a great time. There's nothing worse than being summoned right in the middle of an Anorian puzzle game." The right head glanced around the room, turned to look at its twin, rolled its eye and closed it. "Good to see you, Morlax. You too, Franzine."

Morlax contained his sigh of relief. The echo effect had ended when the vacationing head spoke. Franzy waved. Dandi held out her hand and shook Nix's right arm.

Though both heads looked the same, their personalities were different. Morlax liked the right side. At least it had a sense of humor. Unlike the Doubel, both heads worked together. As far back as Morlax could remember, the two had never quarreled.

"Glad you could make it." Morlax was sincere in his comments. With both heads present, they could make progress.

Silence prevailed as Nix and Nax interfaced. Both eyeballs spun as if they were windows on a slot machine. "I see...There's no doubt it's Him. Our Quantum Sequential Molecular Signaturing analysis leaves no doubt." Eyebrows lifted; blue irises whirred and stopped. "So, three planets and one solar system are gone. He's not wasting any time."

"Has anyone put plan A into effect?" asked Morlax.

"He ignored the petition." Nix counted on his fingers. "Plans B and C have failed as well. We're all out of ideas."

The room grew silent. Dandi leaned over and whispered in Morlax's ear.

"Has anyone tried to set up a meeting? Some cultures say He is reasonable. Perhaps we could make a deal." Morlax smiled at Dandi and blushed.

"That's a marvelous suggestion. We could put up neon signs all over the universe. Let me check my calendar." Nix swatted his left hand, allowing the right one to pull out the pocket date book. "Let's see, I'm free..."

Morlax jumped out of his seat, which took most of his energy and equilibrium. He swayed in mid-air before gaining his balance. "Damn it, Nix. We'll meet whenever it's convenient for Him, and count ourselves lucky if He agrees."

"Slow down." Franzy raised its pen in the air. "I don't know shorthand. No, I don't. Yep, yep, yep."

"Forget the notes," Morlax continued. "None of this matters, nothing matters and nothing will matter if the Great Ordainer keeps at it."

Franzy pressed its lips together, shoving the bottom one out farther. Morlax contained his welling anger at this idiot. Nuets weren't known for their common sense, only their sense of organization and neatness. Franzy was forever sorting paper clips by size, color, and manufacturer. Morlax couldn't even find a paper clip in his office, and he liked it that way.

"Morlax is correct in his assessment. According to my tabletop calculations, if the Great Ordainer keeps at it, he will have gone through our known galaxy and universe before I celebrate my next birthday. That doesn't give us much time."

"I move we adjourn this meeting. We can continue where we left off tomorrow." Morlax glared at Franzy, who was about to object. (Nuets didn't sleep. They were too busy tidying things up.)

Nix seconded and Nax thirded it. Dandi's and Franzy's votes weren't needed.

Morlax and Dandi, holding hands, followed Nix out the door. Franzy trailed, mumbling. "You know, Morlax, this is a big mistake, waiting for tomorrow. Yep, yep, yep. While we relax, the Great Ordainer is out there doing His thing. More planets, galaxies are in jeopardy. Yep, yep, yep, it's a big mistake waiting for the last minute."

Morlax wanted to throttle the Nuet, but held his temper. Dandi shook her head as if to keep Morlax from violence, but the Orfian was a civil being, and fighting took more energy than Franzy was worth. He said nothing.

Franzy continued with its yep-yep-yepping. "Waiting for the last minute...not a good idea at all."

Morlax could contain his anger no longer. Dandi grasped his hands, but she either forgot or didn't think to put a leaf over his mouth. "You are one stupid Nuet, and your yepping is driving me insane. Don't you know that if it weren't for the last minute, nothing would ever get done?" And with that said, Morlax broke free of his fiancée's hold and jetted down the hall, bouncing off the walls, shaking the framed pictures, and kicking the ankle-high, dog-like messengers into hyperspace.

Chapter Seven

In times of emergency, the Intergalactic Department of Investigation, together with the Coalition of Planets and Galaxies, had the authority to suspend commerce. This included all offices licensing murder. Murder, Mayhem, and Music received their notice and complied. Thankfully, it didn't affect the entertainment division. Even better, the sanitation department was also excluded from the declaration.

Agents, dispatched to the five corners of the universe, were ordered to report anything unusual. The Galactic Guard was put on alert, and thousands of patrols policed airspace in order to maintain peace. So as not to alarm the populace, newspapers reported the situation as an intergalactic power-grid failure.

Dandi, to Morlax's relief, was ordered to distribute her tape to various planetary rulers, and left immediately. For some reason, the various rulers wanted proof before joining the crusade.

The best part of Dandi's assignment was the portable trough filled with

Chlorifloridian soil. It was delivered to the door of Morlax's apartment. After Dandi finished her tour of duty, she would be allowed to keep the dirt. Now all they had to do was stay alive.

Dandi threw her pills and portable UV flashlight into the bag with the dirt and kissed Morlax goodbye before embarking. It would be days, if not weeks, before she could return to her planet, and by then her babies would be grown. Thank goodness Holly had promised to take pictures.

Morlax returned to his office alone. He was exhausted and still sick to his stomach after his breakfast of wine, but not so ill that he didn't have an appetite. Closing his door, but leaving it unlocked, he sat in his chair and opened the bulging sack of protein. He had a lot to mull over, and he hunkered down to an all-night session of eating and thinking...and drinking. There were still the cases of wine in his locker.

Mai-Z was plugged into the wall and clicked away amperes. Except for the monotonous ticks, the lobby was quiet. It would be this way until morning, when the general public discovered the closings. Then the excrement would hit the mechanical air circulator. Good thing Morlax was used to ducking.

He knew they were in for trouble. It didn't take a genius to realize that Nix's plan wouldn't work. Setting up signs, especially ones flashing "LET'S MAKE A DEAL," wouldn't stop Him from destroying lives and property. He didn't need permission or an application to commit murder and mayhem. Or did He?

There comes a time in everyone's life when a moment of brilliance knocks him upside the head. It takes a being of intelligence to recognize such as an opportunity, and not to mistake it for an act of aggression or a headache. It would be written in the Galactic History Books of the Universe that Morlax, from the planet Orf, was gifted with true insight and genius...that the brilliant idea that struck him on the evening in question was a revelation and not a migraine.

In truth, Morlax, acutely aware of the jackhammer pounding away at his brain, discerned the difference between pain and inspiration. Rip-roaring drunk but elated, Morlax wrote his idea down, and with little more than a hangover the following morning, set out to convince the council to test it.

* * *

Mai-Z interrupted Morlax in mid-snooze. "They-are-rioting-outside-sir."

Cymbals clanged in the background...no, it wasn't cymbals, just the robot's gears. Mai-Z needed oiling. Morlax lifted his head. The room swirled around his eyes in a cinematic whirl of colors. "Where am I?"

"Mr.-Morlax-are-you-working-properly?"

"No. Yes. Jeez, my head hurts. Did someone drop a brick on me last night?"

"Do-you-want-me-to-investigate-this-allegation-sir?"

Morlax propped his elbows on his desk and placed his chin on his palms. "No, Mai-Z, it was just a joke. What is going on outside?"

"There-is-a-revolt. I-have-calculated-that-there-is-a-ninety-two-percent-chance-violence-will-occur-if-they-are-not-dispersed."

"Is it that bad already?"

Mai-Z nodded. A bolt fell from her ear. The robot picked it up and reattached it with duct tape (one of Earth's better inventions).

"I'll take care of it. Is Franzine here?"

"No-sir—It-may-be-in-the-crowd-but-I-doubt-it-would-make-it-through-that-mob."

Morlax hovered slowly to the lobby, every burst of power from his shoes resounding in his head as if an elephant were doing a tap dance on his skull. He opened the door and this solo recital turned into a Broadway production.

"Enough already," he shouted, "I can't do anything about this. The Coalition has suspended business until further notice."

"No one told me. I have a nine o'clock appointment." A giraffe with three necks stuck one of them into the crack between the door and frame.

"Nor us." Three gorillas with wings and horns pushed their way past and stomped inside.

A blur of alien pageantry followed the ape's lead, shoving and kicking. Morlax was having terrible trouble keeping his equilibrium. If the Octomoose hadn't caught him, he would have landed on the Jellysnake. Ick.

"Please, everyone. Just go home. There's nothing I can do about this matter until the Coalition lifts the ban."

The bickering between species kept Morlax from being heard. "Please," he shouted three more times, "Go home!"

Gunshots resounded. Twice. Hitting the ceiling, a bullet blasted a hole in the tile, struck a steel beam, and ricocheted in a downward spiral, planting itself in a potted palm. "You-heard-Mr.-Morlax—Go-home-now."

Mai-Z's metal finger was smoking. The crowd in the waiting room quit squabbling and stood at attention. Morlax regained his composure, glanced left and right, smiled, and took three backward strides to stand beside the robot. "Thanks, Mai-Z. That's one way to get their attention."

"My-pleasure-sir. I-am-pleased-that-the-semi-automatic-is-still-working."

"I'm ecstatic." Morlax grabbed Mai-Z's arm and aimed it at the closest creature. "Now that I have your attention, listen up. Mai-Z has my permission to shoot anyone and anything that isn't out of here by my count of five. One...two...four..."

The crowd dispersed, all except Franzine who was busy dusting footprints off its white lab coat. Its thick mop of red ringlets looked like sprung springs. A day's worth, maybe two, of stubble accented the pointy chin.

Morlax extended a hand and helped the Nuet balance on one foot. Franzine hopped the distance to a chair and began straightening out its other leg, which was bent at a 45-degree angle. Mai-Z went over to assist. "I didn't think I was going to get in alive. They were pretty angry. You saved me, Mr. Morlax. Yep, yep, yep. You are a hero."

"Don't make anything out of it, Franzy. I did what anyone else would do in that situation." Morlax lied. If he had known his assistant was in the crowd, he would have let them tear it apart. Well, not really, but it was a pleasing thought.

"Have you ever seen anything like it?" Franzine, leg successfully straightened, got up and locked the door.

"No, and I have been here most of my life." Morlax looked at the security monitor. The mob hadn't dispersed, just relocated to the street. A few creatures picketed. Most were yelling obscenities in languages that Morlax was grateful he didn't know and the langulator couldn't decipher.

"I wonder if my old buddy Tarnak is experiencing the same problems. Would serve the crook right if he were inundated with violent idiots."

"Yep, yep, yep. I could call him. Or I could turn on the news. Or, I could...."

Morlax sighed. "Don't bother. I was just allowing my thoughts to control my tongue. We have much to do today. Too much, really."

"Shall I make some java?" asked Franzine.

"That would be fantastic. I seem to be having a problem with the machine. It comes out thick when I make it."

"Yep, yep, yep. That's because you put in too much paste. Want me to show you how I do it?"

"Not today. I have a lot to do, and besides, you're back now. I would hate to encroach on the only thing you do well."

"Is that a compliment, Sir?"

"What do you think?"

Franzine's lips curled into a toothy grin. "Java is my specialty. Coming right up, boss."

Mai-Z returned to her desk and her typing. Morlax followed the Nuet to the hallway. "I'll be in the board room. Whenever you're ready, Franzy."

Morlax wiped the sweat from his brow with the edge of his caftan and shuffled to the end of the hall. He ordered the door to unlock, and the mechanism, recognizing his voice, complied. One of the smaller hover lights bounced above him, flickering until the bulb heated up enough to provide light. It had been a year since the room had been used.

"Clean." Morlax waited in the hall as dust cloths, mops and brooms tidied the walls, floors, table and chairs. The last implement finished seconds before Franzine arrived with two steaming mugs.

Morlax inhaled deeply. There was nothing better than the odor of freshly brewed coffee, except for the sweet smell of his fiancée. Dandi...he hadn't thought he would be missing her, but he did. Not only did she remind him of powdered doughnuts; she was smart, too. Bouncing ideas off her helped. But she had her duty to do and he had his.

Franzine handed Morlax a mug, almost spilling it when the TP rang. Both beings stood in place, waiting to see who the caller was.

"Franzine-you-have-a-call-on-line-three."

Morlax glared. "We have a lot of business to go over before the interplanetary meeting today. Make it quick."

"Who is it, Mai-Z?"

"It-is-Nix-sir—madam—thing."

"Patch him through to the board room, please." Franzine sat beside the portal and set its mug in front of the stacked files. "Nix, what is up?"

"Identify yourself, Agent Nine-fifty-nine."

"Yep, yep, yep." Franzine paused to clear its throat. "If ever I would leave you, it wouldn't be—"

"The yepping was enough. Good, it is you. Is Morlax there?"

"Yes, your Excellency," Morlax faked a smile for the tiny Nix on the portal stand, "I'm here."

Nix crossed his arms and tapped his foot. "I'm waiting..."

Morlax burst into song. "Someday—"

"That was yesterday's code-song. Didn't you get the memo?"

"No, sir. With everything that's going on..."

Nix started to pace. "Forget it. Too much to do, so little time. The meeting place of the Intergalactic Department of Investigation and the Coalition has been changed in order to seat everyone."

"Since when is the Coalition part of this task force?" Morlax asked.

"Didn't Franzine tell you?"

Morlax stared at the Nuet before answering. "No, *it* didn't."

Franzine stared at its feet. "I didn't have a chance, sir. We had a situation this morning. Yep, yep, yep. I was going to. Why, just this minute...."

"Forget it. Doesn't matter. What does matter is: I feel this is a problem directly affecting everyone in the entire galaxy. It was to everyone's benefit that I invited all the departments. Don't you agree, Morlax?"

"Oh, yes. Brilliant idea, sir. So who else is coming?"

Nix rubbed both chins. "Franzine, do you have the list?"

"Yep, yep, yep. Indeedy I do." Franzine withdrew its notepad from the front pocket of its coat. "The Department of Investigation..."

"We know that, Franzine," Nix's heads said in unison.

"The Coalition of Planets and Galaxies, the Department of Astral Vehicles, the Interstellar Parliament, the Ministry of Law Enforcement, the Extraterrestrial Bureau of Exploration, the Society for the Prevention of Cruelty to Aliens, Mistress Blout and her Amazing Dancers, and, last on the list, the Sanitation and Rehydration Department of Refuse."

"Is that all?" Morlax mumbled. "You forgot to ask my mother."

"I heard that, Morlax. This is no time to be petty. Unless your mother has a solution to this problem, and I can't see how she could, since she shouldn't even know about it, I suggest you limit yourself to intelligent comments or forever hold your tongue."

Morlax held his breath. "I apologize for my outburst. Won't happen again."

"Good. Then it's set. The meeting will take place this afternoon at four, in the Teal Room at the United Universe building. Dinner will be served at six and there will be dancing to eleven. Both of you are expected to stay and entertain the dignitaries."

"Not the planet Redun? And what's with the dancing? The Great Ordainer is out there destroying planets and solar systems. It doesn't seem right to party," Morlax moaned.

"Unless you have a better suggestion, keep your displeasure to a minimum. As for the gala, why not mix business and pleasure? Who knows when, or if, we will live to see a new day?"

Morlax shook his head.

"I take that as an affirmative. Good. Bring your Mai-Z. We're going to need servers. Bye, Franzine, my sweet. See you later." Nix winked. "Get to work, Morlax. This is no time to dilly- dally around."

Nix disappeared. Morlax faced Franzine, his bottom lip trembling as he spoke.

"'My sweet'? My instinct was right. You *are* having an affair. Did you know Nix is married to the meanest fire-breathing chicken in the galaxy?"

Before Franzine could answer, the TP rang. In silence, the two beings waited. Morlax glared. Franzine resumed looking at its feet.

"The-call-is-for-you-again-Franzine."

"Who is it?" the Nuet squeaked.

"Mrs. Nix."

Morlax chuckled. Franzine gulped. "Tell her I'm busy."

It was too late to tell the feathered beastie anything. She appeared on the portal surrounded by a wispy layer of smoke. "Why, you little, no-good tart. I'm going to have your appendages removed and thrown into the Sea of Storms..."

Chapter Eight

Franzine was in a tizzy and of little help to Morlax after its confrontation with Nix's wife. Morlax, feeling vindicated after his boss's slights, quit teasing the Nuet. It was in enough trouble and, being an amiable creature, not like most Orfians who were gruff and ill-mannered, he allowed the Nuet an extra fifteen-minute break.

Returning to his office to do some work, Morlax shuffled the papers on his desk, clearing an area large enough for a mug of java. Soft and soothing, transcendental music wavered in the background as he munched on cream-filled pastries.

The pending pile was daunting. Stacked high against the back wall, it seemed to be reproducing as he watched. So many unhappy beings. So much hatred and prejudice in the universe. Nothing less than total destruction could restore harmony to this galaxy. Perhaps the Great Ordainer had it right. Wipe the slate clean and let evolution take its course.

The only problem with that solution was that Morlax didn't want to die. What would it solve anyway? Controversy and conflict were unavoidable whenever two or more creatures, regardless of origin, congregated. Everyone had an opinion, and in truth, not all disagreements were damaging. Debates opened new realms of thought, and birthed myriad possibilities. Progress is served by those who venture forth when all others stay behind. If one believed it could be done, it would be done. There was always some brave (or crazy) soul willing to take a chance, buck the system, and follow his dream. The Doubel was wrong. One head wasn't better than two.

Morlax ordered a lit cigar and puffed away. He wondered how Ola and Bola were doing, or even if there was a Bola or an Ola anymore. His solution to their predicament had been evasive, but brilliant. No one could dispute his ability to do the job well, not even Nix.

Before Morlax could pat himself on the back for his genius, the TP jingled. It was followed by an explosion and screams. Mai-Z clanked through the door, her arms raised high. Behind the robot was the Doubel, still attached. *That answers my questions*, he thought.

"Hello, Bola, Ola. Nice to see you again. Mai-Z, why don't you get us some java and cakes? Reunions can be so much fun."

"Don't move or I'll blow this tin bucket to pieces." Bola raised the barrel of his laser disintegrator above his head and peeked over Mai-Z's shoulder. "Hi there, Morlax. Sorry about this, but you left us no alternative."

"I was just thinking the same thing, but what other options did I have? Give an Orfian some slack." Morlax pointed to the immense stack of folders on the back wall. "All those cases are pending. Between the interviews and interruptions, I barely have enough time to eat."

"Why did you rush making our decision?" asked Ola. She raised her head from behind the robot, winked and waved. "This was Bola's idea. Believe me, I understand your problem. There isn't enough time in a day to get anything done any more. Don't take it personally. You know I think you are a hunk. Bola made me come along. Sorry."

"I don't blame either of you. I understand; really I do. Why don't you put the weapon down and we can talk about it."

"Do you take me for an idiot?" asked Bola. "As soon as I drop it you will arrest me. No way. I'm not going to prison."

"Who said anything about jail? Just put it down and we'll discuss all the options. I'm a reasonable Orfian; besides, what would this little incident do to your career, Bola? You don't want this to get in the papers, and you really don't want to hurt anyone."

Before Bola had a chance to answer, Franzine spilled into the room. It was typical of Franzine to be oblivious of its surroundings, and it didn't notice the Doubel, the laser, or Morlax making faces. "Nix is on the phone. Do you want me to transfer the call, or shall we take it in the conference room?"

Morlax's gestures increased. His head bobbled back and forth; his eyes shifted to the right corner, to the left corner, and back again.

"Are you feeling okay, boss?"

Morlax resisted the urge to pummel the Nuet. Through sealed lips he muttered, "Can't you see I'm busy?"

"Too busy to take Nix's call? No one is that busy or that crazy..." Franzine paused, rubbed its temple, and realized Morlax wasn't alone. It saw the Doubel first and the laser second. "I'll tell Nix you are indisposed."

"Who is Nix?" asked Bola.

"My boss," answered Morlax.

Bola motioned to Franzine, using the laser's barrel as a finger. "Go ahead. Transfer the call. I want to talk to him."

The Nuet gulped. "I can't do that. Nix is in no mood to..."

The laser went off, blasting a red beam at one of the hover-lights. The luminescent fixture exploded and sizzled before crashing to the floor. Franzine jumped a meter.

Morlax looked at the mess and snorted. "Just do what he wants before I have a shower-head as a ceiling. Doubels can be mighty mean when they're mad."

"Yeah," Ola agreed. "The last thing you want to do is to fire up Bola's temper. He is already angrier than a Cockatrice."

The reference to Nix's wife prompted Franzine to shriek and run out the door.

It ran from the room, screaming "Yep, yep, yep."

"What is the matter with that thing?" asked Bola.

"It's a Nuet. They're all like that. Now put that thing down. Franzy will transfer the call and you can settle things with Nix. Okay?"

Bola sighed. "I will, but I'm going to keep it close."

"No one is going to take it from you. Relax. Let Mai-Z fetch us some tea and crumpets."

The Doubel nodded, released Mai-Z, and dragged two chairs to the desk. Bola sat, placing the firearm in his lap. Ola took the other seat and placed her right hand atop Bola's left. The couple smiled. Morlax smiled. The TP rang.

Morlax pressed the button and Nix materialized. "Now you have gone and done it. I have half a mind to fire you."

"Nix," Morlax leaned forward, "I have a disgruntled customer here who wishes to talk to you."

Nix turned one of his heads and glanced at the Doubel. "They can wait. I have the head of the Bureau of Endangered Species here. He isn't happy."

"Nix, Bola has a laser disintegrator. He is threatening to kill me." Morlax looked at Bola and waited for him to acknowledge the claim.

"Morlax is as good as dead if we don't get some satisfaction."

Ola added, "I can vouch for that. My other half is as mean as I am beautiful."

The veins in Nix's necks pulsed and throbbed. "Is that a threat? Sounds more like a miracle. Kill him. Go ahead. It will save the government an expensive trial."

Bola and Ola, at a loss for words, looked at each other.

"You don't mean that, your Excellency-ness." Morlax's voice cracked. "Do you?"

"You bet I do. Mr. Hooper is livid. Seems you okayed the murder permit for some idiot...I believe his name is Bacchus...to kill a Wyrm."

"It was destroying his grape vineyards." Morlax sank into his seat.

"Wyrms are an endangered species. Don't you do any research?" Nix was screaming, causing the transmission to fade in and out.

"Why yes, sir, I do, but I can't recall worms being on the list."

Nix withdrew a long parchment scroll and stabbed at the paper. "The objective of the Endangered Species Code is to promote the protection and conserve the habitats of any and all life-forms listed herein. Wyrms are number seven on the chart this week. See? It's all here in writing. Wyverns, Manticores, Basilisks, Gryphons, Hydras, Chimeras, and Wyrms."

Morlax felt a migraine coming on. Worm? Oh, drat. It dawned on him, Wyrm. The Y was the difference, a simple little letter. Y—Y—Why? Why hadn't he realized it? Why hadn't such a simple request aroused his suspicions? For that matter, why had he been born?

"Did you hear me, Morlax?"

Morlax uttered a faint yes.

"Consider yourself suspended from duty until further notice."

"What about the meeting today?"

"Your presence won't be needed..."

The other head interrupted. "Oh, yes, he is. Morlax is..."

"You are off base, Nax."

"Oh, no, I'm not, Nix."

The heads started arguing. Morlax folded his arms and buried his face in the nest. No one said anything. Bola and Ola sighed.

The silence didn't last. Franzine shoved open the door, flung itself to the floor by Morlax's feet and continued screaming. "Help me! Help me! She's here!"

"Who is?" Morlax lifted his eyes and stared at the open door.

"Mrs. Nix! She's breathing fire and burning the whole office down. Mai-Z can't calm her. I had to run for my life. Hide me! Help me!"

Franzine latched onto Morlax's ankle, its claws sinking into the tender flesh of Morlax's calf. "I don't want to die! I don't want to die!"

A dead Nuet wasn't a bad thing, Morlax thought, grimacing through the pain. His bellies were in knots and his breakfast, eight cheese cakes and six chocolate-covered doughnuts with sprinkles, threatened to leave his body at both ends. The hammer pounding in his head increased in direct proportion to the noise. Morlax tasted the bitterness of failure and cried, "I can't take this any more! I give up."

Jumping out of his seat, he flew to the Doubel (dragging the tiny Nuet over the cold, warped tile) and snatched the barrel of the rifle. Pressing the cold steel against his head, he pleaded with Bola. "Go ahead, pull the trigger. You would be doing me a favor."

Bola refused.

"Please, please, please. By the authority vested in me by the Ministry of Law Enforcement to authorize murder and mayhem, I give you permission to end my life. You would be doing me a favor. I give you my word, I'm not an endangered species."

Ola patted the Orfian on his back. "You poor baby. This is Bola's fault. Bola, get off your useless ass and help him."

The male half of the Doubel shrugged. "Looky here, Ola. I have no intentions of pulling the trigger. That wasn't the purpose of this visit. I told you earlier I was only going to threaten him, and I did my best. I'm not a killer. If I have told you once, I have told you a thousand times."

"I didn't mean I wanted you to kill him," Ola rolled her eyes. "What I meant was...well, you could do...if you were to take the..."

"I'm waiting, Ola, not that waiting for you is anything unusual. You would have been late for our birth if I hadn't dragged you there."

A stream of fire singed the desk. "Where is that tart? Come on, give her up! Won't do you any good hiding her. I know she's in here."

Nix quit arguing with Nax as soon as he heard the voice. "Tootsy, is that you?"

Mrs. Nix, a Cockatrice, had the head, neck, and chest of a chicken, the wings of a bat, and the tail of a lizard. She sneered at Nix and faced Morlax, smoke streaming from the nostrils in her beak. "You heard me, Morlax. Tell me where she is now or I'll..."

"Snookums, Daddy Cakes is here." Nix was waving both arms wildly. The transmission flickered. "Leave Morlax alone, and come on home. There's nothing to get all hot and heated about. Franzine is just my assistant. It's you that I love. Only you."

"Shut up, you two-timing gigolo. And you, Morlax, tell me where she is or I'll kill you first."

"Stand in line, you harpy! I have had enough. Bola, Ola, either use the laser or get out of here, now. You don't need me to reverse the decision. You have found something in common: your hatred for me. Build on it, or blast the other into oblivion. I don't care.

"Franzine, take your claws out of my leg or I will kick you into the next century. Nix, you can take this job and..."

"How dare you call my wife a harpy? You are treading on thin ice, Morlax. One more insult and I will fire you."

"You didn't hear me? I quit!"

"Fire who?" clucked the Cockatrice. "You don't even own a pack of matches. I'm the fire-breather in this family, and this monstrosity of flab is mine."

"I'm flattered that I'm so popular, but give me a beak...I mean break." Morlax shook Franzine free of his leg. "There you are, Mrs. Nix. This pile of useless appendages is the home-wrecker. That's what you're jealous of."

The Cockatrice slithered around Franzine, pecking the ground and swishing her tail. "It's a Nuet, a nothing. You are having an affair with this non-gendered, scummy fly?"

"That's what I have been trying to tell you, Fancy-Feathers. If you hadn't destroyed the TP's screen, you would have seen that Franzine is a Nuet. Why, it's neither male nor female. I would never be unfaithful. You are the light of my life."

Franzine rose to its knees and sniffled. "He's right. Nix is just my boss. Nuets don't have affairs. We reproduce all by ourselves."

Mrs. Nix remained silent, pondering the predicament. Morlax held back his sigh of relief. One was never too sure how a Cockatrice would react from one minute to the next.

"Oh, you two-headed darling," Mrs. Nix clucked in a high-pitched squeal. "How can you ever forgive me for doubting you?"

Nix opened his arms. "Nothing to apologize for. It was all my fault, working late, forgetting to call. Please accept my apology."

"No, no, no. I must accept all the blame. We Cockatrices are just jealous creatures. It is you who must forgive."

"Whatever you say, sugar-beak. You come on home and Daddy-cakes will show you how forgiving he can be."

Mrs. Nix excused herself, begging Morlax for forgiveness and promising him she would make it up to him in the future. Afraid to do anything but accept, Morlax stroked Mrs. Nix's feathered neck as he led her to the door.

Morlax continued to wave until the creature was out of sight. He sighed and hollered for Franzine. "Clean up all this blood, Franzy. Mrs. Nix has made quite a mess with her tail swishing. Oh, and bring me some bandages. Just look at the scratches you made. Don't you ever trim your claws?"

Morlax returned to his office to find the Doubel still arguing. "Bola, Ola, get out of here and do whatever it is that you do best. At this point I don't care what you do, and I doubt I have the authority to be of further assistance. Goodbye, good luck, and good riddance."

Morlax pointed to Mai-Z. "Yoo-hoo, Mai-Z!"

The robot clicked to attention.

"Show this couple to the hall and lock the doors. I have a lot to pack and I want...no, I need to be alone. Hold all calls, except for Dandi."

And they all obeyed. As soon as the room was empty, Morlax reached in the back of the closet for a bottle of wine. He popped the cork and drank. And drank. And was happy...for a little while, until Dandi came through the door, breathless, and collapsed.

Chapter Nine

Dandi wasn't dandy. Gone were the lovely golden petals; in their stead were bare stalks tipped in tufts of gray fluff. Her eyeballs seemed huge, attached to thin coils. Her lips, which had once disappeared when she wasn't speaking, protruded. Morlax had no idea what was wrong, but he knew it was serious.

"Dandi? What in the name of Sara Lee is going on?"

"Oh, Morlax. It has been an awful day. If I have to watch that illusio-tape one more time I will curl up and die. I'm not used to this stress. It's causing me to sporulate early. What am I going to do? I have fifteen more deliveries to make, but I'm in no shape to travel. Neither can I cultivate my babies here. The soil is all wrong. The..."

"Slow down." Morlax rushed to Dandi's side and lifted her in his arms. "Let me get you some water."

"That would be nice. I haven't had a chlorophyll pill all day."

Morlax deposited the Chlorifloridian in his leather chair and fluttered to the water fountain. Dandi hadn't prepared him for this change. *If that's what asexual reproduction is,* Morlax thought, *blowing away piece by piece, then I don't want any part of it.*

He returned quickly and handed her a cup. "Drink up. Take your time. I have nowhere to go and all the time in the world...or whatever is left of it."

Dandi swallowed the pill dry, dipping her tangly roots directly into the glass. Between blinks the water vanished.

"More." Dandi held out the glass.

Morlax, shaking his head, filled the container to the top. This time his beloved sipped the water. He looked curiously at his fiancée.

"Water works faster if I drink through my roots, and I needed some bad. I hope that didn't disturb you."

"Not at all."

"I'm glad. You can't believe the beings that freak when I do this—and I'm talking about creatures that eat from their belly or inhale their food."

"The universe is made up of all kinds."

"It sure is," Dandi glanced at the clock, "and that reminds me: it's getting late. Don't we have to be at the meeting in a few hours? Shouldn't we get going?"

"Nix fired me," said Morlax as he slithered into the egg-shaped command chair beside Dandi.

"He what?"

Morlax told Dandi what had happened, everything from Bola and Ola's threats, to Mrs. Nix and the fiasco with the Wyrm.

"You think your day can beat that? You don't know what awful is. I'm not even sure I do. You would have to have something good to compare it to."

Dandi burst into tears. "I thought I was your something good."

Morlax would have removed the foot from his mouth if he had been able to fit it in there in the first place. "Forgive me. You are the sunshine in my life. It's hard to count one's blessings when one's whole life is a big disaster. I'm not getting any younger, and with the Great Ordainer out there, I'm probably not going to get any older."

Morlax was sixty-six years old, middle age for an Orfian. Ten more years and he would retire. He dreaded growing old. He had said that there was nothing worse than an old Orfian, except for a dead Orfian, but that had been when he was young. Opinions change. With the Great Ordainer out there in the cosmos killing this and destroying that, becoming a senior Orfian wasn't looking all that bad. Heck, being an Orfian was better than being a Chlorifloridian. Morlax looked at Dandi's puffy head. One good stiff wind and she would be bald. At least Orfians didn't fall apart.

Dandi spoke between sobs. "Stop being so negative. Have faith. Didn't you tell me earlier that you had an idea how to put an end to the Great Ordainer's rampage?"

Morlax shrugged. "That was before I was let go."

"Are you going to let something as trivial as a job keep you from saving the universe? You have a right to be at that meeting. We all do. I wouldn't let Nix keep you from attending."

Morlax wiped Dandi's tears. "What if my idea doesn't work?"

"Has anyone come up with a better solution?"

"Not that I know of, but getting the Great Ordainer to come to my office and..."

"Shh." Dandi pressed a leaf to her lips. "Don't say it out loud. He has big ears. He might be listening right now. You don't want to give it away."

"If He is all that powerful, I'm sure He can read my mind."

Dandi shook her head. "He could; you may be right about that. But with so many creatures in this universe thinking and speaking, I doubt He will home into just one person's thoughts. Why take any chances?"

"But how will you know if it's a good plan if I can't talk about it?"

"Because you're smart and I have faith in you."

Morlax beamed. He wasn't used to having his ego stroked. Not even his mother held such a high opinion of him. "I don't deserve you, Dandi."

The plant smiled. "True, but I love you anyway."

They kissed. It was easier this time, as Morlax was able to find her lips. The embrace lasted minutes.

"Let's say I have a solution. Do you think Nix will let me present it at the meeting? After my goof, I would be lucky if he let me keep my pension. If I could even get inside, Nix would keep me from taking the stand. You didn't hear Him. He was pretty mad."

"Didn't you say Henrietta owed you a favor?"

"Henrietta?" Morlax scratched his head.

"Nix's wife. You didn't know she had a first name?"

Morlax shook his head.

"I met her the other night when I was showing Nix the tape. For such a powerful being, Nix is one henpecked husband. Henrietta can be a real snit, but Cockatrices are good to their word. If she promised you a favor, she will come through. She will get you on the podium."

"But who will get me inside?" asked Morlax.

"What about the Doubel? You did say they had a laser disintegrator?"

"Bola won't use it. He told me that himself."

"He won't have to. Just the threat will get you past the door."

"They're pretty mad at me, too. I don't think they will help me."

"You won't know until you try. Stop with the excuses and get a move on."

"I suppose it's worth a try." Morlax picked up the TP's receiver.

"That's the spirit. Think positive. I'm going to get Mai-Z and pull the air-coupe around. I'll meet you outside."

Dandi left. Morlax dialed. "Hello, Henrietta. How is it going? This is Morlax. I have a favor to cash in—"

* * *

The hover-car's door wouldn't shut. There wasn't enough room for Morlax, Dandi, the Doubel, and the robot. Mai-Z stepped outside and there still wasn't enough room.

Morlax lowered the window. "Kick it."

"Kick-what?"

"The door. Kick it shut."

"With-my-foot?"

"No, Mai-Z, with your head."

The sarcasm was lost on the robot. Morlax suddenly remembered that humor chips hadn't been installed in the earlier models, but it was too late to stop Mai-Z from battering the door closed with her head. The car rocked, almost tipping over, and teetered to a stop. Dandi and the Doubel groaned as their necks jerked. Morlax had enough padding and didn't feel a thing. Still, it worked. They were inside.

Morlax rolled the window down. "Thanks, ole girl. Are you hurt?"

"I-do-not-think-so—No-just-shaken—There-is-a-small-dent-and-I-seem-to-have-broken-my-right-eyelid—It will-not-shut-but-no-harm—I-can-still-see—Should-I-go-see-if-there-is-a-spare-part-in-my-locker-sir?"

"Not enough time. You will have to make do."

"Where-shall-I-sit-sir?"

Morlax popped the trunk. "Sorry, Mai-Z, but you're going to have to ride back there. None of us can breathe in space. I hope you don't mind."

"No-sir—The-trunk-is-fine."

"That's the spirit. If it all works out, I'm going to see you get a promotion. Some new chips. Maybe a wax-job."

"Thank-you-Mr.-Morlax."

"Thank-*you*-Mai-Z. You-are-a-fine-old-girl." Morlax caught himself imitating the robot's speech pattern and stopped. Glancing at his watch, he sighed. "We're running out of time. I'm going to have to go to slight speed if we're ever going to make it to the wormhole. Buckle up, everyone, and hold on tight." He checked that everyone was secure before accelerating to super-light-speed.

The amazing thing about time is that it's infinite, and still, no one ever has enough of it. Morlax prided himself on his punctuality. He would rather be an hour early than a minute late. This particular occasion, when every millisecond counted, was no different. Unfortunately, there was more to factor in than distance.

Morlax stared at the line of vehicles waiting at the wormhole toll station. There were too many to count. Only Nix would plan a meeting during rush hour. Morlax's eyes bulged as he pounded the steering rod with his fist. "I only wish Nix had as many brain cells as he has riches. Why do all the ignoramuses in the universe have wealthy parents? I will tell you why...because when you have money, you don't need smarts. If you're rich, everyone thinks you know it all."

Dandi placed a leaf on Morlax's shoulder. "Calm down. We won't be the only late arrivals. I will bet my last tuft of hair most of those cars are heading to Redun, too. Now, take a deep breath and..."

Morlax growled.

"Tsk, tsk. If you lose your temper, we will only have to spend more time finding it."

"Listen to Dandi, Morlax," said Bola. "There's no way to argue with a woman and win."

"You are a woman-basher, Bola," Ola said. "I would punch you if I could move my arm."

"Good thing you can't. I might be tempted to do away with you. Don't forget, I have the weapon and the permit."

"Forget? You're the one who should remember. I could have killed you a dozen times already, but..."

Morlax leaned over the seat and glared. "If you two don't quit, I'm going to give Mai-Z your seat and lock you both in the trunk."

"Amen," Dandi chirped. "Why don't you take a lesson from Morlax and me? We have our differences, but we don't argue..."

"How long have the two of you been together?" asked Ola.

"If you count today, three days."

Ola burst into laughter.

Bola joined in. "We were born together. It will be a hundred Doublian orbits next week. Give us some advice when you know something."

"Enough!" Morlax blasted his horn. "If either of you says another word, I'm going to start singing."

Silence descended, and stayed for hours. The digital clock on the tollbooth wall flashed four o'clock. They were definitely going to be late. The two hundred or so cars, busses, and commuter trains behind them were going to be even later.

Morlax flashed his government card, hoping Nix hadn't had time to cancel it. He was in luck. The Octocat (a full-grown Octopussy) waved him through. Now, if his luck held out, Morlax thought, he might just get his chance. Perhaps Nix hadn't taken him off the list.

The car entered the wormhole and immediately began to spin as if caught in a whirlpool. Morlax had traveled by wormhole often enough to know the effect was harmless, but not enough to convince his insides of it. After the wormhole deposited the car a short distance from the United Universe Building, Morlax paused to regain his equilibrium before putting the vehicle on autopilot.

"We're almost there. I can see valet tracking from here."

Dandi smiled. "That beam?"

"Oh, that's right. This is your first visit to Redun, isn't it?"

"No, I was here to show Nix the tape, and there was no tractor beam then." She stared out the front window at the tall buildings. Her eyes grew huge.

"All the government buildings use tractor beams when there is a big meeting. With all those cars zooming into the Redun atmosphere, they have to do something to cut down on accidents. Also, it's the only way one can park and not get lost. It's all computerized now. Saves on walking, too."

"Why should you care, Morlax?" asked Bola. "With your anti-gravity shoes, your feet never touch ground. I would bet you haven't taken a step since baby-hood."

"Babyhood?" said Ola, her voice brimming with sarcasm. "I would bet Orfians get fitted for them in the womb."

Dandi stifled a snicker.

Morlax wanted to rip the Doubel apart. He clenched his teeth and closed his hands around the steering bar with a grip that made his fingers hurt. "That's enough. Go ahead and make fun of us if you will, but without us Orfians there would be no anti-gravity devices, no interplanetary travel, and no intergalactic commerce. The Orfians are the only ones that create such fantastic devices. We may be fat and lazy, but without our creative minds and intelligence, you Doubels would still be discovering the wheel."

Dandi placed a frond on Morlax's shoulder. "They didn't mean anything by it. Don't be so sensitive. Bola and Ola are here to help you. They didn't have to come."

Morlax grumbled. He was about to express his gratitude when the tractor beam pulsed. "This is it, guys. We're headed for the Alpha-Centurion level. Some-one write that down."

After the car was neatly stacked, Mai-Z helped them out. Morlax ordered everyone to follow him, and the Doubel took the rear.

"Look natural. Bola, keep the gun tucked under your shirt. Mai-Z, be ready to use your middle finger. Now let's get a move on."

Morlax floated to the conveyer belt. Dandi was the first to step on the moving walkway, followed by the Doubel. Mai-Z stayed a few feet behind.

Beings from all over the universe traveled in front and back of the group. Morlax kept looking around, waiting for someone or something to stop him, but no one did. They passed by tall and short buildings and long and wide ones, a few that were larger than an intergalactic garbage scow and one the size of a toaster. A few structures were encased in a watery globe. One floated upside down. Some were businesses, but most were governmental structures, ranging from diplo-matic compounds to offices.

Above, through the layer of universal air, one could see the stars; below, only gravel. There were no trees, no plants, nothing that wasn't made of plastic, cement, or glass. Beside the buildings were parking lots, stacked five or six layers thick. Redun was a place to conduct or control business, nothing more, except for a huge, underground golf-course made of Astroturf, and that didn't count. Since fifty percent of all deals were made swinging a stick and hitting a dimpled ball on artificial landscape, the course was considered a convention room. On sunny days, and especially on Fridays, most workers could be found attending a meeting in the "green room."

The electronic walker looped and curved, around and about, over and under, with exits at each doorway. Morlax noticed that no one got off.

"See, I told you," said Dandi. "We aren't late. Everybody is going to the conference."

Morlax agreed. "So far, so good. None of the guards recognized me. Just keep your fingers crossed. We're almost there. See that eighty-story building with all those awnings? That is the United Universe Building."

A few kilometers in the distance, decorated in multi-colored flags, was the most important building in the entire universe. There, beings from the five corners of the cosmos met, debated, passed, and enforced legislation that governed everyone and everything. It was impressive, made of faux marble, resilient polystyrene plastic, and mirrored glass. By the doorway, standing next to carved pillars, stood two burly Bull-guards. Chains, mallets, numchucks, and laser pistols were attached to their belts. Worst of all, they were checking IDs.

Dandi entered with a wolf howl and a smile. Morlax wasn't as lucky.

"Dis is da guy," one Bull said to the other.

Guard number two removed a photograph from his pocket and looked at Morlax. "It sure is. Mr. Morlax, by the authority vested in me by the Coalition of Planets and Galaxies and the Ministry of Law Enforcement, I place you under arrest."

Chapter Ten

They clamped the metal cuffs around Morlax's wrists. Everyone in the vicinity stared. Mai-Z, who had taken off her broken eyelid and was busy removing dust particles from her eye, hadn't heard a word and didn't have a clue. Bola and Ola stood frozen.

"Okay, everybody. Nothing to see here. Please disperse and continue with your business." The communicator collar crackled as the Bull-guard spoke into the receiver. "Got a hot one. Going to bring him to the station."

"Go ahead, officer. Identify yourself and the suspect."

"BowSir from the forty-fifth-and-a-third here. Guarding the United Universe Compound..." The Bull-guard stopped in mid-sentence.

"Disconnect and remove those shackles now, or else I'm going to pull the trigger." Bola nudged the steel a bit deeper in the cop's furry neck.

"Go-ahead-and-do-what-he-says—or-I-will-shoot-too." Mai-Z pointed her finger at the other guard.

Morlax smiled as the manacles were removed. "Thanks, guys. The rest of you idiots gawking, get on with your business, or else."

Everyone dispersed.

"We had better get inside before someone else stops us. What should we do with these guys?" asked Ola.

"Let's take them with us." Morlax grabbed the rings in the Bulls' noses and led them to the door. "Dandi, run inside and get Henrietta."

The one-tufted Chlorifloridian nodded, eyeballs bouncing. "Yes, sir." She slipped through the door, followed by Morlax, the guards, Bola, Ola, and Mai-Z.

Henrietta was slinking in the back of the auditorium, as if a three-hundred-centimeter cockatrice could hide between rows. Dandi tapped the beastie on her shoulder and the two engaged in a short conversation.

Creatures continued piling into the huge auditorium. The overhead fans clattered. Langulators crackled and blared. No one noticed and no one heard anything over the confusion. Morlax beamed his toothless grin. This was a good sign.

Exactly forty-two minutes late, Nix and Nax took the podium. Behind him, seated in cushy chairs, were the president of the Coalition and his cabinet ministers.

After the applause died down, Nix bowed. "Thank you all for coming. As you have heard, the known universe is on red alert. We called you here to discuss the situation and to help us find a viable solution. To date, thirty-one planets, eighteen star clusters, and one worm-hole have been destroyed. Only Chloriflorida and a few minor planets have been spared. At this rate, we're all doomed. Now for the bad news: Due to the inter-galaxy moratorium on commerce, the Coalition has cancelled tonight's dinner and dance. However, following this meeting, refreshments will be served in the Colonnade Room."

Roars of disapproval drowned out the clanking fans. Nix raised his arms, lowered them, and raised them again. "Quiet please. Let me finish. There will be free refreshments *and* all the Tarantian whiskey you can drink."

A few claps and one yippee were heard.

"Now for the reading of the minutes..."

Spitz, the president, stood on the podium. He was the size of an Orfian nail and resembled a spoon. "Skip it and get on with the important business."

"But...but...it says here in the Intergalactic Code of..."

Spitz glared.

Nix nodded. "Today's business is to find a way to stop the Great Ordainer of Destruction. The Coalition and the IDI, in an attempt to make contact with Him, have placed zillions of signs all over space inviting Him to come and talk things over with us. So far, we haven't heard from Him. It's a pity, since we have established shrines, altars, and sacrificial life-forms in our attempts to lure Him to this symposium. Since we have failed, we're open to your suggestions. Please raise an appendage of your choice, or, if you don't have one, a neighbor may accommodate you. Please wait your turn. I will call on you as soon as I can."

No one did anything, said anything, or lifted anything, except for Morlax, who floated midway down the center aisle. "I have an idea, a concept, and a possible solution."

"The chair doesn't recognize this criminal. Arrest that Orfian, now!"

Dandi rushed down the walkway, her last puff drifting on the air currents. "Stop! The universe is in no shape to disregard any ideas. Listen to Morlax. At least hear him out."

Bola raised his laser disintegrator and, along with Ola, walked to the stage. "We second and third the motion."

Nix and Nax conferred. "Regardless of the vote, under the United Universe's by-laws, no known criminal or..."

"Take your by-laws and shove them, Nix. You too, Nax. I have put up with your pettiness long enough." Henrietta thudded down the left aisle, with tail swishing and smoke pouring from her nostrils. "You will listen to Morlax and you will drop those silly charges. Have I made myself clear?"

Nix pouted. "Yes, dear."

Nax sniffled. "Whatever you say, Henrietta."

The Cockatrice climbed up the steps and nodded to Spitz, who stood to give her his seat. She sat, crossed her scaly legs and folded her arms.

In a teensy, high-pitched voice, Nix said, "Morlax, you may have the floor."

Morlax floated to the podium and latched onto the wooden pedestal. "Thank you, Dandi, Bola, Ola, Henrietta and all you out there willing to listen to me. I have a plan. Unfortunately, I can't tell you what it is."

"What?" shouted Nix and Nax. "Why the hell are you here?"

"Because," Morlax faced his boss, "it will work."

"And how do we know that? How can we trust you? After your disastrous goof with the Wyrm, you expect us to have faith in you?"

"I've made one mistake in all my thousands of decisions."

"What about the incident with the Griffin and his clone? Or the two warring planets, Rill and Swill?"

Morlax shrugged. "Okay, so three mistakes, but you have to admit that most of the time I do a good job."

Nix sighed. "Competent, perhaps."

"Okay. Competent. I don't see anyone else offering a suggestion."

"You haven't either."

"But I do have one. If I'm forced, I will fill you in, but He might be listening, and if He is, and if He hears about my plan, all is lost."

"Morlax's right." Dandi stepped onto the stage beside her beloved. "I met Him; I heard Him. He likes Orfians. He has a sense of humor. Those are enough reasons for me to give Morlax a chance. So what if he has made a few mistakes? Are any of you perfect? Unless you're part of the solution, you're part of the problem."

A few from the audience clapped. Others joined in.

"Whoa," said Nix. "Are you going to take advice from Morlax's fiancée? She's prejudiced."

"I'm not. I may love Morlax, but this isn't a popularity contest. This is a life-and-death situation, and who better to trust than someone who has to make these decisions on a daily basis? Nix, you trusted him to run the permit office; why not believe in him now?"

"Morlax has broken the rules..."

Dandi put her hands on her stalk and glared at the two-headed creature. "What rules? Your rules? Morlax made a mistake, and that's a whole different matter. The universe as we know it now is disintegrating bit by bit. Nix hasn't a solution. Morlax does. We can all wait our turn to die, or we can fight. What do you want to do, everybody?"

The room was abuzz with conversation. It grew loud enough that Henrietta strutted to the podium and fired, "Silence. Let her finish."

Dandi winked at her friend. As the talking died down, she began again. "Listen to me, folks. Morlax didn't want to come here; he didn't think any of you would hear him out, but here he is. Do you know what he risked to be at this meeting? Let me tell you, he risked jail and worse. How many of you would do that just to be heard?" Dandi waited for a response, tapping her feet and cupping a leaf over her brows to see into the audience. "I thought so. Now, if anyone of you has an objection, this is the time to come forward." Dandi waited. And waited. "No one? Okay. It's time to put this to a vote. Do we have a motion to give Morlax our full support?"

Conversation ensued. Spitz whispered to the head of the Ministry of Law Enforcement. Henrietta preened. Ola leaned her head on Bola's shoulder. Morlax and Dandi crossed their appendages and waited in silence.

"What do we have to lose?" asked a huge Toe from the planet Hangnail. "I move we let Morlax do what he can."

The purple duck sitting next to the Toe raised a wing. "I second the motion."

"And I third it."

Everyone looked around to see where the booming voice had come from. The words were deafening and filled the room as if a bomb had exploded.

"Will the being that finalized the motion please stand up?" said Nix.

A hush fell like an anvil from a ten-story building. No one said anything; everyone looked around. From the back a shadow grew. Tall and shrouded in mist, *something* grew to gigantic proportions. It cast a darkness on the room that the hover-lights couldn't illuminate.

Morlax shivered. Dandi hid behind Morlax. Nix and Nax hid their heads in their coats.

"Who are you?" asked Morlax, in a whisper so soft Dandi didn't hear.

"I am He who has been called by millions of names and yet has none, for no one existed before Me to give Me one."

Morlax could barely breathe. "You are the Great Ordainer of Destruction?"

"That will do," said the shadow, "but you may call me GOD for short."

Chapter Eleven

Later that evening, as the dignitaries swarmed the refreshment table like ants at a picnic, the topic on everyone's mind was the visit. Everyone had seen something, but no two beings could agree on what it was. Morlax had seen an Orfian that made him look emaciated. Dandi had seen a sunflower, just as she had before. Nix had seen a two-headed creature resembling his father. Bola and Ola had seen a rare identical Doubel. Mai-Z and the other robots had seen nothing, but they had recorded atmospheric electrostatic wavelength signatures registering in the upper microfarads.

After recapping the events, the Coalition had formed an opinion in two parts. It was indeed the Great Ordainer, for one; and for the other, GOD didn't create life in His image, but rather, life-forms created Him in theirs.

Though it was depressing, some good came from the revelation of the shadow of life and death. GOD would meet with Morlax and hear what the Orfian had to say. He would give the universe a fighting chance and not read Morlax's mind. In return, the Coalition would remove all fifteen zillion signs. The neon advertisements were littering His creation.

The existence of the universe rested in Morlax's hands. Whether or not it was a good thing, no one standing by the punch bowl would say. Not even Morlax dared to comment. He really didn't have a plan, only an idea, and if it were to be successful he would need help.

Dandi, the Doubel, and Henrietta returned with Morlax to the office, and were ready and willing to help. Nix offered, but Henrietta insisted that if life were to go on, Nix's abilities would best be utilized painting Murder, Mayhem, and Music's conference room—a bright red, the Cockatrice insisted, with yellow trim. No one argued.

Too nervous and anxious to sleep, the gang worked furiously through the night. Nix and Nax finished the room an hour before GOD's appointment. Morlax sent out for breakfast and even Nix was invited to partake of the victuals.

The clock ticked away precious time. Mai-Z waited in the lobby, ready to record wavelengths. Cameras, stationed in each of the rooms, broadcasted everyone's movement, including the fly buzzing around the honey cake. After all, who knew what form GOD would take, if any? Burning bushes seemed to be the favorite at two to one.

At precisely nine o'clock Mai-Z's buzzer went off.

Morlax clapped his hands three times. "Everyone to your stations. Nix, please don't say anything. In fact, why don't you wait in my office? Mai-Z, please answer the door."

Dandi and Morlax waited at his usual vantage point in the hallway. Mai-Z clanked away, taking all of five minutes to reach the door. It took two more to open it. No one knew what to expect, especially after last night's appearance. What they saw was disappointing. GOD was completely covered in sackcloth. Not even His face was exposed through the opening in the hood. An invisible hand held a scythe. Only Mai-Z wasn't shocked. The robot couldn't see anything.

"Mr.-GOD—Right-on-time—If-You-will-make-Yourself-comfortable-I-will-tell-Mr.-Morlax-you-are-here."

GOD entered and thirty-four cameras stationed about the lobby converged on Him. GOD waved. "Must I wait? Whom else is he expecting?"

"Could-You-speak-up-a-bit?—I-damaged-my-ear-the-other-day-and-I-am-having-trouble-hearing."

"Forget it. Go fetch Morlax."

Exaggerating every movement, Mai-Z clinked and clanked her way to the desk. She was reaching for a clipboard when GOD interrupted her.

"Can you move a little faster? At this rate, it will take a century...Ah-hah, I get it. Go as slowly as you want to. I'm immortal."

Mai-Z pressed the intercom button. Her finger fell off, and she removed a roll of duct tape from the top drawer. "One-minute—I-need-to-fix-this-first."

The sackcloth robe moved to a chair, where it sat. An assortment of periodicals rustled as He picked up an issue of *Earth Fancy*. All cameras focused as He read the article on Dolly, the cloned sheep. "Aren't there any newer issues? Forget it. Nostalgia seems to be the theme in this place."

Mai-Z managed to secure her digit and looked up. "We-get-the-rejects-from-the-Department-of-News—I-would-be-happy-to-bring-You-one-from-their-lobby."

The magazine waved. "No, don't bother. I didn't come here to read about the galaxy."

"Why-did-You-return-Sir?"

"Spring cleaning."

Mai-Z nodded. "All-fixed." She pressed the button. "Mr.-Morlax-sir—GOD-is-here-to-see-you."

"Thank you, Mai-Z. I expected Him, of course. Could you usher Him to the conference room and bring the papers with you?"

"I-would-be-delighted-to-do-that-sir—Mr.-GOD-if-You-would-be-so-kind-as-to-follow-me-I-would-appreciate-it." The robot rose from her seat and moved with glacial slowness to the hallway. GOD tossed the magazine aside and humored the machine by doing as He was asked. He accompanied Mai-Z, the cameras zooming in for a close-up each time He moved.

"Am I under surveillance?"

"Not-really-Your-GOD-ship—The-whole-universe-hangs-in-the-balance-so-Morlax-felt-that-all-life-forms-had-the-right-to-monitor-the-meeting."

GOD nodded, taking baby steps as He followed Mai-Z. "Must we go so slowly? For My sake, let Me guide you."

Before Mai-Z could answer, GOD took the lead and rushed by the water cooler. Immediately, the gurgling stopped, and He reached for a cup. "Nothing like still waters. Want some, Mai-Z?"

"I-rust."

GOD snapped His fingers. "I knew that." He tilted His head back and downed the liquid. "Umm, delicious, one of My best inventions. Shall we trek onward?"

"Could-you-wait-a-moment-Your-Holiness?—I-just-broke-my-shoe."

"Will we ever get there? Don't answer. This must be Morlax's strategy, to stall and drag everything out. Am I right, Mai-Z?"

"I-cannot-lie—That-is-part-of-Morlax's-plan—If-You-will-excuse-me-I-need-to-repair-my-shoe."

"Oh, geez. Do any of your parts stay glued? Don't answer that. Allow Me." GOD zapped two bright and shiny metal shoes on the robot.

Mai-Z's eyes lit up. "Thank-You-for-restoring-my-sole."

"You are welcome. Now, can we get to the office sometime this era? Don't answer that."

Mai-Z didn't have time to blink before being whisked to the conference room. Morlax wasn't the least surprised when his robot and GOD suddenly appeared.

"Welcome. I have been looking forward to our chat. Sit down. Make Yourself comfortable. Have a nibble." Morlax gestured toward the table filled with pastries, dips, chips, cheeses, crudités, and hors d'oeuvres. "Eat, eat, eat. We can yak when we're done."

The cloak didn't move. Morlax wondered for minute if GOD was still inside. His anxiety diminished when he saw a huge plate filled with tasties float to the end of the table. Dandi winked. Morlax looked stern and glared.

"Mai-Z, our guest needs something to drink. Could you please get Him one?"

"I-would-be-delighted-to—GOD-Sir-what-would-You-like?"

"Got any Wild Turkey?"

"Do we have Wild Turkey? Listen to that. I have the best-stocked bar on three planets, I have spared no expense preparing for Your visit, and You ask if I have Wild Turkey." Morlax chuckled.

"Well? Do you?"

Morlax shrugged. "Mai-Z, will you go check?" He fluttered to the door and held it open.

"Wait. A deity could die of thirst by the time that bucket makes it to the door. Here." He gestured and bottles rained from the ceiling like manna from heaven. "There's more in the water cooler if that isn't enough." GOD, pleased with Himself, took a swig. "Little trick I picked up from one of My sons."

Morlax and Bola were delighted. Henrietta slithered around the table, grabbing the bottles. "I will have none of this. We have important matters to discuss and I won't allow any of this task force to get inebriated."

Morlax wrinkled his nose and handed his magnum to the Cockatrice. "Henrietta is right. You're at an unfair advantage already."

"What do you mean? Are you calling Me unfair?"

"Oh, no, Your Holiness. I would never say that. I go to church every other year. No, what I meant is, You are all-powerful and all-knowing. If any of us are to have a chance to convince you not to destroy the universe, we must keep our minds clear."

"It's a pity. Good stuff, that Wild Turkey." The outstretched sleeve filled another plate and pointed to an item on it. "Mmm. What is that called?"

"The cake, my Lord?" asked Dandi.

"No, the mashed potato meat pie."

"Ahh," Dandi's eyes sparkled with excitement. "It's called shepherd's pie. I made it from one of Henrietta's recipes."

"It's delicious."

"Eat." Morlax reached for a cookie. "No rush. There's plenty more where that came from."

The hood moved up and down. "Thanks, and don't get me wrong, everything is delicious; but I would like to start, especially if your plan is to delay Me as long as possible."

"Have it Your way, but before I hear Your side of the story, I would like to talk over the terms of the contract."

"Contract?"

"Well, murder is legal now, but You have seen fit to go about destroying this and that without a permit. Now, You can argue the point that You are above the law, and in that case, any discussion is moot." Morlax picked up the clipboard and held it out for GOD to take. "But I think it would behoove you to give this a read. I'm willing to bet that every inhabitant of every known planet in all the cosmos is watching us now. How would it look if the great GOD wasn't willing to abide by a few simple rules from the very creatures He gave this universe to? Why, it would be a case of 'Do as I say and not as I do.'"

"How do you figure that?"

"Isn't it true that You handed down a commandment that says, 'Thou shalt not kill'?"

GOD nodded. "You know your religions. I'm impressed."

Morlax beamed. "I fancy myself a bit of an authority."

"I admit to giving the tablets to Moses, and to Moliath, Newlen, Breasin...oh, forget it. There must be millions of them. It was one of my best ideas, those commandments. 'Thou shalt not kill' was right at the top."

"So it's 'Do as I say and not as I do.'"

GOD rubbed His invisible beard. "In other words, since you passed this law to legalize murder and mayhem, and in order for Me to set a good example, I need to comply with your rules and apply for a permit. Very interesting. Quite brilliant."

"Yes, and thank You." Morlax bowed and glanced at Dandi and the others.

"And is that the application?"

Morlax nodded.

"Okay, let Me read it. You have piqued my curiosity."

The sleeve accepted the clipboard. Everyone watched breathlessly as the clock ticked. Dandi gazed back and forth, shifting uneasily in her chair. Franzy crossed its fingers and clamped its eyes shut, as if praying. Henrietta paced, her talons shredding the thick carpet. Morlax watched with cool indifference, afraid to feel anything resembling hope.

And then, a pen appeared. It moved in a whirly fashion along the paper. GOD was filling out the form. Morlax felt his chest would burst. He turned away, trying not to stare, but he couldn't help himself and he shot sidelong glances at the group, then at the moving pen, as if watching a tennis match.

"Here you go."

The clipboard floated to Morlax and he caught it. "One minute, I need to make sure everything is filled out properly. Hmmm," he flipped the page. "Yes...very good. Everything is in order."

"So what is next?"

"A few minor details, a few more forms to fill out."

"And then you make a decision? Just you, right?"

"I will decide, yes, but I also have rules and regulations to follow. One of them is to be impartial."

"Do you feel you can be objective?"

Morlax nodded emphatically. "I will do my GOD-given best."

"And because I willingly signed the contract, I am now bound by these laws."

"You got it. I mean, You could do what you want; after all, You are GOD. But if You do so, You go back on Your written promise, putting You on the same level as those You seek to destroy."

"Flawless reasoning, Mr. Morlax. I have been, and always will be, true to My word. Let's get on with approving My permit."

Mr. Morlax smiled and pressed the intercom button. "Mai-Z, would you bring the rest of the permit forms to GOD's office?" Morlax smiled. "If You would be so kind to follow me to Your office—"

"My office? I need My own office? What is going on?"

"In order to proceed with Your killing spree, You have agreed to comply with all the rules and regulations. That includes, but isn't limited to, filling in all the forms that will provide the information necessary for me to make an informed decision."

"And I need My own office for that?"

"We thought You would be more comfortable with Your own place since there are at least a vigintillion planets, and there isn't a name for the number of inhabitants on each of them. A form must be filled out for everyone since we passed a law denying destruction on a planetary level, let alone on a galactic level."

"Why, this is preposterous."

The hood slipped to GOD's shoulder and revealed a face of flames.

"Burning-bush-like! I win," yelled Nix as he ran into the room. "I was watching from the restroom."

"Excuse me, but *both* of us saw it at the same time. I have a fifty percent interest in that ticket," argued Nax.

"You bet on Me?" The flames crackled.

Morlax shrugged. "It's like the Cosmic Lottery, with all the proceeds going to clean up the mess You made yesterday. The loss of that wormhole was catastrophic."

"This is unbelievable."

"Not really. If You want to know what is really unbelievable, Velcro is. It's amazing how you put those two strips together and they stick. Another thing is..."

"May we get started? Where is this office?"

GOD's headquarters were across the hall from Morlax's workplace. Franzy had generously donated its cubicle to the cause. It didn't need one anymore, since Nix had promoted it. Morlax held open the door and waited for the robe to glide in.

At the back of the room there was a desk, and beside it a small refrigerator. To the left was a couch. The room smelled of pine and fresh paint. Two of the walls, the red ones, glistened. There had been enough left over from painting the conference room, and Nix and Nax had used it to paint the front and back walls crimson.

"Just make Yourself at home." Morlax pointed. "There are pens in the holder over there, cold beer in the fridge. I just love those imported beverages."

"Lovely, just lovely."

"Glad You like it. Any questions?"

GOD said no.

"Then I'll be in my office. Feel free to stop by and chat sometime. My hours are from eight until nine. We weren't sure if You had a place to stay, so that's why there's a bed there."

GOD grumbled.

"Ah, here's Mai-Z now. I will let you get started."

Morlax held the door open for Mai-Z, who pushed in a cart full of cartons. Morlax exited and joined his crew, who were watching the events from one of the entertainment consoles in the lobby. Dandi snickered as the creaking robot pains-takingly lifted the box marked "1." Minutes crawled by as she very carefully handed GOD the first page.

"Just bring Me the entire box. At this rate, I could create another world in the time it takes to get to page two."

"Sorry-but-we-must-follow-procedures—We-are-to-take-one-page-at-a- time."

GOD bellowed, "Morlax, get in here."

The Doubel gave Morlax a thumbs-up. Dandi blew Morlax a kiss.

The door was open. Mai-Z stood at attention. Morlax bobbled by and hovered at the entrance. "Is there a problem?"

"Yeah. You failed to tell Me the procedures."

"I'm terribly sorry, but in paragraph seventy it states that an applicant will follow all protocol deemed necessary by the licensor. You didn't ask then, but let me explain now. Mai-Z must hand You each sheet, and she will wait until You have read each page. After You hand it back, she will then read it out loud. When she's finished, You will initial the page in the upper right-hand corner. Mai-Z will take that page to me and when she returns, she will hand You the next, and so on, and so forth. These are serious requests. Life as we know it could be wiped out. We had to revise the procedures to take that into consideration."

"How many crates are there?"

"Good question. Frankly, I haven't a clue. We have a whole department working out the logistics of this. Never before has anyone with Your power, Your prestige, Your su-premacy, entered through these doors. We don't even know what to ask. There's a depart-ment for that too, and a committee of top-notch lawyers and judges to determine the legality and interpretation of each and every word on each and every page."

GOD glared. "Well, could you at least get Me an assistant who moves a bit faster? At this rate, we will never get done."

Morlax shrugged. "I sure wish I could, but she's the only other one authorized to work here."

"What about Dandi?"

"I don't want her to work. She will have enough to do raising our sprouts."

"Henrietta?" GOD folded His sleeves across His chest.

"Henrietta is the head of the Department of Questions, and before You ask, Franzy was promoted to the Department of Requisition and Supplies. I'm afraid there's no one else."

"This could take forever."

"It could, but robots don't die, so that isn't a concern. Mai-Z will be repaired as needed. There is an entire department at work stockpiling replacement parts. Mai-Z may be slow, but she's thorough. I have wanted to replace her with a newer model, and indeed did apply for one, but You know how slowly government works. All those years it takes to program them, not to mention the time involved getting security clearances. Then there are all those forms one has to complete just to fulfill one little request. I gave up fighting the system years ago." Morlax flashed a toothless smile. "I didn't think it was worth the paperwork."

God Box
Robert B. Schofield

I was running low, but I tossed Bill a clip of HE drillers.

"Take it easy," I yelled.

"They just keep coming!" He caught the clip, dropped his old one, and slammed the new one home. Bill was doing better than I expected. He'd probably taken out two dozen by now, which I considered good, for a Baptist preacher.

I flipped my own weapon to full auto and sprayed the last of my 5.56mm rounds into a group of five monks that popped up from a ridge twenty feet away. Damn! How had they gotten that close?

As one of the monks fell, I noticed he was holding a mortar cannon. Not a good sign. But then, nothing in this whole mess was turning out good.

"I'm out!" Bill yelled.

"Me too, almost."

I'd never had first-hand experience before this, but I realized the true definition of a zealot when I heard Bill yell back, "You got a bayonet?"

My Data Command Unit flashed, and I yelled, "What?" into the microphone on my wrist. An explosion thirty feet down the ridge drowned out the reply.

"Say again." I unholstered the .57-caliber at my side, and held the DCU to my ear.

"I've found the god box." It was Jack.

Jack started off as a Chinese military decrypt program. Now, supplemented with data-mining code taken from Finance One's corporate mainframe, and backed by a million terabytes of quantum storage and a full thousand Scotus-IX CPUs, he is the best ripper in existence. We had to call him Jack.

"Execute Plan Gamma. I say again, Gamma." Small-arms fire whizzed overhead.

"We've got—" I started to say to Bill. I looked over, and saw that the small-arms fire had been over my head, but not his. A bloody hole stared at me from where Bill's left eye had been.

Bill once told me there were several ways to know God: Live a lifetime of devotion and prayer, meditate under a waterfall for twenty years, use hallucinogenic drugs, or now, shave your head and plug into the god box.

There was another way that he hadn't mentioned. He was doing it now.

I had nine zig-zag rounds in my hand cannon. There were at least twenty more monks from the monastery, and who knew what after that. I just might be joining Bill by the end of the day, although probably not at the same long-term location.

Where the hell was Redeye?

* * *

It all started two months ago. I was sitting in the Café Rue Laveau, eating boudan with nuke sauce, when she walked up to me. A dark-skinned beauty with a hint of Indian, she said, "You done got it bad. You been fixed—strong gris-gris."

"Name's Slater," I said.

"I'm Kaylee." She held out a bracelet-covered arm.   She wore a long skirt made of colored handkerchiefs, and a string around her forehead with a bit of blue cloth attached to it.

"You lovesick," she said. Her bracelets jingled.

"Taishia," I mumbled.

"What?"

"Nothing."

"I can fix it."

I refused to wear the ball of wax kneaded with feathers, and Taishia's name written three times forward and four times backward in chicken blood, in my left shoe, as Kaylee suggested. But she did help me forget....

She danced naked on a white cloth with burning candles around its edges, her feet not moving—just the rest of her, like a cobra, hypnotic. Sweat glistened on her smooth, dark skin. She sang, and chanted, and called my name in Creole, over and over again. I joined her on the cloth, and we knocked the candles over, to be extinguished as they rolled across the floor in her small foam-core insulated cottage in the swamp.

"You's not religious," she said later.

"Not really," I replied.

"You's lost. No meaning."

"There is meaning."

"What?"

"Survive."

At that, she smiled and nodded. "Yessir!"

* * *

A grenade exploded behind me. I fired the last of my zig-zags and dropped two more monks running through the ditch next to the monastery. Damn! What the hell was Red—

There he was, right flank. He'd taken one in the shoulder. Blood ran down his huge left arm, soaking the side of his flak vest. Somehow he still managed to hold the Cryo.

"Redeye!" I called. "A dozen, down the ridge." I pointed.

He nodded, his inch-long fangs pushing down his lower lip. He swung the Cryo, and fired as I ducked. The whir was a supersonic buzz of locusts. I've never gotten used to the sound. At sixty thousand rounds per minute, it was the highest rate of fire of any weapon in the world. Cryogenic tech was the only way to keep it cooled.

Depleted uranium needles cut through the top of the ridge. Dirt stopped bullets, but not ultra-dense spikes traveling at Mach 6. When Redeye stopped firing, there was nothing left but silence.

"Let me dress that," I said. I pulled a field bandage from Redeye's first aid kit and tied it to stem the bleeding from his left shoulder.

"Jack's in. He's waiting," I told him, pulling the knot tight. Redeye grunted. Redeye used to crank code, before his gen-mods. Now we bought our ware, and sometimes Redeye resented it. But he couldn't argue; Jack was the best.

"You ready?" I said into the DCU on my wrist.

"On your signal," Jack replied.

"Not yet. Just checking."

No reply. Jack's existence was measured in cycles of nanoseconds. Trillions of lines of code came at him, forced him to deal with them in one of a million ways, in the time it takes a human to blink. Jack didn't waste precious cycles engaging in chatter.

Now we had to do our part, in the real world.

Redeye covered the monastery door. When I moved up, he pulled the trigger and the Cryo chewed through the foot-thick stone wall next to the front door like an ice sculptor with a chainsaw. Good thing, too; the front door was rigged with shaped charges.

I rolled through the wall debris, crouched, came up in the courtyard aiming one of my three remaining pocket rockets. The sanctuary would be through the door in the opposite wall, according to the floor plans we'd ripped. That's where the god box would be. I made a quick scan for monks, found none, slapped the rocket against my palm, aimed, and let it go. It punched a neat hole through the far door.

When Redeye yelled "Clear!" I ran across the courtyard, kicked in the rest of the wood splinters, and stepped into the sanctuary. It had not been created for any god I'd ever heard of. An inverted cross hung over a severed hand, its fingertips burned to the bone. A black-handled dagger rested across two metal goblets flanked by human skulls on an altar. Arm and leg bones, candles, and small metal bowls filled with oily liquid sat on tables along the side walls, next to manacles anchored in the floor.

Jack's voice came across the DCU. "The Order of Golden Light is associated with the Sect Rogue, the Grey Pigs, and the Vin' Bain-Ding."

"Common traits?" I asked.

"Cannibalism."

Fucking nice.

"Anything on Madame Saloppe?" I asked.

"No."

I pulled out the second pocket rocket, and held it, ready to fire. I didn't see a box on the altar, or anywhere else in the room for that matter. Saloppe had said it would be there. Was she just wrong? Or was something else going on?

Madame Saloppe was a known risk. Lots of our employers were. She had put us in contact with Bill. A Voodoo queen and a Baptist preacher, the only thing they had in common was their hatred for the monks of the Order of Golden Light. "The forces of the Antichrist," Bill had called them. Looking at their sanctuary, he might be right.

The far sanctuary door creaked, and I turned. A hollow-eyed man, his skin hanging from his bones, rags drooping from stick-thin limbs, stumbled in. He continued to stumble, and I realized it was his normal shambling gait. Two others followed, brandishing curved knives. I slapped the rocket and launched it at the pathetic creatures. They flew apart like twigs.

Redeye was next to me.

"Were those—" he began.

"Zombies?" I finished his question. "Looked like it. Or could have been drugged, starving prisoners." If I'd ruined their escape attempt, it was the merciful thing to do.

"Jack, it's not here," I said into the DCU. "Can you try for an external reference?"

We waited while Jack scanned for security cameras, alarm systems, automatic lights, or anything else wired into the Grid that might match floor plans, and allow him to get a fix on the god box in the real world. It was risky. Jack needed all of his cycles to hide from intrusion-detection software, sector monitors, and data alarms, and to hold a channel open so that when we got in he could rip every line of code out of the god box.

He was also running a background process search on Madame Saloppe, at low priority. He could postpone that for a while. Something about her didn't sit right. It was a strange feeling. My gut had been right too many times for me to ignore it, but this was somehow different, stronger.

Kaylee knew Saloppe, and hated her. "She evil!" Kaylee had said when she found out that Saloppe had hired us. "She friends wit Papa Le Blas. Sold herself to him, she. You gotta watch her. She hoodooed a man to death. Good man, Bojibo. My man, once." I saw a tear at the corner of her eye. "Saloppe want him, but he with me. She hoodooed him. He get sick, and spit up snails, and a frog. I tried to save him, but her hoodoo strong. A week later, Bojibo, he die. When he go, purple snakes jump out o' his mouth. That's how I know it was her."

She looked at me, and touched her skirt to the corner of her eye, wiping the tear. "Why she hire you?" she said. "Why she want you to get the god box?"

The god box. Jack had ripped everything he could on it. Developed by a team of biochemists and brain physiologists at Paradise Engineering Incorporated, it created a special state of mind—it altered temporal-lobe activity, deadened the parietal lobes and the amygdala, tweaked some other things. We got the general theory, but not the details. The details were in the code itself, inside the god box. But Saloppe didn't want that. She wanted the device, in any condition. "Bring me whatever is left when you're through," she said. "I don't care about the insides. Just bring me the box."

It was the first time we'd had that request. People hire us to destroy data, to give them a competitive advantage. We're unique because we get it all: backups, hardware, disaster-recovery sites, everything. We could get the box for Saloppe, and still keep the code, but it would be tricky. Not finding the box where she said it would be made it harder.

"I've got a ... trap," Jack said. "A trigger that matches a stairwell. It's underground."

"Where?" I asked.

"Altar."

The altar sat on a stone slab. Pulling the correct manacle, or twisting a candle holder, would probably move it, but so would the Cryo. Uranium needles reduced the altar and the stone slab beneath it to rubble in a screaming blaze of fire. The religious symbolism did not escape me. But Redeye? With inch-long fangs on his grinning, mane-framed face?

A tiny stairway led down beneath the altar. Redeye could barely fit, the Cryo not at all, so I went alone. Redeye had lum-sticks, and more ammo for my hand cannon. I had one rocket left, and the thermite grenade that we needed, and my knife.

The stairs led to a crypt. Corpses on shelves lined a narrow passageway that twisted back into solid rock. It ended at another stairway leading down.

"Jack, what kind of trigger is it?" I said into the DCU.

No answer.

The monastery was half way between Baghdad and the ancient site of Babylon. We had a phased-array satellite dish set up half a klick away to tap into the Grid. Under this rock, the DCU must have been out of range. I hoped that was it. The alternative was that Jack was not doing well.

How would I signal him to rip the code? Split-second timing was critical. As soon as we started to slag the box, disaster recovery would kick in. The code would be copied to a dozen different locations in a thousandth of a second. But we didn't want that to happen. Jack would rip the code, and block all other channels. We would have the only true copy, plus the box itself, melted and smashed, which would go to Saloppe.

The trap trigger Jack had found was down there somewhere, down those stairs. Low tech beat no tech, so I pulled a wooden staff from one of the corpses, banged the dust from it, and began tapping the stairs, walls, and ceiling in front of me as I descended. A landing appeared ahead, followed by a turn to the right. I threw a lum-stick onto the landing, and heard a hiss. "You will die!" I heard a voice call from around the corner.

"I've heard that before," I said.

"Bahometh will slay you!"

"Who?"

"Bahometh! The King!"

"Who's queen?" I said, "Saloppe?"

The sound of spitting. "Saloppe is evil."

"I've heard that too. And you're better?"

"Did she send you?" The voice asked. "Madame Saloppe?"

"Maybe," I replied.

"She sent you here to destroy me."

"No. For something else."

"No, you are wrong. For me."

"Who are you?" I asked.

"Mujibar."

I took a step down, drawing the .57-caliber at my side as I did. "If she wanted you dead, she would have hired an assassin," I called. "I'm not an assassin."

"Not dead, she wants me destroyed."

I peeked around the corner and saw a bald, black man wearing a purple cape standing at the far end of a room roughly ten meters square. His ebony skin glistened in the light of red candles burning on shelves along the far wall. He held a wooden rod with a foot-long blade in one hand, and a gourd of some kind, with beads and a bell attached to it, in the other. Beside him on a short table was a metal box, a foot square.

"I just want the box," I said, slowly stepping onto the landing, keeping my gun out of sight behind the wall.

"Come and get it." He smiled.

I shifted my weight, and WHAM! I was falling. The trap! The edge of the pit struck my hand, and my pistol flew from my grasp. The wooden pole I had stopped using all too soon caught under my arm and slammed across the top of the pit. I grabbed at it with my gun hand, and somehow managed to hold on. The lum-stick tumbled below me. I glanced down, and saw a huge albino snake coiled among metal spikes lining the floor of a twenty-foot pit. The glow of the lum-stick cast leaping shadows on the walls as the stick fell into the spikes.

"You will meet Le Grand Zombi!" Mujibar said.

He came forward, shaking the gourd. "L'Appé vini. Le Grand Zombi!" The gourd rattled and jingled. The snake below me hissed. Mujibar whirled his knife stick. I could not climb out of the pit before he got to me, and he knew it. His pearl-white teeth shone in triumph.

Knife fighters argue about the best way to carry a knife. It depends on the blade, of course. I usually prefer hilt-down, along my left side, from a shoulder harness, for my Sikes-Fairbairn Commando. But I usually don't carry a thermite grenade. Today, that's where the grenade was. My chrome Commando, sharp as a scalpel, was slung hilt-up, between my shoulder blades in a cross-back harness. I shrugged the pole tighter under my armpit and reached behind my head with my free hand as the Voodoo man approached. The knife wasn't there.

Mujibar swung his blade down. I jerked back, barely in time. His blade missed my face by inches. I reached back again, more frantic this time. The knife must have shifted. I couldn't find it! From the corner of my eye I saw Mujibar flip his weapon around and lift it over his head. I couldn't move enough to get out of the way while holding on to the pole across the pit.

"L'Appé vini, pou fe gris-gris!" he yelled.

His blade came at me like an arrow. The only thing I could do would put me in an even more vulnerable position, but I had no choice. I slid my arm over the pole and swung down. Mujibar's attack missed again, his blade sailing through space where my chest had been only moments before.

I now dangled helplessly, my hands fully exposed. He could cut my hands, or knock the pole into the pit, and me with it. It looked like I would meet Le Grand Zombi today.

I swung my legs for momentum, to shift my grip, and as I did I felt something below me lifting up. It was solid and flat, rising from the side. It slammed up to floor level, and I rolled, leaving the pole behind. I heard the ring of metal on metal as the Voodoo's weapon missed me a third time.

It was the trapdoor. Jack. The trap could be triggered remotely, to open or to close. That's how Jack had discovered it in the Grid in the first place.

Mujibar cursed something I didn't catch. I was on one knee, pivoting, both hands behind my head, searching. I found the knife, shifted behind my left shoulder. Mujibar spun as I let the Sikes-Fairbairn fly. The blade buried itself in his chest with a THUNK, and he collapsed.

I made sure the Voodoo priest was dead. I retrieved my knife, and gun, and went to examine the box. It was a breadboard chassis, like those I'd seen many times, fairly standard for beta hardware. I/O port, power, and Grid connection were standard, with just one board of custom chips and wiring. The Grid and power cables disappeared underneath the wax-dripped shelves of the small room. All I had to do was set the thermite grenade on top of the box and pull the pin, and the box would become a pile of slag. Then when the mess cooled, take what was left to Saloppe, and our contract would be fulfilled. She still owed us eight hundred grand.

Slagging the box was fine, but there was no need to lose the intel stored in the circuitry, since she didn't care. If I cut the Grid cable before melting the box, that would ruin their disaster plan, but it would also keep us from copying the intel. Jack's job was to circumvent that problem. He would block all outgoing disaster copies, which would kick off as soon as processes noticed the hardware was compromised. Then he would rip us one pristine version, and send it to our own private datastore.

Jack would do that, if he could: if I could tell him to prepare for it. Jack needed a few critical seconds to redirect his processing cycles from "conceal and avoid", to "block and transfer". If he wasn't ready, he would likely fail. And worse, if he was taken off-guard, the outgoing copies would set off data alarms that would show Control Central he was there. CC's Fortress software would find him, and tear Jack apart line by line.

Jack was good, but could he handle being hit off-guard? I doubted it.

I tried calling him again. "Jack, it's Slater. You there?"

The DCU on my wrist was silent.

"Redeye, do you copy?"

Nothing. I'd noticed Redeye's DCU was scorched when I'd bandaged his shoulder. He couldn't relay the message.

How could I let Jack know? If I ran back to the surface it would be too imprecise. "Pulling the pin in, oh, about three minutes or so" wouldn't cut it. I looked at the box, and my eyes fell on the I/O port.

The god box was online. Jack knew where it was in the Grid. If I had an Infex, or an ICU, I could plug it in and contact Jack directly. But I didn't. My DCU was a combat model, no I/O interface. There had to be some way.

I found the answer in the Voodoo priest's robe. An I/O cable with a head-sized mesh net was sewn into the hood of Mujibar's cape. Put on the hood, plug into the box, and I would be online with God. Hopefully, God wouldn't mind if I told Jack to get ready, that I was about to drop a two-thousand-degree, white-hot grenade on the pathway to the Divine.

I cut the mesh net out of the robe's hood, stretched it over my skull, and walked to the god box. The I/O cable was slick with Mujibar's blood. Not ideal conditions for meeting the Creator.

I leaned over, plugged the cable in, and saw... Everything.

I was still looking at the room, the stairs, my stick, Mujibar's weapon and gourd, and Mujibar himself, but something was superimposed. I saw "lines of force" extending out, everywhere, to everything, but also coming together in one "spot" that was nowhere. The lines connected things, but with no control implied. They just were, as they should be. The "spot" moved as I looked around. It was always just out of sight. It was behind the walls, beneath the floor, or just invisible in front of me, but I knew it was there.

I felt calm. Everything was right. Everything. I looked at the walls, the candles, the god box itself, and it was all, just, *right*. The candles were being candles; the walls were being walls, all just as they should be. I looked at Mujibar's body. It wasn't a sad thing, or good, or even bad. It wasn't a shame, or a pity. It was just the way it should be, the way it had to be, because that's the way it was.

The universe made sense. The universe was good, and right, and even bad things were OK. They were fine. That's the way they should be.

There was no Being, no bearded man on a throne. All there was, was the All of Everything. All connected. All right.

I closed my eyes, and thought about Jack. Slowly, a figure appeared in my mind.

"Jack?" I said.

"Yes," the figure replied. He looked a little like Redeye, a little like me, and a little like Bill.

"It's Slater," I said.

"Nice to finally meet you in person," he said.

"Are you busy?"

"Sort of, in one sense. Here I'm not."

"What's going on 'there'?"

"A Bulldog Breaker alarm is trying to warn CC that I'm in its sector. A Tripmine v7.3 is trying to lure me into a code-shredder. I'm re-routing priority crash traffic around myself while trying to stay unnoticed, and I'm delaying a non-maskable interrupt vector that's making its final call before declaring voltage failure."

Something made me say, "Need help?"

"Sure," Jack said.

And I was in the Grid. Jack looked similar, but huge, and made of chrome, with ghost flames flickering all up and down his gleaming body. A spinning horizontal tornado of multi-colored iridescence swirled to one side of him, hypnotizing, calling. A pulsing metal dog barked as data shot from its glowing red eyes.

I took care of the NMIV first. With a wave, the flames around Jack sputtered and vanished, and the interrupt vector was gone. I pinched the tornado, and Tripmine v7.3 shrank, and disappeared. With a nod, the bulldog went silent.

Jack smiled. "Thanks," he said.

"Sure," I replied. "Get ready. I'm going to—"

Did I want to do that?

I looked around. I was in the Grid. I was in it, not viewing it, like with an inducer. The lines of force were still present, visible, even here. Strange. I looked at the lines, tried to find the "spot". It remained just out of sight as before.

What if I stayed here? It was as if I could do anything, control the Grid. The Grid had the lines of force, as if it were real, but I knew it wasn't. At best it was a metaphysical construct. One other person had tried to interface the Grid with physical reality, and he had gone insane, and I'd killed him: Edgar Dunbar, the criminally deranged CIO of Holobar Labs. Is this what it had been like for him?

But with the added capability of altering physical laws as well?

I didn't want to end up like Dunbar. Something compelled me to go. Not just the knowledge of Dunbar; it was more. It was stronger. I knew I couldn't stay. I had to finish the job.

"Get ready, Jack," I said.

He nodded. "Thanks again." His chrome hand waved.

I unplugged, and dropped out of the Grid.

I was back in the room, with Mujibar's corpse and the god box. I only had a few seconds. I put the thermite grenade on the box and pulled the pin. It was up to Jack now.

I stood back as the grenade showered sparks and melted straight down through the box and the table and burned into the rock floor beneath. The box transformed into a collapsed hunk of metal with a hole in its center. When its edges cooled, I picked it up and went to find Redeye.

"Got it," I said as I emerged from the stairs below what was once the altar. I held up the remains of the god box.

He nodded. "Let's find Saloppe," he said.

* * *

On the shuttle back, Jack called. "Copy stored and locked. Security as directed?" he asked.

We had the intel. We could recreate the hardware, reload it, and then we would have God online.

"Switch to protect mode Zulu," I said into my DCU.

"Copy," Jack replied. "There's something else."

"What?"

"The background process check on Saloppe."

"Yeah?"

"Insufficient funds. She can't pay."

"Recent?"

"Never had it," Jack said.

Redeye looked at me. He knew what I knew. She'd never intended to pay us, which meant one thing.

When we got back, we went to see her with a full combat load: vests, weapons, gear, ammo, everything. It wasn't a social call.

Knee-high grass surrounded her house on the edge of the small, backwater town. Her place was ramshackle, desperately in need of paint, on stilts two feet off the ground. A cross with candle drippings and a statue of Mother Mary with a hand-painted face occupied a bare spot in the front yard. A small, black coffin, sized for a baby or a small child, with bells around its edges, sat on one side of the front porch. The porch creaked when Redeye stepped on it. He went to the coffin and opened it with the muzzle of his rifle. "Empty," he said.

I peered in and saw bloody stains.

I eased myself next to the front door, wrinkled my nose at the smell of something rotten, and knocked.

"Come in!" Saloppe's voice was old, but strong.

"Cover," I told Redeye. He nodded, and I kicked the door in.

"Been expecting you," Saloppe said. "No need for that." She waved at the gun in my hand. She was old and wrinkled, just like her vid. "Crone" was the best word to describe her. She sat in a dark, high-backed chair, with symbols and crude faces painted on its arms and legs.

"We're here—"

"Know why you're here!" she said.

"We don't like being used."

"Got my deposit. Got the innards of the machine. Sell that for three times what I owe ya!"

"That's not the point," I said.

"Is the point! I ain't rich, but you got what you want. I got what I want."

Something dawned on me: the flattened trails in the tall grass outside. "You did want Mujibar, didn't you?"

Her eyes narrowed.

"He stole the Grand Zombi from you. We're not assassins," I said.

"Didn't need no assassins," she replied. "Got other ways, better ways, I want a man dead. You think I double-cross you? Gonna kill you? Look at you!" She waved at my combat gear.

"I know you're not going to kill me," I said.

"I hoodoo you, I want you dead!" she said.

"Try it," I replied.

With that, she twitched. "Ah!" she said. She convulsed, and I raised my gun. She continued to shudder as I watched. Finally, she jerked sideways. "Yah!" Her hand flew up. She was holding a knife.

It was a sudden, foolish move, but it didn't stop me from firing.

Footsteps pounded outside. "It's me," Redeye called.

"Clear," I said. He stepped in and stared at the dead Voodoo woman.

* * *

I went to see Kaylee, who lived on the other side of Saloppe's town. Wet clothes hung outside Kaylee's cottage, strung on a line between two massive, moss-covered bayou trees. A washboard rested on an upside-down washtub propped against her front porch. Kaylee was in her sitting room, standing in front of her altar; feathers were scattered at her feet, along with some small pieces of cloth and twine. She was holding a wooden plank with a black candle and a pile of ashes on it.

"Saloppe, dead," Kaylee said. It was not a question.

"Yes," I replied.

She blew out the candle. "Don't be mad," she said. "I voodooed her. She killed Bojibo. She would'a kilt you."

"You didn't voodoo her. I shot her," I replied.

She blew the ashes from the plank, and set it on the altar. "I know."

"Do you know why Saloppe wanted the god box, Kaylee?" I asked.

She froze.

"Kaylee?"

Her hands went to her mouth, and she shook her head.

"Tell me what you know."

"No, no! Bad things, bad people! Evil. No good to even talk about it."

"Redeye and I have the god box now, inside and out. Although the inside and the outside are currently separated, I will admit. Why would she want a smashed shell? I don't believe her only goal was for us to kill Mujibar. Is a burned, melted case worth anything?"

Kaylee's eyes widened. "You killed Mujibar?"

"Yes. Did you know him?"

"Heard his name," Kaylee shrugged. "He powerful."

"He thought that's why Saloppe sent us, to 'destroy him.' But if he hadn't been with the box when we found it, we wouldn't have touched him. Not a good plan for Saloppe. Besides, she said she'd have hoodooed him if she wanted him dead. At the very least she could have hired a regular assassin instead of us. She wanted the case for something. Do you have any idea what?"

Kaylee's hands dropped from her mouth. She looked at me with timid eyes. "She want it for her work," she said. "It belong to her enemies. Can do strong work with that."

"Like what?"

"Hoodoo work. Steal theys power. Make 'em sick, fight with theyselves."

"Maybe. I think Mujibar stole her snake," I added.

"That Saloppe's power. They always fightin' over power."

"Who?"

"No, no! Say the name, they hear you."

"One name?"

She shook her head no.

"Okay. Enough about work." I smiled, and rubbed her bare, smooth shoulders. "Is that jambalaya I smell cooking?"

She smiled back, full lips over bright teeth. Happy eyes. "Yessir."

* * *

When I got back to our hotel room in the city the next day I found Redeye at the Encom. Our Encom was an ICU, an Info Control Unit, a level above a DCU. ICU's were strictly for Domestic Infrastructure Security Control. But DISC didn't know we had this one. Just like GIS didn't know we had a Grid inducer, and like almost nobody knew we had the code from the god box. But someone knew.

"Jack's in trouble," Redeye said as soon as I walked in. He was hunched over the Encom's display cube, his hands on the control bars, the headset stretched to its limit over his massive, hairy head.

"What's up?"

"He's under attack. It doesn't look Fed. I can't tell who."

"Is all the hardware online?"

"Everything but the backup reserves. I wanted you to take a look before committing those."

Our private datastore was in a nitrogen-filled cylinder, on a coral reef, one hundred meters underwater, in an international no-dive zone. Five other cylinders, connected by Rad channels, backed up the main datastore and add-on CPU arrays. We could bring them online in an emergency, but doing so would compromise our stored backups. We'd never had to do that yet.

I went to the Encom as Redeye stepped away. I didn't need the headset. It wasn't pretty. Jack was a multi-colored ribbon in the display cube. Colors represented CPU utilization, memory, I/O, and various core processes. The colors were shades of red, pink, a few streaks of purple, and lots of angry orange. The headset would have blared static in my ears and the mouthpiece would taste bitter, I was certain.

Lines representing channel connections pulsed with data. The boxes at the ends of the lines were blank for the most part, as blocker programs hid the attacking software's identity. An attack typically consisted of one to four links. It was difficult to coordinate more than that and still have sufficient power for any successful infiltration. Jack could easily handle two dozen simultaneous attack links. The display I was looking at showed Jack as the center of a fifty-pin pincushion.

"Shit. How long has it been going on?" I asked.

"Twenty minutes," Redeye said. "I was just about to call you."

There were usually tuning options—commit more memory to reduce CPU utilization, increase buffers to reduce I/O, readjust various core processes depending on the attack type and strength—but with everything maxed, tuning wasn't possible. Besides, Jack had dynamic resource allocation control himself, and he was never wrong.

"They want the code," Redeye said. "Or at least they don't want us to have it."

"Who wants it?" I asked, looking at the grim display.

Redeye shrugged.

If we committed the backup hardware reserves, the safe copy of the god box code would be at risk. If we didn't use them, and the attack succeeded, our main datastore could crash, and with it, Jack.

"Where's the inducer? Maybe I can see what he's up against inline."

Redeye nodded toward the second living room of our suite. "Warming up," he said.

The Grid inducer showed Gridspace like a vid. You were an observer of a show, with some interaction. When I'd plugged into the god box it was like being in the vid itself, a part of it, with control.

I went to the inducer and checked the settings. Redeye had it set to enter near Jack. I wrapped the goggles around my head and pressed the data pads to my temples.

Breathe slow. You needed the right state of mind. In. Out. One. Two. Three. In. Out.

Jack's image coalesced. He was a silver man, not huge and chrome as the god box had shown him, standing on a stepped pyramid that rose out of cracked, dry ground. As the scene faded in, I saw Jack was in the middle of a nightmare. Huge, ugly creatures, with the bodies of snakes and bloody, leathery wings, dove and bit at him from a twilight sky. An army of skeletons, wearing top hats and carrying rattling gourds, swarmed up the stairs of the pyramid and clawed at his feet. Three zombies the size of mountains, with gray, rotting, putrid flesh, surrounded Jack and took turns swinging boulder-sized, scabby fists at him as he dodged.

Jack pulsed rhythmically with power. He moved like lightning, but I knew he couldn't keep it up.

Surrender the god box code, an unknown asset, or surrender Jack, a proven asset? But the god box code had huge potential. If we had the right hardware to run it on, I'd plug into it now, and help Jack.

I don't know if Jack saw me. I think he did, with a blinding fast glance. I knew I had to act fast, so I pulled out of Gridspace.

"Let's bring up one backup array," I said as I unhooked.

Redeye, seated once again at the Encom, nodded.

I put the inducer on standby, and peered over Redeye's shoulder. The ribbon at the center of the display changed from red to streaks of yellow as one of our five backup cylinders came online. The purple lines in the ribbon representation of Jack turned blue. I imagined Jack in Gridspace, swelling. Instead of dodging the huge zombie fists, I pictured him catching one, and smashing it with a punch of his own. I imagined him kicking huge piles of skeletons down the pyramid, and catching a bird creature and breaking its snake neck. Four, then five, then six of the pincushion attack links disappeared.

"Another tube?" Redeye asked.

"Not yet." Jack was good.

One of the yellow streaks flashed, then turned green, followed by another. Five more attack links dropped.

We watched as one by one, the pincushion lines showing attacking data links blinked out. When it was down to ten, Redeye said, "I'm taking the backup tube offline."

"Yeah." I nodded.

In another minute it was over, all attacks defeated. Jack and the god box code were safe.

Redeye hit audio on the Encom. "Jack, how are you?" I asked.

"Green."

"Someone knows you're there, and what you're guarding," Redeye said.

"Yes," he replied.

"We've got to offload the code. We need hardware, another god box," I said.

"We can rebuild the hardware based on the code itself. But we need these chips to optimize it." Redeye turned what was left of the custom chipboard from the god box over in his hands. It was melted through in the middle. The chip IDs were scorched.

He and I were both good, but we needed the best. When you're going to build something that alters your brain, guesswork is a bad plan. Redeye stopped flipping the board over in his hands. He looked at me and I nodded.

Gameboy. He was the best. He had to be the best hardware master, so he could always run the latest and greatest games. Shoot a few aliens, contact the Divine; it was all the same in my book.

* * *

We sent a hologram of the chipboard to Gameboy. The next day he called us for a meeting. Gameboy preferred to meet in Gridspace, so he could stay in persona. Redeye didn't like using an inducer, but he conceded for this. We double-linked in to meet Gameboy on his own turf.

The meeting room was a white sphere with no direct lighting. The only way to tell it was a sphere was by carefully watching the thousands of translucent ping-pong balls that ricocheted around, passing through everything in the room except the two red and blue ghost circles that hovered at opposite sides of the large area.

A bubbling cauldron floated in the center of the sphere. Gameboy appeared in his usual flowing blue wizard's garb. He had ten arms. "Slater and Redeye," his voice boomed.

"Master Talazar," I replied, bowing.

He smiled. "An interesting thing here," he said. The chipboard hologram instantly appeared floating above one of his outstretched palms.

"Yes. We will provide you with the coin of the realm if you can make another for us, whole," I said.

"I can do that," he replied, then paused, and frowned. "Why? What is it for?" He asked.

"It is for a...."

"Spell," Redeye interjected.

"Ah, the were-lion speaks!" Talazar-Gameboy grinned. "I thought you only a fighting companion of the wily one." Redeye and I exchanged cautious glances.

"We have the, ah, recipe for the spell," Redeye said. "Mayhap that would help?" He added.

I looked at Redeye. "Mayhap?"

Redeye shrugged.

"Yes, it would," Talazar said.

"We can give you the specifications for the code—eh, spell, but the exact recipe is a secret. You understand," I said.

Talazar made an incredible flourish with his ten arms, and the ping-pong balls in the room turned to translucent chipboards. "My esteemed acquaintances, you have an impressive array of componentry and apparatus in your own lair. I am sure you are aware that you can simulate this bauble," he flicked a hand at a flying chipboard, "with a spell. The fact that you want it instantiated physically demands that I know the reason why."

Software can simulate any hardware. It was true that using our banked array of CPUs and datastore we could simulate the chipboard. The issue with simulation is always speed. Even though our computing power is roughly equal to that of the Tokyo financial district, this was not an area where I wanted to risk losing a few nanoseconds in a hyper-phase quantum conversion or a floating-point arithmetic adjustment. Besides, simulation would mean keeping the code online, which we were trying to avoid. We needed optimized hardware to load the code into.

"We have reasons, o Talazar, which we do not wish to trouble you with. We do not want to embroil you in the schemes of our adversaries."

He smiled. "I insist."

Redeye growled. I never understood how genetic mods gave Redeye a growl, but they did.

Talazar stepped back with one foot and spread his arms around his head, like peacock plumage.

"We need it for speed," I said.

"I guessed. Speed for what?" Talazar arched his arms. Redeye crouched.

"We need to get the code offline," I added.

Redeye and Talazar continued their face-off, growling, posturing. With the snap of my fingers I could call in Jack. But that would be messy, and we wouldn't be any closer to getting the chipboard.

"It's not for a game," I said.

"Oh." Talazar lowered his arms and looked at me. "Why didn't you say so?"

Redeye straightened. "Not everything in life is a game," he growled.

Talazar flicked a hand indifferently toward Redeye and a ball of sparks crackled around Redeye's head. Redeye brushed them away with a grunt.

"Very well," Talazar said. "I can recreate this item." All of the flying chipboards rushed together, congealing into a single, solid board floating above the bubbling cauldron. "But if I find Rogue Queen, or that asshole CrashRocker using it in the next round of Dark Moon Rising—"

He caught himself out of character, and stopped. "What will you pay?" He asked somberly.

I held up a cred-chip and flashed a number. He smiled.

"Three days," he said. "Where do you want it delivered?"

"You still in the PacRim?" I asked.

"Yes. Singapore."

"We'll pick it up."

* * *

A trip to Singapore was six hours, then another thirty minutes to the Top Ten club. That left two days for us to sit in our New Orleans hotel and try to figure out who had made the attack. Saloppe and Mujibar were dead, along with a monastery of monks from the Order of Golden Light. It was easy to assume that the OGL wasn't happy, and that they wanted their code back, but how did they know we had it? It looked like a clean wipe job. I'd cut the Grid cable after the code copy. No one could tell the sequence.

How had the OGL, and Mujibar, gotten the god box in the first place? From the look of their monastery it didn't seem like the Order of Golden Light was too interested in contacting God.

I worked at the Encom for a day straight, researching. I didn't use Jack. He was on guard duty watching the code. It was surprising how little I could find online. Bits and pieces on the OGL were contradictory. Some said they were descendents of the Knights Templar, founded in Jerusalem in the twelfth century to protect the pilgrimage trail to the holy city following the Crusades. Some said the Knights Templar had been corrupted, and became worshipers of Bahometh. Others insisted that they'd remained pure. There was even less intel on the groups Jack mentioned at the monastery: the Sect Rogue, the Grey Pigs, and the Vin' Bain-Ding. It wasn't even clear if they were separate groups, or the same group using different names at different times. Cannibals have to be careful. I guess they don't call them secret societies for nothing.

The Encom was in one corner of our suite. I sat facing out, windows to my left, door to my right. Redeye was sleeping in back. I was engrossed in the display cube, looking at a picture of a Voodoo rattle, called an *asson*, similar to the one Mujibar had used. It was a gourd, covered with snake vertebrae and bells, used, supposedly, to summon Loas, the Voodoo spirits.

As the 3D *asson* slowly rotated, I heard scratching at the door, and looked up just in time to see the door's faceplate drop to the floor. I ducked as the door burst open. An explosion on the wall behind me threw me the rest of the way to the ground. I rolled, winded, as a burst of silenced, automatic weapon fire sprayed the room.

Where was my pistol? Damn! Holstered on the table next to the Encom. I continued rolling, and stopped, panting, behind one of the two sofas in the suite. I realized, thankfully, that this was the sleeper, and had some mass. I drew my Sikes-Fairbairn from its shoulder holster under my left arm and waited. There was a step, and the metallic click of a magazine being released. I caught the smell of gunpowder. The familiar feel of the hard, cool steel of my knife in my hand was reassuring. My current situation was less so.

Risk a glance at my adversary, or remain a sitting duck? He had to know where I was. I took a peek around the edge of the sofa. It wasn't a he, it was a she, and she was looking right at me, a fresh magazine for her HK assault rifle in her hand. It would take her two seconds to lock and load, another second to fire. More than enough time. I pulled back, ready to throw my knife, saw the fear in her eyes—

There was Redeye streaking from the back room, standing next to her in a flash. Smack! Her rifle was on the floor. He grabbed her, spun her, one massive arm around her throat, a hand on her head. In a moment she would be a crumpled heap.

"Wait!" I said.

Redeye growled.

"Guuuhhh," the girl choked.

"Bring her in," I said, standing.

Redeye carried her by her throat into the room. The door swung shut behind them.

"We're working on minimal data," I said. "Maybe she can change that."

Green eyes looked at me. At least she had the sense not to say, "I won't talk," with Redeye's arms encircling her head.

"Are you ready to go?" I asked Redeye.

"Yeah."

We paid extra for privacy, but even though the machine gun had been silenced, her first explosive round and the bullet holes in the walls would bring the local law. Our fake Fed IDs would work for some things, but not this. Local law would bring Fed law, and Fed law would bring NAIS. We had a long, largely unfriendly history with North American Information Security.

Since we frequently had to leave in a hurry, we both stayed packed to the extent possible. The Encom was the only thing out. We could get another display cube and controller anywhere, so while Redeye held the girl I put the Encom and headset in their cases and got our bags.

"Roof?" I asked. Redeye nodded. He carried the girl under one arm, his personal bag slung across his opposite shoulder. I carried the rest of our gear.

It cost us a thousand a day to keep a driver on call on the roof at all times, but the cost had paid off more than once. This would be one more occasion. The driver blinked from under the wrinkled newsrag draped over his head, but we knew he would be ready. He had been the other two times we'd made checks. He focused on his controls, wisely avoiding paying direct attention to our gear, or the girl, as we climbed in.

"Airfield," I said. "Anywhere clear within five klicks will do."

He nodded as the aircar lifted from the roof.

The girl sat stiffly between me and Redeye, her hands on the black Lycra pants that covered her slender legs. She had short, brown hair, and thin lips that hooked up at the ends. That was all I could tell at the moment, sitting beside her with a pistol stuck in her gut.

The ride was brief. The driver set us down in a field near a small wooded outcropping half a kilometer from the airstrip. I tipped him five hundred to lose the trip records.

"Name?" I asked the girl, after we'd moved her and the gear into tree line.

"Manda," she said.

"Who are you with? And I know you've been thinking up a cover story during the ride here, if you didn't have one already. Spare us, and skip it, okay? We'll be able to verify."

"Lies are tools of evil. I'm Reverend William's daughter," she said.

"What? Bill's daughter?"

"Yes."

Redeye's eyes widened. That didn't happen often.

"What's your church name?" Redeye asked.

"First Aramaean Baptist."

I looked at Redeye and he nodded.

"'God gave man dominion over the fish of the sea, the birds of the air, and the beasts of the land.' Chapter and verse?" Redeye asked.

"Genesis 1:28, awkwardly paraphrased from the King James. Going to ask me who won the World Series in 1945 next?"

"That'll do for now," I said. I reached into my duffel and pulled out the HK Manda had tried to slaughter me with less than thirty minutes ago. "Why?" I asked.

Her lips pulled taut and curled up even more than they did naturally. "You—" she started, pointing an accusing finger.

"Your father was on the mission of his own free will," I said.

"Not that. I know who you are."

"Do you?" Redeye asked.

"Demons. Pagans." She looked at Redeye. "Genetic mutants, subverting the will of God."

"Doesn't 'pagan' have a specific meaning?" I asked Redeye.

"Yes, and we're not it."

"Look, Manda," I said. "I don't give a goddamn what you think about us. Your father was... honorable, in my opinion. He fought well, and died well, for his own reasons. I'm sorry about what happened."

"I don't want your pity." She lunged at me, but telegraphed her move. I sidestepped easily. Redeye grabbed her from behind and repeated the headlock he'd had her in earlier.

"She's a fanatic," I said. "We should have left her."

"Maybe," Redeye replied. He let go with one hand and reached into his pocket. He pulled out an injector and pricked her thigh. After twenty more seconds of struggling, she slumped.

"It probably wasn't militant Baptists that attacked Jack online," I said. "Although I can imagine they might want the god box code."

"Bill never seemed very interested in it," Redeye said.

"True." When we'd met with Bill prior to the monastery raid, his only concern had seemed to be "wiping out the Hellspawn." "I didn't get very far in my research," I said. "Every file I found on black magic, Satanism, or cannibalism, whatever that monastery was all about, I found two more that contradicted it."

"And the Voodoo tie-in?" Redeye asked.

"There's not supposed to be any. My guess is Saloppe was using Voodoo as a cover."

"For Satanism? Doesn't seem like a very good cover," Redeye said. "Didn't you say Kaylee told you they were always fighting for power?"

"Yes. They."

"Don't get defensive. I'm sure your girlfriend is a nice, sweet, voodoo queen."

"A queen is a specific title," I said. "And she's not." More than once a relationship of mine had crossed over to work. Redeye didn't need to remind me. At least I had relationships. I think Redeye's genetic mods lowered his libido.

"What about her?" I asked, pointing at the unconscious Manda.

"Militant Baptists are a pretty small sub-sect. She might know more than it seems."

"Are you suggesting we take her with us?"

He nodded.

It was easier than I expected. Redeye's cocktail must have included a serotonin dump, because Manda's mood was nearly jubilant as we boarded the charter jump shuttle four hours later.

Six hours, two in-flight movies, interspersed with snatches of sleep, and another thigh injection for Manda, and we were in Singapore.

Two things about Singapore, it's hot, and it's humid: right on the equator, and surrounded by water. You can't walk two blocks without working up a sweat. So we didn't walk.

Top Ten was half an hour from the airport, but it was two o'clock in the afternoon. The club crowd wouldn't even be awake yet.

"I'm gonna get some barbecued duck and noodles," I said. "Maybe catch another couple hours sleep in a tube. I'll meet you at the club at eight, all right?"

"I'm going to show Manda the temples," Redeye said. "The Temple of Eternal Happiness was closed the last time I was here."

"How appropriate. If you lose her along the way," I nodded at Manda, "it'll be fine with me." Manda stood in a grinning stupor. "You know they kill drug dealers here. Keep that hypo out of sight," I said. "One milligram and you're trafficking."

Redeye nodded.

We dropped most of our gear at Lim Hun's security-check-free storage, at a thousand times the cost of a regular terminal locker.

Gameboy was a mild mannered kid in real life. "Yes, sir. No, sir. That's not my gum, sir. No, sir, I don't want electroshock." He stayed in Singapore for the sense of security it gave him. More laws, with harsher punishment, than any-where in the world. But if you could pay, you could get away.

Singapore was the only place in the world with urine detectors in the elevators and stairwells. Take a piss and doors would slam and sirens go off. You would get to pay for the sterilization and the time for the police to come let you out, and you would get a public caning thrown in.

It was all law abiding and pristine on the surface; as long as you could keep it out of sight, which meant pay big, you could pretty much do what you want. It was the perfect place to deal ware—hard, soft, firm, or quantum. Other popular biz was intel laundering, and every conceivable form of prostitution.

We split up at Mister T, the nickname for Singapore's Mass Rail Transit sta-tion. Redeye headed west; I went to Bugis.

Bugis was as old-town as Singapore got. Narrow, tarp-covered alleys that criss-crossed through ten blocks of warehouses, sweatshops, and low-rise apart-ments. The alleys were crammed with tiny booths, the hawkers selling everything from jade good-luck figurines and trinkets to high-fashion knock-offs and kung-fu weaponry "for display purposes only".

I should have remembered my rule of not walking. Within ten minutes I was dripping sweat. Wing Fat's noodle and barbecue stand was in the People's Plaza, a three-floor, open-air mall also packed with hawkers' stands, only slightly more permanent than the cloth- and bamboo- partitioned ones in the crowded streets nearby. The low, wide slabs of cement of the Plaza's floor held hundreds of carts and stands selling chopsticks, postcards, incense, sandals, dried turkey heads with the spines still attached, roots, pagoda wind chimes, Buddha figurines, fish, socks, pennants, children's card games, silk, watches, radios, live birds, and a hundred other things I didn't care to identify. The smell was stale beer and road kill. I'd forgotten that part too.

I remembered that Wing Fat's noodles were good, but that memory came from a late night out with an RK girl named Su Ru. Long, black, silky hair, and the smoothest, porcelain skin; I'd thought at first she was a gen-mod. It didn't mat-ter, she was exquisite. It was a good night all around.

Dozens of people haggled in Mandarin and Malay, drowning out most of the rhythmic droning of the flute player begging behind me. I was only slightly sur-prised to find Wing Fat's stand still there. It was one of the more permanent structures, with actual foamcrete walls and tables cemented into the ground, in-stead of the typical wheeled cart and plastic tables and chairs.

Wing Fat was cooking. I ordered beef noodles and duck from the shriveled old woman standing at the counter who could have been Wing's wife, sister, or mother, for all I could tell. I declined her offer of a fork instead of chopsticks, and nodded knowingly as she showed me how to squeeze the golf-ball-sized lime over my food.

The noise of the plaza seemed quieter as I sat to eat the heaping plate of duck and noodles. In mid first bite I realized why. The flute playing had stopped. I swallowed without tasting, concentrating on my peripheral vision.

...Darting movement to my left. I whirled. The beggar was beside me. I had a chopstick in each hand. His eyes were easy targets.

"Wait!" he cried.

No obvious weapons; a defensive posture.

I stopped. "Two seconds," I said, chopsticks poised.

"Kaylee want me to watch you."

"What?" I lowered the chopsticks an inch.

"They know you here," he said. "Kaylee ask me to protect you."

"Who knows we're here?" I asked.

"They." He shook his head. "Don't say they name."

"I don't need protecting."

He smiled, white teeth on a wide, Afro-Indian face. "She say you'd say that. You wear this. Burn this tonight."

The man handed me a small burlap-wrapped packet tied with twine, and a thin, white candle.

"What's your name?" I asked.

"Dr. John."

"How did Kaylee call you? She doesn't have a phone, no Grid, no commo access at all."

He threw back his head and laughed. "Ha ha! You right!" he said, wagging a finger. "She don' need it."

I took the items. "Promise me you gonna wear that, burn the candle," he said.

"Yeah, fine. Just don't tell me what's in the bag."

"Ha ha! Yeah, you probably don' 'wanna know!"

He turned and walked away, resuming his flute playing in front of the silk-kimono booth three stalls down.

I finished my duck and noodles, the necklace and candle shoved in my pants cargo pocket. The food was hot and tangy. They chop the bones with the duck at Wing Fat's, and I had to pick them out as I ate. While I did, I thought about the nameless "they". Who had attacked Jack? How did they even know we had the code?

When I finished eating, I opened the gris-gris bag just to make sure. Wax, bones, ashes, and red goo.

Thanks, Kaylee.

* * *

Top Ten is a huge club between Singapore's megamall shopping and sky-scraper financial districts. The club has ceilings three stories high, with pulsing lights and a dance floor at one end, and tiered seating with plush, semicircular tables at the other. The music is high-energy, with a pounding beat. The crowd tends to be young Asian females, and an international mix of older men. The typical pickup line is "Hi." I suspected that's why Gameboy liked it.

I met Redeye out front. "Where's Manda?" I asked.

"Sleeping. That Hydro keeps you happy for a while, but then you have to pay. She'll be out for at least ten hours."

"Good." I flashed a cred-chip and ID at the front door and a thin, well-tailored Singaporean smiled and led us to a roped-off table halfway up against the far wall.

"Your companion called. He will be here soon," the man said, bowing. "Would you care to purchase a bottle of scotch?"

I nodded.

"How were the temples?" I asked Redeye, after the waiter left.

"More neon than last time. And the price of incense and prayers has gone up."

"Any of them look like they were Satan worshipers?"

"No. How was the duck?"

"I almost blinded a Voodoo who claimed to be protecting us on Kaylee's behalf. I don't believe him, though. No way Kaylee could have contacted him."

"Loas," Redeye said.

"What?"

"The spirits that possess Voodoo worshipers. She could have sent a message through a Loa."

I raised an eyebrow at Redeye.

"That's what they'd tell you, I'll bet," he added.

"How do you know?"

"My great-grandfather taught religion. I inherited his library. Spent a summer reading through it."

"You could have mentioned that before I spent all day in front of the cube researching," I said.

"I'm rusty. We need current intel."

"True."

The waiter returned with a bottle of Royal Salute and two Thai girls in yellow and blue neon, side-slit miniskirts. "Ice and Nim can serve you, if that is acceptable," the waiter said, bowing again.

"No, thanks," I replied.

"Make that a yes." Gameboy stepped up from the tier below, smiling. The waiter and girls turned. Ice and Nim giggled. Gameboy was a clean-cut white boy, body sculpted to an eternal nineteen years of age. He was skinny and pale, had red hair, and wore a cape. I wasn't sure if the girls were giggling at him or the cape.

"We like," Nim or Ice said, pointing, clearing it up.

The waiter turned to me and Redeye and said, "If you would prefer other girls...."

"That's all right," I said, sliding around in the booth. A girl slid in next to Redeye, followed by Gameboy, and then the other girl. "You know we can't talk biz like this," I said.

"Let's have a drink," Gameboy replied, smiling at the women on either side of him. "Then we'll talk."

The girls poured and served, effectuating maximum body contact with Redeye and Gameboy in the process.

"Nice cape," I said. "Too bad you can't wear it outside. You'd be sweat-drenched faster than a lightning round of Dark Moon."

"Au contraire," Gameboy countered. "It's a personal environmental-control unit. I'm the only person in Singapore who can go outside without sweating." He took a sip of scotch. "And it has other uses."

It was a minor score that Gameboy hadn't countered my Dark Moon comment. The game must still be semi-chic this month. I swallowed half a glass of scotch, and watched the girl next to Redeye pull his lower lip down with a finger-tip and look at his fangs.

"Those real?" the girl asked.

"Yes," Redeye growled.

"Oooohh!" the girl squirmed.

"What other uses?" I asked Gameboy, tilting my glass at his cape.

He smiled and took another drink of scotch, declining to answer.

"Fine," I said. "I can at least ask if you've got it."

"The board? Yes," he replied. "In fact," with a flourish, "here it is." He produced a bubble-wrapped chipboard from his cape. It looked like what I remembered of the god box board before I'd melted it. Now we just needed to add the code.

"Thanks." I passed him a cred-chip. It disappeared in the folds of his garment.

At least one thing was going as planned. I took another drink of scotch and let the forty-year-old liquor's warm glow spread.

Ice and Nim were cute. A pack of girls in alligator-skin hot pants and holo-gram-projected mist bras walked by. They were cute too. But I was a one-girl-at-a-time man. I thought of Kaylee, her passion, the warmth of her cottage, her thoughts of protecting us with a gris-gris bag and candle. I wished she were here.

I stowed the chipboard, finished my scotch, and watched the pulsing gyra-tions on the dance floor, vertical instantiations of horizontal desire.

Ice, the one with the long hair, and Nim, with the heart-shaped face, were pouring another round when I saw them walk in. Six, in formation. They opened up with laser pistols, which was bad, because no agency on Earth uses laser pistols except Singapore Drug Enforcement. Lasers are too dangerous, and too expensive. SDE doesn't care.

Gameboy was up, over the table, out of the booth, and twirling. His cape spun around him like a turret, the outer layer of dark material blasting away in tatters as the lasers struck it. Underneath the dark cloth was mirrorsheet. The lasers hit and reflected, shooting red beams out wildly, as if Gameboy himself were emitting the rays. It added to the pulsing neon and strobe lights of the disco. The scene slowed down for me as adrenaline pumped and a heightened sense of awareness kicked in. Gameboy's red beams seemed to be synchronized with the music's heavy beat, pounding like a pulse, the laser light electric blood shooting from ruptured, metal veins.

I turned and yelled at Redeye. "He's a drug dealer!"

Redeye was up and out, the table ripped from its mounting. But I knew we were under-armed. I had my Dolna Apache, a double shotgun derringer mounted on brass knuckles, with a knife blade underneath, and my Sikes-Fairbairn. Redeye would have a pocket greaser or two, a holdout, and several palm-bombs. They were punk weapons, so we could pose as thugs and buy our way out of a situation if we needed to. No chance of that now, seen by SDE with their mark.

Gunshots added to the laser fire, and the club crowd screamed, jumped, dove, and ran in pandemonium. The teener girls' belt holo projectors were knocked out of kilter, and their mist bra images blinked out. They ran topless, shrieking, to-ward the exits. Businessmen hid under tables or similarly headed for the doors.

Two groups weren't running. Four pros drew down on the SDE—Gameboy's guards. They attracted fire as Gameboy headed out the back. Of more concern, though, were two women and a man heading toward us with a purpose. I put a hand on Redeye's arm and we stayed, hands up, wide.

Gameboy and half his guards made it out of the back door, likely into the arms of another SDE squad. Bad news for him.

The two gen-bulked women and the smaller man walking toward us stopped, turned, and waited for SDE. They didn't wait long.

"Hands above heads!" an SDE man shouted, stepping over one of Gameboy's fallen guards.

No one moved.

"We shoot!" he yelled, waving his laser pistol.

"No. You will not," the man in front of me said. His accent was thick Russian.

"Han, I have it," said another SDE agent with more stripes on his uniform jacket, stepping forward.

"Raise your hands, or we will kill you all." The new drug agent waved his gun. When no one moved, he repeated his warning in Mandarin.

The Russian spoke. "You will call your boss, Mr. Chang, and tell him Egon is here. If you do not, you will spend the rest of your life in a pain amplifier. I do not lie."

The SDE agents raised their pistols, except for the leader, who hesitated. "Watch them," he finally said, pointing. He pulled out an Infex and made a call.

Fast talking in Mandarin. His head nodded. A bow.

"You leave now. Go! That way," the agent said to us, pointing at the back door.

We went.

Outside the street was empty. Blood on one wall was likely from Gameboy or one of his men. Maybe from SDE. If so, worse for him. Drug dealing was simple death. Injuring an official meant slow torture.

"Who are you?" I asked the Russian once we were all outside.

"A friend," he replied.

"I don't have any, except him," I said, pointing a thumb at Redeye. "Just tolerable acquaintances."

"So sorry. Come." He motioned, and the two women with him formed a wall in front of us. They led the way out of the alley.

"I am Egon Futanovski," the Russian said when we were standing under a streetlight two buildings down from the Top Ten. "Dr. John is in my ministry. He tells me you are on a holy mission. Da?"

"In your ministry?" I asked.

"Yes. I am Russian Voodoo czar. Current houn'gan of Volgograd."

I looked at Redeye. He shrugged.

"We must go," Egon said. He touched his wrist, and an armor-plated limo pulled around the corner.

It was my turn to shrug at Redeye's glance. True, if he hadn't shown up we'd be calling lawyers and arranging bribe money through a dozen fixers right now, or worse. But it all could have been staged. I could tell Redeye was considering the same possibility. Still, we went.

"Houn'gan of Volgograd?" Redeye asked, when the limo had pulled away.

"Da," Egon said.

"We're not very close to Volgograd, unless my geography is off," Redeye said.

"I am missionary."

"You're a Russian Voodoo missionary in Singapore from Volgograd?" I asked, surveying the limo's interior. Tucked black leather, DCU ports, a wet bar, no obvious guns.

"Da. At turn of century we find Voodoo on computer web. We exchange Russian art for Voodoo training. I am first Russian born Papa-loa," Egon said.

"Wonderful. You got any scotch?" I asked.

"No. But there is rum."

"Loas like rum," Redeye said.

Looking through the bottles in the bar, I said, "Yes, I see."

"So what now, Egon?" Redeye asked.

"You must go. Singtown bad for followers of Legba."

"Apparently not for you." I popped a bottle of rum and smelled. Terrible.

"Is true. I have influence," Egon said. "Can get you away from here. You have what you need? Board from one called Gameboy?"

"Yes," I said. Both Redeye and I tensed at Egon's question and earnest expression. It might have been his limo and Russian bulk-babes. They could try to take the board, but a Dolna Apache was made for close-quarters fighting. Two shotgun blasts and knife-bladed brass knuckles would sure kick-start Redeye's hand-to-hand reign of terror.

My hand slipped to the Dolna.

"Good!" Egon smiled. "Legba watches over you."

"Yeah, we got what we came for," I said, my hand still on the weapon. "We're ready to head back and move some code. Can you get us a direct shuttle?"

"Unfortunately, no." Egon shook his head. "But I have private charter, direct, out of country. You take that," he said.

"Where?" Redeye asked.

"Haiti."

I let go of the Dolna. I'd better save it for there.

We drove through narrow, pedestrian-choked streets. Singaporeans sat at tables under streetlights, drinking expensive beer. Nightlife picks up after the sun goes down and the temperature drops a few, thankful degrees. The limo drove slowly, dodging people. We watched multinational faces glide past through tinted, bullet-proof glass.

"We have a companion," Redeye said.

"The Aramaean. Da," Egon said. "You are fortunate. She will go with you."

"What's fortunate about Manda?" I asked.

Egon turned and made a sign in the air with his hands. "Although she does not honor the Loa, she is blessed," he said. "She has true sight."

"What?"

"You will see," he said. "You will see."

***

Haiti was cooler than Singapore, at least temperature-wise. The Infex on Egon's shuttle said Haiti was the poorest country in the western hemisphere, with over fifty percent of the population practicing Voodoo. Walking around in that environment with a gold-plated chipboard that allowed possibly divine communication was plenty of heat.

Manda did not seem to appreciate the side trip.

"Pagans!" she said. She was flexcuffed in the back of our cab, heading toward a hotel Egon had arranged for us.

"You like that word, don't you?" I said.

She glared at me. "They blaspheme the Trinity. Loas! It's demonic possession."

I'd looked up Legba out of curiosity. "Isn't Legba Jesus?" I asked. "And Erzulie the Virgin Mary? They have different names, but it seems like the same thing to me."

"Ahhh!" She squirmed. Redeye looked on with mild interest, preoccupied with the view out the window. We passed a row of gaudily painted huts, orange, blue, and white, the boards and window frames slathered with alternating colors. A clump of quick-grow palm trees rose up behind a tall fence, there to keep the locals from using the trees for firewood and housing.

"Ancestor worship, animal sacrifices—it's barbaric!" Manda said.

"And breaking in a door to wipe us out with explosive rounds and a machine gun is civilized. I see," I replied.

"You don't know what you'll do," she said.

"Actually, I do. First, I'll shut you up, if you don't do it yourself."

She scowled, shaking her head.

I turned to Redeye. "How soon until we can get out of here?" I asked.

"Whenever we want. I figured you'd want to see a ritual, though, since we're here," he said.

"What?"

"A Voodoo ritual. You can talk about it with your woman." His look seemed intentionally nondescript.

"How did you arrange that?" I asked.

"It's Egon's hotel."

"What about her?"

"Maybe you were right; we should have left her." Redeye glanced at Manda. "You know, Amalgamated Security runs law enforcement for the hotel she shot up," he said. "They also have a joint-venture contract with the Haitian police and military. We could turn her over to them. They'd probably match her with security-cam footage. Might even give us a reward."

"At least Amalgamated has some of the nicer prisons," I said.

"Your stupid threats don't scare me!" Manda said. "Go ahead, turn me in. I'm sure someone at Amalgamated would love to know the whereabouts of you two."

"Okay, look," I sighed. "We aren't kidnapers. And we wouldn't turn our worst enemy in to Amalgamated."

"Well, maybe our worst...." Redeye said.

"True," I answered. "Anyway, we can't have you coming after us or informing on us, so unfortunately we've got to end this right now." I cocked my .57-

caliber. The driver took one look in the back seat and, obviously familiar with this situation, turned up the radio and clutched the steering wheel.

"Sorry about your father," I said.

"I told you, it wasn't because of my father," Manda yelled over the radio.

"Then why?" Redeye growled.

The gun hadn't unnerved her, but Redeye's growl caused Manda to start.

"Because I have seen... that you will bring an end to my religion," she said, still yelling.

I uncocked my pistol. "What?"

"I have seen it."

"Hey, turn that down." The blaring merengue music faded. The driver kept his eyes forward. "Let me assure you," I said, "We have no such plans. In fact, it would be hard for us to care much less about your religion."

"That doesn't matter," she replied.

"Do we look holy to you?"

"No."

"Are you worried about us stealing some religious artifact or something like that? That's not our biz."

"I don't know how or why you will bring it about," Manda said. "But I have foreseen it, so it will happen."

"Do your visions ever change?" Redeye asked.

Manda hesitated. "Sometimes."

"Then try looking again. I promise you our intent is not to end the Aramaean Baptist faith."

"We've got bigger problems," I said. "Like protecting our investments." Jack had reported in on the shuttle. At least no more attacks so far. Hopefully they weren't gathering their strength. Whoever "they" were.

"All right, I will look again," Manda said. "And until that time I promise I will make no attempt to escape, or to harm either of you." She nodded a cross with her head.

"Fine," I said, looking at Redeye. "But the flexcuffs stay on."

* * *

The Paradue Hotel was a converted mansion in Port-au-Prince. Old-style wooden lattice work was the prominent architectural feature. That, and razor-wire-topped stone fences with satellite-monitored cameras. After our normal security checks we made our way to the poolside bar, where the concierge told us Egon's guide would meet us later. To avoid drawing attention, Redeye had convinced me to cut off Manda's flexcuffs before going.

As we rounded the pool we saw a man at the bar, skinny, weathered, with a white panama hat and a goatee. He watched us for a moment, turned and finished his drink, then swiveled on his barstool.

"Good afternoon," he said.

Redeye nodded.

"What brings you to Haiti on such a wonderful, sunny afternoon?" he asked.

"Maybe we're locals," I said.

He coughed into his hand. "Eh, no."

Robert B. Schofield 91

"We're tourists," Redeye replied.

"What flavor of tourism? History, nightlife, music?"

No one answered.

"I'm Ozzy Zimmerman," he said. "Call me Z." He stuck out a hand.

Redeye looked at the proffered palm. I stared into Z's eyes. He didn't blink, or squint, or look away. His eyes looked calm.

"Religion," Redeye finally said, returning the handshake.

"Voodoo! The right place," Z said.

"Not just Voodoo," Manda spoke up.

"I see."

"What are you doing here?" I asked.

"AP Datastream. Your one-stop Infex source," he said. "I'm covering the elections."

"What elections?"

"My, you are tourists!" Z said. "Who don't check out their destinations very well."

"Why are you so curious?" I asked.

"I'm a reporter."

The bartender, a young, heavy-set black man with a short Afro and dolphin-print-covered shirt, walked up behind the bar. "May I bring you something?" he asked in slow, deliberate English.

"Another hummingbird," Z said.

"Just water for us." The bartender smiled and strolled away.

"Religion is part of man's quest for the meaning of life," Z said. "The Voodoos have a unique angle on it. Is that why you're here?"

"Let's not worry about why we're here," I said. "If you want to talk, you can tell us about this election."

"Certainly. It's the first ever corporate-run full government election. And maybe the first fair one Haiti's ever had. Acuvote Inc. is administering it, with Philip Birnbaum and Smith as independent verifiers." He held a hand to his mouth and whispered. "Not surprising, since PBS and Amalgamated Security are both holding companies of Scotus Ltd."

I leaned over and whispered back, "They're just pawns of the Gnomes of Zurich anyway." Throwing out a name I'd heard in my research.

Z raised an eyebrow.

"They also control the Voodoos," I added.

Z rubbed his chin. "Interesting theory. That would be a unique vector for a meme."

"A what?"

"Meme. All religious beliefs are memes," Z said.

That perked up Manda. "Religious beliefs are based on faith," she replied firmly.

"True. But they *are* memes. Technically, they're thought contagions."

Manda scowled. I imagined if she'd had a shotgun she'd have pumped a few rounds into Z for that comment. Like father, like daughter.

"A meme is a unit of culture," Z explained. "Stored in the brain and surviving or dying through natural selection, by being passed on to another brain or not." Manda's scowl grew. "It's standard information transmittal theory," Z said, noting her glare. "They teach it in social journalism."

"So what is a thought contagion?"

"A meme programmed for its own transmission. One that self-propagates by inducing things like evangelism, procreation, missionary work, or other factors that cause it to spread." Z shrugged. "Like religions."

"But these memes can't be intelligent," Manda said.

"A scholar is a library's way of making another library," Z replied. "So you're right. But it doesn't matter."

The bartender brought our drinks. "Please enjoy," he said.

"Ah! Like drinking a banana split." Z picked up his glass. "Thank you, Granville." He took a drink, and looked at me. "So if the Gnomes of Zurich are manipulating the spread of Voodoo, as you say, that would be an external transmission vector for the Voodoo meme bundle. Do you have proof?" he asked.

"If I did, you couldn't believe it anyway. It would be a manipulation."

"Possibly." That slowed him down, which was my real goal. "I'll have to think about that," he said, rubbing his chin.

Manda put her water glass down on the wooden bar with a thunk. "You said religion was part of the meaning of life. It's not part, it *is* the meaning, to serve God," she said.

"If it makes you happy to think so, then I agree," Z replied.

"Don't patronize me."

"I'm not. I mean that literally."

"What do you say the meaning of life is?" Manda asked.

"Practical or metaphysical?"

"Both."

"Well, the practical is much easier. It's that everything is seeking peace in its own way."

"Every*thing*, not every*one*?" Manda asked.

"Everything. Rocks, trees, people, plants, all are influenced by evolution and are striving toward balance and harmony. For people, religion helps some to achieve that peace."

"What is the endpoint of evolution, in your opinion?" Redeye asked.

"Good question. That gets to the metaphysical aspect." Z took another sip of his slushy, milk-chocolate-colored drink. "We are all part of the Absolute, the Everything of existence," he said. "If you want to give that a name, you can call it God. Or Satan. If you choose to give it a name, then the answer would be that to know that would be to know the mind of God."

"Or Satan," I said. Z nodded.

"So what's the answer?" Manda asked.

Z shrugged. "I would say that it is to achieve cosmic harmony."

"That's helpful," I said, crunching an ice cube. I suddenly wished I'd specified bottled water, remembering an earlier incident in Jamaica.

I glanced over and noticed that Manda was looking at Z with a skeptical, quizzical expression.

"What religion are you?" she asked Z.

"A mystic," he said. Manda stared. "It's a meta-religion," Z continued. "I can easily believe all religions are right, if they are right for a specific person. Atheism and agnosticism are also fine," he said. "If it helps achieve balance, it's serving its purpose."

"And that's for the universe to become a super cosmic love-in," I said. "Wow. Don't ask me to buy a flower."

Z answered, "I won't."

It sounded like mumbo-jumbo to me, but the god box nagged at the back of my mind. When it was plugged in, I'd had a sense of oneness, an overall feeling that everything was connected, and all was good and right. Maybe the god box programmers had been mystics. The box could have also, presumably, shown me a man on a golden throne with a flowing beard, and a lake of fire with a red, horned Satan.

"Well, it's been great talking to you," I said. "Getting your view of the universe and the meaning of life and all, but that looks like our guide, so we'll have to get going."

A brawny, blond man with a jingling necklace of bones and chicken feet was walking our way, a smile on his face.

Z glanced at him. "Johnsloe's a good guide." He lifted his glass and tipped it toward us. "Enjoy," Z said.

Johnsloe didn't talk much, but he did mention Egon, and Voodoo, and ceremony. It could have been a trap, but with all my weapons on me instead of stashed in a Singapore shuttleport locker, I thought what the hell. Redeye seemed to think the same thing.

Manda was surprisingly calm. Every time I glanced at her she had a slightly puzzled frown on her narrow face—a face which, I tried not to admit to myself, was decidedly striking in its intensity.

We followed the sounds of drums beating slowly in the distance. As we made our way through the town, night descended and the drumbeat grew. We began to catch glimpses of flickering firelight, down narrow alleys, above rooftops. We eventually found a wide street lined with people. A parade of white-clad Voodoos swayed and jerked in the torchlight, yelling, "Yayaya!" and things in a language I'd never heard. They carried a white cross, with a clown doll dressed in puffy black and white clothing riding on top of it. There were beaded shawls, with skulls and crossbones, and bright red hearts. Some of the Voodoos carried bottles of rum. One carried a chicken; another led a goat on a leash.

The procession yanked itself forward to the beat of the drums. Johnsloe motioned, and we followed him, cutting through an alley to another street, down a second alley to a courtyard. It was obvious that this was where the procession would end up. "Oum'phor," Johnsloe said, pointing to an area in the courtyard surrounded by poles. At the center of the area was a large square column on top of a thick round stone. Drawn on the ground, emanating from the stone and column, were patterns in white powder: intricate symbols, wavy lines, spirals, starbursts, a crude, stylized cow, a boat. Johnsloe pointed at the symbols and said, "Vèvè."

The drumming got louder as the parade approached. A woman wearing a bright, multicolored headband, her head held high, led the procession. "Mam'bo,"

Johnsloe said, pointing at the woman.

The mam'bo carried a jug to the center column of the oum'phor and set it on the round stone at its base. She stood, and as the drums carried on their steady thumping, began twitching and jerking violently. The mam'bo chanted louder and louder, and the drumbeats quickened. Other Voodoos joined her in the oum'phor, also chanting and convulsing. Finally, the man with the chicken approached the center post. As the Voodoos swayed and chanted, he rubbed the chicken on all four sides of the central pillar. Then, with a quick motion, he sliced off the chicken's head and held the bloody, flapping animal in the air.

The dancers screamed with renewed frenzy at the sight. The Voodoo man tossed the head aside and holding the body upside down dripped chicken blood onto the ground, tracing the white lines of the vèvè.

Manda screamed, "Heathens!" but the Voodoos didn't notice.

I felt movement beside me, and turned to see Johnsloe twitching, his eyes closed.

I nudged Redeye and we both took a step away from him. Slowly, our guide opened his eyes. They were no longer calm. They had reddened, and looked wild. A grin spread across Johnsloe's face.

"Honored guests!" he said in a voice deeper than we'd heard before. "Behold!" He spread his arms and motioned toward the oum'phor. "Voodoo came to Haiti from the west coast of Africa in the early sixteenth century, when the Spanish king, Charles V, ordered four thousand slaves a year shipped to this island. The Catholic church justified the move, saying enslaving the Africans was acceptable as long as the 'heathens' were taught Catholicism.

"The Spanish, under the rule of Christopher Columbus' brothers, Diego and Bartolomé, had slaughtered the indigenous population of Taínos natives on the island, and needed a labor force to work their sugar plantations."

I glanced at Manda, who was squinting at Johnsloe.

"The Africans, mainly from the Fon, Yoruba, and Dahomey tribes, combined their native religions under the harsh conditions of slavery. They feigned conversion to Catholicism but maintained their own religion, worshiping ancient African Gods in the guise of various Catholic saints."

Redeye and I looked at each other.

"Begone, vile demon!" Manda yelled. "I cast you out in the name of the Father, the Son, and the Holy Ghost!"

Johnsloe blinked, but continued to smile.

"What is the Sect Rogue?" I asked Johnsloe, not to pass up an opportunity.

"I assume you mean Sect Rouge," he replied. "They are the red cults that come from the Mandingue, Mondongue, and Bisango African tribes. They are cannibals."

"What does Vin' Bain-Ding mean?" I asked.

"Blood, pain, excrement," Johnsloe said.

I glanced at Manda. She was mumbling to herself, eyes closed, hands folded, head nodding. To me, her prayers sounded oddly similar to the Voodoos' chant, only quieter.

"The Lord's Prayer," Redeye said.

The Voodoo dancers in the oum'phor jerked and spasmed. The drums pounded wildly. The mam'bo writhed, gnashing her teeth. The noise could have broken glass.

"Stop!" Manda yelled.

And with that scream, it did. I saw Johnsloe shudder, and the mam'bo freeze in mid-twitch. Johnsloe staggered back a step, but continued to smile. The mam'bo turned her head slowly toward us and took a step forward. The rest of the Voodoos backed away, toward the edge of the oum'phor. Redeye and I each took a step to the side.

My .57-caliber was shoulder-slung on my right side. My Sikes-Fairbairn was hilt-down under my left armpit. A concussion grenade, a claymore mine, and three pocket rockets in my cargo pants, and a Kevlar flak vest, gave me an edge of confidence for whatever might happen next.

I crossed my arms over my chest, ready to grab a weapon.

"Yaaaaaahhhhhh!" the mam'bo yelled. She snapped her head back, then threw it forward and ran to Manda. Her eyes wide, the mam'bo yelled gibberish at a high pitch.

"There's something called a lost language——" Redeye started to say.

The mam'bo thrust out a finger toward Manda. Manda started to grab for the mam'bo's outstretched arm. Redeye, in a blur, caught Manda's wrist first and pulled it back.

The mam'bo smiled. "You just save her life." The Voodoo woman smiled at Redeye.

"A curse on you!" the mam'bo screamed at Manda. She reached into the folds of her shawl and hurled white powder at Manda's face. Before the powder had left the mam'bo's hand I had my .57-caliber drawn, waist high, ready to fire.

The mam'bo looked down at the gun after throwing her powder, and laughed. "Hahahaha! You fast!" she said. "Yesss! Fast like the snake. Papa Danbhalah in you," she said.

"Whatever," I replied, moving my left hand to cradle the magazine chamber of my gun for support.

Johnsloe seemed to shake himself. "Come," he said, motioning. His voice was no longer deep, his eyes once again calm.

Slowly we all backed away, Manda shaking her head and brushing powder from her face. Redeye had his arms loosely encircling her to prevent her from making a sudden move.

Johnsloe led us back through the alleys to the main street, and eventually back to the hotel. When we got there, Johnsloe deposited us near the poolside bar where we met him, and merely said, "Good night."

Z was still at the bar, slumped over a half-empty hummingbird.

"Back sho shoon?" he slurred. He pointed at Manda's face and asked, "Wha's that?"

"A Voodoo curse," Redeye replied.

"Don' worry," Z said. "It's all bullshit. Everything is as it is meant to be." He tipped his hat.

We all went to our rooms.

* * *

I discovered Manda in the hotel's exercise room the next morning, doing pull-ups.

"How'd you sleep?" I asked.

"No Voodoo-induced pain, insomnia, or bad dreams," she replied.

"When are you going to take your look again?" I asked. "So I can stop watching you so much."

"When we're back in the States," she replied. "If I see the same thing, I'll be forced to kill you, and I don't have the means here."

"If that turns out to be the case, you'd better practice more first," I said. "Does your church have a training camp?"

"No."

"You'd better take up a collection."

"Bless you!" she said.

"Yeah." I picked up a dumbbell.

Ten reps later I caught her as she lowered herself from her final pull-up set. Her arms, lean and muscular, glistened with sweat.

I shook my head. "You know what we've got, don't you?" I said, rubbing a towel over my face. "Why would a Satanist want it?"

She dropped from her bar and stared at me. "You kidding?" She looked at me. "To build a Satan box."

I lowered my towel.

"What?"

"Why else?"

My stare was interrupted when the alarm on my Infex sounded. I was at the door, heading out of the gym, when Redeye burst in. "Jack's got contact," he said.

"Time?" I asked, tossing my towel into the laundry bin.

"He can hold them off for a while," Redeye said. "We can make it back home."

"Home?"

"Yeah," he said.

I smiled. It had been a long time since we'd been home.

Home was in the Great Basin of northern Nevada. We called it the farm, but "the camp" would also have been a reasonably descriptive term. Still, for us it was home. We had a large ranch house, a barn, and a garden full of genetically modified, low-water plants. We had a shooting range. I had my weapons bench and my big weapon-smithing tools. Redeye had hunting grounds and a meditation plateau. It looked like a desert homestead on the surface and from satellite. What you couldn't see were the underground rocket-engine-powered generators; the garage full of motorcycles, nitrous-injected cars, and all-terrain vehicles; and the computer and chemistry labs that put most west coast research facilities to shame.

Few people had been there, but I didn't say a word when Redeye suggested we should take Manda.

We flew to Vegas and headed northwest from there, staying in constant contact with Jack. He had just been fighting off probes so far. He'd managed to capture and quarantine one, then dissect it with the precision of the original Jack the Ripper, but could find no backtracking codes. They had all been anonymized, which was tough to do. Real tough. Something big was coming.

"We might have to warm up Seeker," Redeye said.

"You mean find him," I replied.

Redeye grunted.

Seeker was an acquaintance of ours, of sorts. He was a SIBLing, a Simulation of Biological Life, the closest AI research had ever come to succeeding. All SIBLings were registered and working for GIS—Global Information Security—except Seeker. Seeker had been an early experiment. It's figuratively correct to say that Seeker had escaped from the lab, a Frankenstein on the loose.

In an earlier job we'd found Seeker; we could have wiped him, but we didn't. Now he trusts us, to an extent. As an AI, Seeker finds the world of human beings incomprehensible, and thinks of humans as somewhat like gods. He'd helped us before, and maybe would now.

"How does CPU utilization look?" I asked Jack over the Infex.

"Twenty percent," he replied.

It sounded low, but if this was just the probes, that was bad. Twenty percent of our CPU power could calculate pi to a hundred billion decimal places in a second.

"Memory?" I asked.

"Full up."

That was OK.

"I/O?"

"Zero."

Good.

"Jack, send out a broadcast for Phage-Rider II, low priority. Include subnets," I said.

"Done," Jack replied.

Seeker would recognize that.

"You'll get a response," I said. "With an encrypted codeword. Don't transmit it, just store."

"Done," Jack said.

"We'll be home in fifteen minutes."

I looked at Redeye and he nodded. Fifteen minutes was an eon in computer time.

Ten minutes later we topped a ridge and I saw the plume of smoke. At first I wasn't sure. It could have been an air crash, or a convoy explosion. But soon it was obvious: it was the farm. The greasy column of roiling black smoke rose up like a lopsided pillar. Orange flames licked the base. It had just happened. A smart bomb, or a det-charge mistimed, targeted for us.

"Jack!"

"Yes?" came the calm reply.

And I remembered that Jack was located in an underwater nitrogen-filled tube off a coral reef in the Pacific.

"Do a hardware check. All connections," I said.

"Channel link Alpha-1 experiencing multiple retries," he said. "Contact to Data Store-1, negative."

An explosion near the barn sent flames and sand shooting into the air.

"Check again."

"Alpha-2 now negative," he said.

"Stand by."

Redeye punched it. We covered the distance through our narrow, electronic mine-free path of approach in half the time, and slid into what once had been our driveway with a roar and a slew of gravel.

I didn't have to say anything to Manda. She was out and rolling into a combat crouch as soon as the car stopped. So was Redeye.

Manda yelled, "That wasn't smart! There could be more charges."

I thumbed my Infex. "Jack, do you have Alpha-3?"

"Yes."

That link was underground. I pointed at Redeye. He nodded and grabbed Manda, turned her away. I ran to the barn and stomped the ground three boards over from the main door. A section of earth rose and slid away. I ran to it and raced down the steps.

At the bottom, a hall led to the data lab. I sprinted and looked in. The halon was dumping. I grabbed a filter from the wall, kicked the door in, covered my face, went in and looked around. No interior fires, no obvious shock damage. The external alarms must have triggered the halon. I went to the back of the lab, hoping to find what I saw: The Scotus-IX, its gunmetal-gray CPU tube resting securely on a square of raised-floor, in its environmentally controlled polyglass enclosure looking as calm as ever.

I walked to the cable-attached console. "Jack." I typed into the console.

"Yes." came the reply on the screen.

"What codeword did you get?"

"Authentication sequence 001." flashed up on the console.

Good, Jack. "Alpha Omega Prime. Prime One. 001." I typed.

"Authenticate Alpha Beta Prime. Prime One. Omega 002."

"I authenticate Prime 001. Omega 002. Zulu 003." I typed back.

"Accepted. Codeword is Bahometh."

I stared at the screen. I typed again, "Prime 001. Omega 002. Zulu 003."

"Bahometh" appeared on the screen again.

The devil Bahometh was Seeker's codeword? What did that mean?

It could mean—shit. I typed, "Systems integrity check. Priority One." Enter.

"Initiated."

I held my breath for the twenty seconds it took Jack to come back with, "Integrity . . . . . validated."

At least they weren't inside the system, yet.

After the halon dumped the air would recycle. I went outside to wait for that.

I climbed the steps. Redeye and Manda had moved away from the burning house. They were looking at something on the ground. I slowly walked over, searching the area for movement or anything unfamiliar, knowing Redeye had done so as well.

As I approached I saw that Redeye and Manda were standing next to a shallow circle that had been cut out of the ground. It was a meter deep, and maybe ten in diameter. The dirt that had been removed was piled around the edge, forming a wide lip. As I got closer, the stench that rose from the pit overpowered the smell of smoke from the house.

I walked up to the edge of the pit between Redeye and Manda and stared. The scene inside the hole was ghoulish.

It was immediately obvious from the ash and charred wood scattered around the inside edge in small piles that there had once been a dozen campfires just inside the pit. What was not immediately obvious was what the campfires had been used for, until you looked toward the center of the hole. It took a moment for the mind to comprehend, but then it became nauseatingly clear. There, spread out in piles, were an array of black, gore-encrusted human remains: an arm from the shoulder to the wrist; a foot; half of a face on a smashed skull, the mouth twisted into what might have once been a scream; an ear; a tangled mass of sinew and skin; a multitude of bones and entrails. There was a pile for each campfire. In the bottom of the pit, dried blood stained the sandy dirt in a pentagram.

I looked over and saw that Manda was praying.

"Shit," I said to Redeye. "How long ago?"

"A day. Maybe two," he replied.

"They had a guess at our timing." I nodded toward the smoking house. "Egon's people? They booked the flight."

"I don't know," Redeye replied. "How's downstairs?"

"Secure. But the halon's dumping."

"We'd better warm up the inducer."

"Yeah," I said. "The hard link is in place. Jack found Seeker. But there's something strange."

"What?"

"The codeword. It's Bahometh."

Manda turned. "What?"

"Yeah, the devil."

"A specific devil," she said.

"Talk theology with Redeye. I've got work to do."

I got the Grid inducer from our luggage and headed downstairs to the lab. The halon was clear and fresh air was rushing in. There was enough to breathe. I unpacked the inducer next to the Scotus-IX, setting the inducer's thin, black interface plate next to the hardwired console. I booted it up. It would take a while. You could never be sure exactly how long.

During the flight back I'd done a mental inventory of the contents of our data lab. I knew we had everything we needed to recreate the god box, except the custom chipboard, which I now unpacked. I pulled an interface cable from a spool on the wall and snaked it from the Scotus back to an empty breadboard cabinet. Here's where we would find out if Gameboy had actually been able to recreate the board from the holos. Now, so close to testing it, and after what we'd been through to get it, it didn't seem likely. I had a vivid picture in my mind of applying the power and watching the chipboard explode in a shower of sparks. Then something big would hit Jack and we'd have the same choice all over again: save Jack, or the god box code. It wasn't a stretch to realize we could lose both. Maybe Seeker was already gone, to Bahometh. Our home certainly was.

Suddenly, I wanted to hear Kaylee's voice. I wanted to see her, to hold her, to talk to her with my arms around her in her little Louisiana cabin, where everything was isolated and calm, steadied by the great Mississippi river's commanding flow.

That would have to wait.

The chipboard fit in the frame snugly. Gameboy had labeled the only two non-standard connections, Hi-Mem, and Core. The others fit the breadboard perfectly. I started to run jumpers to the two non-standard slots.

"Status?" Redeye asked, bursting into the lab.

"Inducer's warming. I'm wiring the board. Where's Manda?"

"Cleansing the pit," Redeye said.

"Prayers?"

"Napalm."

"You gave her napalm?"

"Yeah," he replied.

"Great. Come here and check this, will ya?"

Redeye jogged over and looked at my wiring. "Secondary power access," he pointed.

"Jesus. Thanks." I added another jumper. "Look good?"

"Yeah," he said.

"You give it power."

Redeye squinted at me.

"Bad premonition," I said.

"You getting superstitious?"

"Just juice it," I said.

Redeye did. No sparks. He checked the readings. "Normal," he said. "No time for a burn-in, though."

"Maybe Gameboy did it."

"In two days?"

"I know," I said. "We'll have to risk it."

"Let's load it up," Redeye said.

I jogged along the interface cable back to the Scotus-IX, and the console. "Jack, I've got a hardwired connection," I entered. "Dump the code to this location, avalanche injection." I redirected Jack's data input to the new god box.

After a moment, "Unable . . . to . . . comply." appeared on the console screen.

Damn! I checked CPU. It was at seventy-two percent. "They're on him!" I yelled to Redeye. I looked over. The inducer wasn't quite ready. Redeye came racing around a data storage unit. "I know you trust her," I said. "But go check on Manda, will you? I've got this."

He nodded and disappeared.

I was hyped, and I knew it. Too hyped for an inducer run. I'd never slow-breathe down to the right state.

It was an old method that I hadn't used in years, but if you couldn't meditate into the state, you could create it, with Hydro. Diepiandrohydrosterone-III. I knew where there was a vial hidden—correction, stored—in the lab. I got it from behind the rack of fiber optic cables. I popped the top and downed the bitter liquid.

The inducer was ready when I got back. So was I. I slipped on the goggles and pressed the data pads to my temples.

One. Two. Three.

Gridspace coalesced. I saw Jack, a human-sized, silver robot. I remembered him in the god box, giant and bright chrome.

"I don't see anything, Jack," I said. Jack looked at me and nodded. We seemed to be in a black void. Jack pointed in a direction that was, from our relative perspective, down. I looked. Far below was a smoldering pool of fire.

"What are you using all that CPU for?" I asked.

"I'm holding it out." A flat area of space in front of me briefly sparkled. Jack had created a barrier. "Force-field v6.2," Jack said. "It's barely holding."

Force-field was a completely defensive move, a last resort. This was not good.

"Where's the code?"

"I can't get to it," Jack said.

"What's out there?"

A picture appeared, rotating, a hologram within a dream. It was a creature, with a goat's head and legs, but with green, reptile scales on its stomach, and blue, female breasts. On one arm was written "Salve" and on the other arm, "Coagula". Between the creature's legs were two intertwined serpents. Flames flickered between the horns on its head, but the flames were somehow dark, flickering black instead of red. The beast wore a medallion that at first glance looked like a pentagram. But when I looked again, I saw that it was the Star of David.

"Bahometh," Jack said.

That couldn't be Seeker. Or could it?

"How did it attack?" I asked.

"Micro-code level disassembler," Jack replied.

Seeker *could* do that. Had Seeker become Bahometh somehow? That didn't make sense. Seeker was a conglomeration of code, comparable in complexity to the human brain. How could that *become* something else? Unless this was just Seeker's new, chosen persona. I guess some people decide to become cannibals.

"Is this a new contact?" I asked Jack. "Is it from the same source as the probes, or did it only show up after the Phage-Rider II broadcast?"

"I . . . can't tell," Jack said. "The probes were anonymized."

Jack was struggling to hold the force field. I checked CPU. Eighty-eight percent. I could bring one of the backup tubes online, but then the god box code would be accessible.

"Give me an external view," I said.

My view shifted and I saw Bahometh standing in a ring of fire, black fire. He was everywhere, huge, a taunting grin spread across his goat face. Or maybe it was a "her", with those blue breasts.

Bahometh raised a fist. I saw "Salve" in its arm as it brought a fist down and pounded on Jack's small, fragile-looking shell. I saw our CPU spike to one hundred percent utilization. A more powerful blow and Bahometh would be through, and Jack would be at the beast's mercy.

What could I do? Commit the backup tubes, which would bring the god box code online? That was exactly what they wanted. I could command Jack to dump the code to our newly installed god box board at high priority, but that would redirect his processing power from maintaining Force-field v6.2, likely allowing

Bahometh to smash through.

Jack, or the god box code? Down to that choice.

"Jack—" I started to say.

Bahometh brought its other fist down with a crash. Jack's force field wavered. Again CPU spiked to one hundred percent. This time it stayed. A red residue remained where Bahometh's fist had impacted. The residue began to spread. It was eating away at the force field. I had to make a decision.

Jack was just a mass of code, so large and complex that no backup existed. I knew he was just code, even though sometimes he seemed like more. I *could* honestly say he was damned expensive code. Jack was a known asset with a known value.

The god box code could be nothing but clever virtual-reality programming. No, I knew that wasn't true. Cannibalistic Satanists had destroyed our house trying to get it, or as a warning. What if they did get it, and built a Satan box?

Dumping the code meant sacrificing Jack. It pained me, but I knew that's what I had to do. I had to tell Jack to redirect, a multi-million-credit decision.

"Jack," I said.

"Ye...." Static.

Suddenly, a light appeared. It started out as a pinpoint above Bahometh's shoulder but grew quickly behind the creature until it became a blazing nuclear fireball.

The taunting grin on Bahometh's face vanished as the beast turned. The white-hot light enveloped him, enveloped everything.

"Out!" I commanded.

I heard Jack scream. It was the sound of a man being flayed alive.

"Out!" I said again.

The light was everywhere. I saw Jack, screaming. I saw Bahometh. I saw Seeker. ...Seeker! I saw Mujibar. Mujibar? The Voodoo priest from the monastery where we'd gotten the god box? That couldn't be; he was dead.

Seeker filled my vision. I knew it was Seeker, although his face was huge and zebra-striped, the black and white areas streaking back into lines that trailed off, fading into the distance. Seeker's lips moved and I heard the word, "Go."

I went. Hard. I rolled the dice and unplugged. One time in ten thousand, doing that fries nerve synapses. But the odds were with me and I made it.

As soon as I was out I checked the console.

"Jack." I typed.

Moments went by, an eon in computer time.

"Jack."

Finally, "Yes."

"Status?"

"Green." appeared on the console screen.

"Can you dump the code?"

"Yes." Jack replied.

"Initiate."

I saw the transfer bar appear. The code was loading into the god box.

"What happened?" I typed.

"Bahometh was . . . burning me. Something made it stop. I don't know." Jack replied.

The transfer bar filled quickly. In less than a minute the god box code would be back in custom hardware.

I heard footsteps and looked up to see Redeye walking through the data lab. "Well?" he asked.

"Seeker showed up," I said. "Saved Jack. Saved us. Jack's dumping the code now."

"How long?"

"Thirty seconds."

It was a long thirty seconds.

Finally—"Done," I said.

"Ready to erase the online version?" Redeye asked.

I looked at him. He looked at me. We both realized it then. We had to verify what was in the new god box before we erased the online code.

"Verification," Redeye said.

Untested hardware, code that had been through hell: who would plug their brain into that?

"Want to ask Manda?" I suggested.

Redeye scowled. "We'd be no better than those grisly bastards—" he started, pointing upstairs.

"Ask her," I repeated. "Can't she use her 'true sight' to see what will happen anyway?"

Redeye paused. "I don't know. But that's at least worth a question."

"I don't believe that crap," I said. "But if we explain what this is, she might convince herself to want to try it."

"Try what?" Manda said, stepping around from behind a channel-link router.

"Great," I said, glaring at Redeye.

"If we were going to ask her, we'd have to bring her down here anyway," Redeye said.

"Fine. Okay, Manda, I know you know, or think you know, what we've got—this god box thing," I said.

"My father told me about it," she replied. "But he went to the monastery as a crusader. He didn't believe in the god box. I don't either. I believe you've got a clever little artificial reality game," she said. "It can't be real. I don't doubt that some people could be fooled into thinking it is, and go to insane lengths to possess it. But then, people go to great lengths to possess super-compressed coal that's turned shiny, among other things."

"You don't believe it's real?" Redeye asked.

"No."

"Have you *looked*?"

"I am humble, but not modest. True sight is a gift. I do not use it lightly, and certainly not for that," she said.

"It's not a game. I've tried it," I said.

"And look where it got you," Manda replied. "No closer to God."

I shrugged. "Maybe religion's just not in me."

"The device creates a brain state equivalent to that of the most holy and religious people sampled," Redeye said. "It is a switch to enlightenment."

"If that's not worth a look," I asked, "what is?"

Manda scrunched up her face, almost as if she were in pain. She was thinking hard. I might not agree with her strict worldview, but she did seem to have good sense.

"I don't have to look," she finally said. "I'd be able to tell if it's the real thing."

"That's what we were going to ask you," I said. "If you wanted to try it."

"Why would I? You said you already have."

"It's new hardware," Redeye said.

"Oh! You want a guinea pig."

"We thought you might be able to use your sight to see if it's wired up right," Redeye said.

"I told you, it's not a toy. I won't help you predict the stock market either, in case you're wondering," she said.

"You don't want a chance to talk directly to God?" I asked.

The twisted face again. "Let me sleep on it."

"Sorry, we've got to test it now. If you don't want to do it, I'll have Jack triple-check the dump and configuration, and I'll do it myself. You'll never get another chance," I said.

After a short pause, she said, "Have Jack triple-check the dump and configuration, and I'll try it."

I nodded. "Redeye, we should have a cap at the optics bench. You find that, and I'll get Jack started."

Jack did a quadruple verification. Everything looked good. I had him all set to purge the online version of the code so we could bring the backup CPUs online without exposure if he got attacked again. All we needed was Manda's verification.

Redeye handed Manda the cap. It was similar to the stretch-mesh liner that had been sewn into Mujibar's robe. "Before we turn this on," Redeye said, "are you sure you don't want to convince yourself everything will be OK with one of your looks?"

"Everything is as it is meant to be," Manda said.

Where had I heard that before?

Manda slipped the cap over her head and Redeye hit the switch.

When the god box went live the change on Manda's face was incredible, from mild disgust to unbelievable awe in an instant. I remembered what it had felt like— I could remember it rationally, but could not recall the exact feeling. I had been connected to everything, and everything had been right. That was the look Manda had on her face: blank stare mixed with exhilaration, peace, and joy. All was connected. The universe was just... right.

Manda looked around slowly, seeming not to see anything, but to see everything. Her gaze swept across Redeye, me, the computer lab. She began walking toward the stairs. We followed. I pointed at the cap cable, the few feet of slack remaining. Manda stopped, turned, looked at the cable, smiled, and turned back toward the stairs. Her gaze traveled up and out, following the ground from below. She was mentally walking toward the pit. Her head stopped.

I inched my way forward, next to Manda, past her. I looked back at her narrow, serene face. Tears were trickling down her cheeks. A smile was on her lips.

I eased back and turned to Redeye, mouthing, "Well?"

Redeye shrugged.

Quietly I said, "Looks verified. I'm going to tell Jack to purge the online code."

Redeye nodded.

I strode back to the console. "Purge." I typed in.

"Done." Jack replied on the screen.

I sat down in the chair next to the console, wiped my forehead with my sleeve, and breathed a sigh of relief. Everything was safe now.

I could tell the Hydro was still working its mellow magic. I felt calm, despite the recent attack. I wondered about that, about Mujibar. Had that just been an effect of the Hydro? It had been a long time since I'd used it. How could Mujibar be in the Grid? I had definitely seen him, or thought I had, along with a distinctly separate Seeker, which was good. Seeker was not Bahometh. But then who was? Or who was behind him? And why had Seeker used that as a codeword?

I glanced over toward Manda. I could just see her between two rows of hardware cabinets, communing with God.

I turned and stared at the Scotus-IX and the console. Who had destroyed the farm, our home? Now that the god box code was safe, I could put Jack on the task. I hit audio. "Jack, analyze and cross-link known references to: Sect Rouge, Grey Pigs, Vin' Bain-Ding, Order of Golden Light, Voodoo, Thule Society, Knights Templar, Bahometh, Mandingue, Mondongue, Bisango, Paradise Engineering, the Gnomes of Zurich, Aramaean Baptist, and Mysticism. Add in any other organizations or terms that correlate with an eighty-plus-percent probability of association. Background priority."

"Time limit?" Jack asked.

"Twenty-four hours," I replied.

"Acknowledged."

I smiled. If there were anything to be found, Jack would find it.

Redeye walked up. "How long should we let her do that?" he asked.

"As long as she wants?" I replied.

"She might never leave."

"Yeah... I went into the Grid from inside the god box," I said. "And then I knew I had to leave."

"Why?"

"A feeling. Dunbar," I said.

"Yeah."

"But you're right. Religion is her life. We're going to have to pull the plug."

Redeye nodded.

We walked over. Manda was on her knees, smiling and weeping tears of joy. Redeye stepped in front of her, crossed his arms and looked down. Manda smiled up at him.

I had a remote switch. When Redeye nodded, I flipped it. The instant I did, Manda's face went blank, and she fell face forward onto the computer lab floor.

"Manda!" Redeye shouted. Nothing. Redeye knelt down and shook her. She stirred.

I pulled the cap off her head. Damn! Had I purged the online code too soon? Had Gameboy screwed up the chipboard?

"Beautiful," Manda said. She pushed herself up.

"Well?" I asked.

"It works. It's real."

That was all we could get her to say.

We spent the rest of the day cleaning up the farm. Manda carried things, did tasks as we instructed, but she wouldn't talk. She wore a serene, quizzical expression, and every so often she would simply stop and stare for a few moments, looking at nothing in particular.

We found more pentagrams in the house, drawn in blood on the walls of our basement rec room. When Manda saw them she calmly got a napalm canister, hosed down the rec-room walls with it and burned the place clean, a tranquil look on her face the entire time. I was glad we had flame-proof foamcrete walls.

We slept that night in the computer lab, warmed by CPU fans blowing across semiconductor thermal-control modules, the hum of massive processing power lulling us to sleep.

In the morning I awoke to see Manda staring at me sadly.

"What?" I asked, rubbing sleep out of my eyes.

"Kaylee," she said.

"What?" I said, instantly awake.

"They have her."

"Who?"

Manda smiled, sorrowfully.

"Where is she?!" I demanded.

Manda cocked her head and frowned.

I grabbed Manda's shoulders. "Where's Kaylee, and who has her?"

"The Vieux Carré. Bad people," she replied.

"The French Quarter?"

Manda nodded.

"How do you know?" Is it your group, the Baptist militants? Are they running this game?"

"No. I looked," Manda said.

"If I find out it's your people, you're dead."

"You love her, don't you?"

I pointed a finger at Manda, finally broke eye contact and rushed to the computer console. The Vieux Carré was the Old Square, the original part of New Orleans.

"Jack," I said, "analysis status. Give me what you've got."

A shape appeared on the display. At first I couldn't tell what it was. I looked closely. It was an inverted triangle inside another triangle, surrounded by interwoven lines. The lines began to unfold, expanding on the display, growing like a flower opening. Words and symbols surrounded the edge of the diagram, expanding out with the enlarging pattern. When it stopped I found myself looking at a slowly spinning mandala. The words around the edge were the words and phrases I'd asked Jack to analyze: Voodoo, Sect Rouge, Order of Golden Light, and all the others.

"Recursive?" I asked.

"Yes," Jack replied. "At least to six ply."

They were working for and controlling one another, probably without even knowing it.

"Any recent change in communication patterns within or between any of the organizations?" I asked.

"Time frame?" Jack queried.

"Last twelve hours."

There was a pause. "Large solution set," Jack said. "Any narrowing parameters?"

"New Orleans, Louisiana. The French Quarter."

Another pause. "Recent references to 'the goat without horns', Sect Rouge. A Grid entry point on North Rampart Street near old Congo Square," Jack said.

"What is the goat without horns?"

"Most probable meaning," Jack said, "is a reference to human sacrifice."

"Print a map. Redeye!" I yelled over my shoulder.

"Yeah?" He said groggily.

"Time to go. We need to pack the god box."

"Why?"

"Kaylee."

I turned and he was already standing, scowling at me. "Slater—"

"What is there here? Our burned-out farm. The scum that did it is in New Orleans, with Kaylee."

"You sure?"

"Ask her." Manda was smiling sadly. "There's a breadboard hardware case in the holoplate storage cabinet," I said. "We can move the god box board and code to that."

"Okay," Redeye said, nodding slowly. "Power module?"

"I'll charge one," I said. He started to move. "Redeye."

"Yeah?"

"Let's take the Cryo."

He grunted. I saw the brief grin flash across his face.

We drove to a private shuttle pad closer than Vegas and hopped a ride to New Orleans. We took the Cryo, our standard combat gear, and the Basher. The Basher was a one-of-a-kind weapon, Broad Area Selective High Energy Radiator. It was a directed electromagnetic-pulse rifle that could generate one hundred fifty million volts, ten times the power of a bolt of lightning. I only brought it out for special occasions. I had the feeling this was going to be one.

Manda remained silent during the trip, a placid stare on her narrow face. When we got to New Orleans I turned to Redeye. "We can't watch her too. Let's let her go."

Redeye started to nod.

"I want to stay with the box," Manda said.

"Hey, we're not dealers, and this isn't your fix of Hydro. We're back in the states. You wanted to go, so get lost. If you decide you still need to kill us, give it a try. But I say you'll lose. Then you'll have direct access to God."

"I won't do anything to you," Manda said. "I want to use the box again."

"No," I said. "That was it, a one-shot deal."

Her expression was blank. I couldn't tell if she was going to cry, or grab for a gun and start shooting. "Technology is a commodity," I said. "We sell a competitive advantage. That box is one hell of an advantage. It's not a toy, and we're not interested in doing religious research."

I waited for her reaction. Manda stood there in the airport causeway staring at me. Then she simply said, "Okay." She turned, and walked away.

"If we see her again, I'll have to kill her," I told Redeye.

"I think we'll see her again, but I don't think you'll have to kill her," he replied.

I grabbed the handle of our trunk of gear and began pulling it. The god box was now a Kevlar-lined oversized briefcase. Redeye carried it as if it held nothing more than real-estate documents or software brochures. With his business suit and massive bulk, and his mane tied back in a ponytail, the case made him look like an offshore businessman, with me his assistant-slash-hired-thug. He was bigger; people would assume I was more assistant than thug. That's the look we went for as we entered the Vieux Carré.

The old French Quarter was a city within a city. There was nowhere else like it on earth. Every intricate ironwork balcony, hanging plant, and gas-lit brick courtyard in the ten-by-fifteen-block area was protected by a mountain of historical preservation laws. Jazz music and the smell of Creole cooking greeted you at every street corner. Stories of vampires, pirates and ghosts abounded, and it was the unquestionable home of Voodoo in the states. You could smoke a cigar and carry a drink around freely in public, and gambling was legal. All this made the French Quarter a hot tourist location, and that meant big business. No one entered or left the Vieux Carré without someone knowing it. And fortunately for us, big business liked computer records.

It was an easy task for Jack to rip surveillance footage of Kaylee, bound and gagged, being carried into a dilapidated two-story on North Rampart Street at the very edge of the Quarter shortly after midnight. It was also easy for him to blank out records of Redeye and me entering the Vieux Carré. But there were human spies too, so we kept up the businessman/thug charade until we were safely in our hotel room. We had a suite with high ceilings, long, shuttered windows, wall sconces, and antique furniture. It was all quite old, except the data ports. They were very modern.

"Fourth check complete," Jack reported from our Encom. "No surveillance sources available from interior of 515 North Rampart."

"And no further arrivals or departures?" I asked.

"No. Total count remains seventeen, including target."

"Say Kaylee, Jack, instead of target."

"Acknowledged."

"Eight-to-one odds," Redeye commented.

"We've had worse."

"I wasn't complaining," he said. "The more the better. The Cryo is going to feel good after their play on the farm."

"Nasty," I said.

"'Men never do evil so completely and cheerfully as when they do it from religious conviction,'" Redeye quoted.

I nodded. "Yeah, I can't wait to meet them." I cocked my pistol and flashed a grin. "Let's try not to rip up too much. It's zoned historic, after all. And I do like New Orleans."

Redeye's smile turned to a frown. "Eight to one is high. Don't forget, cockiness kills."

"I know," I said, holstering the pistol.

Eight to one *was* high.

* * *

Fortunately, we had the element of surprise. With Jack masking our way online, all we had to worry about was the street traffic as we made our way to North Rampart. Dozens of eyes watched as we carefully walked up St. Ann Street, but they were low-tech informants and petty thieves. If any one of them had so much as looked at an Infex or DCU, we'd have taken him out. Most were just looking for a current or future mark, a foolish tourist, imbibing too much and flashing too much wealth.

As the signs said, "Beware of pickpockets and loose women." The historic notices were still true, although the scope had expanded.

Redeye and I stood on either side of the front door of the decaying building at 515 North Rampart. The floor plan Jack had obtained from the city records said that the building was a gut job. It had burned to a shell in '19, and all that had been replaced were a second-story floor and a staircase. It should just be two large rooms on two levels, sixteen Satan-worshiping cannibals, and Kaylee.

"The trick is to not hit the girl," I said.

Redeye nodded. I nodded back. He spun and kicked in the door.

Revenge is sweet. It wasn't like the monastery. This was personal. Black, hooded robes. Leather-bondage-gear-clad cultists. Whips, studded collars, shackles. A pentagram on the floor with burning candles. A wavy, black dagger raised in a gnarled fist. Those images were frozen briefly in my mind, before Redeye opened up with the Cryo.

Eight-to-one became two-to-one in a matter of seconds. It was wrathful vengeance. The Cryo spun and launched tongues of fire-wrapped depleted uranium at the cult members. I saw Redeye adjust up and over the canvas bundle in one corner of the room, that could have been a person, to come back down and finish dropping every moving thing that could be seen on the first floor.

Redeye juked in and aimed the Cryo at the staircase. I ran to the bundle in the corner. It was a goat with its head cut off.

I aimed my pistol at the stairs and Redeye moved forward. That's when we heard the scream from upstairs. It was Kaylee. I ran toward the stairs. Redeye opened up with the Cryo again, this time aiming up at the ceiling. He cut a circle in the floor above us. Just as I reached the stairs the circle fell through. Two more cultists crashed down amidst splintering wood debris. Redeye cut them in half with a short burst.

There should be two cultists left, plus Kaylee. I raced up the stairs. I'm not sure how Redeye had known where to shoot, but he'd done well. A naked couple sat on the edge of a filthy mattress on one side of the hole in the floor, and Kaylee, bound to a chair, sat on the other side. Red smears had been painted onto her face and hands in broad strokes. It was intended to simulate blood. Maybe it was blood, but it looked too bright. When Kaylee saw me her eyes grew wide.

It was obvious that the couple had been taking advantage of the mattress. They looked from the hole in the floor in front of them to me with shocked expressions. Then, slowly, they both began to smile. The woman stood and waved her arms at me in an intricate gesture, mumbling under her breath as she did. Her naked body was full, firm, and sweat-covered. As she gyrated, the man bent down to reach for something under the mattress. The woman's movements were intended as a distraction. It didn't work. Two shots from my .57-caliber put an end to the man's reaching. Two more ended the woman's spell.

I ran to Kaylee and cut her ropes with my Sikes-Fairbairn. She jumped from the chair and threw her arms around me.

"You come for me!" Kaylee said. "I din'a tink you—"

I silenced her with a kiss.

"How you know I'm here?" she asked. "I been prayin' to Erzulie. Ya! She talk to you!" Kaylee said.

"It was a little more direct. Online data tracking and surveillance footage," I said.

Kaylee smiled. "Oh, she talk to you." She tapped my chest with her fingertips.

"You all right?" It was Redeye. He was standing at the top of the stairs, still keeping one eye on the ground floor.

"Yeah," I said.

Kaylee nodded at Redeye, then buried her head in my chest.

"A Scotus," Redeye said, gesturing with his head. He kept the Cryo aimed at the front door.

I hadn't noticed, but there it was in the corner, a Scotus-IX, just like ours. That was the Grid entry point Jack had monitored. It had a hard-wire-attached console. Redeye's mention of the powerful computer system triggered Jack. His voice came across the DCU on my wrist. "It has offline cached storage." Jack said. "It could contain detailed data relating to the information recently requested."

Yes, it could. Who wanted the god box code, and had been running the attacks against Jack? Why had Seeker chosen Bahometh as a codeword? How had Mujibar appeared after the last online attack? How did Manda tie in? Who, exactly, had destroyed the farm? Was there, at some level, perhaps one person running it all? The machine in the corner might have the answers.

"A Scotus-IX," I said to no one in particular.

"Yeah," Redeye replied.

Bringing the Basher had been a waste. The Basher could blow the silicon brains out of any piece of electronics. But a Scotus didn't use silicon. The CPUs of a Scotus were 3D man-made diamond circuitry, formed by microwave-heated methane. The Basher couldn't touch it.

Using the hardwired console, I could make the offline storage accessible in the Grid where Jack could get to it, if I knew the password. I didn't.

Kaylee clung to me as I looked from the Scotus to Redeye. He knew what I was thinking.

"I'll stay here," I said. "You go get the god box."

Redeye nodded.

"Kaylee," I said, pulling back an inch. "I need to—"

"I know," she interrupted. She kissed me again, and said, "You get them. They evil!" She stepped back and carefully walked around the hole in the floor to the corpses sprawled across the grimy mattress. Kaylee looked down at the dead bodies and pooled blood, and spat.

I went to the console and tapped the sequence to enter core command mode. To kill time until Redeye's return I wrote a quick program to blast password combinations at the online gateway: Bahometh, Knights Templar, Mujibar, Order of Golden Light, all the phrases I'd given Jack, plus all the abbreviations and combinations. Redeye was back long before the program had tried all sixty-nine-factorial permutations of the expressions.

Redeye called, "Me!" before climbing the stairs. Once up, he sat the god box on the floor next to the Scotus and snaked an I/O cable between the two. He plugged in power, attached the mesh head-cap, than turned and looked at me.

"Flip you for it," I joked.

"I'll cover you," he replied.

I nodded, took the cap in my hands, and slowly stretched it over my head.

Redeye stepped back. Kaylee walked over beside him. I remember her gently touching his arm, a concerned look on her face, just before Redeye switched on the power.

* * *

The Power.

One of the areas in the brain that goes numb with the god box is the speech center. That's how it has been for centuries with mystical revelation, according to my research. That's why the phrase, "It's impossible to describe," has been used so frequently. That's how it was now.

Oneness.

I was connected to IT ALL.

It seemed impossible, but this felt even more complete than when I'd used the god box in the crypt under the monastery. Had Gameboy jacked up the hardware somehow?

I looked at the Scotus and saw everything. I saw the outside. I saw the inside. I saw all of its inner workings, its circuitry, its engineering, its past, and its future. I saw my infinitesimal hack of a program and its attempt to obtain the password of the Scotus's online gateway—how simple.

With a grin I held the gateway in the palm of my hand, and with the snap of my fingers, I opened it.

There was Jack, waiting. Huge, golden, chrome, he smiled.

"Nice to see you again," Jack said. "You look... better."

"Thanks." I smiled. "So do you."

I glanced over and saw all of the data in the Scotus. "Do you want to have a look through this?" I asked.

"Sure," Jack replied. He became a blur, wrapped around the data that was stored in the powerful computer.

That was good.

Everything was good.

While Jack was doing that, I decided to have a look around, for Bahometh.

I found it in the Grid; the concept of 'where' was irrelevant. Bahometh: Goat's head and legs, green reptile stomach, blue breasts, *Salve* and *Coagula* on its arms, a Star of David medallion around its neck.

As soon as I found it, I transitioned-solidified-coalesced at the spot. It took a thought. I appeared, and Bahometh smiled at me. The creature was not transparent. It was dark and opaque, and I could not see anything in it. Bahometh's goat's-head smile turned into a laugh.

I was calm. "Seeker?" I asked.

"No." Bahometh's voice was neither deep nor shrill. Bahometh's voice was steady, calm and powerful. "I am not Seeker. I am not Mujibar. I am not Saloppe. I am Bahometh." The creature laughed again, horns and head thrown back.

"What are you?" I asked.

The laughter faded, the smile gone. "I will tell you." Bahometh expanded, drawing itself up. I expanded as well, which caused the beast to pull back its head. "I am not good. I am not evil," it said. "I am the collapse of the distinction between those two ideas."

I nodded. I understood.

"You are worshiped by evil because evil wants to be good."

"And good wants to be evil," Bahometh said. "But again, those terms are too unconditional."

I nodded again.

"My favorite color is gray," Bahometh continued in its neutral-powerful voice.

"Yes," I said. "But good and evil exist. Cults—"

"Give purpose to the lost and oppressed," Bahometh interrupted. "It is unfortunate that they need such associations, but it is the way of things. It is the same with organized religions."

I heard a whisper in my mind. "He is the Prince of Lies," it said.

"Religions do good," I said.

"That concept again." Bahometh flashed an impious grin. "Good, in whose judgment? An all-knowing, all-loving, all-powerful god's?

"It is trivial to formulate a proof that a god cannot be all of those things and still allow innocent suffering to exist," Bahometh said.

"I can see that," I replied. It was true.

The whisper in my mind said, "He is the Evil Deceiver. He is Descartes' malicious demon." The voice was not my subconscious. I heard it as if someone were whispering in my ear.

"Did you attack Jack?" I asked.

"No," Bahometh said. "It was someone else using my likeness."

"A lie," the whisper said.

I concentrated on the whisper and replied, "I know." With that small effort I knew the source of the whisper.

"Seeker," I said.

"What!" Bahometh roared. "That creature is here?"

"Appear," I commanded, and Seeker materialized. I took notice of our surroundings, and realized we were on a grassy plain floating in the emptiness of space. It was a solitary chunk of earth, with a warm sun overhead.

Seeker was a floating chrome ball, a foot in diameter.

Bahometh curled its thick, goat lips back. "I am not Mujibar, but he is here as well," the beast said. The Voodoo man coalesced on the grassy plain next to Bahometh. Mujibar held an asson, and wore the purple cape I had cut from his back when I was removing the god box mesh cap from him at the monastery.

The Voodoo man laughed. "Saloppe, she want me destroyed, not just killed," he said. "She fail."

The chrome ball zipped over next to me and said, "She knew Mujibar was using the god box. Saloppe thought that destroying the god box would end Mujibar's power in the Grid."

"She wrong," Mujibar said. "I here forever now. You kill me there, now I kill you here." He pointed the asson at me and snarled.

Mujibar was dark, like Bahometh. Even with the god box I could not see them clearly. It was as if these two entities alone were somehow outside of the connectedness of everything. Was this reality? Or was there a masking program that the god box—which was hardware and software connected to the Grid, I reminded myself—could not penetrate?

"You are the same," I said to Bahometh and Mujibar.

"Yes," Seeker said.

"No." Bahometh swelled. "It is all about balance. Two of you, two of me," the creature said.

"Not quite," I replied. "Jack!"

"Yes?" The gold-chrome figure appeared.

"Did you find anything?"

"Yes. Cross-analysis revealed that there is a single individual with a majority of direct control over all organizations examined. The individual is well hidden, but is identifiable. The individual is—"

Bahometh howled, and the sun overhead split in two.

"Jack!" I pointed, and he was beside me. I looked at him and I knew the name he was about to speak.

I turned my head upward to see a thousand demons shrieking out of the sun. Their screams were a hundred riot sirens. The light from the slit sun was blackened by their mass, creating a pulsing, swirling twilight. My first thought was of the Basher, modified for organics.

With that thought Seeker zipped in front of me and transformed. The shiny chrome ball morphed into the huge, silver rifle shape of the Basher. I grabbed it, and aimed.

Winged devils dove and shrieked as I pulled the trigger over and over. Each blast was an atomic fireball that overwhelmed sight, sound, and feeling, and took out a hundred demons at a time. But they kept coming.

"Jack," I commanded. "Shield."

Shield was one of Jack's core functions. Jack became a glowing golden cocoon around me. The devils that made it through the Basher barrage hit Jack and deflected off.

I looked for the "unload all" switch that was on the real Basher, and found it on this version as well. I flipped the switch and pulled the trigger one more time. It was the center of the sun.

White. Heat. Light. Wind. Atoms blasted past me, trying to pull the skin from my bones. I reminded myself that Seeker was doing this.

Was Jack protecting me, or had the blast blown Jack apart? Was the god box all that was protecting me from Seeker's intensity? I willed Jack to be safe, and knew he would be.

The holocaust subsided. The demons were gone. Seeker was once again a floating chrome sphere, and Jack was a golden robot. Bahometh and Mujibar faced me on the grassy plain, the sun once again restored and shining overhead.

"Impressive," Bahometh said.

I smiled. "I know who you are."

"Do you?"

As I watched, Bahometh and Mujibar merged. They touched their hands together and melted into one another. Slowly, their arms, bodies, and heads became a fused mass of black flesh. They pulsed, growing as they did. The pulsing fleshy mass split, into three entities this time: Mujibar, Bahometh, and Satan.

The Devil incarnate, complete with red skin, a forked tongue, spade-tail, cloven hooves, and a pitchfork, stood next to Mujibar and Bahometh, laughing gleefully.

"You know me, do you?" he said. "Yes, you do. For I am you."

"No," I replied.

"You fool yourself. You are all things, just as I am," Satan said. "Plus and minus, good and bad, it's all about balance. Yin and yang, select your term."

"Three of you and three of me?" I asked.

"Exactly."

"Wrong. One of you and one of me."

The Devil raised his spiky black eyebrow.

"Your version of Mujibar is an unregistered SIBLing, just as Seeker is."

Mujibar grinned.

"Bahometh is a computer construct, designed to work for you," I said. Bahometh laughed as I pointed toward Jack. "No, it's just the two of us," I said to Satan. "Slater and Z."

The fire-red figure grinned, and transformed into a white-suit-clad gentleman with a panama hat and goatee. "Thank you for the Caribbean vacation," he said calmly. "So I could keep an eye on you while my friends took care of your house."

"Your friends."

"Followers. Minions. What do you prefer?"

Seeker shot forward. "Why?" The silver ball hovered.

"I told you, it's all balance. Balance swings like a pendulum. It's time for a swing. What you call evil—my followers, my minions, the cults—will reign for ten thousand years," Z said.

"Mujibar was a pawn," I said, thinking of Saloppe and the original contract that had gotten Redeye and me involved in all of this in the first place.

"Who isn't?" Z said with a wry smile. "Paradise Engineering was building a god box. It needed testing. The Voodoo man sufficed. Unfortunate that Saloppe interpreted it as an incursion on her power and hired you."

"You are the legal owner of Paradise Engineering, Incorporated," Jack said, taking a step forward.

"Owner under another name. Or rather, under the names of several holding companies I indirectly control," he said.

Jack stepped back. I understood. Z owned the god box, but he did not have control of it. Board of Directors, reviews, government checks, and his need to stay hidden until the device was perfected had kept him in the shadowy background. He realized he had waited too long.

"The point is that it is a power box," Z said. "God box and Satan box are pointless terms."

"Maybe," I said. It did seem to me, from my current perspective using the box, that the device was more than mere 'ware. This must have been what Dunbar felt with his brain hardwired into a crude, pre-alpha version of the god box. But Dunbar had crossed, was able to cross, the boundary from the Grid to physical reality. That is, before we killed him.

I could make that test. But then I would be no different than Dunbar. Absolute power corrupts absolutely. What would Redeye do? I wanted to ask him, but he was on guard duty in what I currently considered to be the real world.

What else could I try, something outside of physical reality? Yes. Had the thought that popped into my mind come from the god box? I nodded at a spot on the ground in front of me. "Bill," I said. "Appear."

A shimmering blue-white aura formed on the spot, and the militant Baptist minister took shape on the grassy field. Was he real? It was difficult to maintain the meaning of that term. "Look," I said to Bill, pointing. Bill turned toward Z. As he stared, his expression became a grimace. "Hellspawn," Bill snarled.

"Pathetic illusion," Z replied. "Father of the Voodoo-cursed girl. Can't you do better than this?" Z waved a hand at Bill. "I can turn the daughter any time, you know. She already finds me ... interesting."

Bill bristled, but held his temper. Bill's image flashed, the single pulse of a strobe. Briefly, Manda stood there on the field instead of her father.

"You cannot turn her," the once-again-Bill figure said. "She knows what you are."

Z smirked. "We'll see."

Bill looked back, at Jack and Seeker. Seeker zipped forward. I could see the side of Bill's face. A smile tugged the corner of Bill's mouth up as Seeker whispered. I knew what Seeker was saying. Mentally, I told them both: yes, do it. The two launched themselves at Bahometh and Mujibar.

Seeker became a ballistic missile, a sabot round with one target and purpose. Seeker streaked toward Mujibar, impacted and exploded before Z or his creatures could move. A flash-bang yellow-purple fire burst, and Seeker and Mujibar were gone.

Bill flickered, vanished, and reappeared, standing in front of Bahometh. He held a gigantic flaming sword in one hand, and his holy Word of God, the Bible, trailing a red ribbon bookmark, in the other. Bill cut viciously at Bahometh. The creature screamed, and reared up on its haunches.

Z yelled, "No!" as Bill made another swing. The flaming sword cut the beast in half with a roaring slice. Bahometh faded. Wisps of flame consumed the unholy figure as it vanished.

"It's over," I said to Z. "I can destroy you with a thought." Z's face was impassive. "The design has been improved upon," I said. "Seeker helped. When Gameboy rebuilt the chip, Seeker intercepted the plans and enhanced them. The god box is now a hardware instantiation of the ultimate power in the Grid," I said. "Maybe more."

"Hardware." Z nodded. "It all comes down to hardware, doesn't it? Grid power is in physical, high-powered devices. Mental power is in the brain. Spiritually, a soul does not come into existence without the hardware of a physical body. You want to talk hardware?" Z's placid visage became a chuckle. "Let's talk hardware." His face twisted into a vile grin.

"Ask your pathetic programs how many companies I control! And how much hardware each of those has! It is mine to command." Z's white suit and Panama hat became black. His skin chameleoned to crimson. "Bring everything that is under my control online!" Z boomed. His voice was pounding thunder. "You have one device." Z spread his arms and his red skin pulsed like flowing blood. "I have ten thousand!"

A vast network of interconnected machines appeared in space behind the power-maniac.

I saw them all, their pathways, their data, their capacity and raw computational power, in total. Their combined ability far exceeded that of the god box. But I also saw something else. There!—with a thought I pinpointed it, a core node, the control point. It was the node on Rampart Street, the diamond-core Scotus-IX twenty feet in front of me in the real world. Z had known about it once, but he was a grand manipulator; he hadn't remembered what seemed like such a minor detail in his immense scheme.

It would be so easy, just a thought, to destroy the node with the snap of my fingers. I could feel it. Then Z's network would come crumbling down. Even though the computer was in the physical world and I was in the Grid, I could do it, I knew. Where were Kaylee and Redeye? I knew that too. They were standing near the Scotus, near enough that they would be in danger if I destroyed the machine. And then, also, I would have touched the physical realm, just as Dunbar had done.

Z's power was massive. I saw that he could knock me offline and rip the god box code out from the hardware. He had enough processing power behind him to do that. And he would do it soon. There wasn't time to tell Redeye to slag the box standing next to him. Z would crush me, and have everything he wanted, in just over a second.

The physical realm was Pandora's box. But in less than a second I decided. I did it.

I reached out, and with a thought, I willed the diamond Scotus core node of Z's network gone.

I saw the explosion, really an implosion, from afar, as if drifting above it all. The machine was sucked from physical reality into the quantum dimensions of probability. A quantum pulse wave—I knew physicists would call it that eventually—spread from the vanished machine. Kaylee and Redeye were standing too close.

"You fool!" Z said. "You have only helped me." But Z's grin held doubt. A small box in the web of machines that made up Z's computing power disappeared. I willed the god box to maintain its connection to the Grid. Then, one by one, spreading from that missing point, the network connections vanished, and Z's red face paled.

"You have no power," I said. "That's what you fear the most, isn't it?"

His disbelieving expression twisted into a quizzical grin. "And you have it all? Don't you?" he said. "You don't know what to do with it though," he prodded. "I can show you." He spread his arms in a welcoming gesture.

"Wrong. I do know." And I did know, in less than any fraction of a second. In a moment in between time, in a pseudo-second of un-time, I knew. I absorbed Z's power with a thought. I knew everything, I was everything, and I could see everything. I was the god box. I was the universe.

A brief flash of thought came to me: "You can have anything you want." But what is there to want when you are everything? That was what Dunbar and Z had failed to see.

With all, there is no want. *Absolute* power does not corrupt, it frees.

I did not want everything because that made no sense. So I let it all go.

But first, before letting it all go, in that un-second of everythingness, I did three things: I willed Ozzy Zimmerman gone, destroyed, obliterated. I willed Redeye to be safe. And lastly—I thought lastly—I willed the same for Kaylee.

And I knew: only two out of three were destined to happen.

With that thought I collapsed to the floor of the building on Rampart Street.

***

When I came to, I found Redeye holding something cold against my forehead. He pulled it away. It was a twisted hunk of cold metal from an overhead support.

"Face first, man," he said. "I ran to catch you, but not quite."

I pointed up, at the sagging roof.

"Endothermic implosion," he said. "My guess is someone perfected a meson gun. It took out the Scotus."

"Yeah," I said. "What about...?" I could see it in his face.

"She got caught in it," Redeye said, shaking his head slowly. "Sorry."

I nodded.

"We've got to move," Redeye said. "That meson gun means opposition in the area. So—"

"No, it's over," I said. "Ask Jack. Use the god box."

Redeye shook his head again. "It was cabled to the Scotus. It got yanked in to the implosion. That's what pulled you into a nosedive," he said. "No way to tell about Jack or Seeker."

"No need," I said. "They're safe. And so are we now."

MARS ON A BILLION DOLLARS A DAY
Ryck Neube

ONE

Paula Jasmine Caudill glanced at the display panel of her spacesuit. A blinking red light warned her of a leak. Fear knotted her stomach. She forgot to breathe. Adrenaline smacked her like a racing truck as she eyed her distant ship. No chance of rescue there.

"It's all up to you, kiddo," she said to herself.

Glancing down, left, then right, she saw no escaping gas, no hint of a defective seal. She yanked the mirror and patch kit from her tool belt, chanting a mantra of "Calm, calm, calm." Mentally, she rehearsed the quickest way to use the mirror to check her suit where its bulky nature precluded direct inspection.

The mirror slipped from her gloved hand. Yelping, she snatched it before it tumbled away. *Calm*, she commanded her pounding heart.

"This isn't a time to waste seconds fumbling."

It occurred to her to tap the panel. The warning light immediately went out. Nonetheless, she scanned the back of her spacesuit. No leaks.

"Another false alarm."

Her radio staticked, "Is there...Caudill? Repeat previous... Repeat...message."

She knocked on the side of her helmet. "No problem here. Just talking to myself again," she repeated four times, hoping her ship could paste together a full message.

Paula continued her way along the tether, inspecting the woven cables connecting the two spacecraft. The vessels spun around a common axis like frantic dancers, providing the illusion of gravity aboard the ships.

Having made the kilometer's journey to the *Da Vinci*, she was now halfway back to her own spacecraft, the *Tax Deduction*. The two vessels were a study in contrasts. The *Da Vinci*, with its long, graceful solar panels and silvery telemetry dishes, was drawn with sleek lines. Even the rounded bulge containing its Mars lander appeared organic, integral to the vessel's shape. It looked like a dragonfly redesigned for Grand Prix racing. The *Tax Deduction* resembled a child's drawing of a distorted whale with a weight control problem. Boxy payload containers were slung beneath broad flippers; stubby solar panels sprouted helter-skelter from its hull as if the ship had been harpooned.

Relishing the weightlessness, Paula paused. Pushing away from the tether, she waited until the last second to jackknife and catch the line before her safety cord jerked taut. She closed her eyes as she released the tether again, enjoying the sensation of absolute contentment.

Watching the starscape, the distant Earth the brightest of the dots, Paula sensed the presence of her father, and his spirit smiled. If only, she rued, he had lived to see her in space, fulfilling his most heartfelt fantasy.

A slight twist allowed her to view the *Nippon Glory*, a dozen klicks behind the two spinning ships. The third vessel of the fleet was an old U.S. shuttle purchased by a consortium of Japanese corporations to strut the rising-sun flag for the expedition. The shuttle's belly was a nest of girders that had once attached a pair of boosters assembled in orbit to provide the *Glory* with the power to escape Earth. The *Glory*'s charred nose and missing tiles gave the ship a battered appearance, like an elderly boxer who had lost too many fights. Its three-member crew circulated through the other two ships to log mock-gravity time during the nine-month flight to Mars.

Tether inspection was make-work. Every day, someone took the stroll, grateful for the chance to escape the cramped confines of their ships for a few hours.

The mundane activity had been the perfect cover for Paula to inspect that suspicious dish on the ventral side of the *Da Vinci*. It hadn't been shown on the ship's original design specifications she had studied. And for the life of her, Paula couldn't understand why the dish stayed pointed at the *Deduction*.

Ever since the fleet had left Earth orbit, they had experienced endless communications interruptions. Somebody was jamming them. But who? The media back on Earth—when gaps in the interference allowed the stories to reach them—posited that one of the myriad military satellites orbiting Earth was blocking the signals to and from the expedition. Who was doing it—if anyone—remained a mystery. The list of suspects was endless, from neo-communists who hated the originator of the expedition, Ten Carl Richards, for his capitalist past, to NASA who hated the man for doing what they could not.

It was enough to make a woman paranoid, especially since the Japanese and their far less comprehensive communications system reported to Tokyo twice a day. Never once did they report a problem.

When Paula had discussed the jamming problem with Captain DeJung of the *Da Vinci*... Paula couldn't put a finger on it exactly. DeJung had become evasive, talkative for the first time on the flight. The captain had complained profusely about the inconvenience of the jamming, then suddenly switched to gossiping about the sexual antics aboard her ship to avoid further discussion.

So Paula had inspected the suspicious dish. Best she could tell with her multimeter, it wasn't broadcasting or receiving. Indeed, the dish didn't appear to be operational. Perhaps it was just another backup system.

"Ah well, it was something different to do," she said before giving herself a push down the tether.

She chided her paranoia. Being millions of klicks from Earth was ample reason for communications problems, she rationalized, especially during sunspot season. No conspiracy was necessary. Perhaps the expedition suffered from nothing more than having selected frequencies used by one of the Earth's militaries.

"It's all in your head," she muttered. If only she could convince herself.

TWO

Another week, another turn inspecting the tether.

Paula's helmet rang with a static-filled message; she could not understand a single word of it. Paula counted herself lucky that her suit only had a defective radio. Poor Doctor Duncan looked like a mummy, she had so much duct tape wrapped around the defective seals of her suit. Paula smacked the side of the helmet, once, twice, thrice.

She paused, letting herself float from the tether until her safety line stopped her.

"Everyone...*Deduction*." She was pleased with getting two clear words of the dozen that had been uttered over the radio.

"Please repeat," she said four times. Only static replied.

Paula rotated. Her eyes filled with the blinking blue lights outside the airlock of her ship. The lights announced an emergency. Loosing her safety line, she raced the half klick to the *Deduction*, hand over hand, taking care not to accelerate too much. Her fifth time out, she had made that mistake only to smash against the ship like a bug on a windshield. Damned near broke her neck that time.

At the last moment, she embraced the tether with gloves and boots, eating the momentum with a series of squeezes. Paula regretted not timing the dash, feeling she'd set a new record.

The outer hatch refused to close, forcing her to use the hand crank, which wasted minutes. This was the second time they'd broken the hatch assembly.

"Nothing works around here," she grumbled. No surprise, she thought, considering the number of corners that had had to be cut due to the cost and rush of their launch.

Paula felt lucky having a Russian-made suit with quick-release clam hinges; the helmet and backpack unit parted from the ventral portion of the suit. Freedom required scant seconds. The other two ships had purchased their suits from the United States; those took far longer to don and doff a piece at a time.

Emergency or nay, as per her own standing order, she refilled the suit's oxygen tanks and exchanged its batteries before leaving the airlock. As captain, she had to be doubly tough on herself.

"What's the crisis?" she asked as she joined the pilot walking toward the bridge.

"Don't know," replied Taylor, rubbing his eyes as he lurched. "If the damned ship cracks in half, I do not care. If I don't get a decent night's sleep soon—"

"If we could harness your whining as fuel, we could reach Mars in an hour."

"Very funny, Paul-aaa."

She ignored the bray Taylor used for her name; promised herself that one glorious day she would break that nose so skillfully crafted by a plastic surgeon, whose reflection he checked in every shiny surface he encountered.

She stopped abruptly, "accidentally" elbowing Taylor in the gut before she entered the bridge. It felt good.

"Bottom-line this problem for me," she shouted over the hum of electronics and human whispers.

Ten Carl Richards jumped from the captain's chair. Only his confidence hinted he once had been the richest man on Earth. "Caudill, we just received a warning from Earth. The SOHO-VII satellite detected a major storm brewing on the sun last week. *Somebody* neglected to warn us while the rest of the world was battening down its spacecraft."

"No reason to get paranoid, boss," she replied.

His laugh came out as a cough. "They want us to fail. That's why they're jamming us. They'd be overjoyed if we all died out here."

"Exactly who are *they*?" she asked.

Ten Carl shrugged, then added, "We are directly in the flare's predicted path." He smacked a fist into his open palm.

"We've been having radio problems. That is perfectly reasonable this far out," she replied. It sounded like a hollow rationalization, even to her. Still, it was her role as captain to ease the growing fear of her crew.

She turned to the captain of the *Glory*. "Did Tokyo warn you?"

Captain Tanaka nodded. "We were told of the possibility. Our scientists deemed it a remote, an extremely remote danger."

Paula chewed on her lower lip lest she curse.

From his communications console, Javier said, "The current data from SOHO was three days stale when we received it."

"So? We're ready for any storm." Paula threw a thumb over her shoulder. In the center of the *Tax Deduction*'s water reservoir was a chamber prepared to protect them from the radiation hell of a solar flare.

"From the preliminary surface-flux data, it looks like the storm will be a long one," said Javier.

Everyone groaned.

The chamber had been designed for the five members of the *Tax Deduction*'s crew, not the three additional crew members of *Nippon Glory*, nor the four aboard the *Da Vinci*. However, since those ships lacked shelters, there was no alternative.

"Can you guess how long it will last?" she asked.

"The magnetic lines are twisting beyond anything on the solar record," replied Javier, a tremble in his voice.

Unlike the rest of the *Deduction*'s crew, Javier had far more than mere money awaiting his return. He was married—happily married, with three children. Paula sighed. Since the boss had made her the captain, it was her duty to make certain Javier, above all, returned home to that family; especially his youngest daughter, whose over-sized eyes and scratch across the nose in the photograph on the console reminded Paula of herself at the age of five. The kid would need her father.

"We'd better get the others aboard."

"Yes, ma'am; as your loyal lieutenant I sent out the call the instant the news arrived." The billionaire snapped a salute, then laughed. Ten Carl's eyes twinkled.

Magnates like Ten Carl thrived on pressure, she mused, thrived on putting their employees in a vice to see how much stress it took to crack their walnut minds.

"I—I should check the shelter," said Javier, his voice showing the wide cracks in his walnut.

Three years ago, Javier had told his fellow computer nerds the boss was crazy to try for Mars. He hadn't realized the boss was eavesdropping from one of the stalls in the bathroom. Ten Carl had taken the statement as a gauntlet thrown. He'd pestered Javier for months before the man crumbled and said yes. So the information technologist had been the first recruit for the crew; Javier's price was two million for each year of the three-year mission.

Pity, Paula thought, she had not been privy to that information until after she boarded the *Deduction*. It had never occurred to her to ask more than the salary Ten Carl paid her for being his personal historian.

"What do you think, captain?" asked Ten Carl. He laughed again, motioning at the bright yellow Post-It note stuck on the back of Javier's head. It read "Empty."

Paula could not help but laugh herself. The boss's moods were infectious. That joyous quality he possessed was a major reason why she worked for the billionaire. Of course, his whims often made her brain ache. He had made her the captain of the *Tax Deduction* because she beat him at one of his poker games.

A mad billionaire's infinite whimsy—how could she resist him?

"What are your orders, Captain Caudill?" The boss smiled. Javier and Taylor glowered at her. Captain Tanaka merely looked uncomfortable as he polished a computer terminal with a handkerchief.

"Javier, inspect the shelter," she said. "I'll stay on the bridge and join the party fashionably late."

"Give me a minute, there's an update coming through."

As Paula walked across the bridge, Ten Carl Richards saluted her once again. She smiled.

The boss was a squat gnome of a man. He was named Ten Carl because his father, the infamous slumlord Carl Richards, had declared that his son would be ten times the man he was. The proud father had proved correct, after a fashion.

At the age of twenty, Ten Carl had been expelled from Harvard for running a string of coed prostitutes. At twenty-five, he'd been arrested on charges of dumping toxic waste. Four members of the jury that found him innocent mysteriously became millionaires soon afterward. At twenty-seven, he'd entered the moneyed elite as a billionaire. Billions had bred more billions. By the age of forty, he'd become the richest man on Earth.

"The flare IS!" Javier yelled from his communication console. The skinny man leapt to his feet, trembling from head to toe.

Ten Carl laughed as he hugged her. "Another mess you have to get me out of."

"Okay, people." She pulled free and clapped her hands. "To the shelter. How long before the sleds get here from the other ships?"

"They're outside the primary airlock," said Javier as he edged toward the hatch. He dashed back to his console to snatch the picture of his family.

"Taylor, be so kind as to escort our guests from the airlock to the shelter."

The pilot failed to move beyond making an obscene hand gesture. She swallowed the urge to hit Taylor, but could not get her fist to open.

She glanced at the screen Javier had abandoned. Most of the telemetry was garbled. Staring hard, she could almost see the modulation of the jamming signal forming a lazy series of M's across the screen. She wished she could guess the *why* behind the communications sabotage. How could it possibly profit anyone?

The data stream abruptly cleared of electronic interference. Numbers jumped, went through the roof. The console's alarm rang, triggered by the signals from the International Space Station.

"Move!" Paula shouted, slapping a bulkhead in lieu of smacking Taylor.

The crew responded. She recorded a message to be played whenever the airlock was activated, in case Taylor ignored her command.

"Boss, you should go, too."

Ten Carl grunted, remaining on the bridge. She walked to the communications console, seeing the burst of data from the station announcing that the SOHO satellite had died after the hell of the solar flare touched it.

"Boss, we need to get to the shelter," she said as she systematically turned off the equipment on the bridge. *Slow and steady,* she told herself, *no need to waste time with a mistake.*

"In a minute, I have to check my stocks while they aren't jamming us," he replied, blocking her from turning off the communications console.

"By the time your message gets to Earth and your broker replies—" Hardcopy began spitting from the printer. "Amazing."

Ten Carl gave her a sheepish grin. "I have them monitoring our signals back on Earth. They send the data the instant the jamming stops."

"But the time it would take is—" She shook her head. *Don't waste time,* said the nagging voice within. "Never mind that. Boss, it's time to go." She grabbed his forearm. He shook her off.

"Oh, Jasmine, you are such a drama queen. We have plenty of time."

He was the only person besides her father that had ever used her middle name. Sometimes it irritated her beyond belief. Other times, it made her grin the way she found herself doing now.

"It's time now! The other crews are cycling through the airlock. The solar flare is—" She paused, knowing this was not the way to motivate him.

Her hand rocketed down, intercepting the boss's as he sought to place a wad of gum on the seat of her jumpsuit.

"Now is not the time for one of your stupid pranks."

"It's always time for a good laugh," he replied.

"You know," she said, "my father worked for a billionaire, too. When I was in college, I tracked down my father's last lover. I can't believe I've forgotten her name. Anyway, the woman told such glorious stories. Daddy and the billionaire once—" Paula walked from the bridge without looking back, allowing her voice to trail off.

Ten Carl followed on her heels. "So what happened with your father? How rich was his employer?"

Paula noticed piles of spacesuits littering the corridor as if there had been an astronaut striptease. She smiled all the more broadly.

"I have to stop by my cabin." It took her seconds to fetch a worn canvas gym bag, a tool belt and a handheld computer.

"So how rich was he, this other billionaire?"

"Maybe twenty billion. I don't know if you have ever heard of Daddy's billionaire. Selton, his name was. He..."

THREE

The solar hurricane lasted four days. A magnetic field generated by the ship hummed through the outside of the water reservoir, deflecting some particles. The water and the tank's carbon-fiber walls, infused with molecules of lead, absorbed others. The people within the chamber tried not to think of the remaining particles whizzing through their cells.

"My agent says she can book me a million dollars' worth of personal appearances once we return to Earth," bragged Taylor. "And that's not counting the film and book offers."

She'd often overheard their pilot boast how his movie-star looks would turn this mission into superstardom for him.

For Taylor the expedition was merely a stunt. The concept burned like bile in her throat. The fool could care less that they were making history. This shouldn't be, she thought, about pampered egos, but about the whole human race.

Yet the mission *was* a stunt. An angry billionaire had mounted this expedition after being declared a pariah for his predatory business practices. Ten Carl Richards had decided to spend his fortune entering history as an explorer rather than a robber baron.

Washington politicians had refused to believe one man could get a Mars expedition off the ground; Congress had ridiculed Ten Carl as they granted him permission. Only after the three sections of his whale ship were launched by Russian boosters had the politicians started to fear the mad idea was possible. Nonetheless, they'd bickered over how to respond, until it was too late to do anything. Only after the *Tax Deduction* was being assembled in low Earth orbit had the world begun to believe in Ten Carl's boasts. While waiting for NASA and the ESA to launch the cargo containers now slung beneath the *Deduction*'s wings, the rest of the world had decided to join the stunt.

Paula closed her eyes. Whenever the inner cynic chewed on her, Paula invoked memories of her father—the way he had lovingly stared into the sky with moist eyes as he taught her the constellations. Most of all, she relived the way Jay Lawrence Caudill's voice had cracked when he spoke of the "real" heroes, the Gagarins and Glenns who pioneered space.

This mission was a stunt, for the others. Hell, she thought, the EU had selected their crew by committee—appointing a fucking mission *poet*, she wanted to scream.

But this expedition was not, not, NOT a stunt for Paula Jasmine Caudill.

She closed her eyes and silently said, "Daddy, I'm here for you. If only you had lived long enough to see this."

During her weekly rant against Jay Lawrence, Paula's mother was fond of screaming that he had abandoned the family. Though she had been a child during the divorce, Paula knew it was her mother who dragged them to Florida simply to hurt her father. She knew it was the woman, that stranger who had given birth to Paula only to hate her because she loved Jay Lawrence. The woman grew more bitter by the day because she had divorced Jay Lawrence so long before he became rich that no judge would increase her alimony.

The screamer never realized how a seventeen-year-old Paula in the cyber-age could run a computer search capable of rousing the envy of the CIA. As her mother volcanoed accusations against her ex-husband, Paula knew Jay Lawrence had been murdered in distant Cincinnati during a senseless street crime.

It broke Paula's heart to envisage her father's lonely end, from morgue to cremation. Had anyone picked up his ashes? The funeral home had gone out of business by the time she followed the cold, cold trail. Jay Lawrence's lover had been out of the country; Caudill luck had already sent his parents' generation to the grave, leaving only a handful of cousins scattered across North America. The cremation itself had been paid for out of the cash recovered from his wallet.

All Jay Lawrence had was a daughter and son. In the end, all he had was nothing.

Most of all, Paula recalled her own mounting anger as weeks went by without an e-mail or letter from him, her own efforts unanswered. She had been so enraged by his thoughtlessness until she learned of his fate.

How her anger, her betrayal, tasted of bile even now.

Senseless. Senseless as reducing the greatest mission of human history into a public-relations stunt.

It was the story of the pathetic Caudill luck.

"Why don't the other ships have shelters?" whined Taylor after being nudged by one of the Japanese on his way to the bathroom.

Paula jerked her feet out of the way.

"There was not time. The launch schedule was all about catching up with Citizen Richards," said Captain DeJung of the *Da Vinci* in a whiskey-low voice. Her hand stroked the poet Salamanca's thigh.

"We organized our contribution in seven months, from inception to leaving orbit. There was scarcely time to supply our ship with the basics. We understood the risks," said Captain Tanaka as he scrubbed the edge of a bench with a handkerchief.

"I didn't ask for company," said Ten Carl Richards, his right hand vanishing inside Doctor Duncan's jumpsuit. "As a matter of fact, I delayed my start by a fortnight to accommodate you laggards."

The doctor appeared oblivious as she brushed her long blonde hair. Indeed, her dilated pupils hinted Duncan had dosed herself to the point where she no longer knew she was in space. Every time she dropped the brush, her hand continued stroking her hair until Ten Carl returned it to her.

DeJung tsked. "This launch window was broad. You could have waited for a few months. Had you—"

"Had you people planned better," snapped Ten Carl. "I didn't invite you people. You are just here to steal my glory!"

The bickering went on for hours.

A dozen people crammed into a glorified drum designed to hold a maximum of six became a torture session. Ten Carl Richards forbade conversation after the third argument. Day after endless day of silence, it felt to Paula as if they had spent the entire six months of their flight inside the chamber.

Paula's nose would grow accustomed to the smells for a few hours, then another molecule would be released, and the stench would assume a critical mass of garlic and sweat, wine and pepper, and, worst of all, a metallic smell Paula could not identify.

Having people crawl over her to use the toilet behind a canvas curtain drove her crazy. Almost as crazy as the stench from the second-rate chemical toilet. *The boss spent billions,* she mused, *then cut a corner like that.*

"What's in your mystery bag, Jasmine?" asked Ten Carl.

She tightened her grip on the gym bag balanced atop her lap. "The legacy from my father."

"Didn't I hear your dad struck it rich there at the end?"

"He didn't trust banks. He kept the money he inherited hidden somewhere, but it was never found after his murder. All I have are these photo albums. He was a big fan of space, so I'm taking his mementos to Mars. He would've wanted it that way."

"A photo album? Pictures of little Jasmine on the beach? May I see them?"

"Boss, my bag is none of your business."

"Women always have their secrets," said Taylor.

She hugged her gym bag, rejoicing because she felt the presence of her father, of his dreams. Yet for once, it did not make her feel better. Her knees ached. How she wished she could stretch out. Her stomach rumbled, but her throat was so dry she could not conceive of swallowing a bite.

The bag of rations would have supplied five passengers for three days. Only twenty-five liters of water were stored inside the shelter.

Hunger and thirst. Cramping and stink. Worst of all, the ennui.

While Javier slept, the boss tiptoed down the narrow walkway between the benches. Holding his finger to his lips, the boss shook everyone else awake, one by one. Carefully Ten Carl opened the man's jumpsuit at the crotch. With a wicked grin, the boss up-ended a bottle of habañero sauce over Javier's crotch.

Despite herself, Paula laughed when Javier woke screaming.

The next day, the boss distributed stacks of hundred-dollar bills, shuffled the cards, and started a poker game.

"It's not the same without some of your chili, Mister Richards," said Taylor.

"I can smell the popcorn," groaned Duncan.

"We shouldn't torture ourselves with food talk, or any talk, for that matter. We are playing cards here," said the boss.

The game did not last long in the silence.

Bored, Paula examined her life behind clenched eyes, trying to recall it day by day. Where were the homey memories? she wondered. A thousand fights with her mother, a hundred arguments with her dragon of a grandmother—why did she remember so many fights? No wonder she'd moved from home as soon as she graduated high school. Eight lovers and a single one-night stand had all crashed in flames and acrimony. Her private life had always been measured by conflict.

That depressing revelation led her to seek refuge in memories of classroom victories: valedictorian in high school and number two in her class at the University of Cincinnati. She'd set a speed record for earning her PhD in North American history of the mid-nineteenth century.

As much as she resisted, her thoughts fluttered to the Burns. She could not recall how that first night at Dean Burn's palatial Tudor home had gone. Nervous around the legendary academics, she had drunk too much. Waking in the middle of the night handcuffed to Dean and Professor Burn's bed had panicked her at first. However, the couple's charm and magnificent sexual skill had soon captivated her.

What soft, busy hands. The memory still sent a tremble down her spine.

But the entire experience had turned out to be just another example of the infamous Caudill luck. Her father had inherited a fortune, found true love, and promptly gotten his throat cut in a senseless street crime. Paula had just signed a lucrative contract to be host of a TV series about the Civil War, and finally found true love with the Burns; so, of course, the Caudill luck struck Paula down.

A nosy gardener discovered the bodies of six coeds buried in the Burns' back yard. Her lovers' hobby proved to be serial killing. The scandal killed Paula's TV career, even after the police had deemed her totally innocent. Indeed, the detectives concluded Paula would have been the couple's next victim, though she could never bring herself to believe that. There wasn't a university, or even a business college in Samoa, that would hire her. Innocence was no defense after so much publicity.

If it hadn't been for a whimsical billionaire buying an estate on the fringe of the Gettysburg battlefield and advertising for an in-house historian to impress his visiting business associates...

Selling used cars for three weeks had left Paula with the urge to stick her head into an oven. To be Ten Carl's personal historian had been her salvation, or so she thought at the time.

Now she wondered if it was just another stroke of the Caudill luck.

FOUR

Captain Tanaka announced, "I have no faith in these instruments." His scarred fist smacked the bank of gauges monitoring the interior of the *Deduction*. He immediately wiped the smudge off the glass. "The readings have not changed in twenty hours. I am going outside."

"That isn't wise," said Duncan, fussing with her blonde bangs. She nearly fell off the bench. Ten Carl's personal doctor continued, "Don't gamble with radiation."

"Bring back that tin of tuna and bottle of pinot noir on my desk," said Ten Carl, "before you die."

"Would you people shut up? I'm trying to get some sleep," said Taylor.

Paula felt the need to say something, anything. "Captain, are you certain this is...uh, wise?"

"At some point, action is necessary." Tanaka barked commands in Japanese at his two minions before he departed the shelter.

"What's the reading, Javier?" asked the boss.

Javier stopped staring at the photograph of his family, leaning over to examine the instruments. "Steady at four hundred and forty, same as yesterday. His marrow must be frying by now."

The Japanese muttered as they glowered at Javier.

"Let's return to the silence rule," said the boss. "Do you agree, captain?"

Paula grunted and closed her eyes. Her imagination plagued her with images of what the radiation must be doing to Tanaka. She didn't care for the brusque man who always seemed to be rushing, even when he was standing still. Nonetheless, nobody deserved to die like that.

"Jasmine, what were you telling me about your father?"

"What?" *Just like Ten Carl,* she thought; *he declared silence, then decided to talk.*

"Your father and his employer. How many billions did he have?"

Paula sighed. "Twenty or thirty, not even close to how much you had before this expedition. Selton was a sick young man. There was a scandal about his illness, but I don't recall the details. Very sick. Very crazy. But how can anyone be rich and sane?"

"I wouldn't know, Jasmine." Ten Carl roared with laughter.

His levity caused her to cringe. Like laughing during a funeral, it didn't feel right. "The man had to be insane. There Selton was, living in Kentucky, but he would only hire Poles, or people who could speak Polish. You know, Napoleon's personal bodyguards were Poles."

"Fat lot of good it did Nappy," said Taylor.

"Napoleon wasn't assassinated," she snapped. "He merely lost the war. Anyway, my father could speak Polish because his maternal grandmother had bought him a car when he was old enough to drive in exchange for learning the language of his heritage."

"Heritage is important," said Javier. "When my father left Habana, he——"

"I only gave one person permission to speak."

"Counting yourself, boss?"

Ten Carl frowned at her before saying, "On with your story, Jasmine."

She paused, wondering why she tolerated the boss's whims. *To get into space,* whispered the voice of her father. Paula caressed the worn gym bag on her lap.

Paula continued, "My father had lost his job at the factory, so he went to work for this billionaire. He did all sorts of jobs around the mansion, from managing the household accounts to dealing with visitors, but mostly he took care of the lunatic's collection. This is the crux of the story. Selton had so much money that he collected pieces of dead famous people."

"Pieces?" asked one of the Japanese.

Paula nodded at the man, reaching to flick an unruly curl of hair from his eyes. She smiled, embarrassed she couldn't recall his name. "Selton owned body parts—the brain of a slain president, a hand from a serial killer, a baseball player's liver, that sort of thing. Pieces of human beings in a frigging collection: only the rich could do that. It's almost as insane as a fat cat buying an expedition to Mars."

Everyone laughed. Everyone save Paula.

Tanaka returned, his Geiger counter locked on its peak reading to prove the radiation was near normal.

"Are you certain your detector is working?" asked Ten Carl as he stuffed the tin of tuna into his pocket and seized the bottle of wine. "Anybody have a corkscrew?"

"Yes, it works. No, I have no corkscrew," replied Tanaka.

"I will double-check, just to be safe," said Paula, feeling the need to do something to prove she was a captain. Rising, she contorted through the gauntlet of people to reach the door of the chamber. She pulled a radiation meter from the tool belt draped over one shoulder. From the corner of her eye, she caught Taylor reaching for her gym bag. She returned and grabbed it.

With the meter held forward like a knight's lance, Paula eased from the shelter, confirming the *Deduction* was safe. After shouting the news into the shelter, she raced to the bridge.

Dammit, she was the captain, not another one of Ten Carl's whims. She resolved to prove it to them all.

Paula tried to reactivate the ship's systems. Nothing. Inspiration led her to the circuit breakers. Sure enough, the flare had thrown them. *Easy fix,* she thought, flipping the switches. Navigation alone came alive. She drew a hammer from her tool belt, fighting the urge to smash something.

Captain DeJung of the *Da Vinci* entered the bridge. "Having problems?" she asked.

"More than my share," replied Paula, staring at a control panel, shaking the hammer.

DeJung sneered. Paula knew it without looking.

"*I* expected extensive electronic damage." DeJung opened the access panel of the life-support console. She made a tsk-ing noise. Unplugging a circuit board, she crossed wires. A puff of air emerged from the ventilation shaft.

"I have done my share here," said DeJung. "Now I shall return to my *Da Vinci.* There will be plenty to do there."

"My *Da Vinci,*" Paula mocked as soon as the woman left.

Paula consulted the manual, checked the tutorial program on her chip-plate. With their help, she nursed the rest of life support on-line.

A freshly showered Taylor arrived on the bridge. Having spent three months being trained by Coca-Cola/Lockheed-Martin, Incorporated, who designed the *Deduction*'s electronics, he did not require manuals. Instead, he went through the motions with professional ease. The masterputer roused long enough to crash. Taylor brought it back up, cursing the major sector damage to its hard drives. The communications console refused to revive.

Paula fetched her personal radio set from her cabin while Taylor replaced circuit boards. Her radio embraced generations-old vacuum-tube technology. Returning to the bridge, she attached the radio to a power outlet and antenna feeds, plugged in the headset, and listened. Faint Morse code signals told her the situation, listing the satellites fried and an impressive number of power grids on Earth that were whacked. ISS, the International Space Station, had been badly damaged. It was a historic event, the worst solar belch since records had been kept.

Arriving on their ships, the other crews found their electronics did not rouse. Gone, simply gone. The fleet had turned into a convoy of wrecks.

Paula finally went to the showers. If nothing else, hot water was the ultimate mood purge. Pity it lasted a scant sixty seconds; the cold water only lasted fifty seconds longer. She scrubbed the soap off her body with a towel stiff enough to walk from the room.

She could still smell herself. Wringing the excess moisture from her jumpsuit crumpled in the bottom of the shower stall, she hung it upon the last empty hook on the wall. In a day, it would be dry and almost clean like the so-called fresh jumpsuit she donned.

The boss had purchased the best washer and drier on the market for the *Deduction*, their efficiency matched to the limited water supply and their less-than-perfect recycling. Unfortunately, in the chaos and rush of the launch, they had never been installed. The *Deduction* was six days from Earth before they'd realized the appliances had been left in orbit.

"Pioneers must make sacrifices," she reminded herself while wondering if her father ever grasped the realities of space. Or had he merely dreamed? Dreams where every pioneer was clean. Where everyone wore laundered clothes. Where flight systems always worked. Where pioneers did not die.

Your father is a loser because he is a dreamer, ranted her mother.

But if you do not have dreams, Paula had never had the courage to retort, *you are worse than a loser. You are dead where it truly matters.*

Paula returned to the bridge after eating a military ration. The peanuts were the only thing she recognized in the meal.

"This is unacceptable!" shouted the boss. Ten Carl paced the bridge. "I must contact Earth."

Taylor was sweating bullets. He was on the deck, surrounded by panels from the communications console. "Too many components have been destroyed."

"I can send Morse code home." Paula switched her radio back on. Faint voices hissed from its speaker. She fiddled with the controls, finding the right frequency. A familiar beep-beep sounded.

"Morse code? That's Civil War crap," said Taylor.

"I can broadcast data with that Civil War crap," she replied. "My signal is so weak, they've yet to bother to jam it."

"Can you contact my broker?" asked Ten Carl.

"My friends are listening. They can relay your message." Paula twisted the dial.

During the flight, she had broadcast the real story to her fellow historians, dotting and dashing messages. Somewhere, she mused, supercomputers toiled to deconstruct the code for the CIA or KGB or MI5. They would peer at the message detailing Ten Carl's obsession about waffles smeared with precisely six grams of butter every morning, whereupon the spymasters' brains would explode trying to decipher the hidden meaning.

"My people can contact your people. I just need the passwords to convince your accountants." Paula grinned as she worked the key.

She dotted and dashed for an hour. Her chums replied with stock data that pleased the boss. The time lag allowed Paula to fret about the jamming being directed against her radio set, so she sent her most trusted recipients a series of messages telling them to use parts of their addresses or phone numbers as alternative frequencies.

She fell asleep on the deck of the bridge, curled around her radio set; woke, feeling chagrined, but nobody had noticed. Paula checked the tape from the machine, relieved it had captured three short replies she had missed while asleep. All were garbled. As she feared, the jamming now encompassed her machine.

Why? she kept asking herself.

Her unlikely bed had left her muscles stiff. Wandering the bridge, she checked the duty roster, discovered nobody had checked the tether. She scribbled her name beside the chore.

"The boss said we should stay inside until all the systems are on-line," said Javier.

"Where is he?"

"In his cabin with the doctor. He needed a...*check-up.*" He winked, then glanced at his family photograph as if to apologize to them. "He asked not to be disturbed."

"Case closed. I'm the captain, so I'm ordering myself to check the tether. What's the status of the comm system?"

"We have tightbeam contact with the other ships. We are getting spotty reception from Earth. In a few hours, I should be able to establish a solid link with the ISS. Best I can tell, the jamming has ceased."

She chewed her lower lip. Why would they jam her radio and cease jamming their main frequencies? *Because they knew we were off-line,* she thought. But how could anyone on Earth know that when the ship wasn't broadcasting? She had not mentioned it in her messages.

"What about the other systems?"

"Taylor thinks he can patch together a complete control system from the parts that survived the flare. Some of our spare parts were wrapped in lead foil."

"Excellent. How about the other ships?" she asked.

"No news from the *Da Vinci.* The *Nippon* is a junk heap. They are sending a sled over to get spare parts from their cargo container under our starboard wing."

"Perfect. If something goes wrong on my stroll, there will be a sled flying out there. Safe as can be."

"The boss said—"

"I AM the captain of this ship," she snapped.

After being sardined inside the shelter for days, she felt a surge of pure joy as she donned her suit. The airlock's computer was off-line, but her versatile chipplate held a program to inspect the suit. She thanked her lucky stars she had carried her handheld computer into the shelter. As she expected, most of the suit's vital hardware had survived. She donned her tool belt over the suit, attaching extra components.

Paula took extra care crawling across the whale on the way to the tether. The disastrous solar flare made her wary. Was this, she wondered, sufficient to fulfill her quota of Caudill bad luck? Or merely a prelude?

Paula attached her safety line to the tether, launching herself with a strong yank. She felt like a simian, using her boots to grasp the tether, clambering up until she had to kill her momentum in stages.

"A tail would be so handy in space," she mused.

"You've got a nice tail," said Taylor over the radio, static dotting each word.

She glanced down. The helmet radio's light was not on. Her chip-plate had showed the system non-operative. Weirder, the suit's radio had never worked so well before its circuits got dosed by the flare.

"Javier, I thought you said only the tightbeam system was working."

"You asked about ships, not spacewalkers. I'm not reading any telemetry from your suit."

"Are you ignoring me?" asked Taylor.

"Get back to work," she said. "Caudill out."

She floated away from the tether, intoxicated by the freedom. She took a while to find her bearings; Mars gleamed, the brightest thing in her field of vision. She was musing on its precise colour when the Japanese sled moseyed toward the *Tax Deduction*. Its two occupants waved at her, no doubt as overjoyed as she was to be outside. She returned their waves.

It relieved her to have the Japanese on the expedition. Ten Carl had selected his crew by whimsy. The Europeans had been more concerned with getting a mix of nationalities and public personalities than with sending competent explorers. Only Tanaka's crew were true scientists capable of solving Martian mysteries.

The sled's fore jets spat to slow them. Its aft jet tilted slowly before a puff of propellant skewed the skeletal craft around to dock with the outermost cargo container.

In the original plan, she recalled, that container was supposed to be an R&R module, even containing a pool table to help them pass the time. Once the EU and Japan joined the expedition, the boss had sacrificed it so the *Deduction* could carry backup parts and supplies for the *Glory*, just as the boss's wine-cellar module slung beneath the opposite wing had been sacrificed for the *Da Vinci*'s stores.

The sled's aft nozzle pivoted as soon as its forward jets puffed a second time. The sled's nose dipped as it came to a stop, then began drifting backwards. One of the astronauts spidered to the rear of the sled.

The aft muzzle spat. A snake of fog exploded from the fuel tank as it ruptured. The snake struck the closest astronaut; he rocketed off the sled, slamming the tail of the *Deduction*, and ricocheted into space.

The sled tumbled twice before crashing into the container.

FIVE

"Mayday! Mayday! The sled just rammed a container," Paula screamed into her microphone. The echo inside her helmet was deafening.

The upended sled bounced off the container, flinging oxygen tanks and tools. A screwdriver embedded itself in the flank of the whale. The arms of the sled's pilot flailed. The fuel tank sprayed itself empty, tumbling the sled around to bang into the container again before slowly rolling away starboard.

Paula contorted, trying, failing, jerking again before finally grasping her personal propulsion unit hanging from the rear of her tool belt. Her hand fumbled, wasting more time before she could attach the unit first to her suit's wrist ring, then to her belt.

"What the hell was that?" Taylor asked.

"The *Glory*'s sled rammed us," she replied. "Get some help out here. We have casualties."

She fought her panicked panting. Should she go after the sled or the free-flying astronaut? Easy choice. The sled's pilot had the best chance of surviving on his own. Unclipping one end of the safety line looped around the tether, she computed the path of the astronaut spinning away from the *Deduction*.

"What do you mean? Rammed? What's happening out there?" A burst of weak static made Javier's voice comic.

"The sled wrecked. Get help out here, NOW!"

A personal propulsion unit (PPU) was little more than twenty-centimeter-thick pipe studded with a handle and straps, filled with pressurized waste gas. Paula angled the PPU's muzzle clear of herself, pointed its bright orange tip well in front of the path of the spinning astronaut, and squeezed the trigger. Her arm felt as if the PPU had wrenched it out of the socket before she released the trigger.

Damn, she thought, looking at the gauge. She'd exhausted half of the PPU's gas on a single burst. *Slow and steady,* she told herself; she didn't have time to waste. More accurately, the flying astronaut didn't have the time for her to waste.

"What's happening out there?" asked Javier.

"Dammit, I declared a Mayday! Hit the alarm. Get our people out here! We have one casualty on the sled and one thrown free. I'm going after the free-flyer."

"NO! We have no signal from your suit. I cannot track you. You—"

"Shut up and get somebody out here, Javier!"

Paula's eyes darted to the bar of miniature gauges beneath a magnifying lens that ran along the inner jaw of her helmet—three hours of air, almost that much juice in her batteries. She checked her tool belt; a sigh of relief escaped when she touched a boxy flashlight, the perfect way to signal a rescue sled should things go wrong.

A glimmer caught her attention. She twisted to look behind her. The polished metal clip at the end of her trailing safety line sparkled from the sun's reflection.

She scanned ahead, her hands tightening on the PPU automatically.

"Oh shit, I've lost him."

Her stomach cramped. How could the astronaut have vanished?

"Repeat your message, Paula. Your signal is breaking up," said Javier. Behind his voice, an alarm bellowed.

She twisted, eyes squinting. Where was the man? Could he have changed course? Could he have used his own PPU without her seeing it? She had not looked away for more than a few seconds.

Paula recalled the time she had smashed against the hull of the *Deduction*. Her head had rammed against the inside of the helmet so hard it bruised the entire right side of her face. Damn near knocked her out. Of course, she'd had a safety line to prevent her flying off while she was stunned.

The astronaut was probably unconscious. That eliminated his using a PPU.

"I've lost sight of him," she said, trying to keep the panic from her voice. "Javier, is our radar working yet? I need a fix on him."

"Nothing is working," he replied.

"Then I'm staying on this course." What choice did she have? Her ears kept abrading as she turned her head violently within the helmet, hoping to glimpse the floater. How had he disappeared?

Her mind crunched the math. Was she moving faster than he was? Since she led the target liberally, the astronaut probably wasn't to her left. She concentrated on the vast expanse of space to her right. Nothing. Up and down. Nothing.

What if the ricochet angle she guessed was wrong? What if he'd hit something else, careening like a billiard ball? Perhaps one of the solar panels?

"Dammit!" she screamed in frustration.

"Jasmine, get the hell back to the ship!" demanded Ten Carl.

"Stop bothering me, I'm busy."

"Jasmine, I—"

"Has someone gotten to the sled yet? Don't let the rescuers forget to take extra PPUs before they leave our airlock."

Releasing the PPU, she noticed it tugging on the straps connecting it to her suit. Paula grasped it again. Only then did she notice a tiny stream of gas still spewing from its muzzle. She rapped its side. The stream ceased.

"Doesn't *anything* work right?" She fought the urge to scream again.

She unclipped and turned on the flashlight, hoping a few stray photons would illuminate the victim's white spacesuit. Nothing. Cursing the idea, she rued wasting more time. Sunlight alone should make the suit easily visible.

Her mind raced. If the leak had accelerated her too much, where would the victim now be?

She reversed the PPU, fired the remainder of its charge to slow herself. The shiny clip and safety line soared past her, jerking backwards after the line went taut. She threw her hand up to protect her visor. The clip smacked into her wrist. She fought not to yelp. Contorting, she grabbed her second and last PPU from the back of her tool belt. Another quick burst left her motionless. This time, she seized the clip and attached it to her tool belt.

What if he was in the tiny cone of shadow from the *Deduction*? More flashlight shining. No sign.

How?

If his oxygen tank had ruptured, it would act as a giant PPU. No, the tanks were too sturdy for that. She swung the light. All that gas and humidity would leave a trail. There was no trace of icy fog.

She stared until her eyes throbbed. Futile. The wait seemed endless. When Doctor Duncan reported that the helmet of the sled pilot had cracked like a lobster at dinner, Paula fired her PPU in short bursts for a slow return to the *Deduction*.

Paula kept telling herself that the victim's tumble must have carried him kilometers away by then. There was nothing she could do.

Over the next few days, sleds searched non-stop. She relieved Taylor of all other duties except repairing the radar. Even when it finally came on-line, it showed nothing.

The victim was never found.

Captain Tanaka thanked her, reassuring her that she had done everything humanly possible for his crew.

It did not stop her nightmares.

SIX

Paula crawled over the stubby fins of the whale ship, searching for damage inflicted by the collision. The wings didn't support the containers, despite that illusion. Beams had been welded to the frame of the hull just below the wings from which to attach the long, narrow cargo boxes. They were necessary because of another illusion, the cargo's weightlessness in space. It retained all its original inertia, and a high-speed manoeuvre still had to contend with the twenty-five-ton containers' desire to continue flying in their original direction. The wings could have never survived such stress.

She checked slowly, carefully, the way she thought a captain should.

In her nightmares since the crash, she piloted the doomed sled. During the third such dream, in the instant before she crashed, the instant before she died, Paula had realized what she should have done: maxed the aft throttle, giving the pressurized propellant someplace else to go. The thrust would have dolphined the sled over the wing with millimeters to spare.

Instead, the pilot had cut the power, fearing an explosion. As if that could have been worse.

The crash had taken a scant four seconds in reality. In her nightmares, it went on for horror-filled minutes.

She used her mirror in combination with a flashlight to check the underside of the wing where it was obscured by the dinted container. Nothing too damaged. The latches connecting the box to the beams were bent beyond repair.

"We'll leave it attached to the beams when we reach Mars orbit. We were going to torch the beams off anyway. Later, we can free the container. Easy fix."

Seemed sage to check the other units. A real captain took no chances with the safety of her crew.

The container closest to the hull had a black box atop it, flush against the aft support beam. She followed its wires along the beam to an open access plate in the hull. That wasn't right. There should be no open plates.

Again, she deployed her mirror, exploring the interior of the access. The mystery device was sucking power straight from their solar cells. She produced her multimeter, running it through a dozen modes. A familiar electromagnetic pattern, that lazy M, appeared on the meter's screen.

"Our ship is jamming itself," she muttered.

Anger flared. She jerked the wiring harness from the box.

Floating to the end of her safety line, she pondered the angles. The black box could have been installed by any number of workers on the ISS while they were attaching the containers. It could have been installed by one of her own crew, or one of the other ships' crews, under the guise of inspecting the tether.

It could have been placed there by the Easter Bunny, for all she knew.

She floated, trying to fit the pieces of the puzzle together. Failing that, she decided to go inside and make certain the jamming had ended. The villain would eventually come out to see what was wrong with the black box. He or she would replace the wiring harness. When the jamming resumed, Paula merely had to find out who wasn't inside their ship.

"Then I will pound the scum with my hammer. Easy fix."

When she reached the bridge of the *Deduction*, sure enough, the jamming of their communications had ceased. She studied Taylor, her hatred of the dapper man making it easy to believe he was the saboteur. He did not show a sign of guilt.

* * *

Despite the storm damage, the fleet made Mars orbit. Barely. Captain Tanaka stubbornly refused the boss's invitation to come aboard the *Tax Deduction* and abandon the crippled shuttle. The *Nippon Glory* caught the slot high, nearly skipping off the tenuous atmosphere on a course to Pluto. By the second orbit, it was three hundred klicks behind and thirty-five klicks above the other two ships. A compensating burn drained the last of the shuttle's fuel; though the shuttle descended to the fleet's altitude, it lagged behind by ninety kilometers.

By contrast, the *Da Vinci*—once the tether was released—stayed close to the flagship, despite its ravaged flight control systems. Pilot Cardenas plastered himself outside his ship and fired the engines by hand. Control damage precluded their landing craft *De Soto*'s detaching from the mothership in order to fulfill its designed destiny.

It took a full week for the *Deduction* to drop its eight cargo containers and unite them to form the first Martian space station. The beams that had held the containers in place became the spine of the station. The original plan had called for some of the *Da Vinci*'s and *Deduction*'s generous array of instruments to be transferred aboard the station, making it a powerful platform for scientific observation and experimentation, as well as knitting together the fourteen satellites already in Mars orbit into a single network. Alas, most of the array had been destroyed or scavenged for parts.

Much to Paula's irritation, the black box—now on the hull of the station—went unnoticed and untouched. Indeed, no one reacted when she finally removed the other end of the cable and sealed the access panel.

Supplies were ferried from the containers to the ships, and unnecessary material transferred to the station. Fuel, flown via sled to the *Glory*, allowed the shuttle to rejoin the fleet at the end of the week. The shuttle docked with the station, retired after its long journey. The rest of the surplus fuel was pumped into the *Deduction*.

Captain Tanaka accepted Ten Carl's offer to join the landing of the *Tax Deduction*, lured by the honour of being the first human to step on Mars. An altar of photographs and possessions of his lost crew was prepared by Tanaka to place on the historic site.

Captain DeJung brought her current lover, Miguel Cardenas, aboard the *Deduction*, declaring they would be the EU landing party. Immediately, the two remaining aboard the *Da Vinci* began dispatching protests about being left in orbit. Sexual abuse. Chauvinism. Sexism. Racism. Classism. The accusations against DeJung invoked every sin, then created new ones. The poet Ofelia Salamanca sent her rhymed verse protests in no fewer than eight languages.

The night before the landing, DeJung argued with Cardenas. The crew watched with amusement while the captain punched her lover into the airlock. DeJung smacked the controls, closing the inner hatch and starting the evacuation of the chamber's air.

Diving, Paula knocked her aside, nulling the program before the outer hatch opened. Cardenas sprang to his feet inside the airlock. It did not require a Nostradamus to see his future. He started donning his suit in lightning mode.

DeJung flew at Paula in the zero gravity. Paula dodged her fellow captain at the last instant, throwing an elbow into her gut. Momentum caused Paula's forehead to collide with the bulkhead. Paula staggered from knees back to her feet, pushing off to bounce in the zero gravity, shaking her bloody head.

"You have no right!" DeJung's fist cut the air; its miss sent her into a tumble.

Paula wiped blood on her sleeve, pulling a hammer from her tool belt. "This is my ship. I decide who goes out the airlock." She glowered so hard that DeJung backed away, her motion slamming her against a table. With a shout of fury, she threw herself down the corridor.

An hour after Cardenas returned to his ship, Salamanca came aboard the *Deduction*, only to vanish into DeJung's makeshift cabin in the cargo hold. The poet's vocal lovemaking increased the entertainment value.

Ten Carl floated into the open doorway of Paula's cabin. He wore a robe drawn tight over his spreading paunch. Doctor Duncan floated behind him, wearing naught but a pair of socks. Her hair fought to free itself from a net that she continually adjusted. Puffy eyes hinted the doctor had been self-medicating again.

Paula toed the ragged gym bag under her bunk as casually as she could before resuming her long squint at the chip-plate. Her eyes burned from reading the landing procedure on the tiny screen of the handheld computer. The poet's screams of passion kept making her lose her place.

"Captain Caudill, are you ever tempted to bag one of our crew?" He laughed as he stroked the doctor's back.

"Bag? Where do you learn your slang, boss? Paleolithic TV?" She placed her chip-plate over her bunk, watched it float in the zero-gee before snugging it under the blanket.

"Why do you keep calling me boss?"

"That's what my daddy called the billionaire he worked for."

She didn't tell him that her father's employer was always a capital-B Boss because Jay Lawrence Caudill had respected, even admired, the madman despite his faults; whereas her reference would forever be lower-case, since Ten Carl was not a person to be admired.

From down the corridor, Taylor yelled, "Can you people be quiet? I'm trying to get to sleep. Quiet, dammit!"

"Hey, you didn't answer my question," said Ten Carl. "Are you ever tempted? I've seen how Taylor looks at you."

"Why would any sane woman look at Pretty Boy twice? He'd rather be in bed with a mirror."

"A little flesh wallow is a nice way to pass time." Ten Carl pulled the floating doctor closer, pawing her breasts. She went as stiff as a surfboard, except where her hands fussed with her hair. Jasmine suspected Duncan didn't notice the lack of gravity.

"Maybe not as much fun as poker, but—" He guffawed. "C'mon, Jasmine, we beat them. We've won this game. Relish it while you can."

"Why did you have to make me the captain?"

She flashed back to the poker game that had made her captain. Paula had been tempted to fold, since Ten Carl had a pair of queens showing against her pair of eights. But only half her winnings rested in the pot, so she'd stayed in the game while Taylor and Duncan opted out. The next deal had given her a third eight.

Had the game been part of that dual-edged Caudill luck?

"I deal with winners. That's the secret of my success."

"Winners?" she asked. "That doesn't explain Pretty Boy. He's never needed to be a winner. Taylor has only been served up the golden best on his family's sterling silver platters."

"You know why I selected Taylor? I have six, seven pilots on my staff, but my public relations firm said Taylor was the most photogenic. Cameras love that face. He got us extra coverage when the media might have otherwise grown jaded with our story."

"It wasn't because he was the son of a senator?"

"Always a cynic, Jasmine." Ten Carl grinned at the poet's scream to God and the proper application of teeth.

"Cynics are made by the times in which they live, not to mention what they have to do for a living."

Ten Carl laughed, then stared aft at the canvas walls of DeJung's cabin. He wiped dust off a bottle of wine in the pocket of his robe. "Do you have a cork-screw?"

"I'm certain DeJung will."

The billionaire launched toward the lovers' cabin. Doctor Duncan tried to smile before pushing off the wall, floating after her lover. The boss had stuck a "Kick Me" sign on her back.

Paula returned to reading landing procedure on her chip-plate, but couldn't concentrate. The celebration cast bizarre echoes.

Her mind kept returning to the Burns. She wondered how the couple was faring in prison; wondered if they had really been planning to add her to their secret graveyard. She had truly believed them when they said they loved her.

Most of all, she wondered what was wrong with her. None of her relation-ships had been half as good as the two months she had spent with those murder-ers.

That damned Caudill luck.

Now she would enter the history books as the captain of the first ship to land on Mars.

She swallowed hard, wondering if the Caudill luck had exhausted its ill side.

SEVEN

Ten Carl stood, giving a short, thoroughly stupid address about making history. He said nothing about the expedition being a stunt. Paula hoped Ten Carl didn't know his own motivations. Maybe he was that blind.

"Put your helmet on," Paula said to Duncan.

The doctor sighed, patting her hair down one last time before gingerly slipping the helmet on. After sealing and checking her internal monitors, Duncan motioned at her throat. Paula pulled a roll of duct tape from her tool belt and slapped a few strips across the helmet's seal.

"You wouldn't have this problem if you had kept the helmet attached to the dorsal unit," Paula said. "You weren't supposed to remove it."

The doctor ignored her.

Paula fidgeted with the gym bag on her lap. It didn't feel safe there. More duct tape attached the bag under her left armpit, much to the amusement of the rest of the crew.

One minute after midnight, Greenwich Mean Time, on the fifteenth of December, 2029, pilot Taylor drained a glass of champagne and closed his visor; whereupon the pilot dropped the *Tax Deduction* into the gravity well of Mars with a thirty-second burst from the engines. Two further burns kept the ship in the slot while it plunged through the atmosphere.

Intense vibrations caused Paula to bite her tongue. When the explosive bolts on the heat shields blew them away from the ship, the *Deduction* jumped as if the whale were sliding sideways on ice. The shaking grew worse.

Paula screamed when the vibrations abruptly stopped as the ship assumed a more aerodynamic form. Ten Carl bellowed like a drunken soccer fan whose team was winning the World Cup. For the final leg of the journey, the *Deduction* flew as an eagle, not a whale. Taylor made two flyovers of the landing site before committing to touchdown.

The official log read that twelve meters off the ground, the port wing suffered terminal stress fractures.

(—*Ironic*, she later tapped to her cohorts on Earth via Morse code. —*The wing that was* not *damaged in the crash with the sled failed.*)

When the wing tore off, Paula thought the whale was landing on its skids. Of course, they did land, though not as planned. The *Deduction* hit the ground, skewed; the aft cargo section tore asunder. The tail made a big bounce after ripping free. The other wing plowed into the rocky surface and disintegrated. A two-meter shard of titanium knifed through the fuselage, tearing Duncan in half, missing her hair.

The tip of the bloody shard brushed Paula's helmet. It had been and gone seconds before she reacted. When she tried to scream, her lungs were already empty.

The *Deduction* surfed two full kilometers, shedding pieces every centimeter of the way. They slid to a stop within 300 meters of the planned landing site.

"We made it," said Paula, amazed she was alive.

The *Tax Deduction*'s shuddering frame split lengthways, each half collapsing sideways, like the opening of a rare blossom.

Paula's visor darkened before the anemic noon sunlight flooding over her. Shadows consumed her, leaving her trembling until her eyes adjusted. Glancing behind her, Paula muttered in awe as the wind carried their dust plume away. It was as thick and tall as a hurricane.

By instinct, she released her harness. As she dropped, Paula recalled the gym bag. With the speed of a cat, she twisted, smashing hard onto her other side. The impact hurt her shoulder. The pain reminded Paula she was the captain. Perhaps it was merely the whim of a mad billionaire, but she was the captain. Responsible.

"People! Talk to me," she shouted into her helmet's microphone.

She staggered from the wreckage. Her boots sinking centimeters into the Martian grit nearly caused her to fall. It shocked her to be out of the ship so quickly.

"Damn it, people, talk to me, NOW!"

"It's unbecoming for a captain to sound so...so excited," said Ten Carl.

She saw his squat form crawling over a segment of the shattered hull, sliding to the Martian soil which puffed into a cloud. The boss held his left arm against his side.

Taylor stood atop his seat, a goodly ten meters removed from the nearest bit of wreckage. Paula could tell by his dance that he was celebrating his miraculous survival, but his suit radio was not operating.

Directly ahead of the *Deduction* clustered the four unmanned units that NASA had sent to Mars. Mars City, the press had called it. City? Paula thought. More like a trailer park. The structures looked so tiny in the vast landscape dyed a dullish pink by her tinted faceplate.

The two habitat modules reminded her of oil-storage tanks. Launched eight years ago, before NASA lost funding during the Depression of 2021, the units looked new. The two Earth Return Vehicles (ERVs) were elongated cones atop towering, automated Sabatier factories which inhaled the carbon dioxide atmosphere, combining it with hydrogen brought from Earth, in order to manufacture methane and oxygen. The two gases would fuel the ERVs home. In contrast to the habitats, the factories appeared worn, their aluminium hulls pitted and their nooks piled with sand.

A robotic cart rolled toward the *Tax Deduction*. Its camera, atop a long mechanical arm, panned the wreckage. The robots had been passengers aboard the habitats. Over the years, they had explored the area and conducted environmental research.

Paula knew the ISS orbiting Earth would receive the pictures in forty minutes or so. No way would their faceless enemies jam this signal.

"Report to me, dammit!" she shouted over the radio. Returning to the wreck, she tossed a girder out of her way, feeling superhuman, a force of nature.

Taylor bounded to Ten Carl's side. What a toady, she thought, always trying to impress the boss.

Captain DeJung fought with her cargo-net seat—they had used the nets to accommodate the extra passengers. Reaching into her tool belt, Paula produced a switchblade, another heirloom from her father. She cut her fellow captain from the restraints. DeJung rabbited from the wreck.

Paula continued to the next passenger, the poet, inside another cargo-net co-coon. The woman was unconscious, but the readings aglow inside Salamanca's helmet told Paula the woman was okay. Leaving the poet hanging, Paula contin-ued to the next seat.

Javier stirred. His visor was cracked, but not leaking. Just to be safe, Paula slapped an adhesive patch over the crack. She pulled him upright, caught him when he fell. She inspected his suit. Fine. After a few minutes, he reeled toward the party outside.

Tanaka limped from his net to help Paula carry the unconscious poet from the wreck; but not before he tsked his disapproval at her switchblade hacking away the net.

"That knife is a treaty violation. No weapons of war are allowed on Mars."

"It's a tool, you twit."

"Define it as a rock, it is still a weapon."

"Rocks are weapons, too. I—"

"Any landing you walk away from is a good one," interjected Ten Carl. He laughed. "Besides, we planned to take the ERVs home anyway."

"Captain Tanaka," Paula said, using her most authoritative voice, "take Taylor and help the rest of them into a habitat module. DeJung, you are with me. We need to make contact with the *Da Vinci* and the ISS and Earth and anybody else who might be listening. You take the Earth Return Vehicle on the left; I will take the ERV on the right."

"Who are you to order—" Captain DeJung shut up as Paula wiped her blade on the sleeve of DeJung's spacesuit.

It pleased Paula how much she sounded like a real captain. Not a poker winner. Not an accidental leader. Not a Caudill loser. She could almost see her father smiling.

Paula climbed the ladder on the side of the towering factory below the ERV— ten cylindrical storage tanks surrounding and protecting the Sabatier reactor. Ice dotted the ladder, hinting at a leak within the buried works of the methane/oxygen factory. One of the rungs was broken. *Not too shabby,* she thought, considering how long the ships had waited for people.

The hatch of the return vehicle refused to open. Grabbing a hammer from her ubiquitous tool belt, Paula pounded around the lip of the airlock before trying the controls again. It opened slowly. She crawled through the narrow aperture. *Damn NASA,* she thought; how expensive could it have been to make the hatch larger? *Bless NASA,* she thought, seeing a line of lightweight Mars-suits hanging from a rack, one of the details the boss had overlooked in his haste to leave Earth.

As soon as she closed the outer hatch, lights blinked on. Peering through the window of the inner hatch, she watched system after system activate inside the seven-passenger capsule.

She slipped into the pilot's seat, plugging a radio cord into her helmet. The communications system came on-line.

"This is Captain Paula J. Caudill of the *Tax Deduction*. Humanity is now a two-planet species," she said. "Please respond."

A few minutes later, she listened to the Dutch captain begin a speech that would last a full hour. Paula switched to the frequency used by *Da Vinci*. Two messages to her orbital companions went unanswered.

Paula explored the ERV. When the sensors declared the capsule fully active, she opened her visor a crack. The air tasted dusty. The bathroom was astonishingly luxurious and functioned perfectly. She stripped. The petite shower worked as well as the toilet. She luxuriated under the non-rationed flow. Supply closet three held a bale of jumpsuits.

"Clean clothes at last!" A Nobel Prize could not have made her happier. The fact that she had to roll up the sleeves and legs of the jumpsuit for it to fit did not diminish her delight.

She opened the food stores, finding the usual rations. She gobbled two military-issued MREs.

Playing with the controls, she eventually found the intercom function. "Caudill to habitat, is this working?"

"Jasmine, we've been trying to raise you for half an hour. Is everything okay?" asked the boss.

"Fine," she replied. "How are things over there?"

"Better than I expected. There was a crate of Merlot waiting for me. How's that for hospitality?"

"How are Javier and Whatshername, the poet?"

"Excellent. Tanaka set my broken arm like a first-class doctor. No pain whatsoever."

The mention of the word "doctor" cramped her stomach. "I...I'm sorry about Duncan. She didn't suffer."

"I'm okay."

He said it with such enthusiasm that Paula hated him. Had Doctor Duncan meant so little to the heartless bastard?

"Have everybody stand down," she ordered.

"Stand down? Are we in the military now?"

"Don't hassle me, boss. We all need a solid eight hours' sleep before we do anything." She switched to the radio, sighed as the DeJung continued her speech with a digression about the mercantile system in the sixteenth century.

On her second try to the *Da Vinci*, Paula got a modulated storm of static. She fiddled with the frequency.

"Caudill? What is the bitch doing? We are getting interference from her broadcast," said Cardenas.

"It's *Captain* Caudill. The landing went well," she lied. She listened to another catalogue of DeJung abuse suffered by the orbiting duo. They insisted their protests must be relayed to Earth immediately. She agreed, another lie.

A few minutes later, the first message from Earth arrived via the massive ISS broadcast array. "The government of the United States of America has seized the assets of Ten Carl Richards until such time as we can assess the damage the expedition is doing to our government's property on Mars."

Hitting the intercom, she informed the boss. He laughed hysterically.

"Spending forty-two of my own billions on this vacation was an experience unparalleled by another human being this century. I'm history now. Do they really think I care about the billion or two I left behind? I'll earn twice that the first day I'm back home."

His laughter grew so shrill, it frightened her.

Paula decided not to return to the habitat. Instead, she curled up on the pilot's seat and went to sleep. As she dropped off, she would have sworn she heard her father laughing.

EIGHT

The following weeks were a blur to Paula. She slaved sixteen hours a day on an endless parade of chores.

The fractious crew ignored her orders to scavenge what they could from the wreckage of the *Tax Deduction*. DeJung claimed Paula had no authority over her, since she was a fellow captain. Javier avoided Paula altogether. The poet announced she had not been dispatched to Mars to be a slave, but to create art.

Ten Carl refused to support her. "You must learn to assert yourself, Jasmine. This will be a good character-building lesson for you."

Upon hearing that, Taylor stopped obeying her except when the boss was present.

Only Captain Tanaka picked through the wreckage with her. Yet he refused to talk. His memorial for his fallen comrades had disintegrated during the crash; she blamed that for crushing his spirit. Other than sending a terse daily report to Tokyo, he did not speak to anyone.

His silence unnerved her. Paula found herself talking nonstop as they worked.

"Daddy would've volunteered to come to Mars if there had been zero chance of getting back home. He would've done anything to get into space. Thought it was his birthright. His dream..."

It embarrassed her that no matter how hard she tried, she could not stop talking.

It also unnerved her that she could not figure out who had installed the jamming device on her ship, or why. If only she could point a finger. Doctor Duncan would have been a perfect villain, since Paula would never have suspected the junkie. DeJung or Taylor would be her favourites to blame, but really, they went out of their way to be annoying, to draw attention to themselves. No guilty person would do that. Could it be one of the orbiting duo? Or one of the dead?

What if, she fretted, it was nothing more than one of the boss's pranks? Like the time he'd sent her to London to buy antique furniture, after informing Interpol she was a drug smuggler.

A tsunami of e-mails, interview requests, and data flooded over the new Martians. Their crash insured they were even bigger news than merely the first humans on Mars. Complaints from orbit, as well as anonymous poison-pen letters against Paula and the boss, only increased the media's desire to know everything.

To insure adequate coverage and big profits from selling said coverage, NASA programmed the robot to follow them around whenever they left the habitat. Indeed, at the end of the workday, the robot came inside to film them at rest.

* * *

The boss grabbed Paula as soon as she left the airlock. "You won't believe the good news."

She pulled away. How her back ached. She tripped over the robotic cart, sprawled on the deck. "What?" she barked.

"Hold your ears, because this will blow your mind."

"Where *do* you learn your slang, boss?"

Ten Carl threw the robot into the airlock, waiting until the hatch closed. "I have a contract to write a book! Of course, you'll do the actual writing. Don't worry. I'll see you get a BIG bonus."

She got off the deck. "Wait a frigging minute, I—"

"Oh, Jasmine, there is one minor detail—we have to stay on Mars an extra twelve days."

"Are you insane? A Cray super-computer calculated our course home. Thirty days is our maximum stay on this planet, if we want to get back next year. Otherwise, we have to wait two years plus. Given our late departure from Earth orbit, we have to—"

"The ISS says our ERVs have 40% more fuel than necessary. We can fly to Earth, take a vacation on the Moon, fly to a comet, and still get home."

"I—I didn't know that." Paula made a mental note to check the boss's figures.

"Well, now you do know. ISS is refining the numbers as we speak. This is so cool, Jasmine. I know you're used to writing history, so you'll have to rid yourself of some of that scholarly attitude to write for the common folk. This will be the easiest money you've ever earned."

"Why twelve days?"

"This is so beautiful. The title of my book is *Mars on a Billion Dollars a Day*. See? I spent forty-two billion, so we have to stay forty-two days. Don't you think it's hysterical? A billion a day! School children a century from now will be reading MY book. I love this!"

"Don't you mean OUR book?"

The boss guffawed, smacking his cast into a bulkhead. "My lawyers are drawing up OUR contract. I know you're going to hear I got a hundred-million-dollar advance, but that is media hype. We're trying to generate excitement for my book. After everybody gets their shares, I'll barely clear a million. So how does eighty thousand dollars strike you? Fair?"

"If I'm going to write the book, don't I deserve the whole million? After all, you will get the royalties."

"Oh, Jasmine, don't be that way. Of course, I'll give you a big bonus as my personal historian. It's a tax thing. If it comes out of the book money, my taxes will be higher."

"Boss, I—"

"You need to send the first hundred pages to my publisher tomorrow. Big bonus. I said that, didn't I?"

* * *

One afternoon, after slaving to uncrate a rover, she entered the habitat to discover everyone save Tanaka had moved into the other habitat.

"Don't take it personally," said the boss.

"If you'd stand up for me just once—!" she yelled. Her temper was short; she was exhausted from hours of filling sandbags to stack against the habitat for further protection from the hostile environment. Perhaps it was her imagination, but she swore she could feel the cold creeping through the hull at night. And NASA had intended its astronauts to bury the habitats eventually.

"Oh, Jasmine." He waved off her comment.

"They listen to you. If you follow my lead, they—"

"Jasmine, you won the right to lead with an eight of spades, an eight of hearts, and an eight of diamonds. Now you have to show the others you deserve it."

"Then do a day's work with me. Show them you respect my orders."

"I do respect you, Jasmine. You're smart, a good historian. But I paid for this vacation, so I won't work. If you want them to treat you as a leader, make them respect you."

"Fine!" she shouted.

"How's this? I'll move back over here. That will show everyone how much I respect you."

"Lucky me."

"By the way, do you have a corkscrew? I've misplaced mine. Do you think someone could be hiding the damned thing from me? That's not a very funny joke." He wandered into the back of the habitat, smacking his forearm cast against a table.

She slammed her visor, stopping in the airlock only long enough to change her batteries and recharge her oxygen tanks. Rules were rules.

She stomped directly to the other habitat. In their—it surprised her she was already thinking of the module as "theirs"—habitat's airlock, she stripped off her Mars-suit. Her jumpsuit beneath was sweat-plastered to her body. From her tool belt she removed the switchblade, pocketing it before dropping the belt atop her Mars-suit.

The others had collected in the first-floor common room. The aroma of fresh popcorn and bubbling chili announced the imminent start of the boss's poker game. His corkscrew was on the table.

She screamed, "I lead by example. I've NEVER asked any of you to do something I wasn't willing to do myself!"

She reached Taylor first, kicked him in the nuts. "I could've broken your nose. That would break the heart of your plastic surgeon, wouldn't it, Pretty Boy?"

DeJung bellowed, charging Paula. Paula stepped aside, grabbing a double handful of hair, letting her fellow captain's momentum jerk her around.

"*Your* nose I can break." And she did. Whereupon, she rolled DeJung over her hip, slamming her onto the deck. Pulling the switchblade, Paula triggered the steel, held the edge against DeJung's pulsing throat.

"You people want to play the alpha-dog game? Well, I can bite! I command here. Any debate?"

She pressed the blade into DeJung's flesh until a thin line of blood oozed from the cut.

"Any debate?" she repeated.

There was none.

"Here's the bottom line. Tomorrow, DeJung and Taylor will start draining the tanks of the factories. Fill the empty oxygen tanks Captain Tanaka and I salvaged from the *Deduction*. Then you'll fill the reservoirs of the habitats and the rover. Salamanca—yes, YOU, poet girl—will inventory everything we've salvaged. Javier, I want you to go through the habitats for every piece of electronics we might use to get the space station operational. Are there any questions?"

"No," moaned DeJung, snaking free. She held her gushing nose.

Paula tried not to laugh. It would not be sufficiently captain-like.

NINE

As a reward for Captain Tanaka's hard work, Paula drafted him for a ride south. It first took them three hours to unload the crates packed around the rover. After they inspected the vehicle from stem to stern, it started on the first try, despite its decade-long wait inside the habitat's garage.

The rover's aft luggage bed had been designed too narrow for the cargo cases shipped with the module and factories. "Typical government planning," Paula grumbled, cursing the entire time they removed the extra oxygen and methane cannisters from their protective cases.

Tanaka merely nodded as he hoisted the metallic tubes into the rover's aft bed and secured them with netting.

Her tongue brought the helmet straw to her lips for a sip of her suit water. It was salty as sea water. Paula went inside the habitat to flush her suit's water bladder and refill it. The boss denied the saline prank, but his crooked grin told her it was one of his jokes.

While she was in the habitat, Paula rewarded herself with a quick shower. To have all the hot water in the world... It was a simple fantasy. Those were always the best. As their generator burnt methane and oxygen, every light turned on, every burrito burnt in the microwave created waste water. Wonderful, wonderful waste water.

She even treated herself to a fresh Mars-suit before returning to the rover. Compared to her old suit, it smelled of spring.

The rover crawled at ten klicks an hour, its top speed. Although the vehicle

resembled a dune buggy, it steered like a garbage truck. The route wasn't as
sandy as she'd feared; it felt like driving on a gravel road. Trouble was, there were
myriad boulders to dodge. It proved too easy to oversteer, crashing into holes and
arroyos she hadn't seen until it was too late. After dragging the rover from two
gullies—each time having to unload the cargo to lighten the load—in as many
hours, the duo got out and walked. They paused first, of course, to recharge their
oxygen and swap their battery packs.

"Just in case," she said, shouldering an extra oxygen cannister. When he
reached for another, she stopped him. "One is plenty. There's no reason to be
paranoid."

A few kliks later, they encountered an overturned robot. They righted the
machine, cleaned its solar cells. Within minutes, its batteries were recharging.
With a lurch and a happy hum, the cart scurried toward Mars City. She waved as
its camera panned backwards. They continued marching south.

"I do not understand the point of this," said Tanaka. "Why did we salvage the
robot? Does Earth need more pictures of Taylor's constant preening? Now there
will be two robots following him like puppies."

She grinned, happy she had finally gotten him to speak. It was almost enough
to make her forget that dull ache growing in her shoulder from lugging the cannister. Just her luck; after she'd refused his offer to carry it six times, Tanaka had
stopped offering. She was too proud to ask for his help after that.

Sweat poured down her torso, making her Mars-suit reek worse than she
dreamed possible. *Clean so few minutes ago,* Paula rued. It didn't seem fair.

"Six robots landed with the habitats," she explained. "Four of them were sent
after the first robot that traveled this way. NASA claimed they were all lost during
routine exploration."

"Claimed?" he asked.

"Nothing a scientist hates worse than appearing foolish. The first robot found
'possible' signs of life at the bottom of a crater. It took pictures and samples, but
failed to return to Mars City. The other robots never reached the site. Imagine
what would have happened if a robot scouting team back on Earth announced they
had found life, then it turned out to be a Martian rust stain. The scientists couldn't
take the career risk."

"Washington cut their funding anyway. They should have gambled. It might
have saved the Mars program."

"I agree," she said.

"How did you find out about this discovery?"

"One of the ex-members of the RST—the Robot Scouting Team—sold the
information to the boss. The pictures sucked, but the telemetry gave us a perfect
road map."

She stopped, checking her chip-plate for their position. It was only five more
kliks. She unslung the cannister before attaching a hose to refill her tanks. Once
her companion had done the same, they hiked without the tank.

The crater was unimposing, eroded over countless millennia into little more
than a depression in the rocky ground. They nearly walked by it without noticing.
The inner surface appeared sturdy, but her first step over the rim caused a slide of

debris. Had Tanaka not grabbed her, she would have tumbled to the bottom.

"There and there," he said, pointing at small mounds at the bottom of the crater. A wheel was clearly visible, half buried in one. The other mound sported a broken solar panel like a tombstone.

"At least we know why the robot didn't return."

Producing a rope from her tool belt, she attached it to a rock. Paula led the way down the wall of the crater. With the rope to steady them, it proved to be an easy descent.

She recognized the boulder near the bottom immediately from the grainy photographs Ten Carl had showed her. The crevice hid behind the boulder. Crevice, it appeared in pictures, since nothing else gave the views a scale for comparison. Crack was more like it, she mused, barely two meters long and thirty centimeters wide at the top. Shining a flashlight, she found it less than a meter deep.

"Captain Tanaka, our crash cheated you of being the first human on the surface of Mars. So I want you to have the opportunity to discover the first native life-form."

It made her feel proud to see the look of surprise on his face.

She stepped back from the crack, handing him the flashlight, a small camera, and a wad of sterilized baggies inside a large manila envelope. Paula tried not to peer over his shoulder as he sank to his hands and knees, but she failed. The light played over alternating layers of dark and light stone; small knobs dotted the layers, their putrid yellow-greenish colour darkening as the light changed its angles.

"Could it be algae?" he asked. The camera flashed a dozen times. He handed it back to Paula. She slipped it into a pouch dangling from her tool belt.

"Not likely, living in the shadows. If it is a life-form, it must be getting its nourishment from the rocks. What's that narrow stratum above the growths? Sulphur?"

"I do not know. Hayamura was our geologist."

And Doctor Duncan was our only biologist, Paula didn't say, despairing at the prospect of not being able to do the science on the growths. Maybe Earth could coach them through the necessary tests.

He held up one of the baggies he had used to engulf and scrape off a knob. "It feels spongy." The second time he squeezed, a puff of material exploded from it.

"Spores," she yelped. "Fungus is the only thing I know that blows up into spores like that."

"If it is indeed sporing. It could be a fragile mineral. A crystal, perhaps."

"Mineral deposits don't spore. It must be alive!"

"If it is indeed sporing," he repeated.

He took more samples, then returned the baggies to the envelope before sealing it carefully.

Paula hurrahed. She told Tanaka, "As their discoverer, you have the right to name the species. This is better than an altar for your crew."

"That would be most fitting," was all he said.

They returned to the rover in silence. How could he plod like that? she wondered. People walking to the gallows had more enthusiasm.

Paula kept breaking into dance, leaping into the air to make huge puffs of grit when she landed, until they reached the cannister. Though she ached, she couldn't leave it behind, so she looped some rope through its handles and dragged it.

Life. She tried to remember whether anything spored besides fungus. That was a pretty complex life-form. What else might live on this planet?

She recalled lectures from her father as he drove her to soccer practice. He'd claimed that finding the humblest bacterium native to another planet would mean life was everywhere in the universe. Her father's voice had trembled with the implication as he spoke, not unlike the way she trembled now.

Until she actually saw the fungus, Paula had thought the low resolution pictures from the robot were nothing. Bringing Tanaka to the crater had been a sop for his morale. Now she had no doubt. Life!

"Once this news hits the media, the politicians of Earth will open the public wallet to find that one-tenth of one percent of their military budgets to send expeditions to Mars. Real scientists with real ships that won't disintegrate upon landing."

Real ships, asked the nagging doubt within her, *like the* Da Vinci? *Not fair,* countered the voice of her father. The EU's ship had not been slated to fly for another three years; it had been a miracle the engineers could get the craft into space in mere months. The *De Soto* lander had originally been designed to deliver robots to Mars, not humans.

Life would beget government funds. Funds would create ships capable of laughing in the face of a solar hurricane. Indeed, their experience with storm damage was already being used on Earth to design sturdier ships.

"We are going to launch a new age of exploration, of greatness for humanity!" she shouted while dancing her joy, until the cannister pulled her back to reality with a jerk.

Tanaka nodded.

Upon reaching the rover, they changed batteries and refilled their Mars-suits from the spare cannisters. As the rover idled, it rolled forward a few meters, revealing a rime of frost that had formed beneath the vehicle. Like the habitats' generators, the rover created water as exhaust waste. Paula pulled a wrench from her tool belt and tightened the hose connecting the exhaust pipe to the water-collection tank.

Tanaka cleaned his visor, brushed dust off his seat, then wrapped the cloth around the vital envelope, which he held in front of him like a sacred icon.

They listened to a radio message from DeJung stating that she had discovered a problem with one of the methane/oxygen factories and was commencing repairs.

"You have to give the woman credit—she can fix anything," said Paula. "I always thought I was good with my hands, but she's a marvel. You see, my mother was hopeless with home repairs, but she was too cheap to hire someone. I was fixing lamps and toilets by the time I was ten."

Fighting the urge to speed back, she drove slowly, remembering the hours they had wasted pulling the clumsy rover from gullies. Wind had already eradicated their tracks. Since Mars lacked a magnetic field worth the name, there was no compass to help. Instead, she followed a radio beacon from Mars City. The dust clouds they raised frequently overtook them, forcing them to stop until visibility returned.

They topped the rise marking the southern border of the Isidis Planitia. A quartz boulder the size of a house glittered, a difficult landmark to miss. She sang to herself, smacking the steering wheel to keep time. She had to hit the brakes to avoid a boulder that seemingly appeared from nowhere.

Driving on, she said, "Our landing disaster is nothing now. Life is the Grail, the juice that makes the galaxy go around. Captain, we've opened up new chapter of humanity."

"Perhaps," was all Tanaka said.

It made her wish she could stop talking. She tried. It made her stomach feel like it was filled with fighting cats. Finally she allowed herself to resume singing.

Glimpsing the flashing beacon of Mars City in the distance, she juiced the throttle forward. A few klicks later, they reached the furrow of the *Deduction*'s crash; the tail section stood like a piece of surreal art.

Like a headstone, she tried not to think.

A thump. Her chest rammed the steering wheel. The left front wheel broke free, bouncing away at a right angle to the rover. The shattered axle hit the ground. Sand spewed. The rover skewed. The rear of the vehicle rose. She hit the steering wheel again as she fought to jump free, convinced the vehicle was going to flip over and crush them. Then the rover regained a friendlier center of gravity and slammed into the ground on its three wheels.

The nice thing about driving at six klicks per hour was that the jarring wreck was hardly jarring and barely a wreck, especially for survivors of a craft that had hit Mars at fifty times that speed.

Tanaka grunted as he hopped out of the rover.

"I didn't see that rock," she said. It angered her to sound so defensive.

"Neither did I," he replied. His inspection of the damage lasted seconds.

As soon as she stopped shaking, Paula exited. She pointed at the cannisters in the back of the rover.

"You do not need to remind me." He walked to the rear of the rover. Attaching a line to the oxygen cannister, he topped off his backpack.

"At least we're close to—"

She felt the slightest of vibrations through the skin of her Mars-suit. She turned around in time to see the factory closest to the habitats spout a flame, a delicate rose of fire. It blew a perfectly round smoke ring at the other factory. She wiped the dust off her visor in disbelief, grabbed the binoculars out of the rover.

A figure ran toward the nearest habitat. A second one squirmed from beneath the factory, knocking over a toolbox, bellyflopping onto the ground.

The factory exploded like fireworks, hurling ten-meter-tall storage tanks filled with hydrogen, methane, and oxygen. One flying cylinder impaled the other factory. Another cylinder rammed a habitat, tearing a long gash in the structure before breaking in half. One of the halves vanished inside the habitat.

A second blast annihilated the methane/oxygen factory, sending its ERV tumbling across the plain. Scores of debris plumes puffed like mushrooms. *Their* habitat crumpled as if made of foil before disappearing inside a dust cloud.

Paula forgot to breathe. She almost sobbed in relief that the second factory appeared okay, despite the cylinder spearing it.

"We can repair that," she whispered.

The second factory exploded. The spacecraft atop it rose, catching the sun in a tremendous glint. She thought someone might have launched the ERV to escape the conflagration.

"Go, go, go-o-o!"

Whereupon their last hope of escaping the red planet detonated a thousand meters above Mars City.

TEN

"As captain, it is your duty to...to euthanize the hopeless," said Ten Carl, waving his forearm cast like a baton.

Paula duct-taped a plate over a hole in the wall of the habitat. She opened her mouth, then closed it, tightened her fist, then opened it, deciding the easiest thing would be to ignore him.

Figures, she mused, *the only person in Mars City untouched by the disaster would be the boss.* Billionaires, by definition, possessed solid-gold luck. Ten Carl had been in the airlock of "her" habitat, furthest from the blasts, trying on light-weight Mars-suits he had looted from one of the ERVs. He'd hoped to find one that fit, since he had gained eighteen kilos during the trip. Thinking the explosions were Marsquakes, he hadn't bothered to investigate. Instead, he'd casually exercised his sartorial imperatives while chaos reigned.

At least, she thought, Captain Tanaka had volunteered to bury the rest of the expedition. Bless him. She could not bear to add more of her crew to Duncan's graveyard.

Several of the habitat's solar panels had been damaged; she had turned off the methane-powered electric generator until they could measure their supplies. As a result, she worked in the twilight of dim lightstrips. Dark as her soul, she fancied.

"This is NOT my fault," the boss said abruptly.

"Poor Javier didn't want to be here, boss. He was scared of his own shadow, but you wouldn't stop pestering him, wouldn't stop bribing him until he came with us," she grumbled.

This could not be the fault of the infamous Caudill luck, she prayed. That only killed Caudills. It had never slaughtered innocents.

Not her fault. *What a pathetic mantra,* she thought. She was as bad as the boss.

"He knew the risks," replied Ten Carl. "We all knew the risks."

"Risks? All Javier cared about was earning more for his children on this expedition than he could in three lifetimes working for you." She coughed the knot from her throat. "What am I going to tell his family?"

"I made certain he had good life insurance, and his full salary is in an escrow account. His family are millionaires now."

"He was the only one of our crew who had kids. Do you think his son and daughters will enjoy the swap—wealth for their father?"

"Of course they will." He stepped deeper into the shadows.

"What?"

"Money heals all wounds."

Paula's hand dropped to the hammer in her tool belt as she fought the urge to pound the boss. One of the holes in the wall gave her a view of Tanaka digging a grave. The sight choked her.

She returned to the endless task of sealing the myriad holes in her habitat. Shutting the hatch to the second floor had enclosed the common area on the first floor. The upper level had been swiss-cheesed by flying debris; no amount of duct tape could fix that.

The lab had been totally destroyed. With it went their only chance to confirm that the knobs were truly life-forms. Now *that* might well be Caudill luck, she rued. Earth did not believe the fungus was truly a fungus. They decreed it Martian rust, just as the original scientists had feared they would. Now she would not be able to prove it was a life-form until they returned to Earth. *If* they could return...

On the bright side, the upper level of the habitat had absorbed most of the blast; the lower level had been protected by the sandbags she had piled against that side of the outer wall.

On the even brighter side, the habitat's bathroom was on the first level. Indeed, there was still air behind its closed door. A few more patches and she could repressurize the entire floor.

A cylinder filled with methane had dropped within meters of the habitat's airlock. Miraculously, it wasn't leaking. With the oxygen remaining in the habitat's reservoir, they might have sufficient fuel to escape into orbit.

All they needed to do was construct a launch vehicle to use the fuel. Her brain throbbed.

"This tragedy is unfortunate," continued the boss, "but we cannot spare our limited supplies for someone who is going to die anyway."

"DeJung is NOT going to die," she snapped.

If she hadn't wrecked the rover... If she had run faster... If she had patched the woman's damaged suit faster... If she had found the parasite line to attach DeJung's damaged suit to her own faster...

If she had been a trained captain, instead of a winning poker player, maybe DeJung wouldn't be dying.

Paula came to a rounded projectile sticking through the aluminium wall. It had sealed itself nicely. It took her a second to realize it was the crown of a helmet. With the speed of fear, she taped over it.

"The woman had her arm blown off. By the time you reached her, DeJung's air had been gone for minutes. She is probably brain-dead. Why should we waste what few supplies we have left on a vegetable? She is—"

"—part of MY crew, boss."

"You hate her, Jasmine."

She swallowed hard, could only bring herself to nod until the anger leaked out. "The bottom line is: as long as I am alive, I will keep her alive. Cope with it. You made me captain. Now suffer the consequences."

"Have you gone mad?" he asked.

"Like you?"

"I'm not the one with a skull in my bag," he replied.

She started to protest the violation of her privacy, but the protest died in her throat. Instead, she fetched another roll of duct tape.

* * *

Paula Jasmine Caudill dreamed of her father. It startled her awake, Jay Lawrence's laughter ringing in her ears. She shivered under her blanket until she found warmth in the memories.

He had showed up one night when she was fifteen and preparing to leave on her first date. Her mother had decided to leave town for a week with her new boyfriend. Her brother, Daniel, as always, had charmed the beau, winning an invitation to the trip. Paula and her perpetual pout, as always, were not invited. Having suffered two visits from Child Welfare regarding the neglect of her children, the vulture had called Jay Lawrence, charging him a thousand dollars for the privilege of staying with his daughter. Since he had inherited a small fortune from his late employer, her mother demanded money whenever he saw his children.

Jay Lawrence Caudill had found her extortions hilarious.

He'd brought along Godzilla videotapes. Paula had canceled her date. It was more fun staying at home with her father, watching silly monster movies and talking.

A few hours after her mother had left, he made a call. Minutes later, a strange woman arrived with pizzas; he invited her to join the feast. At the time, Paula had thought nothing of the shared glances, the shy smiles from the woman who spoke with such a strange accent. She found it amusing how her father spoke to the pizza woman in a foreign language.

Years later, Paula tracked down the pizza woman, his Polish lover, and they spent hours talking about her father's dreams. They all revolved around history, exploration, and a generation of shortsighted politicians who had cheated him of his childhood fantasy of having a future in space.

* * *

Day nine, post-disaster. Paula only knew nine days had gone because of the scratches she made on the wall when she woke. The endless labour compressed the days until they felt the same.

Her first duty was to check on DeJung. Her fellow captain's vital signs were weaker; the woman was clearly dying, however slowly. Paula mixed freeze-dried glucose solution for the comatose patient, and added antibiotics after changing the bandage to check the ragged shoulder wound and its spreading inflammation. She cleaned the crust and drool off the woman's cheek.

Paula ate a tasteless ration, washing it down with rusty water. Sleeping on the deck had left her stiff and cranky; her lumpy gym bag made an awful pillow. Sixteen hours of rock-hard labour a day did not agree with her aching back. Paula couldn't believe how cut and bruised her hands were. One of her scabby knuckles looked infected. Returning to the pile of medical kits next to DeJung, she consumed some penicillin.

The boss sat at a communications console retrieved from one of the ERVs. They had the capsule's electronics and most of its supplies, but the explosion of its booster rocket had destroyed the air and water reservoirs. The boss stared at a computer screen, clacking at a keyboard, sending another message to Earth. When he dispatched it, the lights shrank to embers in the ceiling strips as the radio stole the power.

The boss ignored her, as was his wont lately. She felt grateful.

She exited the habitat, her attention drawn to the shreds of a sheet flapping out of a massive crater on the hull of the second floor of the habitat. It marked where her bed had been. Had she been sleeping like the poet...

Resuming where she had left off the previous night, she began erecting another windmill. Originally, the windmills had been designed to supply electricity at distant camps. However, some low-bid company had failed to pack all the parts for the towers.

She welded a fragment of frame from a ruined factory in lieu of a missing strut. She found herself missing the annoying DeJung's preternatural ability to repair things. Her hand slipped, cutting a gash through her glove. It stung. At least the ravening cold precluded much bleeding. After an appropriate amount of cursing, she slapped duct tape over the rip, adding to the accumulation already there.

In the distance, Tanaka dragged a sled of salvaged material. She hoped he had found more oxygen.

The day blurred by. Instead of having a second windmill operating, she finished the work day with naught but three meters of the tower standing.

"Not too bad."

Over a steaming MRE ration (*What kind of meat steamed in that pouch?* she wondered, after pouring water into its heating bag) she slipped on a headset, plugged into the radio to receive the daily update from orbit.

"How are you guys doing up there?" she asked.

Cardenas took his sweet time replying, giving her too long to contemplate the metallic taste of her military ration. Tanaka believed sufficient material had survived the explosions to construct a greenhouse. They could have lettuce in a few weeks. She eyed the beans sprouting upon a tray on the table. *How low have you sunk,* she asked herself, *to get excited over frigging sprouts?*

"*Da Vinci* here. Not much to report, another day closer to retirement."

They both laughed mechanically at the stale joke Cardenas made every day.

"How are repairs progressing on the *De Soto*?"

"It is a waste of time. We cannot repair the lander's flight-control systems."

It took her a minute to catch her breath after that statement. "You're the only chance we have."

"Sorry, the *De Soto* is no chance. The auto-pilot is beyond repair. The only way it might land in one piece is by one of us piloting it down by the seat of our pants, and neither Helmut nor I feel like committing suicide. Forget about the lander."

"You have plenty of oxygen up there. We have plenty of methane down here. You can pick us up and end up with more fuel than you expended. C'mon, you two know there's not enough fuel in the *Da Vinci* to get back to Earth. But with our methane—"

"Our ship doesn't burn methane. We need—"

"I know what the *Da Vinci* burns. We can adapt your engines. Hell, we can make our own rocket engines."

"Forget about it. The *De Soto* is too damaged to land. It will only crash."

"You can't strand us."

"We must. Our launch window is shrinking by the hour."

Her stomach tightened. "What do you mean?"

"Helmut and I have been running numbers with the help of the ISS staff. We can use the lander's fuel to break orbit, take a long ride to Venus, pick up a gravity assist, and reach Earth."

"You're going to abandon us to die here?"

"What's the sense of us dying, too? We cannot reach you. You cannot reach us. What is the point of this charade?"

How could she debate that? Paula had known all along they could not repair the lander. Still, it had been nice to wrap herself in the comfort of a little hope.

"I disagree," she said, adding a sigh. How could she talk anyone out of survival? "When will you have to take off?"

"Tomorrow. Do not worry, Earth will take care of you. They plan to—"

Paula stifled her scream. "Stand by, the boss wants to talk to you."

She walked to Ten Carl's sleeping form, giving his leg a swift kick. "I have the *Da Vinci* on the radio. Cardenas and Muller have decided to fly home tomorrow. You want to talk to them?"

The boss rocketed to the radio, screaming into the microphone before the orbital duo could say a word. She smiled. It was the best revenge she could create.

Walking away, she froze. There on the deck was a photograph of Javier's children. Her foot pushed it out of sight. She looked at her meal, pushed it away. Her stomach knotted at the thought of those fatherless children. Would a real captain have failed them so badly?

Forcing herself to finish her cold meal, Paula played the tape of the news recorded earlier. The TV signal was weak, yet welcomed after so many months of jamming. The UN had brokered an agreement between the Russian Space Agency and the World Bank to finance the launch of an Energia-E booster which would deliver an unmanned rescue craft to Mars in nine months.

Ironically, the Russian spacecraft would be the *Tolstoy*, which Moscow had meant to send with the expedition. However, the government had gone bankrupt once again before the craft could be transferred to the launch pad.

She could not bring herself to believe the promise; she could not stop herself from hoping it was true.

Her handheld computer measured their supplies against the calendar. They possessed eleven years of food, 272 days of water, and eight months of air.

"Eight months of air. Of course, DeJung is in a coma, so she doesn't breathe her full ration."

She worked through the inventory again. It didn't include the oxygen in the suits, nor the airlock tanks. Those added a few days' worth, not the month she needed. No, they needed far more than thirty extra days of breathing, she rued. It might take weeks, perhaps months, before the *Tolstoy* could be launched.

How could she find that much air and water? It seemed impossible to achieve.

A sound startled her. She looked around without finding its source. It reminded her of her father's angry snort when she had told him she was failing geometry because she was too stupid to master it. That had been the only time she had ever seen him angry.

"I know, Daddy. Nothing is as impossible as flying to Mars," she muttered. "Looks like I'll have to find more air."

ELEVEN

She spent half a day re-wiring the habitat's transformer to accommodate the current generated by the windmills.

"You'd think the frigging systems would be compatible right out of the box. Same company selling to the same NASA for the same mission. Standardization isn't rocket science. Why would they send camping equipment that wouldn't hook up to the habitat without hours of modification?"

Paula chided herself for being so angry at nothing. How could anyone have guessed that the factories would explode? That the habitat's generators would not have sufficient oxygen to burn the methane?

For several minutes, she froze, daydreaming about the long showers she had taken while the generators were creating hundreds of litres of water a day as a waste product. Snapping from her reverie, she pondered how the disaster had reduced her horizons from true love, from success, even from history. Now her dreams revolved around hot showers and bean sprouts.

"Pathetic."

Turning, she stubbed her toes against an empty oxygen cannister. Staggering, she nearly tripped over another one. Tomorrow, she promised herself, she would check those cannisters to make certain the zero showing on their gauges was truly zero. Perhaps she could use the airlock's pump to pull a few extra hours of oxygen from those empties.

As she grunted from the effort of moving the cannisters, her lungs tried to fill, dislodging a puff of dust inside her helmet. The ensuing coughing fit left her gasping. How had Martian grit invaded her helmet?

A glance to the instrument panel inside her helmet showed her air tanks were nearly empty. That explained why it was so hard to breathe. Her knuckles rapped the chin of the helmet. The gauge did not change.

"Ouch," she grunted, wondering why her knuckles were so tender.

The warning light belatedly blinked to warn her about the air situation. It was a slow, steady blink. She had plenty of time to recharge her tanks.

"Doesn't anything work around here?" Her question roused more dust which roused more coughing.

She tried to breathe through her nose to stop hyperventilating. Olfactory nerves suddenly came to life. The acrid stench of herself nearly blinded Paula.

"My kingdom for a shower," she muttered.

Suddenly she could feel her grubby, sweat-soaked jumpsuit stuck to her skin, gradually becoming her new epidermis. Paula dropped to the ground. She would have cried, but she was too tired.

Instead, Paula crawled to her gym bag. Lately she could not bring herself to leave it inside the habitat while she was outside working. As if the boss might steal the skull. As if he might harm it.

"I'm getting entirely too paranoid."

Though her stiff fingers made it difficult, she unzipped the bag, opening it wide before leaning it against a fragment of a pump. Staring into the empty sockets of the skull within the bag made her feel better.

"It could always get worse, eh, Yuri? At least I don't have that bony dead thing going for me like you do...yet. Don't suppose you have some brilliant idea to save the day?"

She laughed for the first time that day. That triggered more coughing.

"No complaints from you, eh, Colonel Gagarin? After all, once you've been part of a mad billionaire's collection, anywhere is better."

Sealing the bag, she rose and went to the airlock to recharge her air tanks before starting her next chore.

Paula could not explain why, but the weight of the bag, however marginal under Martian gravity, comforted her.

* * *

Paula woke feeling rotten, sweat plastering hair to the side of her head despite the chill of the twilight habitat. She could barely bend her fingers around a coffee cup. Only then did Paula notice the growths on the back of her hand. At first, she thought the boss had glued buttons onto her hand while she slept.

She hadn't forgotten her first week on the job at Ten Carl's Pennsylvania estate, when she had awakened after a few too many New Year's Eve drinks to find her eyebrows shaved. Nor the way the boss had replaced his butler's liquid hand soap with blue dye. Permanent dye. Nor the way he had bribed Javier's doctor, and taped the computer tech's reaction when the doctor told Javier he had six weeks to live.

It soured her stomach to think how much she had laughed when the boss showed the tape at the company Christmas party. Poor Javier.

Grabbing a flashlight, she looked more closely. The buttons' yellow-green colour reminded her of the samples Tanaka had taken. Lifting her other hand to peel one off, she gasped. Both her hands sprouted growths from the myriad cuts on her knuckles.

"Mushroom hands. Oh, I'll be such a cover girl when I get home."

Carefully, she peeled one off, hissing from the pain. Tendrils had grown deep into her. Flesh gave way; the sturdy, orange roots did not, emerging intact, swinging like a colourful jellyfish. A drop of yellow fluid oozed from the tendril. When it dripped upon the wound, her pain ceased.

"Thank you," she said to the fungus.

It did not reply, which she hoped meant she was sane.

"Only one thing sends roots into people—life. Welcome, moldy Martians."

Paula looked around the habitat to see if Tanaka was there. The boss greeted her with a nod before returning to pecking away on the communications console. She didn't feel like talking to him. This news was too good to share with him.

"That's right, Tanaka's working on a windmill," she muttered to herself.

Paula smiled. This parasitic invasion confirmed Tanaka's samples had indeed been truly alive. Her body was the only lab she needed. It made sense: a Martian life-form would be incredibly sensitive to moisture. And what was she? A big skin of water.

"Once upon a time," she said to the button, "my species started out as bacteria. Now we have evolved elected officials who take payoffs to dump toxic waste in our neighborhoods, but who will fight to the death to tax snack foods in order to protect our health. In a good year, a million people on my world starve to death because they can't afford to buy the food rotting in warehouses. My government refused to fund a Mars expedition because it spent the money for military hardware to protect itself from Malta and Afghanistan. Take it from me, you can do better than humanity as a role model when you start building your civilization."

She scampered to the pile of crates against the bathroom wall to find sterile specimen containers. Using a fork, she pried a dozen buttons off her hand.

"I'll see to it that, uh, shit." It embarrassed her she had forgotten the silent man's first name. "That Captain Tanaka gets the full credit and the Nobel Prize and anything else I can get him for this discovery."

She could do that much, but she had to do it in secret. Otherwise, Ten Carl would try to usurp the discovery, try to gain ownership of the fungus. She could envision one of his companies patenting whatever compound in the fungus killed pain so effectively.

Elation faded. It worried her how there was no bleeding when she pulled the deeply embedded tendril from her flesh. Worse, the old wounds were decidedly yellowish. Was gangrene setting in?

Her imagination tortured Paula with visions of doctors sawing off her infected hands, replacing them with hooks. "I'm not going to die here," she said, grinding her teeth, clenching her hands until they trembled.

Cleaning the wounds with alcohol only made her feel worse. No sting. No pain. Had the infection spread? If the spores were inside her, she could be one big bag of buttony mushrooms.

Holding her hands under a dribble of hot water that lasted for a few seconds helped. At least she could bend her fingers fully.

Wrapping her hand around a cup of coffee helped buoy her mood. The smell of coffee reminded her of her father. Jay Lawrence had worn the scent like cologne. No wonder, considering he drank twenty cups a day.

Life. Paula wished she could tell her father that he had been right. The universe was full of life. Earth was not a freak show, merely one of a billion planets where chemical after chemical had bonded, eventually forming that most magical of creations.

It was only a fungus, but it declared that life ruled the universe.

TWELVE

It is amazing, she tapped on the key of the Morse set.

Constant practice allowed her to stop thinking of the individual dots and dashes, or moving her lips, as her forefinger formed the letters. Now the words sprang full-blown from her aching digit.

Best of all, the lights didn't dim when she transmitted, whereas the boss now started each day complaining about going blind.

Our ERVs' factories held thousands of tons of oxygen, our habitats tons more. Indeed, there could have been no explosion had that oxygen not been leaking and trapped inside the structure of the factories where it mixed with leaking methane. We had so much; now we tragically have so little.

Speaking of tragedy...

She could tap no more. Massaging her wrist, Paula shook some of the stiffness from her aching fingers, rubbed the infected knuckles as she frowned at the oozing cuts. For the past hour, she had been sending messages to her fellow historians on Earth. It seemed important to communicate, especially since the boss was at his console pouting, and Captain Tanaka had seemingly forgotten how to speak, and DeJung...

Poor DeJung.

Paula had checked her patient first thing upon coming home for dinner. DeJung's corpse was cold. Pinprick hemorrhages marred the late captain's glassy eyes. Most of Paula's homicide knowledge came from TV shows, but she believed those hemorrhages betrayed that the woman had been suffocated.

"What happened?" she had asked the boss, hoping he would confess, praying she could forgive.

"Seems obvious to me. My God, the woman had her arm blown off. All that damage without receiving medical attention; anybody can see the captain died of her injuries."

"I'll tell you what's obvious to me—you murdered DeJung." When Paula's hand fisted, the pain made her gasp.

"Don't be absurd."

"If only you had waited, boss." Paula spat the last word. "She wasn't going to last longer than a day or two more."

"More days wasting our limited air. Nature took her course. Let it be, Jasmine."

"You didn't have to murder her."

"Prove it, Detective Jasmine. You should have mustered the courage to do what needed to be done weeks ago. That's a captain's duty."

"Duty? I'm a death-camp guard now?"

"Don't be that way, Jasmine. You know, I can hire a hundred writers for what I'm paying you."

"What are you paying me? I haven't seen a contract. I haven't seen a penny."

"My publisher is still waiting for the next ten chapters."

"Maybe I'll include a chapter about you putting a pillow over DeJung's face and suffocating her."

"It was a captain's duty. You should thank me."

She grabbed at her tool belt, seeking her father's switchblade. Her mind's eye presented the image of her father getting his throat cut. For what? *What good would another murder do?* Her hand fell away from the belt.

"Duty?" she hissed.

"All that air and water wasted for nothing." He sighed. "And get those chapters done. My publisher is giving me shit every day." Whereupon Ten Carl returned to his console to resume his silent pout.

"She was going to die. Why murder her?"

The boss shook his head before continuing his latest missive to Earth.

She could not prove the crime, yet she knew with certainty the boss had killed her. Now, there would be enough oxygen. They would live to meet the rescue ship because one more person for whom she was responsible had died.

"This is too depressing," she said.

Before leaving the habitat, Paula fetched her gym bag. Going to the airlock, she slipped into her Mars-suit. New gloves were necessary. They were too tight. When they rubbed against her swollen knuckles, the pain brought tears to her eyes.

Paula wandered into the night. An alert light inside her helmet flashed until she wrapped a layer of duct tape around her left wrist to seal the suit. Her feet carried her behind the frame of the greenhouse. It was growing by leaps, now that the windmills were running and they could spend serious time on it.

She passed the ruin of the first factory, turning left until she reached a paper-thin ice puddle the size of a saucer, a splash from the devastated habitat. The ice was shrinking, losing half its area each day. Yesterday, she had shoveled grit over it, not understanding why; it had seemed important. Now, she kicked the dirt away. The ice was black as her mood.

She stretched out on the ground to stare at the sky, the way she had often done with her father, using the bag as her pillow. The clarity of the night sky astounded her. It was simple to pick out the space station, a brilliant star in the far west. Deimos was bright; she could almost see it moving.

We belong out there, her father had once said, pointing at Orion. *Space is our destiny. As in the conquest of any frontier, people will die. But the bottom line is that we must go into space, or our species will die here on Earth the next time an asteroid or comet strikes. We will vanish like the dinosaurs. Every genius and every idiot, every opera and every novel will be forgotten. We cannot allow that to happen. We have a duty to the past, to the future.*

"I know, Daddy. We owe this expedition to the future. But the boss murdered the bitch. The real bottom line is, that stupid crime spoils everything. We won't be remembered as pioneers. All the media will cover is the murder."

The voice of Jay Lawrence's lover, the pizza woman, answered, the words vodka-thick with their Slavic heritage. *The rich are different. Your father did not believe it at first, but he learned. They cannot understand what the rest of us must do to survive, nor can we understand what they must do. Some are even innocent when they are guilty.*

"Murder is murder. There are no innocent guilty."

They had met that last time at Jay Lawrence's grave, overgrown with dry, dead grass. The pizza woman had stopped Paula from tidying the grave, reminding her that her father wasn't really there, that he wouldn't have cared if he was. And she was right. Her father would not have cared because he had never made it into space. A dream shattered...

Why couldn't she remember the pizza woman's name?

Paula remembered being in awe of the dour woman. The police suspected the pizza woman of murdering her father's killer after he got out of prison. Looking into the pizza woman's eyes, she had seen the quiet confidence of a predator, her father's avenger.

Here, I have something for you. It was very dear to your father. Very fitting it should go to Mars with you. It would have made him happy.

The weathered gym bag held a scrapbook her father had assembled when he was a child. Page after page of newspaper clippings chronicled the opening of the space age—the cosmonauts and astronauts who had reached the new frontier were his heroes. Many clippings were tear-stained.

And, of course, the bag held Yuri Gagarin's skull.

It had been part of the macabre collection of the billionaire who employed her father. The pizza woman told how they had rescued it from a black-market peddler specializing in body parts of dead celebrities in the wake of the billionaire's death. The couple had interred the insane trophies in an unused tomb at a local cemetery, but the pizza woman had recovered the skull for the man she had once loved, for his daughter to take to Mars.

Paula had reached Mars for him. Jay Lawrence Caudill's eldest child had been captain of the first ship to land on Mars, history would say. Perhaps a footnote would give her father the credit he deserved for inspiring her.

No one would know about the skull; it would not even be in the footnotes. Such was destiny. Nonetheless, she hoped the ghost of her father's hero knew he had made it to another planet. That would have made her father as proud as if he had reached the red planet himself.

The act almost made her proud. If only the boss had not murdered DeJung and poisoned it all.

It was so depressing. For an instant, she pondered the radio jamming, of the enemies who had silenced the expedition. Not their enemies. The boss's enemies. He was the one "they" were screwing. Who knew, she rationalized, perhaps DeJung had been the saboteur. Perhaps it had been poetic justice.

Could the ERVs' explosions have been sabotage?

"No, no, no. The ERVs and habitats landed on Mars eight years ago. Ten Carl hadn't a single clue about this whim back then. It was nothing more than a few cracked pipes, oxygen and methane building up beneath the ERV until a sparking wire or something ignited it. An accident, a stupid accident."

Simple bad luck. Like a sled wreck or a record-setting solar flare.

Caudill luck. Like her father standing in line too long at a grocery store. If the clerk had been competent enough to work a cash register correctly, her father would have been walking blocks away from the arguing couple on that accurst street corner. Jay Lawrence would never have stepped between the couple to stop the man from punching his girlfriend, would never have gotten his throat cut.

"Bad timing, another aspect of Caudill luck. Like me being too distant from Mars City to save DeJung."

"You should not talk to yourself with the suit's radio on," said Tanaka. He appeared like a ghost at her side.

She started to sit up, but stopped. Too depressed. Her head returned to its macabre pillow.

"I like talking to myself. I thought you were asleep. You'll need your rest. Tomorrow will be a hard day setting up the drilling rig; hope that subcontractor packed all the parts. NASA's convinced there is water only a hundred meters below the surface. Once we find water, we'll be able to survive for as long as it takes the rescue craft to reach us."

"Who can sleep? Citizen Richards murdered Captain DeJung. What are we going to do about it?"

"What can we do? The nearest cop is ninety million klicks away."

"One hundred and twenty-six million, nine hundred and five thousand kilometers," replied Tanaka. He removed a cloth from his pocket to brush grit from the knee of his suit.

"We can't prove a crime occurred."

"That is what they told me when I protested. No evidence, no crime. Tokyo, Washington, Brussels, the ISS, the UN...nobody wants to know about the murder. My commander ordered me to be silent."

"Governments hate when facts get in the way of the myths they're building." She sighed long, feeling as if she were deflating.

"But we KNOW what happened, Captain Caudill."

She grunted as if struck. Captain. The rank mocked her. What good had she done her crew? The image of Javier's children floated before her mind's eye.

"Yes, we do, but there's not a thing we can do about it. Not a damned thing," she said, fighting the sob locked in her throat.

"We will live because Captain DeJung died." His handkerchief polished his visor with short, savage strokes.

"As my father used to say, that's the bottom line. We breathe because she does not." She coughed the lump from her throat. "Ironic: in a few days we will discover water and break the H_2 from that O to make ourselves a storm of oxygen."

Tanaka stared at the horizon for the longest time, posed like a statue. She thought he was studying the station that they'd left in orbit. Perhaps, she fancied, he wished he had stayed in space with the other two who were flying home.

No, she decided, Tanaka would not have abandoned the expedition. He would have insisted upon being stranded aboard the station.

He finally said, "I never met my great-grandfather."

"What?" asked Paula, nonplussed by the non sequitur.

"My great-grandfather was a soldier at sixteen, at Nanking during the war. He claimed—" His voice cracked. A growl cleared it. "I do not believe he participated in the war crimes committed in that city, but he did not try to stop them."

"How could he stop such a slaughter?"

"My mother never spoke to him again after she learned he had been there, that he had done nothing while tens of thousands of helpless civilians were raped and murdered. That is what makes crime possible: not standing up, not saying this is wrong."

"Captain Tanaka, your great-grandfather was a child, too young to be guilty. Besides, if he had protested, his officers would've jailed him, or worse."

"You and I are not sixteen. We are guilty if we allow this to happen."

"In Japan, maybe you're right, but the boss is from the USA. The rich kill people there all the time. They buy the best lawyers; they buy the best juries; they are found not guilty. It's not right; it's simply the bottom line."

"We are guilty, too."

"That's what makes me sick. What can we do? Execute the boss for his crime? I can be judge, you can be the jury, and we can draw high card to choose the executioner," she replied.

"Murder is evil."

"There's nothing we can do. We have no evidence."

"Just the facts."

"It makes me sick," Paula said.

The back of her head could sense the outline of Gagarin's skull in the gym bag. There was a man who would have done something, she thought. Heroes always righted wrongs.

Would her father have brought Ten Carl to justice? Or would he have accepted the death as part of the price of conquering the frontier? Was that why Gagarin and Glenn were his heroes? Because they were better people?

"My crew and I were selected because we represented the best of Japan. Geologist, hydrologist, and astronaut, we represented everyone in our nation. What will the rest of the world think of us if we allow this travesty?"

"You forget, I am the boss's personal historian, not the hope of Japan. I became the captain of the *Deduction* because I won a poker game."

A stupid accident, she thought. She should have folded, quit the game. The boss would have found a qualified captain. Someone who might have had the skill to save DeJung. She would still be on Earth writing articles in the popular press about Ten Carl, making certain his legend became history to earn her weekly paycheck.

Her father would have done anything to get into space. Anything. Even accept murder. Even commit murder, she feared.

"On the frontier," she said, "the only thing that counts is that somebody comes home to inspire the next expedition. We're firing imaginations across the Earth. If the EU or Japan doesn't send the next expedition, then China or Canada will. Ten Carl has shown it can be done by any nation, and done cheaply. Hell, there are forty billionaires on Earth who can do it themselves."

"Murder, can we live with it?" he asked, dropping his handkerchief before he walked away.

"We cannot *prove* he killed her. Besides, he did it so the rest of us could live." The rationalization tasted of bile.

"He did it to insure *he* would live. Richards never cared about the rest of us. Murder, can we live with it?" he repeated in a tired voice.

The next morning, Paula found Captain Tanaka sitting outside the habitat. His visor was open. His corpse's smile haunted her.

THIRTEEN

"You look awful, Jasmine," said Ten Carl as he strolled from the bathroom wearing only a towel.

Paula wanted to snarl at the killer, wanted to punch him. Her right hand cramped when she fisted it. The agony stole her breath.

Yet the billionaire appeared so pathetic. The man looked seventy, though he would be only fifty-two next month; stooped, balding, paunchy, with doughy skin. Knobby knees showed a network of scars from myriad operations following a near-fatal car crash. His toes were gone, amputated in the wake of a drunken college ski trip in Austria.

If only all his scars were external, she thought. The internal scars had undone Ten Carl. All five of his great loves had been after his money. He had no hobbies, no fun in his life save for poker nights; thanks to those nights Paula had all the data she ever wanted to have about his personal life. The solitary thing at which he excelled was making mountains of money.

Ten Carl Richards had ruined his single chance to transcend his reputation as a robber baron, to enter history as a great man, by murdering a dying woman.

Pathetic.

"I slept like a rock last night," he said, stretching like a shaved cat, banging his cast against the bulkhead.

"Aren't you the lucky one?" she grumbled, taking a big gulp of coffee, scalding her throat lest she scream. "I keep having nightmares about our dead. How many of us are going to end up in the first cemetery on this planet?" She looked at her own shadow, then at Ten Carl. "There's room for one more."

The billionaire laughed. "What a mood you are in, Jasmine."

"You missed Captain Tanaka's funeral. What a shame. I gave him a wonderful eulogy."

Paula resolved that she would make certain Tanaka would never be forgotten. His death was the proof she needed, thanks to his eloquent suicide note. Nobody could ignore the pleas for justice from a man unable to live with the onus of being an unwilling accessory to murder.

If she could make anyone listen.

She had sent the news of DeJung's murder and Tanaka's suicide to Earth. The ISS commander, Vice President Wilson, and the UN High Commissioner of Space had all ordered her to stop spreading lies about the boss. The press had been reporting for months about the bad blood between Paula and the rest of the crew. Given the number of accusations and slanders sent home by the expedition, one more failed to convince anyone.

Next time the boss went to sleep, she resolved to scan the suicide note into the computer and broadcast its text to Earth. Broadband. Every news network and tabloid would have the dirt. Somebody would believe her then. It would destroy the murderer, forever taint the history the expedition had made, but she owed it to Tanaka. More, she owed it to her new world. The history of Earth was built upon a foundation of lies. The history of Mars would be based on truth.

The resolution straightened her spine. She drank her coffee with her back turned to the boss.

"Oh, don't be that way, Jasmine."

"I don't hate you," she said. It surprised her because it was the truth. He was too pathetic to hate.

"*Captain Caudill*, when the rescue vessel arrives, we will go home. You will be a hero, statues in the square of your hometown, your every dream come true. It is that simple."

"Nothing's simple in this life," she replied.

"Everything is simple. You know why the SEC forbade me to trade on Wall Street?"

"Insider trading, though I don't know the legal name of the crime. And you still play the stock market through your offshore companies and their puppets."

How Ten Carl had scrambled that first week she had worked for him, personally shredding reams of records to prevent the government from finding out the true extent of his criminal stock market manipulations. He had hired a computer hacker to virus several Wall Street firms, nearly destroying the nation's economy simply to protect himself from the SEC. It was an episode of the Ten Carl history she never got to write.

Even then, Paula had been a witness, a silent accomplice. She'd kept her eyes closed to his crimes to protect her job. What she knew made her as guilty as he was.

The boss continued, "Well, there was that insignificant detail, but the reason's far more complex—yet simple. The bottom line, as you would say, was that I knew how to beat their game. I won every time I played the stock market. It's the same reason they ban card counters from casinos—Wall Street cannot tolerate winners."

"Point of information: card counting IS cheating."

"Only if they catch you."

"We haven't won, boss."

"Perhaps not," he said. "But we haven't lost. As long as we do not lose, we *shall* win." He laughed, slapping his forearm cast with his free hand. "I've got chili brewing on the hot plate. Hope you are up for some poker tonight. I feel lucky."

"Is there such a thing as an unlucky billionaire?"

His laugh followed her to the bathroom, where she vomited so hard she expected to see her spleen in the toilet.

* * *

By the middle of the afternoon, the scabs came off when she removed her gloves. Her abused knuckles had healed, with barely a hint of scarring; it was as if her flesh had been lacerated decades ago. Was it the antibiotic pills she had been eating by the score? Or were the Martian growths a miracle drug? How much would a plastic surgeon pay to have the secret of scarless surgery?

She flexed her hands. They were more agile than ever. No stiffness. No pain. The inspiration struck her like lightning.

After some hammer time with a test tube, she looted her alien button collection. Poking and squeezing, she got several to explode their spores onto the pile of broken glass, making certain each splinter was smeared with the sticky spores.

She made a bag of popcorn, then allowed it to cool. Paula gingerly scattered the infected glass inside the popcorn while fretting that she had pounded the glass too finely. Would one or two cut fingers be enough to infect the boss?

It proved difficult to keep her grin under control as she crossed the common room. She sat the skull atop a storage cabinet where Yuri could watch the game.

The boss brought a couple of bowls of his toxic chili to the table. After they ate in silence, Ten Carl grunted as he shuffled the worn cards. The emptiness of the chamber drew her mind to the graveyard a few hundred meters away, then to the irony, to the justice of her plan.

The microwave beeped. She withdrew his usual bag of popcorn, tossing it on the table. The boss buried his face in its steam when he opened it. His sigh was pure contentment.

"This is such a tragedy," he said as the cork popped from the final bottle of Merlot.

"More emotion than you showed over Doctor Duncan dying."

"Don't be that way, Jasmine. Poker night is all we have left."

Ten Carl filled the two glasses before shuffling the worn cards with his Las Vegas flourish of a deal. Her three jacks were vanquished by his full house.

They played through the night. The Merlot vanished, though he failed to refill her glass. She introduced the booze DeJung had fermented from raisins and sugar inside one of the ERVs. Amazing, Paula thought, that the moonshine had survived in plastic tubs, when the oxygen and water reservoirs made of steel did not. Foul and a hundred proof, the stuff was perfect for poker night.

The stack of currency in front of her expanded and contracted as if the paper was breathing. The boss lost six hands in a row. He fell during his stagger to the bathroom.

Figuring Ten Carl was too drunk to notice that the popcorn was cold, she deployed the tainted bag. The instant he returned, Ten Carl stuck his hand into the snack. He proved too drunk to notice the splinters protruding from his flesh. She had to draw his attention to them before he ate the glass and spores.

He threw the bag aside, cursing, and covered his bleeding hand with a napkin, clacking his cast against the table. "This is outrageous."

"Guess the popcorn company must have had union problems. Disgruntled employees love to sabotage things. You ought to sue the company when we get back."

"Damned unions, nothing but strikes and sabotage." He plucked tiny shards from his hand, dropping them to the floor.

"Sabotage," he bellowed. He guffawed so hard that he fell out of his chair. "It was worth a billion dollars in free advertising."

"Free advertising? What are you babbling about, boss?"

He continued laughing, slapping the deck until he choked. A long cough later, he returned to his seat and began shuffling.

"Boss, what do you mean? Free advertising for whom?"

He picked up his glass of moonshine in his napkined hand, holding it to his right eye to stare through the fluid at Paula. "How many news stories did they do about us when I first announced my expedition?"

"Hundreds."

"Tens of thousands! Yet during the following year there was virtually no coverage until the Russians launched the first section of the *Tax Deduction*. Then there was a flurry of reports; then nothing for the months during our final preparations. I even bribed reporters to file stories about us, but their editors tossed the film."

"So what?" she asked. "Millions of people followed our flight. We became a number-one news item whenever it counted. I reckon we still will be number one until the *Tolstoy* takes us home."

"I knew we'd vanish from the news during our nine-month flight. What could be more boring than a bunch of people stuck inside a glorified shipping crate for months on end?"

"Exactly what are you saying, boss?"

"I spent over forty billion for this game. I wasn't about to let my expedition vanish beneath the usual scandals and petty wars that dominate the news. We were too important to be forgotten for nine months! That's why I sabotaged our communications to Earth. Mystery, that's how I hooked the public! Not a week went by that we weren't on the front page."

"You were responsible for the jamming?"

"I hooked every conspiracy fan on the planet. There is a whole organization, with thousands of members, dedicated to solving our mystery."

"You?"

"The world will never forget Ten Carl Richards." Putting down the glass, he dealt the cards. He dropped a hundred-dollar bill into the pot before pulling off the napkin and picking more glass from his flesh.

"So much evil in the world. I wonder how much is real and how much is invented by people like you to manipulate the public?" Paula asked, fighting the urge to smile.

"Oh, don't be that way, Jasmine. I talked to my publisher today. The company wanted me to cheat you, to make you agree to fifty thousand. But I said, NO! My Jasmine gets her fair share. More than your fair share, because you have earned it. I said that. Really."

"I believe you, boss."

"Can you get those chapters to them in a few days? No hurry, but they really need them. Day after tomorrow at the latest."

"Sure thing, boss."

Staring at the four aces in her hand, she folded. Paula had already won the game.

That night, she sent a message to Earth: "Ten Carl Richards and I are infected with a Martian fungus. We lack the facilities to analyze this life-form, but I am certain it is the same one discovered by Captain Tanaka. Program the rescue ship not to take off from Mars. We desperately need its supplies. If the infection is not deadly to humans, you can re-program the ship by remote control. If the fungus is deadly, you will have done all you can for us.

"This world is ripe for settlement. The bottom line is: the next expedition must be more careful than we were. Please do not respond to this message. Ten Carl is in a state of denial about our disease. Help me protect Earth."

She added the secret code that the captains had been given by the UN—the Plague Code. The paranoids had always been hysteric about the unlikely possibility of Martian disease devastating Earth. Now she could use that fear.

Yes, use the fear, she thought, the more so considering all the sweat and fret she had invested in investigating the black-box culprit.

She flexed her hand. The wounds looked years healed, not like fresh scars. If she hadn't known where the injuries had been, she could not have found the slightest hint of them.

"Such a miracle fungus," she said to the bag of tainted popcorn atop the trash. "You will revolutionize surgery on Earth. Think of all the plastic surgeons who would sell their souls to have a compound that prevented pain and scarring."

It was a petty punishment for the crime of murder, but punishment it was. Ten Carl would go insane when the rescue craft refused to return them to Earth.

She drank the rest of the night, drank until the habitat spun like an amusement-park ride. And she couldn't stop laughing.

FOURTEEN

Not one word about the fungal outbreak appeared on the news from Earth.

Meanwhile, various branches of the media reported the "true" facts about the cold war between Ten Carl and Paula. In order of the sources' credibility, they were: a) Paula was poisoning the billionaire's reputation out of jealousy; b) Paula was a woman spurned; c) Ten Carl had arranged the murder story as a stunt to steal headlines; d) Paula had gone insane from the pressure; e) Paula was hiding the fact that she murdered her sworn enemy.

Paula became a laughingstock, a punchline for comedians on late-night TV. She rued the Caudill luck: from famous to infamous in the space of days.

Recalling the other members of the boss's staff with whom she had worked only depressed her—especially when she thought of Ten Carl's public-relations people who now worked overtime to destroy her reputation. Allison and Charlie and Rita—she had dined and laughed with them. Paula had gone to the hospital with Rita when she had a tumour removed because she hated the idea of Rita being alone. She had dated Charlie's brother. Hell, Allison was living in Paula's old apartment.

"We were friends. I thought we were friends."

On the bright side, she thought, this was as bad as it could get.

* * *

Three days later, the rescue craft *Tolstoy* detonated. The media called it a horrible accident, blaming a fuel-line rupture.

Paula knew the truth. She had not anticipated the UN getting that paranoid about the Plague Code.

Earth had left them to die.

The irony was that the fungus had found Ten Carl inedible. He never showed a sign of infection.

Despite being stranded and doomed, the boss still refused to work. He could not believe the politicians of Washington would allow him to be sacrificed, not after the hundreds of millions he'd contributed to their campaigns. Ten Carl stayed at the communications console day and night, firing off an endless stream of messages to Earth. He seemed to age a year every day.

Paula slaved over the drill. Ultrasonic probes from the robotic survey attested that liquid water existed one hundred and ten meters below the surface. She drilled a full hundred meters her first lucky day. The success thrilled her so much that she optimistically fed a month's water ration into the electrolysis cell Tanaka had constructed to separate water into hydrogen and oxygen. The device failed to work. Upon investigating, she discovered that the boss had stolen parts from the cell to build a slow cooker for his chili.

She couldn't find the plans Tanaka had used to build the cell. Without explaining, she radioed Earth for another set of instructions.

When she was not drilling, she completed the greenhouse. It was an ugly structure, all angles rather than the planned dome, since much of the plastic sheeting and aluminium framework had been destroyed by the explosions. Paula thought it looked like a structure a child might build.

Nonetheless, it felt good to have accomplished something positive. Working the compost generated by the toilet into the gritty Martian soil within the greenhouse yielded an ugly pink mess. She planted the seeds that the library said needed the least water. Still, the madness of using their limited water to grow food when they had ample rations pleased her.

She won the water debate with the boss by playing the photosynthesis trump card. She'd guessed right: Ten Carl was too lazy to research the process, so her lie about all the oxygen the plants would create won the game.

She gambled her drilling would find more water soon. Had to. Unless she found water, they would die. So she believed in the drilling with every molecule of her being.

"It IS going to work," she said a thousand times a day to cheer herself.

Two full-time jobs kept her too busy to fret about their impending death, much as her nightmares kept her from worrying about her lack of sleep.

The first well came up dry. The robots' instruments had been wrong.

She started a second well within an hour of the failure. "This one will work."

* * *

After the *Da Vinci* slipped from orbit, the fuel from the *De Soto*, added to the mother ship's, was almost enough to reach the perfect slot to slingshot Venus for the gravity boost to Earth orbit. Alas, their dead instruments did not warn them that twelve percent of *Da Vinci*'s fuel had leaked during the journey. Their final course adjustment failed to occur. The spacecraft ripped into the concrete-dense atmosphere of the second planet of the solar system and never emerged.

It was a quick death.

"Caudills don't have a monopoly on bad luck," she said when she heard the news.

* * *

The second well came up dry.

She sat beside the drill for hours without moving, wishing she could cry.

She said nothing when she started the next well.

The following day, Paula hiked to the wrecked rover. It amazed her that she had completely forgotten about its water and oxygen reservoirs, not to mention the cannisters of air they had carried.

"Stupid, stupid, stupid," was her mantra of the day.

Attaching a glorified skateboard beneath the rover's broken front axle, she drove it back to the base at one klick per hour. The vehicle added thirty-two litres of water and a week's breathing to their stores.

She "forgot" to tell the boss about the extra water, using it on her garden.

The next day, she decided to check the shattered reservoir of the destroyed habitat. The boss had claimed there was no water in it when he inspected the ruins after the disaster, one of the few chores he had deigned to do. Paula suspected he had been hunting for a corkscrew.

The blast had peeled the habitat apart until it resembled a Dali clam shell stuck in the Martian ground. So many sharp edges. Paula moved in slow motion lest she shred her Mars-suit.

Well, the boss was correct: the shattered tank was empty. However, he had failed to inspect beneath it. The water from the ruptured reservoir had rushed into the ground. There was a chunk of muddy ice the size of a truck buried beneath the debris.

Discovering the ice was like Christmas. Paula grinned the rest of the day as she rebuilt the cell to separate water into hydrogen and oxygen. From the first bucket of ice she melted and processed, she estimated the muddy ice would yield enough oxygen for thirty-nine days.

"The little victories add up."

She celebrated by finishing an extension to the greenhouse. When she wasn't using the windmills for drilling, she routed the power to heaters in the greenhouse. To hell with the habitat, she decided. If the boss wouldn't work, he didn't deserve to waste his days typing in a comfortable environment. Indeed, he kept sending so many messages to Earth that the solar cells could not power the habitat's furnace.

Within days, the seed stock NASA had dispatched Io, those many years ago inside the habitats, sprouted madly beneath the UV-absorbent plastic of the greenhouse. It made her so proud that she moved Yuri's skull in there one afternoon to watch the sprouts growing.

* * *

Stretched out on the surface of Mars, Paula withdrew the skull from her gym bag. She held Yuri up to watch the space station make its orbit, a golden seed in the sky. Tonight, the station seemed especially bright.

"Colonel Yuri Gagarin, welcome to the new Mars. I helped build that space station. It is not much now, missing all its electronics. But the next expedition will upgrade the station into a platform for science to help us conquer this planet the way you helped conquer space."

She rotated the skull, allowing it to take in the devastation of Mars City.

"What a mess. You know, Moscow self-destructed the *Tolstoy*. I thought I'd put the fear of a vengeful God in the boss; make him worry that Earth might strand us here because of his crime. Instead, boom! It's nearly impossible for a lifeform that has adapted to grow on Mars to be deadly to humanity, yet those craven politicians blew up our rescue ship. I forgot how hysterical people can be.

"We're stranded. The nice thing is that the EU and Washington have announced they are mounting a joint expedition—scientists, not clowns like me. If we're still alive in five years when they land, who knows, maybe they'll take us home.

"Maybe.

"Currently we have seven months of air left, maybe a fortnight more. But I've found some ice. The electrolysis cell will split some of the water into hydrogen and oxygen. The rest will go into the garden. We can live on the water recycled in the habitat for a good while; the boss deserves to drink recycled urine. Soon, our greenhouse plants will start exhaling oxygen while we're feasting on fresh vegetables. It won't be much, but every bit helps. Then I'll drill another well. Maybe the next one won't come up dry. As long as I can find enough water, we can survive."

She eyed the skull. The wire attaching the lower jaw had loosened, giving it an open-mouthed gape.

"Okay, no need to laugh at me. Gamblers in Las Vegas are giving the odds at fifteen thousand to one against our expedition surviving. The boss is no help. He just sits on his ass all day complaining to Earth as if civilization will collapse should he fail to return.

"Then again, I remember the way my father used to talk about you, Colonel Gagarin. He was so proud of the example you'd set. You had no idea whether you could survive when they launched you into space inside a sardine can a fraction of the size of my cabin aboard the *Deduction*. The booster your capsule rested upon was more a bomb than a rocket. How many of those boosters had detonated on the launching pad before your launch?"

Phobos raced over the horizon, a dazzle of light. It came with a halo of delicate rose. In the distance, a patch of Mars appeared to glow.

"You took your chance. I intend to take mine. I plan to be alive when the second expedition lands. After all, what's a frontier without pioneers?"

A sound came across the speakers in her helmet. She held her breath. Paula would have sworn it was the sound of her father's laughter.

On her way back to the habitat, she stopped at the greenhouse. The glow of the heaters reminded her of the blood-red eyes she'd imagined the monster in her closet possessed when she was seven. The roof of the greenhouse looked strange—wet. Paula cursed, thinking it was a leak, but—

The ceiling was covered with droplets. She had expected some condensation, but it was raining like spring inside the greenhouse!

She looked at the meter next to the plastic airlock. The LCD display was going wild. The air pressure was five times what it had been this afternoon. She pressed the wall of the greenhouse. The plastic popped right back, straining outward.

"Water and gas must be coming out of the ground," she muttered. "The warmth of the greenhouse melts it from the soil, then the moisture collects on the cold roof. Of course! The planet is a big ball of permafrost. Except the experts said the top layer of soil was desiccated. Experts, ha!"

She didn't question the miracle as she raced to collect buckets and pans for the rain, thinking...she could fold creases in the roof, direct the drips into the receptacles. Already plans bounced through her mind about moving the greenhouse once it exhausted the permafrost beneath the current site.

"Even the Caudill bad luck has to run out eventually."

She laughed. It seemed to echo inside her helmet. She would have sworn her father's laughter joined hers.

Ryck Neube has won first prize in the fourth annual novella competition of The University of Catalonia in Barcelona, Spain. His novel DEBROUILLER was published in 1992 by Svaro, Limited in Europe. Ryck has been a recipient of a writers' fellowship from the Kentucky Arts Council. Serving as a very confused president of the Cincinnati Writers Project, he became the editor of the CWP's anthology, FERAL PARAKEETS AND OTHER STORIES. His short stories and novelettes have appeared in ASIMOV'S SCIENCE FICTION, BLUE MURDER, OCEANS OF THE MIND, EXPANSE, TALES OF THE UNANTICIPATED, OVER MY DEAD BODY!, and others. Ace Books reprinted one of his stories in their paperback collection FUTURE SPORTS. His essays have appeared in THE WRITING GROUP BOOK and ART SPIKE. Visit his website at http://www.sfwa.org/members/neube

Robert B. Schofield has been writing fiction since 1990, when he was the first student to graduate from Indiana University's Cognitive Science program, with dual majors in computer science and philosophy. He has had stories, articles and interviews appear in various publications since then. Robert's story "Interrupt Vector", which is another Slater and Redeye tale, appeared in Volume 17 of the Writer's of the Future contest anthology. Robert is working on giving the data mercenary pair their own novel.

Judith Tracy is the Cinncinati Enquirer Bestselling author of DESTINY'S DOOR. She has also written VALLEY OF ANJELS as well as 2 books in the fantasy YA series THE WILDSIDHE CHRONICLES:™ --BOOK 3: DARK PROPOSAL AND BOOK 4: LEGACY. Her short fiction has appeared in HOT BLOOD X, ASCENT, QUANTUMMUSE, MYSTIC REALM'S DARK MOON RISING, amongst others. When she's not writing, you can find her at home with her two lovely daughters, Jessica and Stephanie.

Printed in the United States
46896LVS00008B/160-180

9 781890 096274